Ewan Lawrie spent 23 years in the Royal Air Force, 10 years in Cold War Berlin and 12 years flying over the rather warmer conflicts that followed. He began writing during long boring flights over desert countries, and what started as a way of killing time soon developed into a passion.

Nowadays he spends his time in the south of Spain, writing and teaching English to Andalucians and other hispano-phones. Though he has had stories and poetry published in several anthologies, *Gibbous House* is his first novel.

Gibbous House

Ewan Lawrie

This edition first published in 2017

Unbound
6th Floor Mutual House, 70 Conduit Street, London W1S 2GF
www.unbound.com

Typeset by Ellipsis Digital Limited, Glasgow
Cover design and illustration by Mark Ecob

A CIP record for this book is available from the British Library

ISBN 978-1-78352-089-3 (trade)
ISBN 978-1-78352-161-6 (ebook)
ISBN 978 1 78352 111 1 (limited edition)

Printed and bound by Clays Ltd, St Ives Plc

1 3 5 7 9 8 6 4 2

'He has no identity; he is continually in for – and filling – some other body'

John Keats in a letter to Richard Woodhouse,
1818

Dear Reader,

The book you are holding came about in a rather different way to most others. It was funded directly by readers through a new website: Unbound. Unbound is the creation of three writers. We started the company because we believed there had to be a better deal for both writers and readers. On the Unbound website, authors share the ideas for the books they want to write directly with readers. If enough of you support the book by pledging for it in advance, we produce a beautifully bound special subscribers' edition and distribute a regular edition and e-book wherever books are sold, in shops and online.

This new way of publishing is actually a very old idea (Samuel Johnson funded his dictionary this way). We're just using the internet to build each writer a network of patrons. Here, at the back of this book, you'll find the names of all the people who made it happen.

Publishing in this way means readers are no longer just passive consumers of the books they buy, and authors are free to write the books they really want. They get a much fairer return too – half the profits their books generate, rather than a tiny percentage of the cover price.

If you're not yet a subscriber, we hope that you'll want to

join our publishing revolution and have your name listed in one of our books in the future. To get you started, here is a £5 discount on your first pledge. Just visit unbound.com, make your pledge and type **gibbous10** in the promo code box when you check out.

Thank you for your support,

Dan, Justin and John
Founders, Unbound

Gibbous House

Chapter One

I had no sooner buried my wife than I received a summons to the reading of her late uncle's will. Truth told, I was not a man brought low by grief. Numb and distant, perhaps, but three long years of watching death's shadow hover had sucked the compassion from my soul. I was not aware of any inheritance that Arabella might have expected, but a trip to the Inns of Court in London seemed a pleasant diversion.

I was walking through the kind of fine rain that falls with more insistence than any thunder shower. The streets were wet as the mud smeared, like a noxious dubbin, on my boots. Carriages slurped past me, and the cries of street vendors were muted by the moisture in the air. I turned into Hawthorne Lane. Number 15 was not in the best of repair; only the stout, studded door seemed to have received any maintenance in the past few years: the timber was oiled, the handle and knocker gleaming in spite of the weather. A brass plate fixed below the knocker read: 'Bloat & Scrivener'.

I was not even to meet with a partner, as the lawyer's letter instructed me to ask for a Cartwright, *sans titre*. I gave the door a firm rap with the knocker. Scarce had I loosed my grip but the door opened.

'Moffat.'

It seemed neither question nor invitation. The speaker drew the heavy wooden door aside and motioned with his eyes, and I followed him into a dark, narrow hallway. The gloom inside was dispiriting. Sconces held unlit candles, and the faint smell of damp decay lingered even after I brought my 'kerchief to my nose. I followed my less than garrulous guide down the corridor. He stopped abruptly and dealt a murderous blow to a door that seemed ill-prepared to receive it. Then he turned the knob with a delicate twist of his finger-tips and melted away.

'Come in, come in,' came the enthusiastic, reedy cry. 'Ye'll be Moffat, then.'

I recognised the Scots accent of my native Edinburgh, though mine own had long since faded away. His was a most peculiar voice: high-pitched, with unexpected modulations, as if a moderate student of the bagpipes were practising on his chanter. No less odd was the appearance of the man himself. He might have been of middling height had his lower limbs not revealed the effects of a childhood diet like that of the worst slum-dweller. His head was uncommon large; the forehead bulging forth made his hairline seem to recede, though it plainly did not. I warrant that looking directly down at his head from above would have revealed an elongated oval. His nose was hooked and his chin curled up, as like to meet it. Were it not for the striking blue innocence of his eyes, he would have been the very image of a singularly malevolent Mr Punch.

He introduced himself as Cartwright, though of course I had guessed as much. Wishing me good morning, he pushed a meagre pile of papers fastened with a grubby, once-red ribbon in my direction.

'Thaire ye are, it'll aw be thaire.'

'But, Mr Cartwright—' I began. 'It's Cartwright, naw but Cartwright.' 'Well. Let it be so, but I understood there was to be a reading of a will?' 'And for why? When ye are the only fellow these papers consairn? And ye'll no be reading them here!' he added curtly.

With that he ushered me out: laying not a finger on me, he propelled me all the way into Hawthorne Lane as if by the force of the will under his enormous brow.

To my chagrin, if not to my surprise, the rain still hung mistily in the air. Two boys running towards the Wig and Feather careened into my person. It was all I could do to preserve my dignity and balance. I checked my pockets and my purse. Only my half-hunter was missing. I wished the thieves well on it, for the watch had told no time since my wife had become ill. Some may think me at once sentimental and callous, for though I had wound it not once since the day she took to her bed, I let it fall to thieves without a second thought, and this only one scant week after her death. Both charges I will not countenance. I had my reasons, though I do not care to share them. At least not yet.

I hailed a hansom cab and cursed the inclemency of the weather once more as the nearside wheel slurried my boots and trews.

'Cheapside, The Chaste Maid Inn,' I said as I settled in the seat. The driver's grunt was eloquent and bespoke a premium on the fare. As much for the indesirability of my destination as the elegant cut of my clothes, no doubt.

'A rare place, sir,' the driver said gruffly as we arrived.

'Rare enough,' I allowed, paying in coin.

'You'll not find another such in Cheapside.' The bark of his laugh was echoed by the crack of his whip and I was forced to leap clear of the carriage to avoid the splashing mud.

Be assured that places like The Chaste Maid were, in fact, none too rare in many parts of London. Its custom comprised the rough butchers and slaughtermen of the Shambles and the more rakish of the commodity brokers from Goldsmith's Row: young blowhards in search of women who made mock of the hostelry's name. My room was cheap, as it needed to be: I had made nothing of my modest means in the years of my wife's illness. Capital needs growth and I had tended mine but poorly.

Passing through the public bar, I noted Thackeray, the landlord, hugger-mugger with two hulking brutes who appeared to know little of either silverside or silver trading.

The staircase at the rear was dark and unwelcoming, but it led to my room and I took it at a gallop. The bed was little more than a cot and the remaining furnishings were as ill-matched as the load on a totter's van. I threw my topcoat and hat on the stained bedding and rummaged in the coat for the red-taped packet of papers.

They were varied: several folded sheets of good vellum, two of the new-fangled lozenge-shaped 'envelopes' for the Penny Post and one curious parchment with a broken wax seal. The parchment was clearly an older document, though none appeared new. The Penny Post had delivered the two envelopes to Bloat & Scrivener over a year ago. I sat on the cot, pushing the soaking topcoat toward the bolster. I had no intention of remaining another night.

Unaccountably, I trembled as I opened the parchment. It bore the palsied hand of the aged, the tremors marring the cursive beauty of the copperplate. I began to read.

It being the year of our Lord 1838 Anno Domini, and I, Septimus Coble, of Gibbous House, Bamburgh, Northumbria, being of sound mind, do make this my last will and testament, voiding all and any extant or anterior wills and codicils.

I do leave all my possessions in sum and total to the husband, should there be any such person, of my great-niece Arabella Cadwallader née Coble, on condition

*that said party do move himself and all chattels
to reside in Gibbous House without delay on being
apprised of the contents of this my last will and
testament.*

Signed and sealed by Septimus Coble in the presence of:

*Jeremiah Bloat
and
Cartwright*

This 27th day of February 1838 Anno Domini.

I felt sick to my stomach. I could be rich, but at what price?
The proximity of Northumbria to Edinburgh filled me with
dread. Border country.

Coble's will had dropped from my hand and lay like a
discarded playbill on the rough planks of the floor. I picked
it up, folded it carefully into a crisp square and hid it in the
lining of my hat. The Penny Post letters drew my eye: I recognised the hand on one. The rounded, feminine curves and
the idiosyncratic angles of the descenders and ascenders were
indubitably those of my late wife, although I had not seen her
pick up a pen in the last two years of her invalidity. I tore the
letter from its cover. The handwriting was less sure, no doubt,
than in her days of robust health, but the very fact of it was
a facer indeed. I began to read.

Esteemed Mr Bloat,
I have received word from a confidential source that you
may be in possession of some information that could
prove to be to my advantage in the fullness of time.
Should it be within your power and not constitute any
breach of faith, trust or confidentiality, would you apprise
me of any expectations that I may have?

I regret, as I am an invalid, that I am unable to attend
your chambers. Therefore I petition you most respectfully
to reply at your convenience,
Cordially yours,
Mrs Arabella Moffat, née Coble.'

Laying it to one side, I picked up the other. A masculine hand, also recognisable; I had but moments ago read its owner's last wishes concerning the disposition of his legacy. I drew the letter from its enveloping lozenge; if it had been read more than once, it had been treated with extraordinary delicacy. The missive began abruptly, without salutation or preamble. Whether it was read by Bloat, Scrivener or, God's grace, Cartwright, was therefore unknown:

Be in no doubt, I hold yourselves responsible should my
great-niece be so misguided as to believe I hold her in
any kind of affection. Whence she knows of any legacy, I
should be most gratified to be enlightened, as your
lawyerly selves were left in no doubt by mine own
instructions as to the extreme confidentiality of this

matter. I urge you not to enter into any correspondence
with Mrs Arabella Cadwallader née Coble, on pain of a
suit on which I should have no hesitation in expending
my not inconsiderable fortune.
    Coble

The queasy feeling in my abdomen was no mere hunger pang.
I thought only of the name Cadwallader, by which – to my
knowledge – my late wife had never been known.

Chapter Two

Sustenance was necessary, even though my appetite had vanished, leaving only a bitter taste in my mouth. I shook out my topcoat and laid it out to dry on the floor by the draughty sash window. The letters, and the blank sheets of vellum, I placed in a pocket of my frock coat. Picking up my hat from the bed, I looked at my ageing attire in the cracked cheval and repaired to the public bar.

Thackeray's confederates were nowhere to be seen and glad I was of it. The man himself was behind the counter dispensing a pint of porter to a broker who seemed altogether too young for his impressive whiskers. The same observation could not have been made about mine host. He was a man, as we were wont to say then, in the prime of life: his whiskers put one in mind of J.C. Loudon's most extravagant feats of topiary. Less aesthetically pleasing was his shirt, which had long abandoned any pretension to a state of whiteness. It was heroically stained and, no doubt, scented by the fruits of his labour. This garment, which would have been commodious for the majority of humanity, strained to hold in his paunch.

It was not blessed with a collar, and by dint of a nod to the custom of wearing a cravat, was topped off by a filthy look-ing rag.

He addressed me in his usual servile fashion, which, though no trace of insincerity showed in his mien, aroused in me a sense of being ridiculed.

'Mister Moffat, 'ow may I be of service? Porter, claret, gin for the... gentleman?'

'I'll have a plate of chops, Thackeray, and some honest beer.'

It was ever thus. Thackeray had no reason to think of me as anything less than a gentleman. However, he lost no opportunity to slight me by pause or intonation. My circum-stances did not allow me to make protest or restitution, though I sorely wished they did.

I seated myself at the table furthest from the door. The landlord himself brought me a pewter tankard, which he filled from a pitcher of beer. From past experience I knew my comestibles could arrive post haste, but would more likely come at Mrs Thackeray's convenience, which was to say none too soon. Eurydice Thackeray filled the role of cook in The Chaste Maid and never was a cook more inconve-nienced by the prospect of culinary duties. Despite her euphonious name, Mrs Thackeray was more oak than nymph and she certainly reminded no one, least of all Thackeray, of a sweet maiden.

Through the inn's grubby window, I caught sight of one of the brutes who had been speaking with Thackeray earlier. He peered through the square of glass, fixed me with a malevolent eye and gave me, I swear it, a savage nod and a wink such as Jack Ketch might give Mr Punch.

I should like to say the reverie with which I filled the wait for Mrs Thackeray's inconvenience concerned plans to spend my newfound wealth, or of fond memories of the wife who had brought me such unexpected fortune. But it behoves me to confess that I spent the time, and I know not how long it was, ransacking my past for the faintest trace of a Cadwallader.

Even without the dubious benefit of their leathery flesh, the stripped bones of my lamb chops hardly covered any less of my platter. I tossed some copper coins on the trestle top and resolved to quit The Chaste Maid to take some air. Halfway to the door, I reconsidered the prospects of an improvement in the elements and mounted the stairs once more to recover my topcoat. To my surprise, it no longer lay before the window. Indeed, it was absent altogether. All too present were the bedclothes, strewn as they were about the room and garnished with the few items of personal clothing I had left in the scabrous tallboy next to the cheval mirror. One of the brutes had been spying on me through the window before I began eating. Thackeray would provide some answers, I hoped. I threw up the sash window and looked down at the street outside. It appeared that come dusk a lamplighter would be searching for his ladder.

In the public bar, the landlord was smearing a tankard with a rag as filthy as the one adorning his crop. He lifted his chin in acknowledgement of my regard.

'Mr Moffat,' he said.

'Thackeray,' I rejoindered, and held his eye in the hope of provoking discomfiture.

In a few moments, he rewarded me with a grudging, 'I'll send the missus up. All right?' He lifted his eyebrows at me.

'Indeed, it is not all right. Who was he?'

He ran a finger around his neck for all the world as if he had a collar on his shirt.

'The both of them were Peelers, sir. What could I do?' For once it seemed his deference was genuine.

'Could they not have used the stairs, man?'

'Sergeant Purewipe and Constable Smackle were both in the Runners before. Out of Bow Street. Old 'abits die hard, Mr Moffat.'

'What did they want? Did they say?'

For answer I received only a shake of his head and a look of pity for the ninny who would ask such a question in expectation of any answer. I lifted a salute of sorts to the brim of my hat and wished him good day.

Mercifully, the rain had stopped. Steam rose from the mud in the streets, and the day was bright and clear, as were the sounds of London itself. Still intent on a walk to clear my head, I braved the mud and the street vendors and headed toward St Paul's.

Cheapside, like most of London, was overrun with Cheap Johns, watercress girls, flower girls and the like. Shouts of 'Scissors sharp as like to cut themselves! Only a shillin'!'

melded with the plaintive cries of watercress girls of barely eight years old hawking 'Creases, creases four bunches a penny'. I tossed a penny to a smut-faced girl in a yellow bonnet and turned away as she held out the wilting bunch of greenery. Arabella's child would have been the same age, I supposed.

The day being so fine, and cheered by this contrast with its earlier misery, I embarked upon a circumambulation of the cathedral, if only to distract myself from the thought of the two officers. Turning left from Cheapside into the Old Change, I turned right on Church Yard. At the foot of Ludgate Hill, a crowd had gathered. Moving closer, I perceived they were watching a performance.

A stall like that of a Punch and Judy show, only far more capacious, was almost blocking the thoroughfare. It seemed too grand to be wheeled along by its proprietor, however strong he might be, and yet I saw no dray or mule in its vicinity. Drawing nearer still, I apprised myself of the nature of the show.

Wooden figures japed around the stage, jerked by strings manipulated by an unseen hand. In no way were these movements natural; they were more like the jerkings of the palsied interspersed with episodes of St Vitus. I had seen such shows before – they were still known amongst their performers as 'The Fantoccini', though the fashionable preferred the term 'Marionettes', proud of having seen the Gribaldi Royal shows at the Adelaide Gallery on the Strand. Arriving *in medias res* detracted not a whit from the entertainment's comprehensibility, the show being a hotchpotch of imitations of circus acts and lampoons of actors from the legitimate theatre. A hurdy-gurdy player provided an infinite variety of musical accompaniment to the clacking of the stringed dolls.

As I watched, they began the final figure. It was introduced as 'The Scotchman' and a riot of plaid and whiskers appeared onstage, then capered energetically in a 'Highland Fling' not even a Scot would have recognised. I made to leave as the hunchbacked proprietor begged some indulgence of the audience, while his assistant played a magyar reel. A voice like a cracked bell assaulted my ears. 'Wait, sir. Wait. Did you not enjoy the spectacle?'

It was no London voice, but neither was it Italian as one might have expected. I felt the hunched figure must be German or Gypsy and his blunt looks did not gainsay me.

'I liked it well enough, except for the last,' I replied.

'Then remove a sum from your payment accordingly, sir. That is fair, is it not?' He tugged my sleeve for emphasis.

'I am not bound to pay for street entertainment.'

'Ah, a Scot yourself then.' And he cackled, mouth wide open, showing an absence of any teeth and the presence of brimstone breath.

I was shaken to the core, furious at my origins being divined, and I snatched my sleeve from his grasp. I stalked off to cries of 'Keep your balsam for the catchpoles, you nimmer!,' which showed that he was a Londoner now, whatever he had been before.

The walk cleared my head, though I could not help but

think again of the bailiffs. There was little for me to fear from them. Gibbous House should bring enough 'balsam' to satisfy the lowest of thieving nimmers. It was time to go north and play the hand out, no matter what other cards might fall.

London's capricious weather had again taken a turn for the worse, but I held to my resolve to quit The Chaste Maid that day, July thirteenth, 184_. Clouds had covered the setting sun and no amount of crepuscular carmine could mitigate the gathering gloom.

I intended to inform Thackeray and depart forthwith, but on entering the inn I remarked on both the relative paucity of custom – given the hour – and the presence of Sergeant Purewipe and Constable Smackle. The landlord was busying himself cleaning some brass that had not felt the touch of cloth since the Regency.

Purewipe fixed me with his hangman's glare and enquired, 'Mr Moffat, Mr Alasdair Moffat?'

I allowed that I was, since plainly he knew already. He cleared his throat, as if uncertain how to begin.

'Ah... it concerns a timepiece. We... have reason to believe it is yours, since your name is engraved upon it.'

'Mine is not an uncommon name in some parts of the Commonwealth, Sergeant,' I said, remaining cool and awaiting developments.

'It's not yours then?' Smackle sneered.

'I did not say that, Constable.'

'Well, is it, Mr Moffat?' Purewipe was clearly the more dangerous of the two.

'It might be, Sergeant. I had the misfortune to be relieved of mine earlier today in Hawthorne Lane. Not the only crime of which I was the victim today, in truth.' I smiled at the two brutes.

Purewipe coloured. Perhaps his collar was a little tight.

'Might you have a witness to the theft, sir?' There was gravel in his voice and I felt uneasy.

'My pocket was picked, Sergeant. No one sees a dip. Surely my word... ?'

Smackle gave a snigger. Purewipe held up a hand.

'Your watch, sir, was but recently found in the hand of a corpse.' He raised his eyebrows.

'By you, Sergeant?'

'As it happens, sir.'

'Did you find a coat nearby?'

He had the good grace to blanch at this and I surmised that the Peelers had been indulging in a little private business to augment their admittedly pitiful income. He straightened his shoulders and leaned his glowering face into mine.

'Mr Moffat, I have a message for you... ' He looked over each shoulder, as if someone were likely to come down the stairs with a billy club. He went on, 'Go north, Mr Moffat. Go north.' He tipped me a salute.

They were almost at the door when I asked, 'Who was it, Sergeant? The unfortunate?'

I was hardly surprised when he answered, 'I believe he was known as Cartwright, sir.'

Whether it was a matter of his belief – or certain knowl-

edge – was moot. I suspected that he had learned something of my business from the deceased legal minion, in any
event. I would have supposed that they presumed that I
had despatched Cartwright, had I not already assured myself
that they themselves had done it. It would not have been the
first time such fellows had removed an inconvenience on
another's behalf.

Thackeray had a wary eye on me as I turned to face him.
He remained quite expressionless as I bade him prepare my
account for settlement, merely intimating that my debt to him
was in the sum of three pounds. I presented him with my bill
of exchange, adding, 'In the sum of three guineas, in recognition of the pains taken for my comfort.'

Answer gave he none. He merely tore my bill into tiny
pieces and jerked his head toward the descending figure of his
spouse, carrying my valise down the stairs.

I would make for the coach north, but first I had need of
more funds than I had and I made for a gentleman's club I
knew, where a man might make a little tin at cards. My baggage I left with a man known for his relative honesty in the
environs of The Chaste Maid. I had frightened him more than
once into being so in his dealings with me, at least. The sky
once again looked as though it had a mind to rain. I turned
up my collar and made my way to Cockchafer's.

I felt the rain on my face as an affront. Even in Whitechapel,
the sun ought most surely to appear from time to time. The
wheel of a dustman's cart splashed my trousers and boots,

which was less an inconvenience than the spores of dusty filth that a fine day might have engendered. In consequence, I was wet, cold and hungry. I had come directly from a game of Écarté at whose table there were gentlemen even less careful of the laws of honest gaming than I, otherwise I might have been less hungry and most certainly warmer.

Dorset Street was my destination. As expected, it was narrow, dank and filthy. My mood would not improve if I did not encounter Tess Hamilton at the very end of the close. She had learned her business from Ikey Solomon, and, though I did not hold out much hope for the receipt of anything approaching the value of my pilfered items, I did hope that she would recognise them as items of quality. In sundry pockets of my topcoat I had several gold fobs and chains, a silver calling-card holder in an exquisite design and, best of all, a miniature sapphire cylinder pocket watch made by Courvoisier and Comp. This last was a quite beautiful piece and had it not been for the fact that I was without any kind of address, fashionable or no, I should have kept it for myself. My removal of these items from my erstwhile partners at cards I justified by the certain knowledge that they had cheated from the instant the first hand had been dealt.

I saw no symbol of the pawnbroker's trade. It was a plain entrance with a solid door and few windows. My knock remained unanswered and I gave up after the third attempt for the sake of my knuckles. Moments later, I heard a shrill 'Gardy Loo!' and was thoroughly soaked by the contents of a particularly fetid chamber pot. The raucous laughter that ensued told me that Miss Hamilton was in residence.

'I have pretties, Tess.'

The face under the dirty and crumpled bonnet could be said to have resembled nothing other than a close-shaven Barbary ape. The voice was as high-pitched as a young boy's and emerged from an all but toothless mouth. Furthermore, the filth that issued therefrom would have shamed a lighter-man at the East India Docks. The woman screwed one eye as tight as one might without blocking the ingress of light completely.

''Tis you, Moffat? Truly?'

'Of course it is, my lovely.'

Miss Hamilton let out a cackle, which soon devolved into a catastrophic explosion of phlegm and spittle. Paroxysm coming to a close, she wheezed, 'There is no doubt of it, Mr Moffat, ye're a fair treat. I'll be down momentarily.'

The head disappeared from the upstairs window and I awaited the opening of the door.

'Not seen you since Michaelmas last, Mr Moffat.'

The woman stood on tiptoe and with her arm at full stretch pinched my cheek with a fearsome grip.

'How Ikey would have loved you, Mr Moffat, were you here as a boy. You are the spit of Jack Dawkins himself.'

Miss Tess Hamilton regaled me with the tales of Ikey's favourites whenever I availed myself of her services. I could only conclude the man had been an insatiable old fence. I followed the diminutive figure into such filth and squalor as might suit a mudlark or a midden-fly. She bent to collect a tallow-fat candle from a tallboy that looked relatively new.

'I have no time for furnishings and carpentry. The small pretties, they're the things, Mr Moffat, eh?'

We left the front parlour and entered the scullery. This same space hid behind the staircase, which arose in the middle of the muck and bric-a-brac that might have covered a sofa or a hibernating bear. There was no doubt that some food had been prepared at some time in the tiny space to which the woman had brought us. I could not in all conscience say that it had ever been eaten by man or woman. Which is to say that the smell was, indeed, fearsome.

Miss Hamilton had the misfortune to be both short and rotund. Her bell-like shape gave forth no ringing tones however, her voice being as rough as a sailor's stubble.

'What have you brought me, Mr Moffat?' The woman put her head to one side and fluttered her eyelashes. I was glad that I had not drunk too much while at cards.

I took out what I had taken from the other players while I had been losing to them at Écarté.

Despite the woman's slitted eyes, she could not prevent the gleam from appearing the moment she saw the watch. She rubbed her hands and snatched the watch from my hands. On making a half-turn away from me, the better to use the thin light coming through the hole in the exterior wall, she let out the noise of a self-satisfied cat.

'Purr-etty!'

'How much, woman? I haven't time to waste.'

I was in receipt of a sly look and presumed her offer would not be to my liking. The watch had cost a guinea at the least when purchased, according to the fop who had lost it to my talents as a pickpurse.

'I'll give you two shiny pennies, my prince.'

'You'll give me a crown and like it.' I stood over her but she merely looked up at me, back arched, as though about to hiss. Then she shrugged. 'Sixpence, for your handsome face, then.'

I would have turned her upside down and shaken all the money from her person, had I thought it would do a bit of good.

'A half-crown, out of fairness and honour.'

'But there is only one thief present.' Her laugh was again phlegmy and somehow lascivious.

It is shaming to say it, but I laid her low when I struck her with my fist. I searched her person and found precisely six-pence to add to my limited funds. I searched the scullery. The parlour was an impossibility. Mounting the staircase, I was astounded to come upon one beautifully appointed bedroom as would have befitted a fashionable house in Curzon Street, save for the sackcloth at the window. There was no strong box, no loose floorboard, no hidden compartment and no money. Tess Hamilton still lay where she had fallen. As I departed the hovel, her groaning convinced me that she was not bound for the inferno quite yet.

Chapter Three

It was late afternoon. Baggage in hand, I hailed a carriage and directed the driver to Smithfield in the hope of securing a coach north that very evening. With my inheritance in mind, I considered the prospect of one day having the where-withal to make the journey north on a steam locomotive. For the moment my means remained such that I could afford only a seat on the coach out on the Great North Road, and that outside.

It had begun to feel cold, and in the interest of expediency I decided to avail myself of the Fortune of War's privy. I relieved a sleeping and somewhat portly gentleman of his topcoat. In times past, he might have lost more than his coat at the hands of the resurrectionists who frequented the inn some years ago. Since the man was safe from the anatomist's slab, I left only a penny or two in recompense, for the coat was not in style and a d___ poor fit.

At the hour of eight, the coach was all but ready for depar-ture, save for the absence of an inside passenger. The coachman himself fussed with the traces, but showed less impatience than the clergyman whose red bulb of a nose emerged periodically into the cooling air to the accompaniment of much harrumphing and sighing. I was merely curious: what quality of passenger could hold the departure of the Newcastle coach? After a time, and only shortly before the reverend suffered an apoplexy, the tardy traveller arrived. It was a womanly figure, well wrapped against the elements, though despite the swaddling she was perceptibly young. She moved daintily but determinedly, deigning to nod at the coachman as she waited for him to assist her.

I laughed as the churchman's head attempted the window at the very moment the coachman opened the door. The woman looked up at me, and it is no self-deception to say that I discerned the lineaments of a smile before she averted her gaze. The memory of the journey, like that of so many others like it, sits deep in my marrow, so penetrating was the cold. Inside the carriage the jouncing and jostling from the ruts and potholes of the roads,– so poorly maintained by the Turnpike Trust,– were sufficient that ladies in a delicate condition were often advised against travel.

Outside, where I in my Pantagruelian topcoat had taken post, it was a gargantuan struggle not to be thrown off at every corner. Attempting to grip fast to a moving carriage with hands numb with icy cold is no easy feat; it is a wonder there are not more unfortunate incidents. But I am no tyro in matters of the outside fare and held tight to my post for my life.

By morning, and after a change of horses that could only

have coincided with the pitifully short period of slumber allowed to me, we had reached Stevenage. My travelling companions evinced as little interest in me as I, in truth, could muster in them. However, I felt I could not forego the opportunity to ask of news from London. I doubted that the clergyman had read either the early or late editions, but I did have hopes of the merchantmen. Indeed, for all my confidence that Smackle and Purewipe had not been paid for their efforts from the public purse, it was not sure that they had not later made some official report of Cartwright's death. Or, worse still, fabricated a part for me in it.

Addressing myself to either Castor or Pollux, I began, 'Sir, I am but recently come from the colonies and would know something of London since I spent so little time there before our departure.'

He eyed me as though I had passed him a clipped coin. Then he began to regale me with the most impenetrable arcana concerning the beneficial fluctuations in the price of American cotton and the prospect of the collapse of the Indian manufactories. Attempting to steer the conversation into waters of more interest to myself, I interrupted. 'How very interesting. But changes go far beyond the commercial, do they not? I have heard that London has become uncommon dangerous of late, and this despite the esteemed efforts of the Metropolitan Service.'

Once again I received a look of near contempt from whichever of the merchant twins I had engaged in conversation. It appeared scarcely credible to him that the safety of persons might be more important than the bale price of American cotton at auction. Rather boldly, it might be said, the clergyman's travelling companion – a Miss Euphemia Lascelles – interposed:

'Oh, indeed, sir, of late I seldom venture out without protection of the male persuasion.'

I had little doubt of that.

To my surprise, the reverend, one Nicodemus Parminter, nodded vigorously, the high colour of his cheeks and nose as expressive as those of a pantomime harlequin. 'And neither should you. Why, even a gentleman risks much in parts of the capital! I would never venture into Cheapside but for my calling among the Magdalens.'

I forebore to commend him on the obvious sincerity and depth of his vocation, asking, 'Indeed? And what of other locales, surely the Haymarket or Temple Bar are safe enough?' Parminter began to form his lips to the shape of undoubtable wisdom on the matter, but he was interrupted by the hitherto mute of the merchants. 'Contrariwise, sir. They are not. I had occasion to witness the aftermath of a brutal murder at the Inns of Court today. Off Hawthorne Lane, in fact.'

There was no need to provoke the man to elaborate, as Miss Lascelles leaned across the reverend – who may have reddened still more – to place a gloved hand on the man of trade's knee.

'Oh please! Spare me only such details as are too gross for these delicate ears.'

The merchant removed the hand with a thumb and forefinger, and I looked forward to a more explicit account than even Sergeant Purewipe's official report might have provided.

'I have occasion,' he began, 'to visit the Inns of Court from time to time. A trifling – if a little drawn out – matter of entail on my late mother's side. My lawyers squirrel their precious papers in chambers not far from Hawthorne Lane: Shawcross & Co. They are of sufficient note to consign my dealings with them to various drones who comprise the & Co. rather than any Shawcross. Having concluded my business with them this afternoon, I intended to exploit the respite from the rain by taking the air until the odour of mildewed documents had cleared my nostrils. It was as I was passing a mean little cut-passage that I overheard rough and uncultured voices.'

My interruption bidding him to fix a time for these events was greeted with the glare of Pliny's Cyrenean serpent. Nonetheless, he answered, 'It may have been a little after two, or it may not. One of what I supposed to be the ruffians was instructing the other in the positioning of what he termed the "hevidence". From the grunts and epithets, I presumed it was very heavy indeed.'

He paused briefly, shrugged at the indifference to his needle wit and continued. 'I peered down the alley and was a little taken aback to espy two Metropolitans standing over what was clearly a corpse. Its hand was clutching a watch on a chain, a little unnaturally to my eye, as if he had expired in the act of dropping it. Nearby was a shabby topcoat clearly too large in dimension to have belonged to the departed. The larger of the two policemen gave me a gallows look and bade me depart, so I took one last look at the hunched and pathetic figure on the ground and went about my business.'

Again, Miss Lascelles' indecorous curiosity saved my arousing any more suspicion: 'Oh, how terrible! Who was he, do you know, sir?' 'I do not.' The man paused, to gather his thoughts mayhap. 'But do you know I cannot forget the poor fellow's legs, most uncommon malformed they were.' With that, all fell silent for the remainder of the stage, until the luncheon halt at Buckden. In the silence, I pondered reasons for Cartwright's demise and wished, in vain, to blame all on chance.

I was in a brown study throughout our sojourn in Buckden and missed the departure of the reverend's companion on the southbound mail. On boarding the coach once again, I noted the fellow had reverted to the fractious and fidgeting demeanour I had witnessed prior to the lady's arrival for the coach from London. Perhaps the mantle of piety itched him somewhat.

Castor and Pollux had taken seats each next to the other. Perhaps Miss Lascelles' presence had discomfited them, for they did seem to prefer the company of gentlemen to that of the fairer sex. As we rode in near-companionable silence, my fellow passengers – having lunched in somewhat better style than I – soon succumbed to a post-prandial torpor.

For want of other entertainment, I reached inside my frock coat for the packet of papers the late Cartwright had bequeathed to me. On the point of extracting Coble's will from the lining of my hat and rereading that first, I suddenly noticed that the blank vellum sheets were void no longer. By some arcane means, writing had appeared. Despite having the look of old and faded ink of poor quality it was discernible, though not intelligible, at least not to me. It had the look of the Greek of the Ancients, although I knew enough to scry that it was not.

Frustrated, I put the papers away, staring instead at the moving landscape, watching Huntingdonshire become Lincolnshire and later Nottinghamshire. By the fading light I calculated the hour to be seven or eight in the evening – the coachman was now struggling to persuade the horses that the White Swan was indeed our destination. This inn had stood for some sixty years as the Northgate in Newark-on-Trent, and so we remaining passengers, along with the driver and horses, would be lodged for the night there.

The building itself showed evidence of better upkeep than the coaching inns were wont to endure at that time. The whitewash was recent and the signs freshly painted – there was no doubt that this was entirely due to the inn's proximity to a prospective station of the recently begun Great Northern Railway. Indeed, there was even discussion with the landlord concerning our accommodations. It seemed there were but two rooms available for the coach, the others being let to those passengers recently arrived by other means . By happy coincidence, the coachman preferred to stay at a house kept by a widow near the Market Square. Castor and Pollux, their détente yet pertaining, were only too pleased to share a room.

I made loud noise of my dissatisfaction at having to share, even with a clergyman, but secretly blessed the saving of a shilling.

Chapter Four

All four wayfarers dined at common table and on simple fare. The reverend showed an appetite for port that his nose and cheeks betokened. The men of trade drank little, and I contented myself with a penny gin. The conversation was dull: cotton, slaves and – incredibly – the Taiping Rebellion in far-off China, although I suspect the merchants were less interested in its effects on missionary work than on the price of china tea. Making my excuses, I repaired to the room I was to share with the clergyman, hoping to gain some advantage in the matter of sleeping arrangements.

The bed was large enough to accommodate two men of middling size, a description that might have fit both the reverend and myself, were one not too specific in defining 'middling'. I moved the bolster to the centre of the bed, and betook myself to the side furthermost from the window's draughts. Sleep came swift enough – and departed swifter.

Reverend Parminter fell cacophonously into the room, as if pitched into a gaol cell by an angry turnkey. He was singing in a prodigious–if inexpert–voice, meandering between keys as though determined to visit them all in the course of one hymn. It was not a pastoral exhortation to the contemplation of God; Parminter was bellowing 'Soldiers of Christ, Arise' like a militant missionary converting the Chinee at the toe of his boot and the knuckle of his fist. What Charles Wesley would have made of his rendition, I did not know.

Mercifully, the hymn was one without refrain or chorus, and I hoped the flatness of the note attached to 'more' was the end of my trials for the night. It was not to be. As befit a man of the cloth, Parminter prepared himself to say his prayers. He made several abortive attempts at genuflection before sliding to the floor and sitting cross-legged in passable imitation of a Hindu swami.

He passed an entertaining hour in listing his many failings, a good few of which had arisen due to his efforts to save women of easy virtue, a prominent figure among whom was one who may, or may not, have borne the name Lascelles. He fell asleep where he sat and I profited myself from some hours sleep, thanks to the blessed peace his prayers had brought him.

I awoke with a start to a litany on the virtues of moderation. The dream had been as vivid as ever and I woke before its denouement, although I well knew how the matter ended: in sweated and befouled bed linen, odour, death and resurrection of a kind. I could not help but note that of late the dream had come more frequently and I felt a little uneasy thereby.

A man's good name is a passepartout in the colonies – only

if that name comes from quality does it open doors in the home country. To those born without a name of any description, more doors are barred than in the deepest dungeon. There came a knock at the door, and a gruff shout of 'Moffat! Alasdair Moffat!'

Drawing the door open sufficient only to view the visitor and hide my déshabillé, I peered out. A coachman met my eye and enquired:

'Moffat?'

'Perhaps.'

The man gave a snort of exasperation. 'The mail coach south is without and I'll be on it soon, are ye Moffat or not?'

'Did we say that I were, what of it?'

His face reddened in total measure, save for the very tip of his nose, and he made to leave. I put out a hand and excused myself by intimating that since I had been lately disturbed from slumber, I was still a little stuporous. He muttered and held out a letter, saying, 'Packet.' Without asking for any 'bona fides' or receipt, he left it with me. I threw the letter onto the bed and went about my toilette.

I was still turning the letter over and over in my hands after boarding the coach. Parminter eyed me as if I had refuted the resurrection in the middle of his Easter sermon; perhaps he remembered some of his unusual prayers of the previous evening. Nods so curt as to be discourteous were all I received from the mercantile brethren. It bothered me not a whit. As the wheels clattered over the first of many ruts, I opened the letter.

'To the husband of the late Arabella Cadwallader née Coble', it began.

We regret the circumlocutory salutation to the esteemed recipient of this missive. You, having received it from the hand of a mail-coach driver, will have the advantage of ourselves on concluding your reading. We supposed, quite correctly, if you are indeed perusing this communiqué, that you would waste no time in travelling north to fulfil the requirements of the late Mr Coble's will. We ask you to board a further coach, to Alnwick, on arrival in Newcastle upon Tyne. Should your means be insufficient to cover the journey, please contact the agent at the field office, where arrangements have been made. Sadly, we are unable to advance funds commensurate with onward travel by railway, or for incidental expenses.

We have arranged for a phaeton to attend the arrival in Alnwick of the Newcastle coach every evening until the 31st. You will be met by our representative, a Jedediah Maccabi, who will accompany you to the Harbour Inn, Seahouses. If you would be so gracious as to attend the day following, at 10 ante meridian, the offices of:

John Brown & Son
Notaries Public
11, King Street
Seahouses.

It was signed in a masculine hand with little fuss or flourish. I sighed and folded the letter into my packet of papers and wished the journey away as a prisoner does the days of his sentence. Resolving to feign sleep, I was soon blessed by dreamless oblivion.

Oblivion, but only until Newcastle, where the dusk was falling. All passengers disembarked with none of the insincere invitations, and certainly no exchanging of cards, which might have been expected in more congenial company. I stood by the coach step and watched as the merchants took leave of each other – a little reluctantly, it seemed. The reverend stalked away straight-backed and with nary a backward glance. When I stood quite alone before the coaching house, I withdrew my purse with some trepidation and counted the sum of six shillings threepence ha'penny, of which an alarming amount consisted in worn copper. Still, it was sufficient unto my needs and, forswearing any likelihood of indebtedness to John Brown & Son of Seahouses, I went in search of the landlord to enquire of an outside seat to Alnwick.

Chapter Five

Thirty-two miles on the Great North Road took me from Newcastle to Alnwick, through Gosforth, Morpeth and Felton, where the Coquet is crossed. Signposts pointed to Hexham, Otterburn and Rothbury and, despite this evidence of civilisation, the landscape reminded me that this land was once too fierce for the Romans, who built a wall to keep its inhabitants at bay.

It seemed to me that the further from London coaches travelled, the more poorly were the turnpikes maintained. This final stage of my journey commenced at dawn, after my arrival in Newcastle, and we made slower progress than I would have liked, considering how my night had been passed. After having booked my outside seat the previous night, I took my remaining shillings to Grainger Street and Eldon Square in the hope of finding a suitable establishment to fill my hours, and perhaps my pockets. The streets were all but deserted, and I remembered that a recent bout of cholera had claimed numerous lives in the city. For most of the remainder of the evening, I held my 'kerchief over my nose whilst in the open air. There was nothing for it but to seek a less salubrious area of the city and accost the first likely fellow I met.

A walk of some twenty minutes found me at the other end of Grainger Street in the Bigg Market, whose inns seemed lively enough, although the street lamps stood too close together for my taste. Some tasks were best performed in the shadows, in my experience. No great distance off the Bigg Market itself a figure stumbled out of the George Yard, likely having left the Old George Inn. He turned left along the street. The most promising aspect the figure displayed by the light of the gas lamp was indeed its wavering gait. A drunken dupe is easier deceived, after all.

As I drew nearer and he passed from the pooled light, the lineaments of his shape from the rear began to seem familiar. Nearer still and it became apparent that the fellow was deep in conversation with someone quite invisible to me. By chance he darted into the meanest close, perhaps to relieve himself of some of the quantity of liquid he had evidently consumed. I resolved to relieve the fellow of his purse by more direct means and duly followed.

It was somewhat surprising that the Reverend Parminter did not recognise me as he struggled and twisted to remove the yellow scarf I tightened around his neck. It was only meet that I lean over his shoulder – if only to ensure he knew the identity of the benefactor who had sent him on his way to meet his beloved god. I left the yellow scarf, as I had done on past occasions, reasoning the police would hunt only for a

Hindoo Thuggee, one of those goddess-worshipping assassins so lately subdued in India and still the subject of tall tales. Parminter had a surprising quantity of coin in his purse. I took his watch as I had none, and he would have no need of it to measure eternity.

The coach was trundling through Denwick, little more than a church and three cottages. There remained but a few miles to the Hotspur Tower and Bondgate Within. I planned to alight at The Olde Cross Inn in the Narrowgate and spend a few shillings on a room and board, any plans of John Brown or his catspaw Maccabi notwithstanding. The driver had readily agreed to triangulate the Market Cross and approach it from the Narrowgate; he had not discussed this diversion with the inside passengers and I considered that particular exemplar of Parminter's coin extremely well spent.

As I came gingerly down from the coach, the driver directed me towards the left-hand window of The Olde Cross and he struggled vainly against his Northumbrian consonants to render himself intelligible to me: 'Divvent caal ut the Cross, mind. Caal ut the Dorty Bottles, lookah.' Harry Hotspur's short-tongued 'r ' fought its way through his narrow lips and I had no doubt the man could have passed in the French capital as a native, if all he said were its name.

'Why, man? Why are dirty bottles kept in the window? I take it not as good advertisement in a hostelry.'

'Ivverone caals it that. The laanlaw'll tell yiz, jus' gan ask um. They caal um Robson.'

I took my bag and resolved to ask mine host at the earliest opportunity. It was a curious thing and it piqued my interest.

A room was negotiated at half the London rate, which I could have paid in Newcastle too, had I been able to sleep. Slumber comes hard to me after such events; reverie and revision of the glory keep one enervated, I find. The landlord of The Olde Cross – I still could not bring myself to call it by its sobriquet – was narrow-eyed, gap-toothed and possessed of a forehead so low as to admit the minimum of grey matter for locomotion. Appearances proved deceptive, as I then found.

'Robson.' I waved a hand at him across the counter top. 'Porter; a bottle from the window, if you please.'

In an accent as rustic as the coachman's, if a little less Gallic, he replied, 'Please yoursel', sir. But yiz'll oblige us and gan geddit yoursel', too.'

I had no intention of touching the filthy phials in the window and asked him, 'Will you not serve me, Robson?'

'Not frum those bottles.'

'And why would that be?'

'Why, thiz corsed, man! Hev bin since Adam Collingwood breathed uz last putting those very bottles in the winda.'

A voice came from over my shoulder: mellifluent, educated and not a little seductive, though it were a man's.

'Yes, some fifty years ago, none have touched them since. Utter nonsense, of course.'

I turned to see a tall man just leaving the very prime of youth; approaching thirty years as if intent on remaining there. He proffered his hand and gave the name I least expected: 'Jedediah Maccabi at your service, Mr Moffat.'

Raising an eyebrow, I took his hand. Despite his Semitic name, he was blond-haired, and his looks bespoke Viking blood from an earlier England. His grip was firm and the hand calloused, though his clothing had clearly never been worn whilst performing manual labour. It was immaculate, of the very best of quality – and some fifty years out of date to my eye.

'The coach driver,' he said. 'He drinks in The Bell, by the Hotspur Tower. He's a renowned conversationalist and a shilling buys a lot of gin, does it not?'

It was said with a smile worthy of beatification, although the name he had given me made that somewhat unlikely.

'Indeed it does, Maccabi. Though I believe that you have wasted it even so, I would have met you at the staging post on the thirty-first, I assure you of that.'

'Why tarry, Moffat? Why put off your inheritance, and a change of clothes?'

Why, indeed? An opportunity to lie low for three days and scour the *Northumberland Gazette* for news of Parminter, to savour accounts of Thuggee gangs terrorising the Tyne and to ensure that I was quite clear of any taint of suspicion.

I considered my answer before replying, 'It has ever been my custom to check the mouth of any horse, gift or no.'

Maccabi threw back his head and laughed, a harsh and dissonant sound – it was quite possibly the only unattractive thing about him. It pleased me that there was something I might despise him for.

'Well said, Moffat. But John Brown is a byword for scruple in Northumbria. Would you dine with me? The Olde Cross has a passable table, I believe.'

Who was I to gainsay him? Besides, he had invited me and I presumed all would be to his account.

The room was dark; candles in sconces and oil lamps few in number provided such illumination as there was. The dark, heavily varnished beams and woodwork sucked this light in rather than reflected it. Perhaps the patina of dirt was deliberately maintained to lend credibility to the preposterous legend of the dirty bottles. To me, it just seemed another grubby inn, but I never saw anyone touch the glassware, though many seemed drunk enough to brave more dangerous feats. The table too was darkly varnished, marked with the initials and sundry scratches of the idle drinker. Some may have been the tally marks of the less trusting; of the landlord or themselves, it mattered not. Robson apologised for the paucity of fare available: veal and ham pie, one leg of lamb, a hasty pudding and vegetables. He gave an excuse which I did not register beyond the word 'late'. I cared not if it were the lateness of the hour or his mother, I confess. We spurned the hasty pudding, I because I had not eaten porridge for twenty-five years and never would again, and Maccabi, I presumed, because of the arcane dietary restrictions of his creed.

Maccabi took his leave after pressing on me a final glass

of port and extracting my promise that I would avail myself of his services as driver of the phaeton at ten the following morning. He assured me the ride to John Brown & Son in Seahouses would be no less comfortable than the stagecoach, and that he would then answer such questions as came within his remit. I should like to say I slept dreamless until the dawn, but the dream of Bedlam and its gory end visited me, as every night it lately had, though in all conscience I know not why.

Chapter Six

At five past the hour of ten, I presented myself in front of 'The Dirty Bottles'. The phaeton and Maccabi were not waiting, but drew up the instant I appeared on the stoop. It rankled that Maccabi had not been inconvenienced; I consoled myself, however, that he had merely driven the horse once more around the triangle of Fenkle Street, Market Street and the Narrowgate to give the impression of an ill-mannered tardiness. He did not descend to offer a hand in boarding or loading my admittedly sparse luggage, just smiled his saintly smile. I cursed him silently.

The Great North Road out of Alnwick offers a view of Alnwick Castle from the Lion Bridge, which, as Maccabi began to inform me, was designed by a Robert Adam. The most striking and ludicrous thing about the bridge was the rigid tail of the Percy Lion decorating it, pointing our way along the road. No one knew if the rigidity of the tail was some visual joke in dubious taste or an indication of the sculptor's shortcomings in his art.

Maccabi seemed remarkably well informed about the ancestral seat of the Percy family and began a tedious disquisition about their employment of a gardener whose given name of Lancelot was scarcely less ridiculous than his sobriquet of Ability or Capacity or some combination of the two.

My escort seemed completely unperturbed by my disdain for him, continuing with his inconsequential chatter as though he were entertaining a small child or infirm relative. At one point he reined the horse into the side of the road, just beside a copse. He sat silent in contemplation, for which I was most grateful. It did not last; he began to list the avian riches of our serendipitous stop. Yaffles, screechers, boom-birds, ragamuffins, thistlefinches and I knew not what. If I had had but one of my yellow scarves about my person, rather than in my baggage, I should have despatched him forthwith, no matter what riches awaited in Gibbous House.

As Maccabi brought our carriage to a halt at Seahouses, I withdrew my recently acquired timepiece from my waistcoat and was quite surprised that it was merely the first hour of the afternoon. My travelling companion's prattle had performed some alchemy that made the journey seem as long as Moses' own to Canaan. King Street, though enjoying the benefit of several streets between itself and the sea front, was in the grip of a North Sea fret, which had soaked my outer garments instantaneously. Whenever I breathed in, I could taste the sea on the back of my tongue and felt as chilled as only the North Sea Spring can make one.

Number 11 looked to have been built about the turn of the

century. The window's glass panes were small and dark with dirt, and the bow of the window of uncertain geometry. The door appeared far too ornate for the simplicity of the building: it was of two leaves, and the escutcheon around the lock was brass, in the shape of a lion's head. There was something exotic in the lines, as though the brass had been fashioned in Persia or beyond. The wood was painted a vibrant green that was quite out of place in this Northumbrian seaside town, and the knocker on the door was a miniature, tarnished version of the benighted lion from Adam's bridge. I presumed that this was a later addition to the door furniture.

Maccabi grasped the rigid tail, lifted the knocker high and let it fall, making the solid sound of a beadle's staff on a sack, or the back of a boy. Both leaves swung open to reveal a figure as wide as it was tall, or rather, short. Atop the rotund torso was a head fully as round. Cherubic features boasted the red cheeks of the happy or a devotee of fortified wines. Bold, greying whiskers seemed an extension of the fringe of hair circling his pate. The man's waistcoat was stained and misbuttoned and one of his lapels hung by a thread. A ragged shirtsleeve emerged from the cuff of his frock coat. Maccabi chose to perform the obsequies on the threshold, whether intent on insult or no, I was unsure.

'Mr Brown, sir, may I present Mr Alasdair Moffat, late of... ' He eyed me for a moment.

'London,' I said.

'Quite so. London.'

John Brown's voice seemed to come from a deep pit.

Rough and harsh as the voice of a man half strangled, or hanged, it seemed no more likely to emerge from his cherub mouth as from that of a woman or a child. He gestured, bidding the two of us enter. Inside the hallway stood more furnishings than in an auction house. Eclectic pieces of vari- and purpose: tallboys, commodes, secretaries, dining chairs and one long table on its end, the legs offering us an embrace as we squeezed our way into Brown's office.

It was with some relief that I observed that a functional number of chairs, a solitary large bookcase and one desk comprised the furniture in that room. More disconcerting were the walls, if indeed any such lay behind the innumerable framed items. Portraits, landscapes, life paintings, sporting scenes, cartoons, sketches, incomplete works and several other canvases were nailed to whatever lay behind them. It was such a riot of images that I almost felt nauseous.

I was put in mind of Greek symbols seen long ago on the flyleaves of books produced from a large and dusty trunk, by a man doomed by encountering me, so many years ago:

Από τα βιβλία του μοφφατ
(From the Library of Moffat)

I fixed my attention on Brown. With conspiratorial elbows on his desk – an expensive piece but as marked and worn as a pawnbroker's counter – he began to steeple his fingers in an attempt to strike a more prepossessing attitude. Sadly, his manual proportions echoed those of the rest of his person, and his chubby hands resembled more the dome of St Paul's than any towering spire. However, the voice from the pit ensured no levity, much less mockery, at least from my part.

His hanged-man's voice, full of gravel and brimstone, put one in mind of the very deepest of pits; I myself countenanced no Gehenna beneath my feet, believing rather more in those hells I had seen above the ground. Still, I could imagine his voice as that of Malphas or Halphas escaped from Solomon's urn.

But no demon ever spoke words of such circumlocutory tedium, punctuated with harsh clearings of the throat, sniffs and snorts, with ahs and ums of uncountable number. I remember clearly how he began:

'Ah... Mr... Moffat, is it? Um... Of course it is, yes.'

At which point he broke into a round of percussive non-verbal noises. As the unmusical rasp went on, in so far as I was able to gather, the man was attempting to establish my bona fides without asking me to prove it in any way. Maccabi retained an air of bored insouciance throughout. When satisfied – although I was unsure by what means – as to that good faith, Brown began to explain the legal points surrounding the inheritance. He elaborated on entail, detail and for all that I could make head or tail of any of it, the devil's tail as well. Fortunately, the property had only lately emerged from chancery. The property, as he continued to refer to the estate throughout, had passed to Coble himself by a somewhat circuitous route, though he vouchsafed that Maccabi would describe it when he escorted me to inspect it.

Brown's acolyte stood by at some unseen signal. Taking possession of a most prodigious bundle of papers of varied antiquity, he proceeded to place them one folio at a time before me and bade me peruse each one with diligence. Some required marks or declarations, some did not. I confess I passed into numb oblivion, and the inky words ran before my eyes as if newly writ with no sand to hand. The last bore merely an anodyne form of words:

As heretofore agreed, I pledge full payment
Signed:
Alasdair Moffat

I was on the point of appending that much-practised signature, when Brown asked for a final time, 'Ah... you are quite sure... um... that you are, indeed... ' Coughs and phlegmonous movements quite interrupted him, until he recovered himself enough to say: 'Alasdair Moffat?'

That I surely was. It had been the work of moments to become Alasdair Moffat, a decision taken as soon as the thought was formulated. The symbols flashed across my mind's eye again. As to who I was before that, the name is gone and all who would own to it too. That party left a middling estate near Largs at scarce eleven years, following the unfortunate death of a younger sister. Her mother, being recently delivered of a further son, descended into peculiar hysteria in the presence of the elder. The older boy was despatched with a trunk to the care of a maternal great-aunt in

Edinburgh, shortly after the girl's funeral. How the father must have loved his wife to exile his beloved eldest son so! Senga Campbell, the great-aunt, lived and worked in the Royal Edinburgh Hospital, and had done so since its opening in the previous decade. By the time she received the boy, she was indistinguishable in dress and deportment from some of the patients in Doctor Andrew Duncan's Model Asylum – and as capable of his care.

The boy received no further schooling, of course, but made himself useful in minor ways. Chamber pots were hardly a challenge, but he found the antics of the genuine lunatics a diversion. One fellow was exceedingly odd: for days at a time, on the opening of the judas hole, his handsome face would appear; cultured tones would explain reasonably that due to some unfortunate misunderstanding he, Doctor J____, was incarcerated in error.

Less often, but with lunar regularity, his face would appear at the hatch contorted with rage and insanity and he would try to bite the boy through the bars, as he teased him with some beef on a stick. Several years passed in such amusement until the day his true education began, the day an Alasdair Moffat was consigned to Bedlam by his relatives.

Από τα βιβλία του μοφφατ
(From the Library of Moffat)

Taking the pen proffered by Maccabi, who seemed to have produced both it and an inkwell from behind his coat-tails, I signed 'Moffat' with a flourish. It was a model of authenticity. Brown's smile did not reach his eyes and he seized this last document with unseemly haste, I felt. The ink, unblotted by paper or sand, ran freely, creating unlikely shapes on the vellum. The notary began to take just such pains with the papers that he had encouraged fromme. In such degree was he absorbed that I could feel his very presence withdraw from the room, as it were. Maccabi caught my eye and raised a sardonic brow over his own. I lifted my regard and – to avoid any nausea – fixed my eye securely to a canvas nailed behind Brown's right shoulder.

The edges of the canvas were curling and appeared singed. The colours were dark and the draughtsmanship and use of colour were familiar in style, as was the content. However, I was sure the medium was not so. It was a painting in oils, depicting a room such as many I had visited. A moll, dressed in fashions over a century old, was being attended by her maid, an old and syphilitic jade. The bed was her only major piece of furniture, and a cat posed suggesting the moll's own posture. A witch's hat and birch rods on the wall suggested either black magic or that her profession required her to indulge some tastes out of the common. On the wall behind her I noted the artist had captured the very tawdry tints of portraits torn from ballad broadsheets; I fancied I could scry the appellation MacHeath under the one and Sacheverell under the other. The symbolism of the two philtres of quack salve on the shelf above the likenesses was admirable. It proved my diagnosis of the moll's attendant.

When Brown's grating voice brought me once more to myself , I was on the point of remembering just whose hand I recognised in the painting.

'Ah... Umm... Moffat. Did you want to repair at once to your... ah... property? Maccabi will be delighted to accompany you.'

'That won't be necessary, Brown. I'll find my way easily enough.'

'Oh, but it will,' Maccabi interjected smugly. 'You will recall signing my contract of employment, sir? I did not wish to leave the house after so long as its factotum, and am overjoyed that you are desirous of my continued employment as such.'

I could have fed the insufferable prig his eyeballs with a Coburg-pattern spoon. The documents I had failed to read were clasped to Brown's chest as like to put one in mind of corsets made of paper. The man himself remained mute and motionless, and, for the second time in less than a week, I found myself propelled from a place of business without courtesy or dismissal. Maccabi attempted a light touch on my elbow as we crossed the emerald portal, but the somewhat heavier touch of mine on his ribs thwarted his presumption. He did not gratify me with a grunt, but merely looked me in the eye as any equal might and said, 'I thought... Perhaps... a tailor?'

I was too surprised at his effrontery not to reply, 'Here? I had supposed that Alnwick would house the very nearest!'

'In that you are quite correct, Mr Moffat. However, I have

taken the liberty of summoning one such to the Coble Inn to await our pleasure this very afternoon. He would not depart without seeking leave to do so, I think.'

Had I not already taken against him so, I would have admired his foresight.

'Coble?'

He threw back his head and laughed his unmusical laugh. 'A natural enough name for an inn in a fishing village! It is the local dialect for a fisherman's boat.'

'And my benefactor's given name? How serendipitous!'

Maccabi eyed me closely, and in a voice devoid of humour, declared, 'There is little of chance in names, Mr Moffat.'

Chapter Seven

The Coble Inn was as mean a hovel as ever I had seen. On the weathered sign that hung acrook from rusted iron outside was a symbol, and not the fishing boat one might have expected. As arcane as it was, the symbol reproduced here did seem uncommon familiar. I was unable to place its provenance at the time, however.

The inn's sandstone walls had never felt the mason's chisel, and it stood, or rather stooped, at the point where Main Street touched the shore. No afternoon sun had sweetened the salt spray from the rollers crashing in from the North Sea, and for that reason alone I welcomed the low accommodation as a haven from the elements.

Inside the inn was a single, long room; all the carpentry was rough and unfinished, even the counter behind which the landlord stood. He continued to stand, mute, when I enquired after the tailor. Only the dart of his eyes to a darkened corner convinced me that he was not some tall Galatea into which the carpenter had poured all the dedication missing from the furnishings. Turning to Maccabi, I allowed that our host was a talkative cove. Maccabi grinned and said, 'Hardly that. John Bill is a mute, hasn't spoken a word since he washed up on the sand outside. His brother has never been found, nor even a plank from their boat. Coble placed him here, an uncommon generous act, I should say.'

'And so would I,' I replied, resolving to ascertain if Coble had left me any interest in this property, and to knock it down if he had.

A bent figure had risen as best it could from behind another rustic table. A dark and vigorous voice emerged, its beauty marked by an accent that was testament to the wanderings of its owner's tribe.

'Elijah Salomons, gentleman's tailor, at your service, Mr Moffat.'

I eyed Maccabi's old-fashioned dress and remarked, 'I am sincere in hoping, despite the evidence of my ears, that this is not your tailor.'

His lips grew thin; I had at last punctured his poise.

'No, sir, he is not. Mr Salomons is the best tailor north of Newcastle and south of Selkirk and numbers the Duke of Northumberland among his clients. I am most appreciative of his attending to you here in Seahouses.'

I offered a smile to my servant before turning back to the tailor.

'Now, tailor, take my measure, while you can.'

Salomons busied himself about my person with chalk, pins and a bolt of dark material I found crude and rustic.

'It is for the patterns, Mr Moffat. I assure you I shall choose the best of cloth to make your clothes, but I could not bring every bolt from Alnwick, I regret to say.'

Glancing over at Maccabi, I saw the beginnings of a smirk, but he averted his gaze from me and engaged the mute in a monologue.

'John, John. Join me in a porter, would you?'

John Bill's eyes rolled alarmingly as he gave a savage nod of affirmation. He poured two tankards and I noted none was offered to me.

'A game, a game, John. To while away my employer's fitting, wilt thou?'

The same exploration of every nook of the eyesockets followed by a brutal head movement came as answer. The dumb figure moved slowly from behind the counter and both men repaired to the opposite corner of the room to a table with nine skittles atop it in three rows of three. The table gave the impression of an over-large fruiterer's box set on four high legs. A stout wooden pole stood in the centre of the box. Attached to the pole by a link-chain was a heavy-looking wooden ball about the size of a plum. Maccabi, still addressing his mute companion in the same jovial tones, which, in truth, I could not credit nor countenance, 'Ha, John, take you the first foray among the clothmakers.'

After his ritual of assent, John Bill seized the ball, drew back the length of his arm and let fly at the skittles. It must have taken a throw of some skill, and an unerring eye, to cause the bolus to miss so completely, not only on the first pass but on all subsequent journeys through the pins until it came to rest against the pole.

'Bad luck, John! A farthing every one down, ho?'

The silent giant moved his head in the lateral plane, and held up a single gnarled finger as knotted as a branch.

'A penny?' Maccabi's eyes were wide. 'Gladly, John, on your head be it!'

Maccabi's shy was a delicate thing, the wooden ball passed through clean, carved a parabola in the air beyond the box and – returning at such an angle as to make the square of pins a rhombus – struck a glancing blow at a pin on the point of the arrangement. It toppled slowly and fell at right angles, knocking down some four skittles.

John Bill's carved mouth turned up slightly at one corner before he began his nod and eye-rolls. Taking the wooden ball between thumb and forefinger, he gave it the merest push towards the skittles. It struck just one, which rocked from side to side like a staggering drunk before clattering into another, causing that to strike still another and so on until all five remaining were rolling in the box. The tall figure twitched up the corner of his mouth once more and held his forefinger up.

It was a pleasure to see Maccabi fumbling in his pockets

for the penny. I noticed the tailor, too, had been fascinated by the game as he had left off his sizing of my figure. I looked down at him.

'Of course, you know what they call this game, Salomons?'

He set to again with his pins and chalk, shaking his head. 'No, sir, indeed I don't.'

I told him, 'It's known as De'il Among the Tailors. Perhaps it should be the other way about?'

Several pins fell from his lips and were lost between the coarsely fitted floorboards. The tailor assured me I would be in possession of a gentleman's wardrobe within a week and, as he had taken a pattern of my feet and various measurements below the knee, he also assured me of footwear to complement it. The man gathered his materials and scuttled out into the night like a cockroach startled by the sudden lifting of a carpet.

I looked over at Maccabi, hunched over a second tankard of porter. John Bill had put my retainer so far out of countenance that I considered revising my plan to knock down the inn, should I become its owner.

'Come, Maccabi. Are we ever to reach Gibbous House, or have you some further nonsense to keep me here?'

'By your leave, Mr Moffat, we have one more call to make. It were better done before visiting the house.'

'Well, let's on with it, man.'

His eyes darted to one side and he looked over my shoulder as he spoke. 'Begging your pardon, Mr Moffat, but in truth we cannot take possession today.'

'Why not? It is mine by right even now, is it not?'

'Most assuredly it is. The tide, however, will keep us from it.'

'Tide? You're babbling, Maccabi.'

'Sir, we must needs visit Lindisfarne and the Reverend Ezekiel Harbinger of the Church of Saint Mary the Virgin.'

'And for why? What has this to do with me?'

Regrettably, some of his smug self-confidence returned as he said, 'You were counselled to read the papers, Mr Moffat. The journey is unavoidable, I fear, and we must make haste if the causeway is to be open for our crossing.'

My watch showed a quarter before four. Maccabi intimated that the tide would be in before seven. I strode out of the door and we boarded the carriage; the horse looked as miserable as only a stabled beast can when left to the bitter elements. When I questioned Maccabi's liberal application of the whip to the nag's back, I was informed that the journey was seventeen miles.

The road north was poor as we took not the turnpike, but a road more used to the farmer's cart and his labourers' feet. My faithful retainer eyed me, averting his gaze when it caught mine. Several times he seemed on the point of putting an uncomfortable question, but immediately thought better of it. It gladdened my heart that he seemed to be grasping the true nature of our relative stations at last.

When I had enjoyed his silence and discomfiture for some two hours, we reached three cottages and a church beside a sheep farm, which the man informed me was named Beal. We turned onto the causeway road and after two further miles the phaeton rolled onto the muddied logs of the causeway. The North Sea nibbled at the edges of the primitive crossing and I asked him if he thought we were in time to complete it.

He thought for a moment and then enquired whether I could swim.

Chapter Eight

Complete the crossing we did, although the nag pulling us stepped high and skittish as the waves lapped at his cannon bones. Maccabi's silence allowed me to ponder something that had perplexed me since his unexpected arrival at The Olde Cross. How had he known I would try to avoid his reception? Why was it in his or Brown's interest that I should take up my inheritance? I realised that I had been careless in not reading every pen scratch on the papers presented to me and had missed the opportunity to quiz the notary on the peculiar wording of Coble's will. Regret at my own arrogance was of no use. Plainly, I would have to dissemble, pretend to the servant that he had my confidence as I took up residence in my new home.

The Northumbrian coast north of the mouth of the River Aln is as wild and bleak as any place in England, but never in my life had I seen so desolate a landscape as that on the island of Lindisfarne. Maccabi told me the lands were once populated by monks. What had possessed them to retreat to such a place? I would as soon have seen the face of the Devil than the Almighty in the raging of the sea on the rocks. It was already quite dark as the carriage rolled wearily to a stop, as if it were as exhausted as the horse.

The Church of Saint Mary the Virgin seemed to me a strange name for an Anglican institution, but the building itself betrayed no extravagant popery in its architecture. It was a simple rectangle, with a tower rather than a spire. It was raining again, and I was mightily relieved that the church doors were not locked, though they were heavy with the rain. There were few candles, the pews were simple and void of hassocks or cushions and the stone flags bore the wet footprints of the recently prayerful, although the church appeared empty.

Naturally, several of the stained-glass windows limned the eponymous Virgin, but the light was so poor as to prevent the discernment of anything more than dark pools of colour. I never set foot in a place of religion without feeling a certain distaste. For want of anything better to do, I approached the lectern at the front of the nave and looked at the heavy Bible. It was open at *Matthew 12:40*. The verse was marked;

'For as Jonah was three days and three nights in the belly of the whale, so will the Son of Man be three days and three nights in the heart of the earth'

I slammed the Bible shut, never having cared much for the opinion of revenue men. Besides, there was little in the Holy

Writ that I cared for, of course. A thin, ascetic figure in a cassock emerged from the vestry.

'One should not treat any book thus, much less the word of God, sir.' The good-humoured nature of the voice robbed it of reproof, but I found myself apologising nonetheless.

'I have ever been clumsy, Reverend... or is it Father?'

Once again Maccabi became a passive observer, not deigning to introduce this strange cove but instead studying some stone-carved New Testament admonition.

'As you please, sir, though I am vicar of this parish. I am Ezekiel Harbinger, but you may call me Ezekiel, if you so desire.'

With a dark look at the d____ fellow Maccabi, I made myself known to the vicar.

'Oh, at last you have come! May I suggest we conduct our business in the more comfortable accommodations of the vicarage?'

He laughed and I felt the rage in me. I thanked the stars above that I had learned to curb my passions, or at least to wait for the opportunity to gratify them in safety and leisure. Maccabi and I followed the vicar through the vestry and out of a mean wooden door. The vicarage itself was John Constable's idea of a countryman's cottage and, I thought, just as authentic.

'Somewhat more recent than the church, your home, Ezekiel?'

To his credit his face acquired a little colour. 'It was built a few years ago, thanks to the magnanimity of your late benefactor, Mr Moffat.'

On opening the door we found ourselves immediately in a parlour, where we were not alone. A young woman of perhaps eighteen years stood demurely in the clothes of a lady's companion or governess. Her colour and embonpoint hinted at pleasure at some future time, while her demeanour insisted such time would not be soon. She gave a curtsey as Harbinger announced her name as Ellen Pardoner. Harbinger bade we visitors sit and despatched the girl to bring sherry and seed cake.

The vicar of St Mary the Virgin eyed me closely, as if character could be read from outward appearance. Maccabi continued as mute as John Bill, averting his gaze as Miss Pardoner delivered his libation. I would soon have been quite out of temper had not Harbinger finally cleared his throat and begun. 'Ah... Mr Moffat, with inheritance comes oft responsibilities; particular duties, if you will.'

I interrupted the man with some heat. 'I'll not be gulled of money by idle promises of salvation hereafter, so if you have me here to beg my indulgence I'll gladly disappoint you, sir.'

Again, the corpse's face took a little colour. 'Oh, dear me, no... don't think... No, it's quite another matter, sir.'

Maccabi interjected, in a voice replete with annoyance and misery in equal measure. 'For the love of God – Tell him!' And then he stared once more off towards the vicar's bookcases.

Harbinger held out a hand to the young woman. 'Ellen Pardoner is a ward of the estate, at least until she reaches majority. As such she is... '

I smiled at him and finished his utterance for him. 'A most particular duty that falls to me, I think.'

Maccabi dropped his glass, spilling sherry on the floorboards.

Both Maccabi and I were reluctant to impose on the churchman's hospitality. I failed to see any practical disposition of the vicarage's two bedrooms between three gentlemen and the young woman. Harbinger, though, was insistent. He proposed overnighting himself in the vestry, as he had done in the past, and I proposed that I stay there myself, wishing neither to be closely accommodated with my servant nor interrupted again by the devotions of the devout. Once posited, this plan was accepted. I noted with interest the admixture of distress and delight at the arrangement on Maccabi's features. One could only surmise as to its cause.

At midnight I was in the cramped room of the vestry, under vestments that hung from hooks in the absence of an armoire. Also deficient was any kind of strongbox: the church's entire collection of plate was in a brass-bound chest, whose key was conveniently in the padlock. It turned easily, but the hasp was not so compliant.

The plate itself was a disappointment, tarnished and thin. I contented myself by removing the communion chalice and filling it from one of the bottles of red wine, neatly stacked on the floor in the corner. It was no fine vintage, rather something bottled in a wooden outbuilding on a Breton farm, rough as the callouses on the grape-picker's hands. Perhaps in consubstantiation the flavour would improve, but I doubted it.

Once again my mind returned to John Brown's behaviour earlier in the day. He had seemed most desirous of at once confirming and yet not confirming my identity as Alasdair Moffat. How could he possibly know anything of Alasdair Moffat's antecedents? Swilling the wine in the communion chalice, I thought back on the peculiar circumstances of Alasdair Moffat's death and resurrection in me.

It was true that the man then named Alasdair Moffat had educated me, and well. When I became his companion during his stay in the hospital, he used many names, totally convinced of the validity of each. I learned something of the Greeks from Socrates and Alexander, experienced the grandeur that was Rome from Martial, Trajan and Hadrian. Figures of high culture were on constant parade through the sick man's psyche, and I learned far more than I wished about Michelangelo, James I and the Duke of Buckingham.

This chameleon's education had been such as would have graced a Newton or any polymath, and yet the man was only six years my senior. I was of a height with him, and we were most remarkable similar in outward appearance, sufficiently so as to make one think us cousins of such consanguinity as to prohibit the relations we had in the latter days, even were we man and woman.

I spent so much time with him that, to my certain knowledge, the man known as Moffat never saw the Medical

Superintendent, at least not while he was alive. When his dead, sightless eyes met those of the henchman the patients knew as the Keeper, the latter was quite unaware of their owner.

It was only a short time after the madman's arrival in the asylum that delivery was made of the seaman's trunk. The supervision of its delivery fell to me, as much did in dealings with the man. The rough porters who brought the trunk handed me a key on an iron chain. I gave it to Moffat, who placed it around his neck as though it were an alderman's chain of office.

No sooner were the deliverers of the trunk away than it was opened. Without removal of the chain, Moffat knelt before it and opened it. The expression on his face was that of a man surprised at a mound of jewels, gold and coin, though I saw it contained nothing but books and parchment, and those in poor condition. Had I but known then, as I came later to learn, that many of these tomes were thought lost to the world, why then I should have made better use of that knowledge in the fullness of time.

From that moment on, we would take some work from the portmanteau library of the trunk every day, and peruse it carefully with whichever persona presented itself in Moffat's tortured mind at the time. On the flyleaf of each and every one was inked:

Από τα βιβλία του μοφφατ
(From the Library of Moffat).

On the day of Resurrection he drew out three heavy tomes:

Fama Fraternitatis, The Encyclopedia of the Brethren of Purity and *Avicenna's Canon of Medicine*. One in German and two in Arabic. Would that I had known then a little more of the first two works. In contrast to other days, Moffat – for once it was he who addressed me – laid the books aside on the cot, locked his trunk, and said, 'My Jonathan, I have been your David these long years. Wouldst thou be mine and I your Jonathan at last?'

I had endured his attentions for some three years, but never once had I achieved such transports as he himself did while using me as his catamite. This was a new development; it would surely be a novel experience for me to use him in the same manner, and I assured him I was willing.

He begged me to wear his own apparel and allow him to wear mine. I believed it was merely a spice for his jaded palate, even as he placed his chain and key around my neck. Use him I did, and with no small pleasure. In the small death after the act he smote me mightily on the crown and I knew no more.

Some hours later I awoke to see the purpled face of... whom? Moffat? Surely I was Moffat, as I wore his clothes and had his key around my neck. This other creature lay supine on the floor of the cell, the colour of his face testimony to the apoplexy that had carried him off. Stiffly, and mightily nauseous from the blow to my head, I shuffled to the door. Taking care not to move the corpse, I removed a ring of keys from what had once been my own coat, opened the door and bellowed for help. In an hour, an attendant came; I knew his face, but he saw my clothes and took no account of the physiognomy above them. This ruffian seized the keys from my hand, forced me inward and locked me in with the corpse.

I know not what period of time passed before the Keeper and his orderlies arrived. He checked the corpse and pronounced him as dead as I knew him to be. An enlightened man, he deigned to quiz me, a madman, as to what had happened.

I told him, more or less, allowing the evidence before him to define the actors and their roles. He left convinced that the Largs boy had perished of a fit after assaulting Alasdair Moffat, illegitimate son of the Duke of B_____.

It took me very much longer to convince him that the blow to Moffat's head had driven out the insanity. Some three years in fact.

Chapter Nine

I awoke in Harbinger's overstuffed armchair in the vestry. By the light of a guttering candle, I could read on my recently acquired timepiece that the hour was a little after four. The nightmare had been as ever it was, save for one small detail.

Until this occasion, my eyes would spring open at the point I looked down at the corpse's empurpled face; a solitary drop of blood would navigate the contours of my head to splash on the sightless eyeball of the man who was no longer Moffat. This time, however, I found that the drop of blood fell on a face still more well known to me: mine own.

There were three empty bottles of the dreadful wine to greet Harbinger when he arrived a little after seven. Despite them, my disposition had neither improved nor worsened. His piping voice invited me to a kedgeree breakfast in one hour in the cottage. I was free to avail myself of the cottage's amenities for my toilette, should I so desire. The clergyman eyed the empty bottles of wine, but said nothing. Picking up the communion chalice from the floor, I threw it to him, noting with pleasure that a few drops of the liquid splashed the white of his collar as he fumbled it.

'Ah well, only fitting that priestly vestments be stained with the Blood of Christ, Reverend?' For answer the vestry door slammed shut.

Breakfast was served in a dining room that would have been commodious for a troupe of circus dwarves, if they had numbered fewer than six. We three gentlemen seated ourselves at a Lilliputian table in chairs of corresponding size. Miss Pardoner hovered by the sideboard on which rested a copper chafing dish better than any of the thin silver plate owned by the parish in the church next door. The kedgeree was a fine example, but the fish, though smoked, was not haddock. I complimented the household on the fine flavours of the dish.

'Miss Pardoner prepared it,' Harbinger said. 'I fear I shall miss her skill in the kitchen when I return to my bachelor state.'

I raised an eyebrow. 'In the kitchen?'

Harbinger coloured and began to choke on a fishbone. Maccabi struck him several hearty blows between the scapulae.

My ward, far from running from the room in high dudgeon, turned on me an icy rage. 'Were I a man, sir, I should have satisfaction of you. Though I doubt you would treat a man as you have just done me.'

'Perhaps,' I said. The colour in her face made her suddenly attractive, and the prospect of having her under my dominion more pleasant still. It amused me, too, that she imagined I regarded any honour worthy of defending in a duel. The very notion seemed as outmoded as dancing a gavotte, and just as pointless, in my view.

'In any event, your talents in the kitchen are to be commended, if this be a sample of them. What is the fish? Do tell.' I smiled at her, which drew a murderous look from Maccabi, who seemed more affronted by the pleasantry than my insult.

With remarkable self-possession, Miss Pardoner replied, 'The fish were Craster kippers, Mr Moffat. Smoked herring, caught and cured in town. As Northumbrian as the Coquet river.'

'As you yourself?' I asked.

'Sadly, no. I belong here as little as you do, sir.'

Yes, I savoured the prospect of future days with Miss Ellen Pardoner.

Harbinger survived the lodging of the fishbone in his gullet, despite Maccabi's enthusiastic efforts to remove it via brute force applied to the dorsal region. The tableau cheered me quite as much as the fine breakfast, and then Maccabi addressed me directly for the first time in more than twelve hours. 'Mr Moffat, we must be going if we are to catch the tide. Might I suggest we leave Miss Pardoner to arrange her affairs here. I shall of course arrange suitable means of transport for your... ward in Seahouses, on our way to your new residence.'

'I should say, Maccabi, that I prefer that Miss Pardoner

accompany us forthwith. I am sure the reverend is familiar enough with the young woman's belongings to prepare them for consignment later.'

The man's incongruously jolly voice stumbled over an affirmation, and I laughed.

'I have not the slightest doubt of that, Reverend.'

It seemed for a moment as though Maccabi had not removed every piscatorial impediment to the reverend's respiration, but he recovered himself.

Maccabi and I had travelled side by side to Lindisfarne in the driving seat of the phaeton. The carriage was no high-flyer, thank goodness, as that design did not allow for a driver. Ours was a mail coach, mounted on mail coach springs, and as such it afforded a slightly less harum-scarum ride to the passengers – and the opportunity to further discommode Maccabi by sharing the rear seat with the interesting Ellen Pardoner.

I myself handed the young woman up into the phaeton, while Maccabi found something of interest in the Church of Saint Mary's bell tower. No sooner was I in my seat than Maccabi laid on the slightly recovered nag with a will. His impetuosity merely allowed me a closer acquaintance with Miss Pardoner's undoubted charms. She shrank quite away from me, and I studied her for a moment. Ellen Pardoner was not beautiful, her nose was slightly out of true and her eyes appeared inherited from a shipwrecked sailor of the Armada, which is to say as brown as a colt's. Nonetheless, I felt myself drawn to her, although I must allow that some of the attraction lay in the possibility of baiting Maccabi.

'So, Miss Pardoner,' I began, with a look at Maccabi's ramrod back. 'How come you to be quite the most attractive part of my inheritance?'

She lifted her chin. 'Mr Moffat, I am your ward and not your chattel.'

'Quite so, Miss Pardoner. But are you not promised? Has not Northumbrian society worn away the flags leading to your – or rather my – door by dint of your expectations, if not your beauty? Have you not pledged troth?'

Her eyes grew hot and I knew her for a woman of passionate temperament, though she spoke calmly.

'It seems to me that any expectations I might have had now exist – or do not – according to your own whim, sir.'

'Indeed they do, Miss Pardoner, indeed they do.'

Miss Pardoner begged my leave to refrain from further conversation as she had passed a somewhat restless night. I noted the stiffness about Maccabi's back subside as she did so, and I asked if her repose had been disturbed by an unwanted visitor. The ramrod returned in place of Maccabi's spine, and I was content to continue the journey in silence.

We jounced once more into Seahouses and ere the wheels had stopped spinning, Maccabi had alighted and handed Miss Pardoner down from the phaeton outside the garish green door of the notary's office. My retainer produced a key from a pocket and let our party in. I was quite intrigued – it seemed that relations between the notary and my employee were closer than might be expected. We negotiated the auctioneer's warehouse of a corridor and Maccabi stopped at the door to Brown's office and held up his hand.

'Miss Pardoner. Would you be so good as to remain without?' He declined to give me instruction; I supposed he knew I would not comply. It was plain that my ward was equally disinclined.

Placing my hand on her arm, I said, 'Please, I'm sure my servant has his reasons.'

The utterance served the two-fold purpose of keeping the young woman out and enraging each to my satisfaction.

The Brewster's Kaleidoscope of images that covered the room's walls again induced a dizzy nausea in me, until my wandering eyes were arrested by the sight of Brown slumped on his desk. I noticed the pungent smell of the heavenly demon and the tell-tale pipe in the notary's hand.

'By his face you would not know it, but d___ me that voice must come from somewhere.'

I looked at Maccabi for confirmation but answer came there none. He merely set about righting the cherubic figure in his chair, removing the pipe from his hand and hiding it in a drawer. It was full of papers as varied and jumbled as the ones I had been duped into signing.

This gulling by border rustics still rankled but, as a man of means, I expected opportunity enough to pay them out. Maccabi raised the sash to dissipate the poppy's miasma. He looked to me and pointed at the figure in the chair.

'He must have taken his pipe late today,' Maccabi said. 'He keeps office from two in the afternoon until six, as a rule.'

Then he opened the door to admit Miss Pardoner.

'Don't be alarmed, Miss Pardoner,' said the toady. 'Mr Brown is having his customary nap, he'll awaken soon.'

I saw myself how the young woman sniffed the air delicately – almost imperceptibly – before a tiny curl manifested at the corner of her mouth. The woman became more fascinating at every turn.

Brown emerged rapidly out of the poppy's spell. There were no cloudy-eyed moments of incomprehension, he became aware immediately that his secret was now known to at least one more, and he sighed. 'How unfortunate!'

'How so?' I enquired, and Maccabi gave me a sharp look but held his tongue.

'I do not care to be had at a disadvantage by a fellow such as you, Mr Moffat.'

His rasping voice scraped any respect from the title, leaving 'mister' in the company of choicer epithets he might have used but for the presence of Miss Pardoner. His cherub's chin slumped to his chest, and he said but one word: 'What?'

Maccabi started and placed a hand on the notary's arm. I lifted a finger toward the Jew and shook my head.

'Naturally, I would like possession of the papers I was foolish enough to sign. All of them.'

'Naturally,' Maccabi echoed.

Brown said nothing, nodded and withdrew the disorderly sheaf of papers from the drawer. The opium pipe fell to the floor and its blue and white porcelain bowl shattered. I wondered where the opium lamp was, and how he had sequestered it before the opium took him. My eyes must have been looking for it, for Brown said, 'It is behind the Hogarth. Take a look.'

At first I did not understand. Then I caught sight of the canvas depicting the moll at her toilette in a bawdy house. It was not a painting that I knew of. I approached and saw that the two bent nails holding one side of it to the wall were loose to the touch. Behind the canvas was a hollowing out of the plaster wall, and a beautiful example of an opium lamp on a tray of beautifully lacquered wood. It was as exquisite a piece of Chinoiserie as ever I had seen. How such a thing had arrived in an obscure notary's office in Northumbria, much less the painting, I could not begin to hazard. I drew the Hogarthian veil over the secret place once more, as Brown's grating voice began again.

'The girl is still your ward. Do with the papers what you will – everything is a matter of record at chancery. You will not avoid that responsibility, try as you might, Mr Moffat.'

'I do not intend to try anything of the sort.'

I smiled at the three of them in turn before questioning Maccabi. 'So, your purpose. Why are we here?'

But it was Brown who answered. 'Miss Pardoner is here, but I assume her effects are not, unless you found cartage on Lindisfarne. Jedediah, I will see to it. Get you on your way. Before Shabbat.'

Again, I was put out of countenance by the impropriety of

his relationship with Maccabi, who in truth owed fealty to me, his employer. Perhaps they both assumed I would renege on the contract I had unwittingly signed. If so, they were mistaken in me; there was far more prospect of amusement in keeping him in my employ.

Once more we were aboard the phaeton, the beleaguered horse overburdened by the extra passenger and weary from the exertions of the past three days. Maccabi made as if to lay about the nag once more, but I stayed him with a sharp word, and I was duly rewarded with glances from both him and the young lady, though of quite different characters. I, of course, gave not a fig for his treatment of the beast.

Not so much rolling as roiling northbound, I was surprised to feel anticipation at the prospect of finally reaching my new home. This thrill was dampened somewhat by the realisation that I was travelling the same road for a third time. It was indeed vexing to suspect that Brown, or Maccabi, had gone to great lengths to delay my occupation of Gibbous House.

Catching Miss Pardoner's eye, I enquired how she came to be entangled in my affairs. She gave me as cool a look as possible and retorted, 'Once again, I find your choice of words unfortunate, Mr Moffat. However, if you mean to enquire after the history of my arrival at the home of Septimus Coble, I shall tell you, though it is a tale commonplace in most parts.'

Maccabi's ears seemed possessed of an astounding muscularity, for I could have sworn his right ear extended a quarter-inch in the direction of us passengers. The young woman cleared her throat and began: 'My life began seventeen years ago, in June 183_, occasioning my mother's deliverance from the trials of her own. I do not mean to say that her trials were any greater than those of any wife to a country parson with a living that kept him and his in impecunity, if not outright poverty. My father would have married again, if only to give his babe a mother, but his prospects were no better than his situation, and society did not consider him in want of a wife. My father did not survive beyond my fifth year himself.

'The parish seemed to be my fate, until the new incumbent began a search for any relative of mine with the means and inclination to take over my education. The reverend must indeed have been a charitable man, if charity be measured in years and not affection, for I was eleven years in age before I was collected for delivery to Septimus Coble and his home here in Northumbria.

'I saw Mr Coble daily at dinner. He was distant but made generous provision for me until his death. My tutors were diligent, if uninspiring, and it seems to me I have had an education of a kind not enjoyed by many women of any station. In fact, I had hopes of—'

She broke off, remaining silent despite all my efforts to draw her out. I was not sure if I believed a word of her tale: she was too exotic a bloom to have sprouted from such meagre soil.

The silence became too much for Maccabi as we passed Bamburgh Castle, and he remarked on the renovations. 'The trust has paid a penny or two for that work. More than thir-teen centuries of history in the castle.'

He had slowed the nag's pace – though I scarce believed that possible – to take in the majesty of the place, as he put it. I could not but reprove him.

'Maccabi, it is my belief that time and money is wasted on the past. I am more concerned with the future, mine in par-ticular. You would do well to look to yours. How distant lies the house, for I am heartsick at all this delay?'

His back stiffened and he grunted, 'Just past Budle Hall on the way to Spindlestone.'

Which answer, of course, meant nothing to me, and I told him so.

'Two miles, Mr Moffat. Two miles to your house, no more.'

Chapter Ten

Budle Hall – a featureless block of a house with all of the straight lines and none of the distinguishing marks of the new Palladian style – was some half an hour behind us. Rounding a corner, we came suddenly upon an estate wall that stretched as far as the eye could see. I held my peace, although I was impressed by the extent of my property. Maccabi stole a glance to the rear and I was glad I had kept my composure.

A few furlongs further on, we stopped at a gatehouse. What had once been a building appropriate to its function was alarming in its present dilapidation. Not a pane of glass remained in the windows visible from the carriage. There were slates on the roof, but they appeared to have been dropped from the hand of a giant and left where they fell. Birds' nests were visible through the holes in the roof, but nary a living creature stirred or gave sound. It was as sorry a place as ever I had seen.

Maccabi, his mood apparently improved, leaped jauntily from his seat, producing a large ring of keys from somewhere about his person. A representation of a coat of arms adorned the gates: party per bend sinister, a unicorn rampant was the charge in one field and the other lay bare. Whether the unicorn was proper or some fantastical colour I could not say; I doubted that it was the crest of any family at all.

The key turned surprisingly easily in the lock, given the rusted and buckled nature of the ironwork. Maccabi swung the gates wide with a flourish, made only slightly ridiculous by the discordant screech of the iron. Retaking his post, he drove the phaeton within, neglecting to secure the gates behind us.

The drive was sweeping: it curved and rose up an incline that was injurious to the horse's wellbeing. I looked upward to the crest of a hill. What I could only assume was a dome to rival St. Paul's appeared from the crest. It looked like nothing more than the grey hump of a gargantuan crookback. Maccabi gave his unattractive laugh.

'Your demesne, Mr Moffat. Fitzgibbon House.'

'Fitzgibbon?' I queried.

'Look at it, sir. Just one of the reasons for its more customary name.'

This sight was nothing to the horror that awaited on the other side of the hill.

The disrepair into which the gatehouse had fallen was not in evidence, but Fitzgibbon House was a conglomeration of architectural styles that held no regard to harmony or beauty. The greater part seemed to have been completed when the most ridiculous extravagances of the Baroque style were in vogue. The dome itself was vast and, far from forming the hub of the house, strayed disconcertingly from the centre.

There was nothing of symmetry about the design: the east wing boasted three towers enjoined by a cloistered walk, while the west had four spires of differing heights and construction. The materials of construction appeared to have been chosen by a magpie. Verdigrised copper on one spire, moorish tile on another; sandstone on that wall, yeoman brick on this. The monstrosity had been designed by – or for – a lunatic.

The grounds surrounding the house had not had the benefit of a landscape gardener's eye. It was a vista of spinney and copse interspersed with grassland, which, though not overgrown, was home to numerous sheep. Of all the fates I had ever imagined might befall me, gentleman farmer was not among their number.

The horse came gratefully to a halt in front of the vast threshold. Being Northumbria, the huge doors were flanked by the seemingly ubiquitous lions, tails extended, though any house by the name of Fitzgibbon could have little to do with the Percys. Maccabi reached for the iron doorknocker, wrought in the shape of a monkey's head. He moved it gingerly, although it was clearly of significant weight and unlikely to be damaged by his use of it. He let it give a single knock on the heavy plate affixed to the oak door.

'Am I so fortunate as to have a household full of retainers, Maccabi?'

He shifted from foot to foot momentarily; I had never seen him so hesitant.

'Not exactly, sir,' he said. 'You have a cook, Mrs Gonderthwaite, and, well... '

He did not finish: the door began to open inward without the slightest trace of the creaks and groans I had been expecting. At first it seemed that the door opened by mysterious means, until I heard a voice emanating from about the height of my waist. A deep and heroic baritone emerged from a figure the size of a five-year-old. It seemed that no one in this forsaken land possessed a voice appropriate to them.

'Mr Moffat, Miss Pardoner, welcome. Shabbat shalom, Jedediah.'

I turned to Maccabi and asked the name of the manneikin.

'My name, Mr Moffat, is Enoch.'

'Enoch. It is not customary to address one's staff by their... first names, I believe.'

The dwarfish fellow stiffened his back, puffed out his not inconsiderable chest and said, 'Well that I am not one such, Mr Moffat. I am Professor Enoch Jedermann, once of Vienna, Leyden and Siena Universities, late of Berlin. I am... curator of the Collection.'

He hesitated for the briefest time, and then added, 'At your service.'

'Collection?' My eyebrows would have become entangled with my hair had I raised them any further.

Miss Pardoner caught my eye, and I saw the familiar upturn at the very corner of her mouth. Maccabi looked uncomfortable. The professor displayed the most self-possession I have ever seen in such a minuscule container.

'My great friend, the late Septimus, was an avid collector of certain... artefacts,' the professor said. Then he nodded and repeated, 'Artefacts.'

Looking around, I realised that the eccentric furnishing of Brown's offices reflected the entrance hallway of Gibbous House. Passages narrowed by piles of heaped furnishings led off the hallway and to a staircase that swept up into a gallery under the dome. I felt that the lunacy of the interior might possibly prove to be the equal of that of the exterior.

I enjoined Maccabi to show me the house, and bade Miss Pardoner make herself comfortable. The professor I invited to dine with us at the hour of eight. It pained me somewhat when he replied, 'Forgive me, Mr Moffat. But as it is Shabbat, I took the liberty of bidding Mrs Gonderthwaite prepare the Shabbat meal. It is כָּשֵׁר – kasher – I hope you do not think me too presumptuous. I feel we should respect others' customs, Mr Moffat, don't you?'

Of course I did think him so, but I would not give him the satisfaction of knowing it. I gave him no more than a cursory nod in response before Maccabi began to show me the seat of my fiefdom.

The staircase led up to a gallery off which led several doors to other parts of the house, including both east and west wings. Contrary to the impression created by the elevation of the forefront, the house extended far, if haphazardly, to the rear. Like the hallways, the atrium was crammed with furniture of madcap selection and sundry bric-a-brac. On the gallery, sconced candles threw a faint illumination on the discoloured wallpaper. This paper was in the French style of half a century before, and, though not so bright as it once had been, was a *trompe l'oeil* after those of Zuber et Cie, a depiction of a vast hall of mirrors.

Maccabi pushed the surface of one of the faux mirrors and it swung ajar. He directed me through into a long corridor with some twenty doors to other rooms. He turned to me. 'These are all the usable bedrooms, sir. The west wing is uninhabitable on account of the cats, whilst the east houses the Collection.'

'And where are the servants' quarters?' I asked him.

He replied with a little heat, 'Miss Pardoner and the professor are the only other users of these accommodations, sir.'

I guessed he had but recently vacated them, or I had mistaken myself in the man.

Each door had at one time been painted in a different shade of blue, with the nearest to the looking-glass entrance being the lightest and the last in the corridor being almost black. Maccabi cleared his throat. 'Miss Pardoner has the teal, third on the left. The professor has the midnight-blue at the very end, Mr Moffat. I suggest you inspect the others to see which is the most suitable to your purpose. I shall wait below to show you the rest of the house; I regret that I may not be able to accompany you around the grounds after darkness falls.'

It was no surprise that he wished to be shot of me as much

as I of him. He was a fool if he thought I would not take the opportunity to investigate what lay behind both the teal and midnight-blue doors.

The brass knob was tarnished to the colour of mud, and contrasted sharply with the still-vibrant teal of Miss Pardoner's bedroom door. It seemed politic to peruse her chamber now, as no doubt she would be performing her toilette before dinner. There were few women of my acquaintance who could do such in less than an hour. The hinges appeared to be as ill cared for as the knob, since they groaned and creaked as though they were about to reveal Ambrosio the Monk in the hands of his inquisitors.

The room was plain enough, neither over furnished nor sparsely so. Its papered walls were no doubt pleasing to the feminine eye, although perhaps more attuned to the tastes of a half-century earlier. The porcelain stood neatly and clean on the toilette to the left of a window. What this window overlooked I could not say, for the filth of it was as impenetrable as night. Nor could I imagine what lay beyond: something about my home disturbed me whenever I attempted to conjure its composition in my mind's eye.

The bed was four-posted, and there were holes in its tester. The curtains seemed in better repair, although a tawdry scene was depicted on them: a very poorly executed copy of 'The Marriage of Venus'. I wondered if this had had any bearing on Miss Pardoner's choice of bedchamber, or if she had merely chosen a door close to the ingress for its convenience. The room itself was spacious enough to encompass several large pieces of furniture and a faded Persian carpet of some beauty.

A large double-fronted armoire was on the wall adjacent to the sash window. Beside it stood a tallboy in the same richly dark wood; it might have been mahogany. The drawers opened smoothly and I chose an item of intimate apparel from one of them; it fit snugly in the long pocket of my frock coat. Opposite was a bookcase that contained only three books. Novels, rather. They were the work of the so-called Bell brothers. I opened one at random; Miss Pardoner, or someone, had underlined the following: 'Conventionality is not morality.'

It was a mere fragment of a somewhat longer statement. But the four words seemed sufficient to me to found a philosophy upon. I confess I hoped that my ward's hand had drawn the line under this motto.

At this point the mooted defiler of the tome entered the room. A low and extravagant bow seemed an appropriate greeting. She gave the merest nod and struggled against a smirk: 'I trust you have satisfied your... curiosity, Mr Moffat.'

'There is time enough for that, Miss Pardoner, I promise you.' I gave a somewhat more perfunctory bow and left her to her toilette. It was not until I left the room that I realised it was deficient in one particular. There had been no sign of a looking-glass.

Someone, I supposed it to be Maccabi, had lit candles in the corridor. There was a window of relative transparency at the very end, but it was admitting little light as dusk was falling. The improvement offered by the candlelight was but little and the dark wallpaper above the wainscoting scarcely helped.

The corridor would indeed have been a dismal place had it not been for the inexplicably unfaded shades of the blue doors. Chance and serendipity had long fascinated me, who had charted no course through life but merely profited – or not – from coincidence at every turn. Therefore, I chose a door midway down the sinister side, for no other reason than that it was the same shade as my frock coat.

The brass knob and plate were alike in design to Miss Pardoner's, save for the fact that they were highly polished. As I opened the door, it became clear that unlike the other bedchamber, this would easily welcome a clandestine nocturnal visitor. I took a candle from the sconce to the left of the door before entering. Inside was a window, although it was not quite so filthy: the glass was so clear as to allow enough crepuscular light to illuminate the room, but perhaps not to permit the reading of any papers.

The bed was little different from that of the previous room, though the tester was in good repair, if a little faded, and there were no classical scenes of dubious taste on the drapery. These drapes were a subtle and warm sienna colour, and decorated with a monogram that included a six-pointed star and the letters A and C. Again, I was struck by the lack of a looking-glass.

The furnishings were lighter in colour, there was no hulking wardrobe of mahogany, rather a clothes press. I slid out a tray or two but found them empty. In common with the other furnishings, the wood was highly polished walnut. There was a dresser with porcelain stood atop it, a little high for practical use. Several hair pins were strewn beside the sanitary ware. A silver-backed hairbrush lay next to them, and it looked as though it should have had as companion a hand-held looking-glass, but it did not. In one corner, to my surprise, was a love seat. With my candle, I walked over to inspect it more closely. The upholstery was stained in a manner that I recognised from years of removing linen from lunatics' beds. Neither stain should have been found in the room of a lady of quality.

There was also a handsome leather-bound book with a locked hasp on the seat, also bearing the monogram with the six-pointed star. It was a simple matter to break the lock with the spear-blade penknife I carried in my pocket.

The book was a journal, and inside was the name Arabella Coble.

Chapter Eleven

I was pricked by no sentimentality in finding the adolescent journal of my late wife. I was merely puzzled that such a thing would still lie in her bedchamber so long after her departure from Gibbous House. But my recent apprehension of my wife's earlier incarnation as the wife of one Cadwallader had provoked in me some curiosity about her, such as I had heretofore not owned, and I took up the book. Equally baffling was the immaculate repair of the room itself.

Book under my arm, I advanced to the door opposite the professor's midnight-blue. The shade applied liberally to this door was navy. There was a lever arrangement where the handle should have been. Brass – as the other door furniture had been – neither carelessly filthy nor diligently polished.

I glanced over my shoulder at the portal to the professor's lair. I swung the door wide. The walls were void of paper or hangings of any kind, and painted with limewash. There was a mean cot cramped against one wall, and the room was not large. There was a window of sorts: a tiny square of glass and wood with no apparent aperture. A rough wooden garderobe stood in one corner and in the centre of the rough carpentry of the floorboards stood a chamberpot, or – more correctly – a bourdaloue. The room reminded me of nothing so much as the asylum in Edinburgh. I tossed my late wife's diary on the cot, pleased with my choice of bedchamber.

It was time to inspect the professor's inner sanctum. There were several unusual aspects to his retreat. For one, an entire wall consisted of the most magnificent mahogany shelves filled with leather-spined books and sundry papers, many of which the professor – unless he possessed the agility and balance of a colobus – could have no earthly hope of perusing.

The remainder of the room was almost filled by the largest bed I had ever seen; bare of tester or other drapery, the posts rose like vacant flagpoles toward the ceiling. At last I had found a room in possession of a looking-glass, although it would have been of little use in adjusting one's dress: the entire ceiling was of mirrored glass, though cracked and crazed as if someone had thrown stones at it by the handful. It showed distorted reflections of murals as outrageous as those rumoured to have been discovered in Pompeii and Herculaneum. Indeed, I would not have been surprised if Francis I of Naples had fainted dead away in the presence of such lubriciousness. I wondered how the professor slept at night, or, indeed, if he preferred not to do so.

The professor's library drew my eye: the entire wall of shelves appeared to have the tomes and papers arranged in no discernible order. Plutarch sat cosily beside Pythagoras and both were Pope's *Dunciad* away from the sentimentalist scribbler Dickens. More venerable volumes had titles familiar to me from Moffat's trunk; several of these were beside vellum and parchment documents. I took only a bundle inscribed with a script identical – it appeared – to the magically appearing hieroglyphs on the blank vellum sheets I had received from the unfortunate Mr Cartwright. A volume lay open on the bed, a wavering black line under the words,

> *But it must be thought that the electric principle, that it*
> *may be easily understood from those things which we*
> *shall soon submit, was not added by accidental causes,*
> *but was intentionally implanted by nature:*

It was a book on something called 'Animal Electricity' by one Luigi Galvani, and it seemed to contain more such arrant nonsense, light on which page I might.

There appeared little of a personal nature in the room, at least nothing that I could find among the professor's clothing. Nor was there any trace of an escritoire or writing slope. Evidently none of the professor's duties of curatorship was performed in the privacy of his bedchamber.

That fellow gave a mighty roar of pain as I tripped over him on the way out of his room. I considered I might issue him with a bell so that one might be warned of his approach. No one should be forced to perambulate their home, eyes fixed downward, on account of a midget. He recovered his equilibrium and his patriarchal voice was calm as he said, 'Feel free to borrow anything from my library, Mr Moffat.

Although I fear there is little that is not in your own, or rather in that which comprises part of the Collection.'

My hackles quite rose. 'And how would that not be mine?'

'All writing is posterity's, Mr Moffat, we merely safeguard it for others.'

I eyed him, astounded at the patronising tone emerging from three feet below my own mouth.

'D___ posterity, Professor, and d___ you!'

And I resolved to be rid of the Collection – whatever it might be – and its eminently d___able curator, as soon as I possibly might.

The tiny man stiffened, made a parody of a bow and informed me that, as it soon would be the hour of eight, he would be delighted if I would join him in the library for a libation of my own choosing. It was insufferable; the man was treating me as a guest in my own house. It would soon be time for me to go abroad, in search of relief from danger-ous passions. I feared there would be little opportunity in rural Northumberland. Nevertheless, I remained outwardly cordial to the man and bade him lead me to the library.

We passed back through the *trompe l'oeil* looking-glass and descended the stairs in silence. Choosing our path care-fully through the piled furniture, we made for a fine walnut door leading to the east wing. The professor passed through it and quickened his pace, his gait becoming the scuttle of a roach, the nails in his tiny boots recalling associated sounds. Surprisingly, I had to make an effort to stay close on his heels;

as a consequence, I could take less note of the rooms we passed through than I might have wished.

It was clear, however, that the first – as well as housing *objets de mystère* in every material, of every shape and size – appeared to be serving as the dining room, at least for this evening. The next room was crammed with products of the taxidermist's art; from the largest savage feline to the tiniest wren, it seemed as though all creation, or at least an example of every species of fauna, had gathered in the room. It was as though one of each of Noah's pairs had made the huge journey from Ararat to be rendered glassy eyed and sinister in Northumbria.

The next room was reminiscent of the notary's office, and for that reason I was glad that the dwarf's scurrying pace had not abated, as we passed through the madman's gallery of images rapidly. Then came a room of geological specimens: agates, beryl, topaz, simpler quartzes, fossils, amber. I would have preferred to tarry in it, but the professor's hobnails tip-tapped ever on. We passed through a vivarium worthy of the Zoological Society's garden in Regent's Park, and I shuddered at the slithering behind the foliage-darkened vitrines.

At last we came to the library. A vast room: it was a repository of books such as the fabled Alexandrian library must have been. The dimensions of the room itself were most impressive. In length it comprised two chains. One wall was punctuated by high, arching windows between which shelves were bursting with books of every size and shape. One of the shorter walls enjoyed French windows leading out onto the grounds, but they were of course flanked by more books. The remaining longer wall contained thousands upon thousands of volumes. The ceiling was high and vaulted, six chandeliers filled with an unconscionable quantity of candles lit the room. Other candlebrae stood on every available surface, and there were many. Low bookcases and tables housed further books, and some manner of seating stood by every place where a hand might be laid on a book.

One low table by a chaise and an upholstered seat had but one book; the remainder of its surface, thanks be, was taken up by crystal glasses and tantali. The professor, as yet not putting aside his irritating presumption, poured us both a generous glass of jerez and proposed a toast:

'To posterity, Mr Moffat.'

'To purgatory, Professor,' I replied.

It was not a jerez of the very highest quality, but it was more than palatable. In fact, it was a better libation than had passed my lips in some time. We were still standing, the professor and I, and though it might be expected that the advantage in height that I held would have made him uncomfortable, indeed it did not. Perhaps it was the darkest brown tones of his voice, the biblical quality of his speech or the perfection of his English in contrast with his accent, but he seemed as prepossessed as any man I had ever met. I despised him for it; hated him for making so little of his disadvantage, and so much of his tiny self. His eyes were full of intelligence as befitted a man of his learning, and I searched in vain for something of the sly in them. He kept them on me, scarce blinking, as though quite content to look at me until I began a conversation or died of boredom.

'Professor,' I began, 'you will forgive me if in future my household does not comply with the servants' rituals. As a man unconvinced of the existence of any divine being, I should prefer that any religious observance of whatever marque not take place under my roof. You may do as you please within your own chamber. At least until I have considered the disposition of this household and your place within it.'

He lifted an eyebrow and, although I felt it had a somewhat comical effect, I was unable to laugh.

'Mr Moffat, Jedediah has told me you have been foolish enough to sign unread papers. I see now that I should have believed him. Gibbous House and all its contents form part of a discretionary trust.'

'Professor,' I sneered, 'I thought you were a man of science, not a court room pettifogger.'

'I have studied a modicum of law, Mr Moffat. Do you know what a discretionary trust signifies?'

'I have no doubt that it signifies you will continue to be a parasite on the estate, sir.'

He gave a smile that quite transformed his face. From that of a sweet-faced dwarf it transformed into the physiognomy of a corrupt and evil gnome. 'Quite so, Mr Moffat, if you care to phrase it thus.'

The smile was gone ere he finished speaking and he assumed a pious look. 'It is time for the Shabbos meal, Mr

Moffat. I think you will find it interesting, even though it be a religious observance. I do.'

His tiny boots beat their tattoo back through the hoards of miscellany to the dining room, and I was forced to follow him.

Chapter Twelve

The room was gloomy. Barely four candles were lit in the few sconces visible in between the stockpiles of bizarrerie in evidence, however, there were several bronze candelabra at intervals along the imposing table. In the murk I could see Miss Pardoner already seated. Maccabi hovered as if caught betwixt taking a chair and moving to stand at the wall like a footman. There were three further places at the table. I moved to the head of it, opposite Miss Pardoner.

Discourse over dinner would be at some volume, it seemed. I enjoined Maccabi to take a seat, if he was sure all was in readiness for the repast. He flinched at the imputation that I might expect him to fetch a cruet set or a bottle of port if not. On my waving the professor to the remaining seat, the fellow shook his head and began intoning in an alien tongue, while picking up a carafe containing wine. It was a prayer of some sort. Maccabi's head was bowed, and Miss Pardoner gave me a bold look for the duration of the incantation. I returned it with interest.

Jedermann moved down the table until he stood next to a silver platter with two unusual loaves atop it. The bread had a look of a braid or plait and the dwarf had, as with the wine, a little difficulty in reaching the platter to bestow his blessing on the bread. His domed head appeared over the edge of the table. It was all I could do not to laugh. It seemed a very serious matter for Maccabi and the professor himself, if not for my ward, who appeared to be biting the inside of her cheek.

I smote the table with my palm. 'For pity's sake, when does a man eat!'

Maccabi shook his head while the professor fetched a lit taper from a tall, thin piece of cabinetry that looked like it should be furniture, but which shared no features with any piece that I knew, save that of being made of wood. The professor took only a few minutes to terminate the pantomime of lighting the candles in the holders, the taper being long enough to allow him the lighting of them whilst on tiptoe and balancing on one leg. He sat at last, breathing a little heavily. Looking from my face to a bell at my left hand, he nodded vigorously. I grasped the wooden handle and the bell gave out a sound of less-than-perfect pitch, but of surprising volume.

A sparsely lean and forbidding figure entered bearing a huge covered platter. Her strength must have been a sinewy sort. Garbed in black with hair shorn as short as a man's and so white, in conjunction with the pallor of her skin, as to offer as monochromatic a study of a less-than-matronly figure as ever I had seen, she said not a word. Placing the huge dish on the table, she uncovered a massive pike. It was surrounded by whole grunions and the leaves of an uncommon large lettuce. The professor let out a groan of what I assumed was appreciation. Maccabi explained, 'It is customary to eat fish or meat for the Shabbos meal; we thought the fish would have something of novelty for you, sir.'

I forebore to say that I might have expired from a surfeit of novelty since arriving at the house.

The skeletal Mrs Gonderthwaite assembled our chargers in the centre of the table and began serving portions of the freshwater fish and whitebaits on them. Picking up two of them she made first of all towards Maccabi, who wisely shook his head. Veering around the table she appeared to be making for the professor's place setting. The diminutive fellow, who, despite a complex arrangement of a wooden block and some cushions atop his chair could barely reach his cutlery, held up a hand. At which point I interposed. 'No, no, I insist, Professor. Guests should always be served first, don't you think?'

He made no reply other than an expressive shrug.

Maccabi stood up, with little grace I thought, as he had to steady the chair behind him. He then set about pouring the blessed wine. Noting his decision to begin with me, I waved him towards Miss Pardoner, at least as soon as he had reached my glass. I informed Mrs Gonderthwaite that I expected, as the host, to be served last, and plates in hand she accomplished a graceful curtsey while nodding her agreement.

So, whatever Mrs Gonderthwaite's intent had been in the

apportionment of the viands, I was not displeased to mark that my plate showed much less of the intricate designs favoured by the Spodes Major and Minor than the others'. The woman departed, as silent as a wraith and perhaps as insubstantial.

I waited expectantly. No further mummery being forthcoming, I bade the table commence. Opposite me, Miss Pardoner manipulated her cutlery with less delicacy than one might have expected: she did not, of course, have a simian grip on the handle of her knife by any means. She merely applied her silverware with a methodical and efficient will and seemed to be making very short work of her vittles. Maccabi pushed his fish around his platter like a sulky boy of five. The professor ate at a fashionably slow pace. I raised my glass. 'To absent friends, and those soon to depart.'

Maccabi and the professor reluctantly raised their own. My ward raised hers to the accompaniment of either the most prodigiously lethargic tic, or the most lascivious wink I had ever witnessed.

Mrs Gonderthwaite drifted in and out with a selection of unfamiliar dishes, fish for the most part, fresh and saltwater, hot and cold, pickled and salted, with nary a sign of crab or lobster. Of conversation there was little; on being presented with something which the professor informed me was 'gefilte fish', I enquired if it was the custom to eat so much food at one sitting.

It was Maccabi who replied, 'For us, yes. The chosen are

blessed with an extra soul on Shabbat, and we ensure that it is well fed.'

The professor simply said that he didn't care for moderation, to which I replied, 'No more do I.'

Having finally engaged the fellow in conversation, I bluntly and perhaps somewhat rudely said, 'Discretionary trust?' Tilting my head on one side, I waited for a response.

It did not come from the little man. Miss Pardoner's pleasingly deep but not unfeminine voice informed me: 'It is quite a simple instrument in its basic form, as I understand it. However, Mr Moffat,' here she gave the beginnings of a smile, 'your inheritance is subject to a particular type of discretionary. That is, a testamentary trust.'

She paused. Maccabi looked at the ceiling. I caught a glimpse of the corrupt and evil gnome in the professor's visage and watched him give the barest of nods. Miss Pardoner went on. 'Wherein the discretionary trust shall be a testamentary trust, it is not uncommon for the settlor to leave a letter of wishes for the trustees to guide them as to said settlor's wishes in the exercise of their discretion. In so far as Coble left sundry papers detailing his wishes for the disposition and management for the legacy in trust, you, Mr Moffat, whether you had read the papers or no, might be said to be in receipt of a Fool's Mate. Certainly, with the game barely begun, regarding whatever plans you might have had for the house, its contents or – it pains me to say it – my own self, said game is already lost. And your plans are therefore moot.'

The young woman finished speaking and looked me

directly in the eye. I confess to being dumbstruck. Not at the legal expertise so lightly shewn, nor at the seeming impasse to which I had come: no, I was absolutely captivated by the boldness of the woman, and I wondered what such a woman would not do, given the opportunity and means.

Maccabi and I sat down once more, just as the professor tumbled from his perch in a most inelegant style. Not even this mishap could disturb the dwarf's remarkable sang-froid, and he announced that he would serve the port since he was up, or at least down, from his chair. Luckily the port decanter and glasses had been placed somewhat nearer to the edge of the ostentatiously large table. Having charged a glass for each of us, he drew himself up to his far from considerable height and addressed me thus: 'Mr Moffat, if you would be so kind as to indulge me, a mere guest in your home, to propose a toast of my own.'

I nodded my assent; Jedermann began a rambling anecdote seemingly as preamble for his toast. The academic's voice was strangely compelling for me; so much so that I paid little heed to the wanderings of his speech. No, I spent the time cudgelling my brains in a vain attempt to ascertain quite why this voice intrigued me so. It was, it must be admitted, a fine one. Befitting an actor on the London stage. Not for the principal parts, of course, but it would have done splendidly for the villainous foreigner of whatever stripe, which character at that time was the *sine qua non* of the dramatic arts. Neither was it the contrast I had previously noted between his beautiful diction, coupled with an undeniable erudition, and the starkly alien accent. It was the familiarity of it: I do not mean to say that I had heard *this* voice before my arrival at Gibbous House; indeed not. My feeling was that I had heard somewhere, at some forgotten time, a similar voice, with similar traits of vocabulary and accent. Naturally, I was quite unprepared to find Maccabi and Miss Pardoner both upright and looking at me expectantly with glasses raised. I cleared my throat and my ward offered the toast: 'Next year in Jerusalem.'

Maccabi repeated the toast in a choking voice and I wondered if he had been as unlucky as Harbinger in the matter of fishbones. Certainly, he was affected enough to have a tear in his eye. I raised my glass and tossed off the port. It struck me that there had been quite some fuss for a small household's dinner on a Friday evening. Waving my empty glass, I said slowly, 'Well, I think there'll be a little less formality in future. Or at least such that there is will be of a more civilised kind.'

'Let it be so, Mr Moffat,' Jedermann replied with great equanimity and I noted he had not drunk the toast nor even risen from his peculiar chair.

I espied Maccabi turning a little puce at this point, and hoped to see the spectacle of the professor attempting to dislodge a fishbone from his throat by leaping up to strike the middle of his back. Unfortunately, the bone was swallowed forthwith or there was some other reason for my factotum's antics.

Abruptly, Miss Pardoner stood and, naturally enough, we

did the same. Or, rather, Maccabi and I did. The professor was still struggling to dismount from his complex seating arrangement as Miss Pardoner informed us:

'As is customary, sirs, I shall withdraw and leave you to your gentlemanly pursuits.'

Again, I noted the upward tilt of one corner of her mouth, and I pondered whither she would withdraw, since the accommodations I had thus far seen had not included any manner of withdrawing room. It had amused me to pretend to Maccabi and Miss Pardoner that I knew nothing of their customs and that I was unaware that, in fact, Passover had not yet begun and no matzah had been served. Of course, I was not entirely unacquainted with Jewish custom; how could I not be so, having married the occasionally righteous Miss Arabella Coble?

Nevertheless, Professor Jedermann continued in a most affable voice, 'Mr Moffat, you must forgive us if we have been a little more formal than usual. The Passover meal . . .'

'Yet you are not Jewish yourself, Professor?'

'I am fascinated by all religion. Since Miss Pardoner and Maccabi are Jewish it suits me to indulge them. We have learned much from the Jewish scholars.'

On and on he went, as if I were a student in some lecture hall in Siena, Berlin or Vienna, and as if I gave a bent farthing to boot. The voice continued to nag at me; my mind turned quite inward and I forgot to ask whom he meant by 'we.' I did not hear the word that brought the memory back, I only knew that the owner of the voice that his own so brought to mind had been instrumental in Alasdair Moffat's long-awaited release from the asylum, years before.

Chapter Thirteen

It was a measure of how distracted I was that I gave a start when the professor dismounted from his siege perilous somewhat acrobatically, and, it must be said, with a modicum of grace. He gave an exaggerated bow and excused himself to his chamber, no doubt to savour the acrobatic propensities of some of those figures depicted on its walls. Maccabi gave the sketchiest of bows and an indecipherable grunt. The decanter of port was half full when I poured my next glass, and I placed it nearby for the sake of convenience. Memory found me in Moffat's cell in the Edinburgh asylum on the day of my release: December 24th 183_, and I remembered letters scrawled on mildewed leaves of long-lost books...

The Medical Superintendent, 'the Keeper', as we patients knew him, was present in the company of a tall figure possessed of an authoritarian air and the brow of a polymath. I sat on the cot; my two interlocutors had brought an ill-matched pair of gimcrack chairs in rough deal, and placed them adversarially opposite me in the cramped cell. The

Keeper and the other fellow had been seated for a quarter-hour in complete silence. The stranger had a notebook open and a pen poised, but to that point had written nothing. Abruptly he began with a diffident question: 'Mr Alasdair Moffat, is it?'

'Who else might I be?' I offered.

'Well, begging your pardon, according to the Medical Superintendent's account you might be Napoleon on Monday, Nelson on Tuesday and Nebuchadnezzar by the end of the week, d'you see?'

A reasonable, cultured voice it was. I noted a few uncertain vowels and the hardening of certain consonants.

'It is some time since I have answered to any appellation but Alasdair Moffat.'

I was sitting up quite straight despite the lack of support for my dorsal area. Silence prevailed for a few moments. The other two gentlemen exchanged a look I could not decipher. The interview, thus far, was broadly similar to many I had had with the Keeper.

The exotic fellow spoke at last. 'But before, who were you then?' He gave me an encouraging look.

'It is true I am quite changed from what I was. A new man, you might say.'

'What do you remember?'

'I have a past, surely, as everyone does. Is it remembered or related, innate or acquired; who can say? Not I.'

'So you remember nothing before the attack on your person?'

'Remember? Perhaps not. However, a journal is a useful thing, wouldn't you agree, Mr McKay?'

The Keeper averted his gaze and said nothing.

My interrogator wore a pin in the lapel of his jacket. It seemed a frivolous gewgaw out of temper with the sobriety of his dress. It was a symbol I had seen in several of the books in the trunk. At its base was a number 3 on its side, points downward. Atop this was a cross, then a circle of similar size, with a tiny dot at its centre. The circle seemed to sport a pair of devil's horns. The man spoke again. 'So, Mr Moffat, how would you describe your experience? An old life – changed, forgotten, discarded?'

'A new birth, a virgin birth, maybe.' I laughed at the thought of it.

The man opposite me smiled and nodded. 'Just so, Mr Moffat. Just so.'

The men stood. As he turned to go, I saw that the pin had the peculiar attribute of seeming at one moment a thing of base pewter, the next of purest gold.

I was turned out the next day with a portmanteau containing Moffat's journal, his copy of *Malleus Maleficarum* and spare linen; two gold sovereigns weighed heavy in my pocket.

As the newly cured Alasdair Moffat, it had seemed expedient to depart Edinburgh and Scotland, and I expended a portion of my paltry monies on coach travel to London. In the manner of many foolish young men, I spent my assets rapidly

EWAN LAWRIE

and without considering how I might replace them. I left a hotel of good quality one March morning by a first-floor window, a *modus egressi* I have not infrequently been reduced to since.

Penniless, I found in myself a natural talent for the nefarious: I picked pockets, being careful to practise on the inebriate; I took to carrying a blade, short and vicious, although on most occasions a sight of it produced the purse – and if it did not? Well, I became proficient in the use of it. There was a good living to be made, but it was obvious to me that a footpad could not hope to evade capture for ever. Besides, in the lower taverns I frequented, I overheard whispers concerning a desperate criminal some had taken to calling the Scotchman. Limehouse became too hot for me, and moonlight illuminated my decamping to the East India Docks. I spent a week watching the clippers of the Honorable company sailing into berth.

It surprised me that these ships, narrow of beam and patently incapable of carrying cargo of any great bulk, formed the major part of the empire's merchant marine, at least on the routes to the Orient. Their tall-masted elegance was pleasing to the eye, however, and on occasion I would be engaged in conversation by some grizzled mariner on matters of little consequence. I learned the difference between a clipper and a cutter, and to appreciate the sleek lines of the former with its sharply raked stem, counter stern and square rig. I could not help but notice their cargoes: expensive, low-volume commodities: spices, tea and passengers.

Many passengers were women, travelling with paid lady's companions or offspring destined for education in the home country. Occasionally, there were ladies travelling quite alone, recent widows of East India Company officers, English flowers too delicate for the tropics or, sometimes, women driven home by some scandal or other. I made it my business to welcome such ladies home, avoiding only those with progeny likely to prove an obstacle to my ends. For the most part, it was a matter of offering these ladies escort to their destination, the requisition of a hansom, guiding them out of the dangerous docklands to more salubrious accommodations. Often I would perform these services, and take whatever beneficence they offered. Sometimes I made more lucrative arrangements, the more vulnerable and gullible found their way to a certain house I knew well, as did some of the more promising children. Arabella Coble did not.

But Arabella Coble was already part of my past by now. What profit was there in thinking of her? Perhaps I would peruse her journal in an idle moment at some later time. I felt I should stir myself from the dining room and take some exercise; perhaps I could circumambulate the house and quell the queasiness I felt whenever I contemplated its design. In truth I was unused to superstition's hold, but there was something unnatural about the arrangement of the building, as if it were as much a *trompe l'oeil* as the hall of mirrors paper on the gallery leading to the bedrooms. I was resolved. Taking a last draught of port direct from the decanter, I made my way to the furniture-crammed lobby.

Chapter Fourteen

Of course, I was not in possession of any keys. No matter, I considered that it would be interesting to discover who answered the bell on my return. I swung the door wide and looked out into a starlit night. Turning left I passed the front of the east wing and peered in the dining-room window. The view to the interior was somewhat obscured by yet another item of exotic bric-a-brac: it appeared to be an orrery, although the number of planets was plainly incorrect, since a celestial body unknown to man was stationed outwith the orbit of the newly discovered Neptune.

Even so, it was a beautiful thing, if tarnished, and I wondered that it had not caught my eye during dinner. The next two windows also looked in on the dining room, and the second of them presented me with a sight as like to stop the heart of any disposed to afreets and phantasms. Some large furnishing blocked the view into the room, but it stood some feet back from the glass. Directly behind the grubby window stood a skeleton, displayed, I supposed, for the benefit of students of medicine. I hurried on my way.

In common with the asymmetry of the towers of both the west and east wings, the windows were not placed equidistant along the wall. Again, it seemed as if the architect had been intent on offending every tenet of aesthetics regarding his profession. He appeared to have delighted in odd numbers and an absence of motif or repetition. For example, the windows would be at random any one of mullioned, sash, oriel, clerestory and even, memorably, stained glass. The latter type of window enjoyed a run of three into the vivarium and I was more than grateful for that.

But the most disconcerting of all were two windows that appeared to offer insight into a room through which I had not passed: the withdrawing room I had previously noted as being deficient. The windows were the more expensive double-hung sash rather than the singles of the taxidermical room. It contained two chaise longues, a sofa and a rather grand chesterfield. A long sideboard provided a place for cordials suitable to the most refined of ladies. There were two paintings on the walls, after Gainsborough and Reynolds, or perhaps by those two themselves, strangely – and ironically – close, given that each had been anathema to the other whilst alive. The room could not possibly have existed, but there it was, visible from outside the building, plainly sited betwixt the vivarium and the library.

To my relief, the windows of the library revealed only the extraordinary room in which I had enjoyed a tincture with the wandering professor. It was only when I noted that the candles had been snuffed that I realised that someone had been but recently in the hidden room. Why else had it been illuminated? Who had been stealthily bearing tapers and doubters to all parts of the house? Maccabi had not mentioned any staff other than the insubstantial Mrs Gonderthwaite. My determination to have more than several matters out with Maccabi grew still more forceful with every hour.

I turned left at the end of the west wing. The French windows at the library's end opened onto a generously proportioned terrace. A long sward of grass swept downward, flanked by oaks of some antiquity, and I could see a tiny coal-red light in the distance, moving rhythmically but slowly, as though someone were smoking a briar pipe. Surely someone tended the numerous sheep I had seen on my arrival at the house? The terrain dropped away as the flags of the terrace marked the edge of the library wall. To my left I could see a wall adjoining the main body of the west wing approximately where the library ended, and where the secret room began. This long extension to the rear of the house obscured the wall supporting the dome. I had seen no entry to this part of the building, although almost anything could have been concealed by the disorder in the atrium. Of course it was likely that access to this part of the building was in the mysteriously hidden withdrawing room, but I had discerned no such portal when I peered through the sash windows, and, as I have said, the room was unaccountably well lit.

The long wall could well have been a mole – had it been

at Seahouses, instead of land-locked in Northumbrian hills. It was uncommon long: a furlong perhaps, with not a window to it, although it plainly was the wall of a building. It was possessed of a mansard roof. At the top of the wall itself was a ludicrous arrangement of deep embrasures and high merlons, although the house was scarce a hundred years old, as Maccabi had informed me during one of our interminable journeys in the phaeton. I doubted that the most irrational fear of the Jacobites could have justified the fortification.

Again, at the termination of this long spur, the terrain swept down a steep gradient. A charming lake, little more than a pond perhaps, lay at the foot of the hill. I resolved to walk down to it. It was no more than several chains away. As I approached, I could hear the waterfowl competing with a cacophony of frogs to claim precedence over the water. At the water's edge I turned to look back at Gibbous House. The ridiculous dome had taken a large bite out of the night's full moon and I learned a further reason for Fitzgibbon House's sobriquet.

On the other side of this elongated extension from the main body of the house, a shorter edifice did indeed emerge from the dome. It was almost commensurate with what one might have expected from the bedroom arrangements on the first floor. Disconcertingly, it did seem a little short, as though several of the bedrooms were little more than closets.

Despite this peculiarity, I was in fact more interested in this part of the ground floor for the simple reason that I had not seen it. The first two windows belonged to the kitchen, which was a little small for the house had both wings been in use. A solitary candle guttered on a large table, its flickering light reflected in the shine from numerous copper pans hanging from a rack suspended from the ceiling. The room was deserted, although I did detect an occasional rapid movement that might have warranted the recall of a cat or two from the west wing. At the next window, I truly was discomposed when the cook appeared with an oil lamp before her breast. The woman could have been blind for all she registered my presence a few scant inches away on the other side of the glass. She put me in mind of the anatomical specimen hidden behind the wardrobe, peering out of the dining-room window. Perhaps because she was naked, and would have provided quite as good a guide as to the composition of the thoracic skeleton as that other assemblage of bones.

I passed several darkened windows obscured by the absence of candlelight and the dirt of neglect. The final window in the wall was brightly illuminated; Maccabi was bare-chested. He appeared in a state of some excitement. I caught a flash of blue skirts as someone left his room. A sleepless night for Jedediah, I surmised. I stepped back quickly into the shadows. Maccabi stared, chin jutting, out of the window, the very picture of the romantic hero. Stifling a laugh, I decided to put off exploring the other half of the exterior until the morrow. Retracing my steps, I soon found myself on the terrace outside the library, where my eye was caught once more by the red coal light. I descended the gradient, thinking to place myself some yards to the right of the smoking shepherd.

Though scarce ten feet from me, he remained unaware of my presence. The sheep were skittish but he appeared to think little of it. There could be no other reason for a shepherd to be abroad at this hour save to protect his master's flock. This fellow appeared to be making a very poor effort at his duty and so I felt his fate was deserved. There was a yellow scarf in my pocket, but even the most credulous would not have accepted the presence of thuggee in this isolated place. My boot struck a rock lightly. I bent down and picked it up. It made a fine sound as it cracked the man's skull. Picking him up, I carried him over the brow of the hill. We were looking towards the pond and both frogs and ducks were silent until I threw the shepherd down the slope. He rolled like a misshapen barrel until I heard a splash and the renewed hostilities between the waterfowl and the amphibians.

I cursed the fact I had not kept his pipe as, for once, a smoke would have completed my pleasure. The night had turned cold, although it was almost April. I had quite forgotten how much difference a few degrees of longitude could make to the climate, and how isolation and the absence of civilisation could lower the temperature. The faint sounds of the pond were almost masked by the Northumbrian wind. For the first time, I contemplated turning my back on Gibbous House and all that I had not quite inherited, but a slight unpaid burdens the soul more than any sin.

On returning to the house, I lifted the iron monkey's chin

and swung the knocker as forcefully as I knew how. The satisfying sound that it made produced no satisfactory result, at least in subsequent minutes. On the point of rattling the monkey's brains again, I was surprised when the door swung wide. Blinded by the light of an oil lamp, I fervently hoped that if it were Mrs Gonderthwaite admitting me, she had taken the time to dress.

Fortunately, when my sight had returned, it became clear it was not she, but Miss Pardoner who bore the lamp. She stepped gracefully aside to admit me. There was a touch of high colour on her cheek and her lips seemed a little swollen. It was possible she had had to run to answer the door knocker's summons.

We stopped at the foot of the stairs; forced to intimacy by the Chinese Chippendale desk behind her and the rough oak chest at my back. She retreated a step, leaned against the vulgarly ornate escritoire, and ran her hand along its bevelled edge. I kept my distance – such as could be kept in such confinement. Chin up, head slightly tilted to one side, she appraised me, showing no deference or need to speak. I expressed my surprise that she was not already retired. Her reply was succinct. 'I keep late hours, Mr Moffat.'

'And bad company... ?' I ventured, but the woman remained quite unprovoked, provoking me in her turn with bold looks.

'Miss Pardoner,' I said, gesturing at the blue of her skirts, 'pretty and distinctive though this cerulean hue might be – it is scarce your colour.'

'But I like it, Mr Moffat, it is the exact colour of the Chalk Hill Blue butterfly – a truly beautiful creature.'

She attempted a fluttering of the eyelashes after the manner of an Eliza Wharton. It was not a success; there was nothing of the coquette in her manner. Still I made reply, out of courtesy. 'Miss Pardoner, it is not the butterfly that interests me, but the moth.'

'And the moth, does it perish at your flame?' The telltale corner of her mouth rose once again. She looked momentarily downward, toward the front of my breeches. My blood was up after the despatch of the careless shepherd. The woman had not finished. 'Or do you pin it – spreadeagle, to a board – at your leisure?'

As I mouthed, 'soon, very soon', to the retreating flash of blue, she scampered up the stairs and through the 'looking-glass'.

Having recovered myself sufficiently, I made my way up the stairs to the concealed entry to the vestibule leading to the blue-doored bedrooms. Naturally, I lingered at the teal-blue door. It was only a shade or two distinct from her unsuitable skirts – it pleased me to a large degree that she evinced a taste for the unsuitable. I put my eye to the keyhole on the tarnished brass plate and was thwarted by the key in the other side. It may have been fancy but I discerned the song of Sheba, faint but urgent, from behind the door.

Surprisingly, at the other end of the corridor there was no aural evidence of the solitary vice I expected from behind the professor's door. Perhaps he was indifferent to the tableaux on his chamber walls, or merely treated them as objects of academic interest. Alone behind the navy-blue door, in my monkish cell, I noted that although the bourdeloue remained in the centre of the rough floor, Miss Arabella Coble's journal was now upon the window ledge with a tall candle burning beside it.

Though still troubled by the passions aroused by my adventure on the hill by the pond, I did not indulge them as a lesser man might. It has long been my experience that gratification deferred is all the more pleasurable, for the most part. Moving the candle to the side of the window ledge nearest my cot, I picked up my late wife's juvenile scribbles, let the journal fall open where it chose and lay down to read it.

A C
*Friday 13th May 183_*
Yesterday, Great-uncle Septimus visited the
'schoolroom'. Though it is found amongst the
blue-doored bedrooms, it always puts me in mind of a
gaol, especially in the presence of my tutor. He is a most
vile drunkard, and his hand lingers too oft upon my
person. Mr Snitterton had the misfortune to be asleep
upon my great-uncle's arrival. Uncle nodded once at me
and said but one word: 'So!' He received only a snore
from the tutor for an answer, though his back was
already turned. I am at a loss to understand how the man
sleeps so well in the straight-backed and, frankly, spindly

chairs we have brought from the library to this room. But I think, perhaps, Mr Snitterton is none too long for employment at Gibbous House.

*Saturday 14th May 183_*
It is late and I write in my room by candlelight. Today is yet another Shabbos gone; Gentiles are so lucky; how I wish I might do something on the day of rest. Visit Alnwick, try the wares in the market. Buy a hat at the milliners, waste the day at a coffee shop. I often think we persecute ourselves as much as the Gentiles oppress us.

*Sunday 15th May 183_*
Mr Snitterton cut a tragic figure as he boarded the farmer's cart before the house this morning. How can anyone travel with so few possessions? I was summoned to the library at eleven of the morning. A rare occurence, though I do not complain; my uncle is so serious a fellow, he quite intimidates me. It was not so important a matter; he merely wished to inform me that my new tutor would arrive tomorrow. A Heathfield Cadwallader, such a mouthful of a name. I wonder what sort of man might own to it?

I had read enough to know that my former wife – the woman who stepped down the cutter's gangplank in the East India Docks – was of quite different character to the silly girl who had written that journal.

Naturally, consequent on earlier events, I was not disposed to sleep. Arabella Coble's entrance on the stage of my life appeared equally naturally in my thoughts.

She had been dressed appropriately for a spring day in London, although not in that particular year. It was not foolish to surmise that her apparel had spent several years in trunk in Simla or Shanghai. We were nearing the end of the decade, and the woman disembarking appeared to be of my own age, or the age I purported to be. That is to say, seven and twenty. She lifted one hand to adjust a large white cap with a striped ribbon bow. Her other hand held that of a female child aged between babble and cogent conversation, and so of little interest, either to me or to my business associate. Nonetheless, she cut a striking figure: unusually tall for a woman, she was not possessed of a fashionable silhouette for this decade, or many previous. From the dockside, I marked the usual encouraging signs of a suitable gull: head, and eyes presumably, moving to take in the full panorama of the quayside, searching for some or other expected welcome. This was ever more frequently interspersed with a heave of the shoulders indicative of great sighing. I wagered with myself that the woman would wait longer than the average time before stepping onto the dock. She did not disappoint. The bell from a nearby church had tolled two quarters before she did so.

I pondered the while how best to approach her. For older women of middle age, I usually made a deep bow of greeting and presented a card. The card bore a name I no longer care to remember, I had stolen its original from a self-satisfied lawyer in Limehouse on the pretext of introducing him to a French whore. Such a fool to have followed a man he scarcely knew behind an East End tavern. Still, such lessons are hard-learned, and if a fellow may not benefit from them in this life, he surely must in the next. An unscrupulous printer in the Fleet was happy enough to produce a couple of hundred examples of the card for half a crown – and a promise that I not return to his family home.

Younger women were often less suspicious, but also inclined to mistrust over-elaborate manners. I clicked my heels like a commissioned hussar and made the briefest of inclinations for a bow.

'Captain Crawford, at your service, Ma'am. You were expecting me?'

She began a shake of her head, but stopped abruptly.

'I was expecting someone.'

She looked me up and down, seeming little impressed with my attire. I presumed that her time in the tropics had not enabled her to keep up with the latest male fashions. My wardrobe, at that time, was my greatest extravagance: I felt that I cut a fine figure that day in my red and black patterned waistcoat, russet trousers, lovat tailcoat and top hat. The acquisition of a modicum of good taste was one of the many things that I owed to my late wife.

'And who should that someone be, if not you?' she said, which utterance quite took my breath away. It seemed that we had both been on the hunt for a flat upon whom we might play the crooked cross. However, I found it strange that she did not address me as 'Captain', as politeness required.

Chapter Fifteen

Good memories such as these had ever helped me into the arms of Morpheus, and I passed one of my rare dreamless nights. The light of dawn was struggling through the filth of the tiny window when I awoke. The late Mr Parminter's watch informed me that the hour of six was a quarter gone. The cheery mood I might have expected after an undisturbed night was somewhat dissipated by the chatter and twitter of innumerable birds, which I had no doubt Maccabi could name from their song alone. I was tempted to target the bourdaloue with my morning micturition from atop my bed, but contented myself with a more customary use of the porcelain.

The paucity of my wardrobe was now becoming irksome to me; as I clothed myself I resolved that Maccabi would be the willing donor of a few items to use until the reappearance of the esteemed Elijah Salomons, with his promises of my 'gentleman's wardrobe' within the week. Besides, it would be amusing to wear fashions last worn before the Hanoverian fop stood in for his lunatic father in matters of state – and I expected it would discommode young Jedediah in the extreme to loan me the best of his apparel.

Breakfast appeared to me a capital idea, and, since the peculiar Mrs Gonderthwaite was capable of such an extravagant feast as that of the previous evening, I felt that there was some prospect of a trencherman's repast to begin the day.

The dining room, however, was deserted. I rang the dissonant hand bell, though there was no prospect of it being heard in the kitchen. It would be quite inappropriate for me to seek out the cook in the kitchen, or, God forbid, in her chamber. For this reason I began to explore the room in earnest, to see what other strange items might be found in it.

Naturally, I made straight away for the huge wardrobe obscuring the window. Hard up against it on one side was a chiffonier, beautiful and delicate. Sadly, its mirror was spackled and cracked. A great shame as it was one of the few I had encountered in the house. I heaved it aside without ceremony, judging it to be more easily moved than the ottoman stood on its end adjacent the behemoth of a wardrobe on its other side. There was no sign of the smallest finger bone: the anatomical skeleton had quite vanished, although I was relieved to see the outline of its pedestal in the dust in front of the wainscoting.

A man's pride will withstand many things; he will usually swallow it, however, in the hope of sending more satisfactory victuals after it. Therefore, I took myself to where I thought the kitchen to be. This necessitated the navigation of the furniture-crammed vestibule. The narrow channels through the piled tables, chairs, chaises, wardrobes, armoires, tallboys and whatnots were somewhat confusing, and it was only at a third attempt that I gained entry to the spur containing the kitchen and the servants' quarters. The smell was not one to make me sanguine of a palatable breakfast. It was not the smell of spoiled provisions, exactly, neither was it due to a surfeit of cats, but it was a smell firmly placed somewhere between the two. I was at that point in a sort of ante-room, which led, I presumed, to the kitchen.

Through the door the kitchen was bathed in a gloomy light, as though daylight itself had been poisoned into pallor. The windows I had peered through on the previous evening's perambulation had not been unaccountably cleaned by some unseen hand. Nor were there any lamps or candles lit. Neither, I supposed, had Mrs Gonderthwaite – even in her youth – illuminated a room. She did not that morning, rather the gloom seeped into the room from her spindly frame, mercifully clothed once more in black.

It may be supposed that I did an injustice to the woman, in referring to her as a cook. It is certain that up to that point Gibbous House was not over-encumbered with other servants. Mrs Gonderthwaite wore a chatelaine; perhaps she deserved the appellation housekeeper. I considered taking to calling Maccabi the butler.

The woman appeared to be in some kind of trance or religious transport, at least of a fairly discreet kind. I passed a hand before her eyes in an effort to engage with her. With no discernible change in demeanour, she greeted me fulsomely.

'A very good morning to you, Mr Moffat. What might be your requirements in the matter of breaking the fast this morning?'

I searched her face for a hint of irony and was unrewarded by any sign of emotion, sentience or clue to animation. The woman seemed stuporous, although I could discern no whiff of laudanum. Nevertheless, I took her up on the invitation to stipulate my morning vittles; thinking to thoroughly fox the woman I began a list comprising blood pudding, haslet, lamb sausage, poached eggs, thick back bacon, fried potato farls and china tea.

'Of course, Mr Moffat. Is it just the one or am I to prepare such for the entire household?'

A look around the kitchen revealed dust in every corner. The gleam of the copper pans the previous evening had been illusory, most were dulled to the green of malachite. No hams hung from the ceiling, no links of sausage in the pantry, which seemed in general uncommon bare, save for an uncertain-looking, if huge, game pie. A solitary loaf was blueing with mould on the large and rough table. The butcher's block was bloody and devoid of any meat.

At this point I was marvelling that the room was devoid of the idiosyncratic and serendipitous additions visible throughout the other rooms. At that moment, however, I saw that a highly polished sextant lay atop the stove, where one might reasonably have expected a saucepan. The state of the kitchen made the preparation of a meal for one as likely as Nebuchadnezzar's feast, and so I bade her prepare for four, thinking another meal would provide more sport with Maccabi, even if the food proved no more than phantasy.

The woman seemed unperturbed by the state of the kitchen. On my leaving I sensed she did not stir a whit, but contented herself in the observation of my retreating back. Retracing my steps through the jumble was a little easier, and little caught my eye – although I noted the variety of woods used in the furniture had as many colours as had the leaves of autumn. It was strange that so many pieces – in spite of standing, lying and leaning higgledy-piggledy around the grand hallway – evinced the sheen of a recent polish.

Maccabi dropped a silver spoon with a clatter on the dining table as I swung the door wide. I resisted the temptation to bid him turn out his pockets, but allowed myself a smile at the thought of doing so. In any event, his self-possession had deserted him and already I knew that this – for him – was a rare and discomfiting experience, and, perhaps, my wordless smile would discommode him still more. I said nothing, and took appraisal of his attire.

It being Shabbos, I presumed he would be wearing the best of his clothes. Since I would soon be wearing them myself, I was disappointed to note the predominance of black and white in the palette. Still, the cut and material seemed of quality, despite the outmoded style. His coat, black, was double-breasted and cut away to tails, the waist of it being very high. Two fingers' breadth of an exceedingly dull waistcoat were visible below it. His shirt was white linen and so bright as to beg the question of how it could be got so, above all in this bizarre house with its dearth of servants. The frill of his shirt and the height of his collar were the only extravagance of his dress. I gauged that his boots would be a comfortable fit, being possessed of the beautiful shine that only leather of some age may acquire, if tended with great care.

He seemed to be in the grip of some internal struggle, as though he had noted my close regard of him and could not resolve whether to challenge me over it. Curiosity, or some other motive, eventually compelled him to say, 'You seem uncommon interested in my garb, today, Mr Moffat.'

'Indeed I am, Jedediah. I rather thought you might be so good as to loan me some articles of clothing, until such time as that fellow of yours brings me something more suitable. If it would not inconvenience you, that is?'

Again he struggled with some inner demon, before saying stiffly, 'Of course, sir.'

'Oh, you are most kind, Maccabi. If you would but lay out the clothes you are wearing on my cot by ten on the morrow. I have in mind to escort Miss Pardoner to church in Bamburgh. You would not care to come, I take it.'

He shook his head for answer and departed with unseemly alacrity, I thought.

The dining table was still as we had left it the evening before. Scraps of food littered the plates and the area of table where the professor had teetered on his perch. The decanter of port was empty of all but the lees, although I was sure I had left sufficient to charge a good two glasses.

Some of this quantity lay in a congealed and sticky pool

beside the decanter, indicating that the remainder had been quaffed some hours before. I would have paid a sovereign to have known by whom. Thankfully for my sanity, a tantalus – identical to that from which the professor and I had availed ourselves in the library – stood on the sideboard. One decanter was full of the same near-to-high-quality jerez we had drunk, and I poured myself a generous schooner. I removed to my seat at table with decanter and glass and awaited developments in the matter of breaking my fast.

My disappointment that the next person to come through the dining room door was not the ethereal Mrs Gonderthwaite with my breakfast was tempered by the realisation that it was, in fact, the intriguing Miss Pardoner. My ward was wearing a day dress in a dark shade of a still unsuitable blue, with a lace chemisette and cuffs. She carried a pair of short leather gloves in one hand. The young woman's hair was most unfashionably short and made a pleasant change from the parted and sausage-curled coiffures that were common during that decade. I declared my surprise that she had such a dress to hand despite the absence of her effects, which were still en route from Lindisfarne.

'You would be surprised what can be found within the walls of your property, Mr Moffat,' she replied.

'I should only be surprised, Miss Pardoner, if I ceased to be surprised.'

My reward was the upward curl of her lip, an expression of hers that from the very outset might have provoked me to either violence or lust, or perhaps both in equal measure, but for the heightened enjoyment provided by patience and anticipation. The young woman took her place at table and I felt in need of a spyglass to see her the better. It was most strange to conduct our conversation in the manner of Irish navvies across a canal. Her not-unpleasant voice carried well, and I imagined her on stage as a Cleopatra or Lady Macbeth – though certainly not as Juliet.

'Might we not ride out today, Mr Moffat?'

'Are you not frum, Miss Pardoner?' I asked.

'I was born a Jew, Mr Moffat, though I have spent some years in the care of Christians. I wonder that you should know such a word.'

I felt there might be some doubt as to the truth of the former.

'My wife was Jewish. Septimus Coble's great-niece, in fact.'

'You are no Jew, sir.' She looked at me expectantly.

'Scarce a Christian, some would say.'

'Something of the pagan about you, Mr Moffat, I think.'

She was quite the most brazen woman I had ever met outside Whitechapel, and she was bolder still than many of those. In common with many women of my acquaintance it was not in her nature to allow a silence of any duration; therefore, in the absence of any responding remark from myself, she queried, 'Are we to breakfast on apples and honey this morning, sir?'

I replied that I should be most astounded if we broke our fast at all.

At which point, the dining room door opened wide and the

narrow-boned figure of the cook was preceded by the huge covered salver I had been so surprised at her carrying so easily the previous day. She placed the silver-domed platter on the table at the mid-point and removed the cover with what passed in so flat a character as a flourish.

Displayed attractively was every victual I had specified: the steam rose from the lamb sausage and blood pudding and I could have sworn I still heard their sizzling; the potato farls each had a knob of butter atop, slowly melting and pooling beside them on the polished plate; the white of the poached eggs contrasted sharply with the rich pink of the back bacon, which had proved surprisingly plentiful in such a household. Mrs Gonderthwaite gave me an expectant look.

'China tea, Mrs Gonderthwaite. China tea,' I said.

The lid was replaced with some enthusiasm and the thin woman repaired to the kitchen with as much animation as she had thus far evinced in my presence.

It was Maccabi who returned with the tea. He looked quite ludicrously uncomfortable bearing the silver salver on which stood a fine china tea service. His discomfort most likely arose from the height at which he bore the tray – quite why he felt the need to keep the china level with his gaze was a mystery to me. Perhaps he was as yet unused to such duties. He placed the tray delicately on the table beside the huge domed platter. This done, he looked toward me. I gave a nod and waved at the breakfast feast under its silver cover. There was nothing for it but to use the previous evening's crockery, and he made a good fist of serving Miss Pardoner and myself, prior to serving himself an egg and a potato farl.

I was unable to resist enquiring if it was quite in accordance with kashrut to eat comestibles that had been in such proximity to the meat of the unclean pig. Maccabi said not a word; Miss Pardoner, however, rejoindered, 'Some interpretations of the Torah allow for the eating of treif in situations of dire need, Mr Moffat. On the whole, I have found the Jewish religion to contain much good sense.'

Since I had shared a bed with Arabella, I knew some of what the Torah might or might not permit, but still I wondered what dire need might be in evidence in this case.

Addressing neither party in particular, I enquired, 'Is the professor not in the habit of breaking his fast in the morning?'

Maccabi, seated at last, took his delicate china cup and drained the tea in one noisy draught. My ward said, 'His custom is not to rise in the forenoon.'

Perhaps he lay awake until the small hours contemplating. It occurred to me I had failed to enquire in what discipline the professor had made his reputation. I made great show of emptying my own thimbleful of tea and looked expectantly at Maccabi. The noise as his cup clattered and smashed on the table was as nothing compared to that of his chair falling to the floor. With exaggerated stiffness and formality, he poured my tea, splashing only a little on my coat sleeve.

Addressing the fascinating Miss Pardoner, more to hear what outrage she would commit on decorum than out of any genuine interest, I enquired, 'And in what particular field has the esteemed professor made his undoubted reputation?'

Miss Pardoner appeared not to consider her reply. 'Professor Jedermann is a polymath, simply put. A master of natural sciences, philosophies ancient and modern, an expert on art, a bibliophile of great passion. Enoch studied with the philosopher Johann Gottlieb Fichte, a thing in itself that is remarkable, given the man's expressed desire to remove all Jewish heads and replace them with others containing not a single Jewish idea. I am glad you do not enquire of the man himself; Enoch is a little self-conscious.'

It seemed such a preposterous thing for a philosopher, even a German one, to be: I was unsure as to whether the minx was mocking me in the extreme, or wished to indicate in what high esteem the professor's abilities were held. Equally, I found it strange that a man so tolerant of others' religion would associate with one with so noted a hatred of Jews.

'How comes he here? There is hardly a seat of learning here in Northumbria. A man would have to ride as far as Durham to discuss the most mundane of philosophical posits, would he not?'

It was Maccabi who answered this, a little shortly for my liking. 'He is the curator of the Collection.'

I was quite unable to contain a snort of laughter, and would have made great mock of this portentous statement had not the dining room doors swung wide open. Mrs Gonderthwaite, having recovered her temper, said in a voice devoid of modulation, 'Mr Moffat, there is someone without.'

This utterance seemed a little deficient in the matter of information, but the woman was already gliding to the entrance hall and the house door. Had I not seen her naked, I could have believed the woman less than corporeal.

Chapter Sixteen

Before the door, cap in hand, was a grubby specimen of the local population. His trousers were better called rags and, though his feet were shod, his boots were an uncommon mismatch in colour, design and, it appeared, fit. He was possessed of a prodigious beard but no moustaches, and his pate was as bald as his lip. The single tooth in his head endowed each sibilant with a comical whistle, while his Northumbrian accent rendered intelligibility a hopeless dream.

The bold Miss Pardoner had followed me to the door – although my factotum, strangely, had not. My ward informed me that the man, an itinerant labourer currently employed on the estate, had discovered a body in the pond. She may well have understood the man, but I should not have been surprised to learn that she had observed events the previous evening from some vantage point in the house.

'Tell the oaf to show us the place.'

Miss Pardoner's smirk was again in evidence as I strode out the door and turned right, in the opposite direction to that in which the pond lay.

'Find out the fellow's name, Miss Pardoner.'

'It's Cullis, Mr Moffat. Or that is the name I saw in the account book yesterday, where he made his mark against it this last month.'

We made an odd trio as we walked along the fore wall of the east wing. Cullis was as bent and wiry as an old man, but he was most likely only a few years older than I. Miss Pardoner seemed as youthful and vibrant as a butterfly between a gorse and a briar bush. I hoped she would live longer than any lepidoptera might. We rounded the wing and paused on the terrace.

'Where might this pond be?' I said, looking to the wrong side of the hill.

'Over there to the left, Mr Moffat. Can you not hear the frogs and fowl?'

Of course I could – and I could also see that there was grave danger of overplaying any hand whilst in the company of my ward.

Over by the pond, I pretended no shock or disgust at the sight of the broken body. The shepherd's head was bent at a most unlikely angle and thus I deduced that, as I had thought, whether by the blow from the rock or by the fall the man had been dead before reaching the water.

'Who is it?'

Miss Pardoner had not time to supply the answer before Cullis.

'Wor Lad.'

Which seemed a strange name of eastern European origin to me, until Miss Pardoner explained that it meant the corpse was that of Cullis's younger sibling.

The still-ambulatory of the two seemed little moved by his brother's fate, as far as I could tell. His cap was rolled tightly in his fists and he worked his jaw energetically, but of his strange dialect he uttered not a word. I did not feel obliged to console the fellow, but I did want the cadaver removed from the pond, so I asked, 'Is he for burial on the parish, then?'

The jaw continued its exercise, until Miss Pardoner used her own to more communicative purpose:

'It may not be a matter for the coroner, but perhaps we might send for the constable at Bamburgh, Mr Moffat?'

'And pray tell, whom would we despatch on such a vital mission?' was my counter.

'I think Maccabi would be pleased to go, if I were to ask him.'

'I shall tell him, Miss Pardoner. I shall tell him.'

Maccabi departed with no good grace atop an equine specimen quite as poor as the one that had dragged us both round half of Northumberland.

Miss Pardoner escorted Cullis vivendum and me to the rear of the property via the strange windowless wall to the servants' entrance on the far side. While one Cullis rested in relative peace among the croaking and quacking, the other was left in the care of Mrs Gonderthwaite in the kitchen, although it still seemed as unlikely a source of provender as before. Miss Pardoner and I passed through the kitchen into the servants' quarters.

'Perhaps I could show you these apartments, Mr Moffat?' She raised an eyebrow.

'Are you so well acquainted with them?' I raised an eyebrow of my own.

'No more than I care to be, sir.'

I bade her lead on.

There were rooms right and left off a corridor leading to the building's end. The first door on my right I knew to be Mrs Gonderthwaite's, and I merely put my head around the door to satisfy myself that it contained neither malkin, broomstick nor cauldron. We continued to look into the rooms on the right hand. In contrast with the lunatic accumulation of artefacts and furnishing in the rest of the house, these rooms had merely devoted themselves to the accretion of years of dust and dirt.

The fifth door down was that of Maccabi's recent habitation; on opening the door I saw the cleanliness of it for myself. This, and the meticulous order of the room, I had been expecting. What I had not expected was the sight of Miss Pardoner's teal-blue skirts of the previous day folded neatly on the cot. Her look was frank and I might easily have been convinced of the truth of her words, claiming that Mr Maccabi was quite the hand with a needle and thread, were I as big a dolt as she thought me.

'I wonder he did not offer to tailor my wardrobe himself,' I said.

We left Maccabi's room in silence, but not before I had skewed a picture frame or two and dishevelled the immaculate bedclothes. I derived some satisfaction from this until I caught sight of Miss Pardoner's crooked smile.

The door rattled in its frame behind me. There were two more doors on the right-hand wall; the corresponding doors on the opposite wall were not in themselves opposing doors. Again, the unknown architect's mania for the asymmetrical was in evidence. I tried the door on the left-hand wall nearest that of Maccabi. It was locked, with a serviceable enough mechanism, since my furious boot did not render the room any more accessible.

'Perhaps I should summon Mrs Gonderthwaite... or at least fetch a key from her?'

It was a most reasonable suggestion.

'It will wait for another day.' I limped along the corridor toward the kitchen.

It took all of my self-control not to laugh aloud at the flushed face of Mrs Gonderthwaite as she attempted to repair her déshabillé. Cullis's reaction to his brother's timely reminder of his own mortality had obviously encouraged him to affirm his own vitality in the time-honoured way. For all the woman's ethereality, it seemed she still had a taste for carnal pursuits.

More restraint still was required when I espied the colour the scene and its implications had brought to young Ellen

Pardoner's face. Turning to Cullis, I enquired what tasks he performed on the estate. After Miss Pardoner's interpretation, it was no great surprise that, amongst other things, he carried out the duties of ostler. This accounted to some degree for the parlous state of the two horses that I had thus far seen.

I instructed Cullis to show me the stables, and as he made his way outside without too much delay I inferred that his inability to communicate in any civilised language did not preclude his understanding of it. Miss Pardoner made as if to accompany us, but I waved her away, saying, 'I think we will come to some understanding, Cullis and I, regarding communication. There is nothing he might say which I might wish to understand, and should he lose his facility to understand my wishes – well, I shall beat him, of course.'

Evidently the cook felt only passion for the fellow, and not love, as this declaration provoked not the slightest reaction from the ghostly presence. Not so Miss Pardoner; the high colour returned to her face and I fancied I detected a little shortness of breath. Perhaps I should have allowed her to accompany us, after all.

The stables were set away from the rear of the west wing. The kindest thing to say would have been that they were in no worse repair than the gatehouse. The building itself housed a long row of twelve stalls, the half of which were not in possession of a door to close. Stone-built, the mortar in the walls had long since turned to dust, and so the stables resembled a remarkable feat of dry-stone wallwork, but not one that could be trusted to hold up the roof for much longer. The roof consisted of more hole than slate: the feeble whinnies emerging from behind the few stalls still capable of being secured bore testimony to its permeability.

Cullis opened the door to the first occupied stall. Filthy straw covered little of the dirt floor, and a roan bag of bones covered most of it. It appeared that the two horses put to work in recent days were the most fit. This specimen looked a scant cough from the knacker's. The ostler carefully closed the stall door as if frightened that too vigourous treatment would cause it to crumble on the hinge. Moving to the next door, he was equally ginger in his handling of it, pausing only to say something which I took to be 'foal'.

The door swung wide to reveal a recently come to term mare and something that should by rights have earned the name abomination and not foal. The thing, to my eye, was no more than two hours old, still sticky-slick with birthing fluids. It lay next to its dam, which from time to time flailed with hind legs to push the beast away. It managed to keep one of the heads out of harm's way, the other was bloodied and as dim of eye as the stuffed exhibits in the house.

Cullis's head nodded vigourously after I instructed him to be rid of the abomination instanter. I wondered that he had not already done so, but perhaps such gumption was not common among the local population. The man showed me a further four horses in varying states of neglect. Quizzing the fellow as to the reason for such negligence returned no communication meaningful to me, therefore I told him in no uncertain terms that I expected such beasts as could be saved to be both fed by him and attended by the veterinary. For good measure I added that I expected to save the payment for disposal of the abomination and any horse beyond salvation, since Cullis could see to it himself. He held out a hand. I placed a small silver coin in it, and resolved to discuss the estate's arrangements for my living allowance with the dwarf when he stirred from his chambers.

Turning from the stables, I skirted the feline-occupied west wing. The smell was discernible from without, no doubt permitted to befoul the air by the quantity of broken window glass. Most confounding was the near immaculate state of the roof. I noted one slate hanging askew: there must have been several thousand comprising the roof. The lead looked new. Two doors let into the rear wall of this wing, each was warped, rotted and sealed by a padlocked chain, with a bar athwart the door itself. Naturally, I peered through one of the windows, but there was little to see through the grime and the cat that leaped – hissing – at the pane of glass unnerved me somewhat.

At the gable end of the wing a blank and featureless expanse of red brick soared to the roof: it made one dizzy to look at it. The corners of the wall where the brick met the sandstone of the rest of the building were most jarring. To the front elevation, the west wing appeared more presentable, though the architect's devotion to asymmetry was served here by thirteen identical windows that ran along the front.

These did anything but mirror the hodge-podge of designs of the east wing's variegated glaziery, which numbered at least sixteen.

Chapter Seventeen

It was a fine day and I regretted the absence of any suitable mounts for Ellen Pardoner to ride out upon. I let out a sigh, turned to the front door and swung the grinning monkey's head with some venom, expecting that Mrs Gonderthwaite would appear eventually. The door, however, opened almost immediately. Miss Pardoner offered a sketch of a courtesy which I returned with a bare nod, whilst I wondered if there were anything which she did that was not informed by a most knowing irony.

The very moment I crossed the threshold, the professor appeared from behind the *trompe l'oeil* like a mischievous sprite. He halloed us cheerily from the head of the staircase and waved, savouring the opportunity, most likely, to look down upon us. Taking the stairs with his peculiar scuttling gait, he held up a hand to hold me fast in the vestibule. As his tiny limbs skittered to a halt on the parquet of the floor, he said, 'Mr Moffat, would you be so kind as to attend me once more in the library? I think perhaps you have a question or two about your situation. I shall do my utmost to answer them as fully as ever I can.'

'I would not be so kind, Professor: I prefer that you attend me in whatever place I choose. The library will suit me as well as any.'

The professor accepted this with little outward damage to his equanimity.

'Quite so, Mr Moffat, I forget myself.'

But I thought perhaps that he did not and I caught the briefest glimpse once more of the corrupt and evil gnome I believed him to be.

'You will excuse us, Miss Pardoner,' I said as I turned to that lady.

'It seems I must,' she replied.

I was disappointed to see that she seemed unperturbed by the prospect, and we abandoned her in the vestibule among the vertiginously piled furniture.

This time I led the professor through the dining room, hearing the familiar snick snack of his dainty feet on the flooring. The debris of breakfast yet remained on the table. In the next room, the stuffed menagerie proved more sinister than I had previously thought: one corner at the far end of the room appeared to be dedicated to a collection of the most fantastical chimerae. The unknown taxidermist had created vile corruptions and combinations of fowl, fish and fauna. For seasoning there were one or two examples of the kind of abomination I had seen in the stables. I had read that certain collectors in Bavaria had a taste for such pieces; many purchasers actually believed them exemplars of formerly living beasts.

'A little Germanic for my taste, Professor. And so much effort to create such – unconvincing monsters, don't you agree?' I asked him.

'Much – in science as in creation – is unlikely, Mr Moffat,' he replied.

We passed into the room with the picture-covered walls, where again the queasy feeling forced me onward quickly. In the room containing the geological specimens I picked up a beautiful milky stone and pocketed it. It was the largest opal I had ever seen. I turned to read the expression on the professor's face, but there was none. The vivarium was filled with the sounds of its diurnal occupants. Intent as I was on reaching the library, I did not peer too closely at the vitrines as I passed them, although I had the impression of unnatural forms moving behind them. Thankfully in the library itself, the hubbub made by the slithering and the rubbing of insect legs was inaudible.

I poured the professor and myself some of the almost excellent sherry, and lifted my glass.

'To purgatory,' I said.

'Too kind,' the man replied.

The glasses drained, he held his upward expectantly and, as a good host should, I obliged him by filling it.

'Sssssssoo, what can I tell you, Mr Moffat? What is it you wish to know?'

I could not get used to his accent, the serpentine hiss of his sibilants, the constant confusion of the v and w sounds. At times I felt it verged on self-parody and that he was having a joke at my expense.

There were a number of questions I could have put to him concerning the run-down and ill-cared-for appearance of the estate. I might even have asked him for a calculation of the estate's worth and probable income. Instead, I asked, 'What is the Collection? What is its purpose?'

The little man nodded and it seemed there was a gleam of respect in his eye, as though this were the very question he would have asked, were he in my position. Unfortunately, his answer was as enigmatic as so much else in the house. 'It's purpose is: to remain, to be studied, to be treasured. To add to the sum of knowledge. What nobler purpose could there be?'

This was twaddle of the lowest order.

'But its value, Jedermann, its value?'

'Priceless, Mr Moffat, priceless – as all knowledge must be.'

It being too much of an effort to reach down and throttle him, I contented myself with enquiring angrily, 'Professor, what I have so far seen is a motley assemblage of furnishings, objets d'art and mystère, geological specimens, preposterous exemplars of taxidermy and the devil knows what creatures. What possible motive is there to call such a thing a collection?'

The malignant look reappeared once more. 'Why, Mr Moffat, it has been collected, has it not?'

'By whom? And how?'

'Perhaps you would rather not know?'

I dashed his glass from his lips and he leaped back nimbly as it shattered at his feet. This time I did seize him by his shirt-front and lifted his face to mine. 'How much? How much can I expect per annum, you weasel?'

'If you set me down, I shall show you the accounts, Mr Moffat.'

I released my grip and he landed gracefully, more was the pity. His shoulders rocked from side to side as he scampered over to the very last rack of shelves in the library's corner. Using the lip of each shelf, rather in the manner of a monkey, he clambered to the very highest of them and seized in a fist a prodigiously sized ledger. He jumped to the floor and landed as nimbly as he'd climbed.

He proffered the ledger to me. It was bound in cracked and stained leather; I laid the weighty tome on one of the low tables nearby. I opened it at random to the entry for the week beginning 13th December 182_. Long columns of neat and rounded figures culminated in totals possessing too few digits to offer me encouragement. I flicked the yellowed pages until it lay open at the beginning of the current year. It seemed as though the ledger had been annotated with the express purpose of obscuring the destinations of outgoings and the sources of income.

'Jedermann, a summary if you please.'

It was not a tale pleasing to the ear or the pocket. There were tenant farmers, there were sheep, there was the public house in Seahouses and very little more which produced an income. Furthermore, there were endless purchases of 'sundry goods and portable property'. It was a desperate state of affairs.

'We shall have to sell what we can,' I said.

'We cannot sell anything, Mr Moffat. Those are the terms of the trust.'

I kicked the low table and the ledger fell to the floor cracking the spine, the book an apt metaphor for the broken-down house.

The professor bent, admittedly not far, and retrieved the ledger. I had already turned my back upon him and was perusing the nearest rack of shelves. Once more I was struck by the random arrangement. There had been no catalogue made of these tomes. If anything, the books stood on the shelves with less care for their content or origin than those on the shelves in the professor's own chamber.

The row that met my eye contained an older copy of *Malleus Maleficarum* than mine own, standing at the left-hand end of the shelf. To its right was a sumptuously bound copy of Hume's *Essays, Moral and Political* – the next book was a work by John Dee, the Elizabethan alchemist. Cheek by jowl with this stood a book with something in the Arabic script upon the spine. A tag of paper protruded from between its pages, I withdrew it. It appeared to be a translation of the book's title: *The Polished Book on Experimental Ophthalmology* by Ibn Al Nafis.

Dropping the scrap to the floor, my finger traced the spines of works sacred and profane, ancient and modern, until my eye at last stopped upon a book bound in cordovan leather, blackened with age and the touch of many fingers. The cover bore the symbol on the sign of the Coble Inn. It was a small volume of a size to slip into a pocket. The title on the spine read *Secrets of the Rosy Cross*. I noted the name of the author was *Septimus Coble*. I remembered discussions of Elizabeth's star gazer in the Edinburgh asylum, and therefore, out of I know not what sentiment, placed only this lighter tome in my coat.

At this point the library door opened with a clamour not usually associated with such places of placid learning. A breathless Miss Pardoner informed me that Maccabi had returned and would speak with me if it were not inconvenient. I toyed with inconveniencing the man, but had to admit to myself that, one day, the vice of curiosity might be my undoing. Therefore I followed Miss Pardoner out of the library, the professor tip-tapping behind in arthropod syncopation. As we were leaving the nightmare picture gallery, the professor tugged at my sleeve and whispered, 'There is nothing to worry about: as above, so below.'

I shook off the demented gnome's hand and hurried to meet Maccabi.

Chapter Eighteen

My retainer stood erect and soldier-like amidst the furniture in the vestibule, something I noted with a certain satisfaction. I hailed him. 'Well met, Maccabi. What news? Are the forces of law on their way?'

He shifted from foot to foot. 'Yes. That is, well, a constable is on his way, having instructed the drayman to transport him hither.'

'Indeed, remarkable initiative for a policeman, is it not?'

Again he moved his feet. 'It was the reporter's idea.'

I laughed aloud.

'Reporter? Here? Maccabi, I would have thought you incapable of such a ludic jest!'

'He is from the *Alnwick Mercury*, sir. He happened to be in Seahouses. There was nothing I could do.'

'And why should you have done aught, you buffoon?'

He kept his counsel at that, so I enquired when he thought they might arrive. To which he replied, 'Within the hour.'

'Best someone renders my home into a more appropriate

estate for the reception of visitors, be they only a Peeler and a scribe.'

Maccabi made for the servants' quarters with a stamping gait, although I surmised Mrs Gonderthwaite and Cullis would be of little help to him.

Miss Pardoner was not in evidence – I was unsure as to where she might be. For no other reason than a want of anything better to do, I thought I might take a promenade along the drive to the gatehouse. The day was fulfilling its early promise: the sun was high overhead and the drive descended between the rolling hillocks and unsupervised ovines. The panorama was the epitome of bucolic paradise. '*Et in Arcadia ego sum*' would have been appropriate indeed – but for the unfortunate lack of shepherds. The gatehouse looked scarcely better from the rear. A trellis enlivened the darkened sandstone and provided a home for several dull-coloured avian specimens – the only evidence of life in the building.

The rear elevation was possessed of the remnants of a door, the boards warped and cracked so that tongue had long parted company with any groove. From the scraps of paint that clung to the weathered wood, I could tell that its colour had once been green. I found it a little humorous that someone in the distant past had locked the door. I removed a board at a time and entered the ruin.

Inside, I was greeted by a multitudinous flapping of wings and a screeching that might be associated with vermin. Such the bats were, I supposed. Some flapping of my own dispersed them to their inverted perches in the rotten-timbered rafters. It was a single-story building. The room I had entered was – or had been – a scullery.

Through a void doorway I saw a sitting room, sofa rotted and chewed by some or other fauna. Once inside I saw that it was furnished with a window to the front and a door to another room on the side wall. It seemed in reasonable condition – and it was locked. Once more I perceived a dissonance between the outward dimensions and the internal disposition of the building. The scullery, the only room to the rear of the building, was considerably smaller than the sum of the area of the two rooms to the front, however tiny the locked room might prove to be. On the wall opposite the mysteriously sealed room was a door to the exterior, presumably to enable the erstwhile gatekeeper to facilitate access for visitors to the estate.

I was on the point of leaving when the toe of my boot met with a hard object that slid rattling along the floor. A large and rusted ring holding one solitary key lay on the floorboards, half hidden by the remnants of the sofa's skirts. I picked it up: it appeared to be a key for a mortice lock and of an appropriate size to allow access to the sealed room. It was disturbing to note that –aside from a modicum of dirt, dust and damage from rodent teeth – the door was in unfeasibly good repair.

The key turned slickly and I opened the door, which offered no protesting creak – or indeed any indication that it was in less than daily use. The room was small but could not have squared with the paradox of the scullery's dimensions. It could not possibly have been an illusion of the optical kind, or if it were I could not begin to guess the mechanics of it. The outside of the building was clearly based on the standard box-like shape: to the eye, all vertices were isometric and angles isogonal. And yet.

There was nothing peculiar or noteworthy about the room itself – save that it was in better condition than many in the main house. It seemed that a duster had been in use within the last few days, which was more than could be said of many of the rooms I had seen of late. I could see no items of a personal nature. The furniture was serviceable, if plain, comprising a narrow bed, some drawers and a chair. I was unsurprised by the absence of a mirror. The only remarkable thing about the room was its resident, who sat motionless in the chair. He, for it was a man, showed little emotion at my intrusion into his sanctum. I was foolish enough to attempt to engage him in conversation before I noticed the peculiar leathery texture of his skin and the glassy unblinking eyes.

For me this latest specimen of the taxidermist's art was by far the most disturbing. I wondered who the poor fellow had been, and how he had come to such a pass. At that point, I heard the crunch of wheels coming to a stop.

Withdrawing from the room and quickly locking it behind me, I opened the door to the side and peered out. Two fellows, one uniformed, one not, both a little bedraggled and in the act of removing straw from their persons, were arrived in the back of a farmer's cart. Plainly, I was to play gatekeeper for the reporter and the constable. Moving to the gate, I saw that Maccabi had had the foresight to leave the chain unpadlocked, and with some effort I removed the heavy chain from the iron gates. I looked up expectantly at the passengers. The constable attempted to speak first, but the reporter, who appeared to think much of himself for a fellow with straw in his hat, interrupted.

'Edgar Allan, *Alnwick Mercury*: Constable Turner is here about the body. Show us up, man.'

There was something odd about the man's accent, but I was more concerned about his presumption in judging me a servant of the house. Perhaps I would avail myself of Maccabi's raiment sooner than planned. Nonetheless, I waved them through and followed the cart up the drive, losing very little in distance thanks to the dilatory nature of both horse and driver. The cart pulled up at the doorway, which opened to reveal Maccabi. The man was either prescient or had intended to wait on the threshold until the constable's arrival. To my reckoning there was no vantage point over the drive from which he could possibly have arrived so quickly at the entrance.

The visitors alighted from the rustic vehicle, the reporter somewhat more nimbly than the policeman. Allan's introduction was the same terse, almost brusque, pronouncement he had given me. The constable appeared to have given up hope of getting the first word in any exchange. Maccabi raised his eyebrows at me over Allan's shoulder; I gave him a rapid shake of the head.

He spoke. 'Good morning, gentlemen. I shall show you to the unfortunate fellow's last resting place.'

He addressed me then. 'Moffat, accompany us, we may need to move the cadaver.'

The man was not so dull as to misunderstand that I wished – for the time – to remain incognito, but I felt he could have relished the peremptory tone a little less.

We went, passing swift, on foot to the pond. Allan kept up a rattling farrago of questions that Maccabi wisely ignored, whilst I brought up the rear behind my supposed betters. If the policeman was peevish at this usurpation of his role, he hid it well behind his silence. The angle of the late shepherd's neck was still convincing enough to my eye to be the cause of death. The silent policeman bent down to examine the body more closely. The greater part of it was not underwater, only one leg, and the other below the knee. The constable lifted each leg carefully out of the water and uttered but one word: 'Broken.'

Cullis deceased's tumble down the hillside had been a precipitous one, true, but I was mildly surprised at this intelligence. I stood a little closer, the better to hear any more gobbets of wisdom that might fall from the policeman's lips. The man ran his hands the length of the body, felt the neck with its improbable angle and discovered – I assumed from the wordless grunt he gave when he felt the cranium – the site of the blow I had dealt the shepherd.

Allan had followed this with feverish attention, all the while scribbling in his damned notebook. I was half expecting – no, gleefully anticipating – the next terse utterance from the policeman's mouth, which was, of course, 'Murder.'

Maccabi was completely and utterly unmoved. Allan grew still more excitable, asking me, 'Know him, did you? Like him? Likeable fellow, was he?'

'I did not, sir, I am recently arrived myself.'

If the scribbler had noticed that my own diction was somewhat more refined than his own, he gave no sign of it, merely turning his fervid eye on Maccabi and sending a further salvo of questions in his direction. Maccabi caught my eye with a questioning look and I gave him a nod. The man was no dullard, I had to allow him that.

He began the introductions forthwith; again, for a reporter, Allan proved remarkably unobservant – or the scribbling was proof of a prodigiously unreliable memory. It appeared he had not noticed my sudden promotion to master of Gibbous House. It interested me more that the policeman did not care to make anything of my brief masquerade as a humble servant.

'So, Constable Turner, may the cadaver be despatched to the undertakers? I fear his brother is determined to achieve a rapid burial.'

Turner merely uttered 'Brother?' in the most quizzical manner, and I suggested we all repair to the house to discuss what should next be done. The policeman strode purposefully toward the house entrance, thwarting my intention to herd the both of them in via the servants' entrance. The reporter, perhaps affronted by being ignored, took to reading aloud excerpts from his notebook. It seemed his handwriting was not of the highest quality as, amongst other things, I was surprised to learn that I had in my employ one Zebediah Macindoe and that a shepherd named Portcullis was recently found murdered in a pound.

Chapter Nineteen

In an effort to restore the correct social order, I steered the company into the kitchen; Mrs Gonderthwaite was present, at least in what passed for the flesh, Cullis *vivat* was not. The cook-cum-chatelaine was in a distracted state, stirring the empty air in front of her with a wooden spoon. I bellowed 'TEA' at a suitably insistent distance from her blank face. She came to herself immediately, although quite unstartled, and busied herself with a large kettle. There were some rustic chairs near to a large table and we all, save Constable Turner and the cook, availed ourselves of the little comfort they offered. No one spoke, not even the reporter.

Believing the policeman's silence a clumsy effort to tempt one or other of us into some rash utterance of use to him, I took the opportunity to study him more closely. He was not young, and in common with the men of his age in this area he sported the ruddy flush of the outdoor life. I had been long enough in Northumbria to note the savage winds and it seemed forty years' experience of them tinted the cheeks a vibrant red. His whiskers were fairly restrained for a man of his class; I could not see the colour of his hair for the incongruous top hat, which, I noted, he forbore to remove in my house. I wondered that the policemen themselves did not demand some more practical – and sartorially harmonious – headgear. His uniform fit – as many such garments do – where it might. The dark-blue serge of his tailcoat strained at certain seams and bagged voluminously in others. His trousers were white in colour and still less practical than the hat. The boots had been polished to a high shine, but were a little dusty after their journey in the cart.

I had been sure the reporter would fill the aural void, but he merely contented himself with running his finger along the lines of his notebook and mouthing the words, occasionally looking up as if startled by the surreal world his note-taking had created. It was Maccabi who proved least able to bear the inscrutable silence of the policeman. Clearing his throat, he said, 'Constable, ah... ;' he shifted uncomfortably in his seat, 'surely you don't think... '

His voice trailed off and I was convinced he was squirming under the gimlet eye of the policeman. The Peeler replied, 'I do think, Mr Maccabi. The detection of crime is a cerebral pursuit.'

This was a veritable feat of oratory from the taciturn officer. Allan looked up sharply from his notebook.

'Detection? What do you mean?'

He withdrew a pair of spectacles from a pocket of his coat and placed them so that he could peer over them at the policeman. He then scribbled the word in his notebook

161

and looked up expectantly. Perhaps vanity had prevented him from using the eye-glasses earlier, although I supposed no ocular improvements would improve his pencraft.

'The work of a detective, Mr Allan. Or, more correctly, a detective policeman.'

The reporter scrawled again, but looked none the wiser. The constable went on at some length concerning the collection of clues and evidence, the use of reasoning, corollary and surmise to bring criminals to justice. The very idea of such a person sounded like something from the most outlandish novel. I wished for a little more of his erstwhile brevity. The reporter continued to scribe as though in the role of Jehovah's amanuensis, and Maccabi fidgeted like a bored girl. Had it not amused me so, I would have found it uncomfortable to watch.

Eventually, the *soi-disant* 'police detective' appeared to realise that his proselytising on the innovatory development in the world of police work was hindering the investigation. He stopped in the midst of some many-syllabled neologism, his mouth closing like a gin-trap sprung by an unwitting badger. The reporter gave a great sigh at this development. The constable turned his gaze once more to Maccabi, who had not desisted in his squirming at any point. What possessed Maccabi to utter the following, I did not know.

'The body, Cullis, I should like to see to its removal... If... '

His resolve withered under the stare.

'It's just, his brother... ' . He faltered again.

The policeman let him fidget a little longer, then said, 'All in good time, Mr Maccabi. The brother might be summoned, I take it?'

Myself, I would have found this new departure into civilised speech an unnerving departure. Maccabi relaxed a little, and, voicing his compliance loudly, dashed out to the servants' entrance, presumably towards the stables.

The uncompanionable silence prevailed once more and I was glad of it, idly perusing the peculiar figure of the newspaperman scribbling at the table. He seemed to be about forty-five years of age. I remarked in him the inclination to a furtive and timid manner as observed in such people as are unused to the fugitive life – and who seldom prosper long in it. He was of middling height, dark of hair and with eyes of the wateriest blue, save for those parts that by rights should have been white, which were threaded with a myriad of red filaments. Whether this was a symptom of some undiagnosed affliction or simply a sign of the extent to which his vanity prevented him from wearing the eye-glasses he so clearly needed, I did not know. His attire was, I had to admit, as garish as something I might have worn had I not benefited from the much-needed education in matters of taste that my late wife had given me. His tailcoat was high in the waist and long in the tails. It was violet – not a sin in itself, of course. His trousers, however, were a plaid monstrosity such as might have been worn by one of the more unlikely mechanicals in one of Scott's puerile romances. Perhaps his eye-glasses should have been the first item assumed on rising from his bed.

Maccabi returned in the time it took to note these things – which is to say, in no time at all. He was unaccompanied and prevailed on the constable to make shift to the stables, as Cullis was unable to enter the house at that moment. The reporter leapt to his feet, intent on witnessing the interview. I thought I might follow suit and it struck me that I had theretofore seen no sign of a notebook in Turner's hands. Perhaps an extraordinary memory was another aspect of the new science of detection.

Outside, Cullis was waiting. He had assumed a rough and filthy leather apron over his clothes, although they would not have been ruined by any amount of the blood coating the roughly cured skin. In either hand he held an extremely large and bloodied knife; the one blade was toothed in the manner of a saw and the other visible as being exceptionally keen – even to the naked eye. The reporter looked wide-eyed as though in fear of his life. The policeman was stolidly silent. I considered that this 'detection' seemed to be a remarkably passive activity. Then Maccabi turned to me.

'Have you spoken with Cullis earlier today, sir?'

'What of it?' I asked.

The 'detective' intervened. 'He would like to know if you ordered the disposal of a horse. It appears there is a use for its skin, at least.'

The reporter looked at him like a bumpkin at a magic show. Maccabi looked equally impressed.

'For pity's sake, we're outside a d____ stable, Cullis reeks of horse, he's wearing an ostler's apron and... I am right, am I not, Constable, that the poor fellow in the pond has been a corpse too long to produce such gouts of blood! That's all there is to this wonderful detection; any fool might pretend to be a practitioner.'

I turned to the policeman expecting a deserved look of respect. He gave me something that approximated a smile.

'My father owned the knacker's in Morpeth when I was young. It must have been a greater feat of detection for you. Although, in fact, you mean deduction, Mr Moffat.'

He appeared to stop and consider that he had not wanted to say so much, and then went on in his more customary terse style. 'Strange thing. Corpses, blood. Not a military man, are you.'

It was not a question. Therefore I did not answer.

Chapter Twenty

Maccabi was still looking uncomfortable. I would have given anything for a moment alone with him to ascertain why. In the meantime, Constable Turner turned his gaze to the brother of the deceased. He spoke in a more intelligible version of the local patois; both Cullis and I were able to understand it.

'Mr Cullis. Older brother, yes. On the estate since March, is it?'

Although Cullis's answer was as impenetrable as expected, the look of bewilderment was unmistakable. Turner leaned his face toward the labourer and glowered, the man shrank back.

'I gave you something to remember me by in Felton, man.'

Cullis cowered and shrank further away from the embodiment of authority.

'Been at the old business, Cullis?'

There was no need for words; the shake of the head was violent. Nonetheless, the detective seemed to discern some mendacity, for he delivered a sweeping, open-handed blow to the fellow's head. Perhaps there was more to the ostler's dental deficiencies than a poor diet.

Maccabi, his face a mixture of nervousness and relief, let out, 'So! A suspect!'

Evidently the man had never encountered a representative of the law, much less been on the wrong side of it. Turner said nothing. Allan's pen raced across the page, and he gave a curse as his ink ran out. His pen was some newfangled contraption, which he filled from a bottle of ink carried in his pocket.

The detective uttered one word, eyebrows raised, to Maccabi: 'Suspect?'

Maccabi's reply was immediate, but less effective for the stuttering: 'I mean m-m-merely that the Cullises are known to you, sir, a-a-and could reasonably be assumed to be criminal characters, and th-th-thus under suspicion. I thought a falling out... '

His voice faded like the last of an echo.

'Did you?' Was the illuminating response.

Most unfortunately his discomfort was assuaged by the arrival of the other players in the pantomime. The professor with his scuttling gait, behind the confidently striding Miss Pardoner and the gliding Mrs Gonderthwaite. The policeman offered a polite click of the heels by way of welcome. Then he turned to me. 'The body may be removed, Mr Moffat. But only to the care of the coroner at Alnwick. The drayman and his cart are yet here for the purpose.'

I was about to instruct Cullis to take care of his brother's remains, but thought better of it, bidding Maccabi to see to it and thereby ensuring his being accompanied by the detective and, most likely, the d___ reporter to the pond. Any enquiry as to whence his guilty manner came could wait until another time.

Cullis was dismissed by the professor to clean himself up – and place the horse's hide in the usual place – and Mrs Gonderthwaite apparently found further tasks for herself in the ill-provisioned kitchen. I looked to my ward and enquired,'Did you know of the professor's talents as a taxidermist, Miss Pardoner?'

The imp danced a little jig of frustration and ran a hand over his scalp, while scowling, as if he had been hoping to deny his pastime. Miss Pardoner, in her turn, denied him the opportunity.

'Indeed I did and do, Mr Moffat. It is a fascinating art and the professor has been good enough to inculcate in me an appreciation of some of its mysteries.'

I thought of the poor fellow in the gatehouse, but thought better of mentioning it just then. Perhaps I should have done so.

'Do you leave the skinning of the beasts to such as Cullis?'

'Oh no, sir. I am more than competent with a sharp enough knife.'

It was not a comforting thought, but it was a fascinating one.

'How fortunate that the shepherd was killed with a rock, in that case,' I said.

The professor cleared his throat and wondered, 'Ah... the policeman has been open with his speculations then?'

I supposed he had not, but saw no reason to apprise either of them of that fact.

'Oh yes,' I said. 'I should hardly be surprised if he suspects Maccabi, the fellow should have embroidered an M on his breast pocket. He is surely guilty of something, of that I have no doubt.'

A little scarlet appeared on Miss Pardoner's cheek but she made no further reaction and I had to be satisfied with that. The professor, however, stiffened his spine and spoke with some gravity.

'Mr Moffat, I have ever found Jedediah Maccabi to be the most honest, upright and diligent servant of the estate, I would doubt him capable of the least crime, save that of a surfeit of zeal in carrying out his duties.'

I could not resist a sneer in the little man's direction.

'It is to be hoped, then, that his betters have not called upon him to perform any unsavoury duties, wouldn't you agree?'

I was pleased to note that this riposte deflated the man somewhat.

I excused myself to both and set off to the front of the house, convinced of an opportunity to see Jedediah carted to arrest and ignominy in the company of a corpse. It was not to be. Constable Turner stood in the rear of the cart next to a shroud-covered form that I presumed to be my late employee. Maccabi stood on the threshold lamentably bare of shackles, chains or any restraint at all. The reporter was in animated discussion with Maccabi, who gave an urgent 'Moffat' at my approach. As I drew near, he turned to the journalist and informed him that he was not in a position to offer him board and lodging. Allan was implying that not to cooperate with him could prejudice any newspaper report he might concoct. Such threats must have had little effect on Maccabi, for he remained obdurate. For certain sure, I was unfazed by them and merely extended the house's hospitality in the certainty that the reporter's stay would – at the very least – prove diverting. At that moment the policeman called from the cart, saying that he intended to return and resolve the matter – if not before the day was out, then soon after. He gave me a long look before laying on the whip to little effect and the cart rolled away.

The repeater watch showed one; it was a pleasant afternoon. I bade Maccabi see to the provision of a luncheon for myself and the reporter on the terrace outside the library. Maccabi seemed about to make some unwise remark, but closed his mouth and went about arranging the miracle of food production from Mrs Gonderthwaite's domain. I turned to the reporter. 'Well, Mr Allan, you are a strange fish to wash up on these shores, I think.'

Despite my bantering tone, the man's eyes narrowed to a sharp glare and his voice emerged sharper still.

'What do you mean by that, Moffat?'

He gave a consumptive little cough and spat gelidly to the side.

'I simply meant that you are no Northumbrian.'

I raised both eyebrows to convince him of my innocence of any guileful motive.

'No, no. I am not, at that. I – I have been sometime abroad. My family are... Reynolds from Gainsborough... Lincoln-shire. Edgar Allan is a professional name.'

His accent bespoke the Americas, although he was trying, somewhat unsuccessfully, to disguise it. There seemed little of truth in anything he had said – perhaps that was to be expected of a newspaperman.

We reached the terrace, covered with furniture of iron after the style of the Spanish *rejeria* or the iron-working fashions imported for St Paul's or Hampton Court. I had little time for chairs and tables of this kind: the artful whorls and curlicues in the metal in no way made up for their impracticality and discomfort. I would have preferred banquettes of honest wood. Still, it was indeed a pleasant day and I motioned the reporter to a less fussy arrangement of four chairs and a table of rectangular, rather than the more common circular, shape.

We sat, Allan almost recovered from my remark. He did seem to be a man with a past not quite behind him; a past he would most likely have looked for over his shoulder were he not hidden half a world away from it. I sat in a chair that offered a view of the lake.

The reporter began patting the pockets of his coat, then withdrew a clay pipe. A further search produced a box of blackened metal about the size of a folded handkerchief. Allan opened it and withdrew a white-headed lucifer. He bent to the flagstones and ignited the match so as to avoid any harm to myself from stray sparks. I had never been a true smoker and I never will be such until the unlikely day that someone invents an affordable match that can be used in safety.

Arabella Coble had enjoyed tobacco, although she never smoked in public. I did enjoy watching the pleasure she drew from the pipe quite as materially as she drew the smoke from it. The matches had been the end of the child, and Arabella's decline began shortly afterward. She did not smoke again, but kept a similarly blackened box at her bedside in memory of her daughter. I buried it with her.

The reporter let out a contented sigh and seemed for the first time relaxed in my company. His legs were stretched out before him, crossed at the ankle, and both he and his clothes cut a slightly less ridiculous figure in that pose.

'A man with a smoke is ever in want of a drink, I find, Mr Allan,' I said.

I stood and entered the library via the French windows, and returned with an Armagnac, which someone had hidden behind a row of false spines whose books' contents, had they existed, would have made interesting reading. The 'books' were of homologous design, as though for a private edition of some collection. All but one spine bore the legend: *Collected Writings on Alcoholic Beverages* and an appropriate volume number. On noting that the spines themselves were as new, the experimental hooking of a finger on the only title of exception revealed the Armagnac's hiding place. It would have been an exceptionally captivating tome, purporting to be '*Les Quarante Vertues d'Armagnac*' by one Cardinal Vital Dufour.

The reporter started from a slumberous ease as I placed the glass on the iron table. He looked uncertain as to where he found himself and looked blankly as I wished him, 'Good health, Mr Allan.'

He blinked severally before replying, 'Quite, and your own, Mr Moffat, though I think you more in need of the toast than I.'

The man looked as pale as the worst consumptive and I laughed, thinking his humour both droll and macabre. Allan did not even smile, just drained his glass at a draught and replaced it upon the table.

I offered to recharge his glass but he declined, staring pensively over his eye-glasses. Thinking to pass the time in conversation, I remarked on his unusual attire.

'Manners do not maketh man, Moffat, but clothes,' he said.

He seemed unstruck by the question of what manner of man his own made him, while I replied, 'I believe you may be correct, Mr Allan. A man is known for what he is by his dress; from the beggar in his rags to the emperor in his purple and all other stations in between, we are known by our buttoned and sewn signifiers.'

He considered for a moment. 'But I do believe we might consider more the physiognomy as the clue to character. I have made study of lower characters in Paris and... elsewhere. A noble forehead is rarely seen upon a villain, in my experience. Look to yourself.'

It would have made a cat laugh, the nonsense the fellow spouted. Nevertheless, I did not expect him to react so to what I said in reply to it. 'So, you would know a villain, if you found his corpse in another man's finest clothes?'

The man's customary pallor was empurpled by some fit of apoplexy or rage and amid the choking he spluttered: 'Damn him, Damn that Griswold.' I watched the fellow recover himself with some interest, whilst considering what a truly peculiar fellow this Edgar Allan was.

Chapter Twenty-one

At last, Maccabi and Miss Pardoner arrived, bearing the necessities for luncheon *en plein air*, which were shortly revealed as a cold collation of meats and cheeses. I presumed, therefore, that Maccabi would not be joining us. Miss Pardoner needed no invitation and sat predictably close to the reporter, although I had stood to withdraw the chair next to mine.

'Good day, once again, Miss Pardoner,' I said, evenly.

The reporter, clearly not having recovered himself sufficiently, merely grunted and airily waved a hand. To be sure, he still looked a little puce.

'Good day, gentlemen. I trust these poor comestibles will satisfy? They are little enough – but the best that could be assembled.'

In fact, they were the makings of a good, if simple, repast. The cheese was of a pan-European variety: the fashionably novel Roquefort, Parmesan, Emmental, Camembert and Cheddar. With the exception of this last, it was scarce credible that such cheeses could be found in Northumberland – much less in the kitchen of Gibbous House. They seemed bare of any mould, save of course the blue in the Roquefort. Many a London table would have been pleased to offer such.

The cold meats were more prosaic by comparison, for the most part being the residue of some earlier roast. The ham hock had a suspicious silvering in the pink; that aside, the rolled beef appeared moist and the lamb looked as though some degree of shepherding had – after all – been done by the late Cullis. There was more of the blood sausage from break-fast, sliced cold, blackly crumbling around pellucid, glistening fat. There were freshly baked loaves, so hot as to steam despite the fine weather.

Miss Pardoner made as if to serve. I waved her to her seat once more.

Taking a knife to one of the loaves, I sliced thickly and placed two generous portions on a plate. Spurning the use of a cheese parer, since the cheese was indeed in a remarkable state of freshness, I took up the handles of the cheese wire and noted how much more effective it would be than a yellow scarf. Miss Pardoner laid a hand on mine. 'Just Roquefort, sir. I find cheese so insipid. I prefer meat.'

Her tone was innocent of any guile, although, perhaps inevitably, the corner of her mouth gave an infinitesimal twitch. I cut a generous portion of the blued cheese and placed it with a spatulate knife on her plate. The cheese itself glistened and I was reminded of beads of perspiration on a lover's skin. Miss Pardoner declined the ham, asked for her beef to be from the rarer end of the joint and demanded a further two slices of the blood sausage than the two I had already apportioned.

Mr Allan appeared yet to be in a funk and made no response when I gestured at him with cutlery and plate. Mine own selections reflected Miss Pardoner's tastes and I found that a pleasing thought.

Since both my ward and I had handled our cutlery with some efficiency I was quite despairing of a libation when Maccabi finally arrived with a decanter of something a little too pale to be claret. Still, I was grateful when he poured the three of us a glass, although I was sore tempted to upbraid him as he spilled a drop on the admittedly greying white of my shirt cuff. No matter, his own clothes would be on my back soon enough.

Edgar Allan drained his glass before I had taken a sip, and held it forth for replenishment. Maccabi complied and departed with an indecipherable look at Miss Ellen Pardoner.

Miss Pardoner addressed the reporter. 'Are you quite yourself, sir?'

His visage betrayed that something troubled him more than a little; his reply had the tone of a wistful child who has lost some shiny gewgaw. 'I am quite sure I no longer know.'

For myself, I was sure I no longer cared.

Maccabi had had the courtesy to leave the decanter on the wrought-iron table; I removed the stopper and charged the reporter's glass to no discernible reaction. Miss Pardoner declined the offer and I filled mine own glass with a little more care than Maccabi had. Miss Pardoner gave a polite, and unconvincing, cough as though asking my permission to speak. Her bold stare gave the lie to this semblance of propriety.

'Mr Moffat. I wondered if you might care to discuss Miss Arabella Coble with me. I quite feel I know her. The late Mr Coble spoke of her fondly and often. You will forgive a young woman's curiosity, I am sure.'

I would have, that was indeed true. However, a young woman's dissembling I would have – and did – find less forgivable. It seemed doubtful to me that my late wife had been held in any great affection by a man who had instructed his lawyers: 'be in no doubt, I hold yourselves responsible should my great-niece be so misguided as to believe I hold her in any kind of affection'.

Miss Pardoner's request was merely a gambit of some kind. For that reason I chose to grant it, hoping to descry in what game she had made this opening.

'She was a remarkable woman,' I began. I regaled her with as affecting an account of the family life of persons of quality as had ever been invented – for publication or otherwise. Even the most blurred version of the truth should have, I supposed, shocked the woman to the core. There would come a time to tell Miss Ellen Pardoner about Arabella Coble: that time had not yet come. Though the reporter appeared insensible, it were too great a risk.

Therefore I spoke at length, with as little regard for veracity as Mr Charles Dickens himself – and perhaps with as much sentiment – regarding the paragon I claimed Arabella to have been. I should confess I limned myself in colours less dark than they should have been, but not too much so. A certain verisimilitude was necessary.

So Miss Pardoner did not hear of forgery, deception or hurried departures by the light of moons, gibbous and otherwise. Nor did she hear of occasional forays into the life of the street on both our parts, although admittedly Arabella provided service more often than I, who was forced to remain contented with pecuniary matters and the provisioning of restful ease for tormented men.

Nor did I mention the swindles, the glorious gulling of a minor earl whose climax earned a year's living – and the dying of her daughter left alone that night with the lucifer box. The ending I gave the fantasy was equally unreal, recounting how Arabella had died bravely in my arms after suffering much.

This last was true in so far as it went. My late wife had died raving and ravaged by syphilis with a curse for Alasdair Moffat on her lips.

Miss Pardoner's reaction was disconcerting at first. 'Mr Moffat, you cannot surely imagine that I have not read it?' The woman arched an eyebrow.

I raised both of my own before charging myself with being doubly dull. In the first and less serious indictment: for not grasping that someone had left Miss Arabella Coble's naïve scribblings for me to find – and in the second; for not taking pains to read it.

My ward's statement meant that there was something in the diary revealing of Arabella. How revealing remained to be seen; but since Alasdair Moffat could not have figured in its pages, something ripe must have lain in them to belie the fairy tale I myself had just spun about Miss Arabella Coble.

'Ah, I see... Perhaps a grieving husband should be allowed a little gilding of mourning's lily?' I ventured.

Miss Pardoner's reply fell somewhere between the bray of an amused donkey and the snort of a particularly disdainful thoroughbred. Any subsequent badinage was prevented by the querulous voice of the reporter, who enquired, 'Who... ahem... is Miss Arabella Coble?'

Blinking like a bat before a raised candle, he looked from Miss Pardoner to myself and back again. Not for the first time, my own reactions were anticipated by the unladylike sardonicism of Miss Pardoner.

'No knowledge of Cobles, Mr Allan? Really, I would have thought a newspaperman employed by Northumbria's finest sheet would have a vast supply of information on such influential personages.'

Mr Allan's crest had quite fallen, and I suspected that he knew himself that the *Alnwick Mercury*'s most utilitarian moments came when wrapped around the fresh produce of the town's market on Saturdays. Nevertheless, one would have thought that a reporter would have known something of the Cobles, therefore I asked him, 'How long have you been reporting for the *Mercury*, Mr Allan?'

He made an unattractive and petulant-looking moue and said, 'Eight days.'

This time I joined my ward in the unattractive snickering.

She recovered herself somewhat quicker than I. There was a glint of mischief or even devilment in her eye as she said, 'Miss Arabella Coble was a renegade, a strumpet, a wilful woman and a faithless wife. For all that I know she may have been a thief and a murderess.' She paused and moistened her lips as though suddenly dry-mouthed. 'I wish that I had met her before she died.'

The last of Allan's pen-scratching died away, whereupon the three of us sat in silence, and only one of us was quite comfortable in it.

Chapter Twenty-two

The warm spring sun was making me feel most drowsy. The reporter, surprisingly, seemed able to bear the vacuum without filling it with questions; Miss Pardoner, being quite the most self-possessed woman I had ever had the fortune to meet, was contenting herself with a facade as enigmatic as that of any sphynx. I had learned, where safe, to take the balm of lethe where I could. Therefore, I cannot say if what I remembered next was truly a dream or a simple reverie: suffice to say it was faithful to memory – although who can say how faithful memory is to truth?

Arabella and I had had our secrets; of course we had. She knew me only as Moffat, after all. I in my turn had but recently learned of the existence of a previous husband, viz one Cadwallader. My feelings for her had not conformed to any ideal of romantic love such as might be found in Lombardy troubadours' parchments. Though she did stir my passions, others had done so more violently. It were rather as though in Miss Arabella Coble a bond beyond consanguinity or sense could be found with my own obsessions. I knew it, and I knew it at once on the dockside the day that we met.

My peculiar education and subsequent reading had introduced me to the idea of the human soul. It was my belief that, if such a thing existed and if it were the seat of compassion and other noble virtues, then I was deficient this essential part of humanity. The sense of a similar void in Miss Coble bound me to her more strongly than ever any vow of love could have done. She was a woman as hollow as I.

Truly, she showed no affection for the mite who was holding her hand on the day that we met. Do not think that she was cruel. The child was ever clothed and fed as well as we; but she received not a caress or buss that other mothers might casually have bestowed with every hour. I did not feel undue sympathy; the girl was nothing to me, of course.

Nevertheless, I was not prepared for the grieving after the episode with the lucifer matches.

We had been doing tolerable well with some business involving breach of promise, mostly among gentlemen of trade, whilst we awaited one large fish that would set us up for some time.

One evening, during late summer 184_, Arabella and I were attending a programme of varieties in the song and supper club known as the Mogul Saloon, in Drury Lane. At the table adjoining was an oldish fellow of plain looks in the company of two rather younger male companions. The fellow was quite drunk, florid of cheek and rolling of eye. The younger fellows' clothes were frayed and shining in parts, although the cut was good. I saw the one slap his patron on the back as his confederate began the dip for the older chap's valuables.

I dashed to the table and seized the offender's hand. It was obvious to all what the two men had been about.

'Leave,' I urged him. 'Unless you wish me to call the Peelers?'

The two younger men left. The older man offered his hand. 'C-c-apital,' he hiccoughed. 'Johnny Brougham, fifth Earl of B_____, call me Johnny, cahn't thank yew enough.'

I pumped his hand, thinking that he was correct in that at least.

'Ah... yew and yer lady could join me, p'raps, hmm?' he asked, with all the diffidence of his class.

'Allow me to introduce my sister Arabella,' I said. 'Captain Crawford, at your service.'

Brougham held out a chair for Arabella. There were other women in the Mogul; at that time there were several ladies in society with a taste for the lower entertainments, but there were few in evidence that night. A certain kind of woman would ape the fashions of these adventuresses with far less panache than Arabella was able to manage. Still, Arabella's origins were much closer to these members of the quality than those of the bawds in the company of the moneyed and the meretricious.

We took our seats to the sounds of a singularly bronchitic and less than tuneful squawk. The assembled audience had begun to laugh the moment a man appeared on the raised dais in front of them. Brougham gave a loud whisper in Arabella's direction. 'Sloman, usually on at Evans', jolly good.'

It was a matter of taste, I assumed. Every song seemed to include a sketch of one of the regular habitués of the Mogul. One fellow with a writerly look – and a notebook clutched to his chest – stood up to bow at the mention of Makepeace. I reflected that one ought never to underestimate the vanity of writers. An hour later our new-found boon companion beamed beatifically during a song lauding the exploits of one Supper Club Johnny, although I imagined a few of those watching merited the epithet.

Arabella struck exactly the right note in her performance that evening. For a performance it was; I myself, who knew her to be eight and twenty, would have believed her no more than of majority age. Again, she hid the boldness and self-assurance that I found so attractive behind a flirtatious and, yes, inane chatter. Brougham cut a figure that was testament to the louche and dissolute existence enjoyed by more than one or two of his peers. His swelling abdomen told of port and too many suppers in places like the Mogul.

Naturally, despite the affectation of diffidence, he possessed the supreme self-confidence of all his class: a certain knowledge of the strata of society and his own elevated station within them. Above all, he knew himself to be irresistible by dint of his status and wealth.

Equally naturally, Arabella resisted him with great skill and feigned reluctance.

She resisted Brougham that night, in Evans' the next night,

at Regent's Park Zoological Gardens the following week and on the Serpentine after that. On every occasion I played the chaperone, the doting and indulgent elder brother. As with any man accustomed to having every wish gratified, the denial of one impelled him to strive to attain it. Arabella refused all gifts, as a player at Speculation will spurn a trick in the hope of greater gains. The proffered gifts became more outrageous; we were both sorely tempted by a sapphire and ruby brooch of Indian origin in the shape of a butterfly. However, we remained strong.

The game continued for several months and I despaired of Brougham ever closing his wet mouth on the hook.

Finally, Brougham came to call at a house on Cadogan Square that the fool believed to be ours. A fortunate encounter with the rich and effete son of a cotton merchant in an alley in Limehouse had offered an opportunity for extortion and blackmail, but I had saved the coin for a later day and extracted the use of his London address after his departure for the Grand Tour. A man's reputation in society is a precious thing and, as such, a marketable commodity.

A sham sufficient unto the dupe was maintained by myself, Arabella, and two confederates I had had occasion to use in the past. The office of butler in the service of Arabella and Captain Arthur Crawford was filled by one Crabbit. This gentleman I had encountered one evening in the foyer of a house in East Cheap. He was leaving, having been disappointed in the matter of employment: the man had lost his position due to a leave of absence in the Newgate Gaol occasioned by a discounted bill.

He would hear not a word against his former employer – a noted Whig – as he had settled the debt and turned him onto the streets at one remove. He stood a head taller than I, and retained an air of servility whilst remaining imposing. His age was indiscernible: he might have been thirty or sixty. A butler he looked, a butler he had been, and – for a while – he played the butler again.

One of the younger molls at that same house I engaged to play the maid. With the paint removed, her East End vowels lent her an air of authenticity, especially when she affected the accents of her betters, as many real servants were wont to do. The two of them were an expense indeed, since they had been in my employ since the first week of our machinations, but it was uncertain how long it would take Brougham to bite.

Brougham's call at the Cadogan Square residence was conducted according to etiquette: that is to say, he arrived in a hansom, which he engaged to wait while he presented his card. As was the custom, Crabbit removed this item of stationery atop a fine salver for delivery to the supposed master of the house. Brougham awaited any reply in the vestibule. Crabbit loured down at Brougham. 'The captain has intimated that you may call at four this afternoon. At which time he will be pleased to take tea with you.'

Through a second-floor sash, I observed the simpering fool withdraw to the carriage to wait. I wished him the joy of six hours at the roadside, with – as like as not – only a content-edly snoring driver for company.

Crabbit was despatched to a bakers for fancies and the like; Arabella instructed the jade in the preparation and presentation of tea. I stood outside the kitchen, enjoying the periodic sound of a hand on flesh and the young woman's vituperative reaction to her schooling in the matter. At length, I repaired to the library, pleased that Crabbit and I had thought to remove some of the very best vintages from the cellar to the book-lined room.

It had been no surprise that not a page of a single book had been cut and I had been still less surprised, on using my own knife, to find that whole runs of shelving contained row upon row of blank-paged books. A man so easily blackmailed clearly had received no sort of education: therefore, he owed me a modicum of thanks for the lesson I had taught him.

I settled in a peacock chair to wait for Brougham's arrival.

Came he at last, preceded by Crabbit's second delivery of his calling card. I felt a simple satisfaction at this defrauding of the social niceties. The earl demeaning himself so far as to call on a mere captain – how much more debased would he have felt to know his obsequies were squandered on an adventuring imposter?

On the card's arrival, I dismissed Crabbit with a wave of my fingers. Johnny Brougham's card bore only the appellation appropriate to his earldom. Plainly, as with many of the blood, the surname bare was sufficient. Said card was impressively stiff, as rigid as the rules of its presentation. It was devoid of the déclassé scalloping of edge that the cards of many of those exalted by success in trade affected. The print of an inky thumb may well have been the affectation of Brougham himself, or indeed a mark of Crabbit's descent from his former position.

Brougham was as nervous as a curate among bishops. Do not think he hopped from foot to foot, rubbing one hand on the other in serpentine style; no indeed, he was as stiff and formal as ever I had seen him. He stuttered painfully over the C of captain – and excruciatingly over that of Crawford – all the while executing such a bow as would disgrace the least ingenious of automata. Still more painful were his overtures: the politenesses required before broaching the business of the matter at hand. The man enquired of the current strength of my regiment, my phantastical prospects of promotion within it and of my imagined exploits under its standard. The trick, of course, was to make as little of all three whilst offering not a whit of detail, much in the manner of a Cardigan or a Raglan.

Much as I enjoyed the ridiculous nature of this preamble, it was some relief when I realised he was approaching the purpose of his visit, admittedly in the manner of a cautious dog toward an intemperate feline. However, he had scarce mentioned my sister's name, when I held up a hand and interrupted. 'Modern though it might be, Brougham, my sister and I are not so disparate in age that I would presume to dispose of her prospects in her absence.'

I rang the bell and instructed Crabbit to fetch Arabella.

'And also, if I might so presume,' I went on, 'I am in the hope that you would not consider it an imposition if our friend and advisor were also present?'

He spluttered his assent.

Arabella returned, on the arm of a man whom I respected as an exemplar of his type. Whitscrape, Malachi Whitscrape, attorney-at-law, as full of scruple as need be: he trod a line as thin as his own corporeal form. As yellow as the parchments he signed with conviction and impunity, only the burning coal of his eyes betrayed his true passion: the acquisition of guineas by whatever means. A useful man indeed.

Arabella took the peacock chair that I had vacated on standing for her entry, as politeness dictated. I stood, legs crossed at the ankle, and leaned one arm outstretched along the mantelpiece – a poor imitation of Mr Adam's. There was little warmth emanating from below it: a meagre log fed a feeble flicker in the grate. Brougham, having executed his stiff approximation of a bow in the direction of Arabella, stood, hands behind his back, clearing his throat as if some blockage would hold him silent for ever. Whitscrape, being an insubstantial, pallid fellow, faded until he no more caught the eye than an artfully arranged coat stand.

Brougham began diffidently, with much circumlocution and further adjustment of buttons, cuffs, waistcoat and the irritating bolus in his gullet. I silently wished he would out with his proposal; Arabella sat demure with eyes downcast.

'And so... Captain, not to delay further – and I hope I am

not indelicate in my haste – I have the honour this propitious day to ask for the hand of your sister Arabella in marriage.'

He let out a huffing sigh as if these very words had been the obstruction that had caught so in his throat. And perhaps they were: we had presented Arabella as a woman of few prospects, being only my sister-in-law and as such having no claim on the house in Cadogan Square and little more than fifty pounds per annum, thanks to a legacy on the distaff side. In short, his prospective bride had been bound for a life of genteel poverty. It said little for his own desirability amongst his peers that he was yet a bachelor, or that he would be tempted so far beyond his circle, no matter what the prize.

A glint in Whitscrape's eye signalled his continued presence in the world of men and I took it as a sign that Brougham had said enough.

'You have chosen well, Brougham. My sister will make you a fine consort. We accept your proposal. It does us both great honour, I'm sure.'

He gave another of his stiff courtesies to Arabella, this time accompanied by a most repulsive leer. It was time to spring the gin and see how much the ermine would forfeit to escape its jaws. 'And we are both, I am sure, cognizant of your extreme generosity in the matter of the responsibility.'

He nodded, still mooning at his prize.

'For indeed,' I went on, 'a man might marry many women, even at an age as advanced as my sister's own... '

Brougham's head swivelled, perhaps he felt the trap around his legs and could not turn to face me.

'But only a rare individual would take a widow... '

The eyes bulged; mayhap he was wriggling his leg and the teeth of the gin were paining him somewhat.

'And she the mother of a poor fatherless child.'

Brougham let out a bellow of pained rage and threw a look of venom toward a suddenly more visible Whitscrape, who gave him a very satisfied nod. Brougham did not address his enquiry to me, but to the lawyer: 'How much, you viper?'

Whitscrape named a sum, not inconsiderable. It seemed that Brougham's reputation, though of some pecuniary value to himself, would not have withstood a suit for breach of promise.

Later that evening, in possession of the earl's bill, we wound the enterprise up in style. Several colleagues of the maid's more normal place of employment were enjoined to attend an evening of libation and dancing. Crabbit disported himself shamelessly with several of these. Arabella invited some blades of her acquaintance, who, naturally, brought along acolytes and parasites in equal measure. Only Whitscrape and I disdained to invite friends to celebrate the success of our venture: the lawyer, I presumed, because he saw no profit in it, and I because there were none to whom I cared to extend an invitation.

The most satisfactory outcome of the evening was the despoliation of the house in Cadogan Square; it filled my soul to know that I had extended a little more in the way of education to the owner of so many blank-paged books.

Less satisfactory was the scene in East Cheap. The house

in which, prior to the gulling of the earl, Arabella, the child and I had taken the attic rooms was a blackened gap between the grey teeth of the rest of the terrace. It was smoking still. Several bare-chested men, quite blackened by the smoke, stood exhausted in front of the ashes. There had been no hope, of course, of any timely extinguishing of the inferno. These men were neighbours and relatives of those who had undoubtedly perished. The London Fire Engine Establishment did not venture into East Cheap: for who there would – or could – pay premiums on the least expensive of policies available from such as the East London Fire Insurance and Mutual?

Arabella was already pale, fatigued by the attentions of several of her invited blades and not a few of their coterie. She stood motionless before the pyre, at once beautiful and terrifying. Caring not for her clothes or shoes, she ran into the pile of ashes and fell to her hands and knees, scrabbling in the ash. By outrageous fortune her hand clasped around a blackened metal object just as two of the brawny fellows seized her and bore her away.

The burns were not serious, merely a reddening of the hands, mostly caused by the heat from her own lucifer box, an item perhaps not suited to the role of demure young lady and, consequent on this, left this past few weeks in the attic rooms with her child – and an equally dead older woman whose name I do not remember.

I held Arabella close in the overwhelming stench of burning and smoke.

Chapter Twenty-three

Indeed, I must surely have been dreaming on the terrace of Gibbous House, since I awoke with a start; a woman-ish scream – evidently produced by Edgar Allan – pierced the silence. I supposed the scream might either have been as a result of the flames coming from his frock coat or of Miss Pardoner's stalwart efforts at extinguishing them by beating at them with a no-longer white cloth, late of the table's surface.

Allan, having fought off the ministrations of Miss Pardoner to his smouldering apparel, fixed me with a rheumy eye. 'If your dreams did not disturb your slumbers, Moffat, they did disturb mine. Who is this Brougham you have been muttering about, sir?'

I chose to ignore him. However, my ward declared herself to be equally interested in the identity of the fellow who stalked my dreams. I confess I was somewhat nonplussed, and before I had collected my thoughts she added, 'A noble fellow, I'll warrant.'

'The man no more exists than Springheeled Jack. Enough

of this nonsense, miss, I'll join you for dinner. A man must have some time to call his own.'

Before I had made good my departure, Miss Pardoner added, 'You would find few to agree with you in London, Mr Moffat, from Peckham to Cadogan Square.'

Her rejoinder almost gave me pause, but I showed her my back nonetheless.

My first intention was to reflect in my monkish apartments on a further course of action towards achieving some pecuniary advancement from my current position. But by the time I operated the newfangled brass lever on the door to my cell, my proposed activity was transformed into a determination to read Arabella Coble's diary with diligence.

It was with some alarm that I noted that the journal lay not on the threadbare counterpane where I had left it. This alarm subsided when I caught sight of the book, spine up, covers splayed, on the boards beneath the iron bedstead. It might well have fallen from the bed whereon I had left it, but I had been sure that Allan's womanly squeal had awakened me – and not some seismological phenomenon. For the journal was heavy, the leather binding being of quality and the paper within it, too. The hasp that had surrendered all too easily to my spear-blade penknife was of metal, gilt or possibly even gold, having been marked easily by the blade. A substantial book, with many pages.

It was astounding to see that the book, which I had assumed would contain little after Arabella's anticipatory speculations concerning a certain Cadwallader's arrival –

which revelations occurred only a little way into the tome – was inscribed to the very last page. Beyond, indeed, for the endpapers and the inside of the cover were bedecked with an inky trail resembling a spidery imitation of my late wife's writing as I had known it. The very last words were written just so:

'Ware the homunculus, "Alasdair",' and a line meandered downward from the extravagant serif at the foot of the letter 'r' to the bottom edge of the book. Thick black strokes in another hand had written

θάνατος

Which strokes taken together meant Thanatos, the Greek god of Death.

Alongside were other Greek letters, which looked familiar. I removed from my pocket the volume purloined from the library, on the flyleaf of which a similar hand had written

ΜοΦΦατ

And yet I knew I had seen these symbols before, long before I had met Arabella, in the library of the man who had been Moffat. Alongside these letters was a drawing depicting the symbol that hung outside the Coble Inn at Seahouses.

I slumped, aghast, onto the cot. It was no great revelation that my late wife had been in the habit of keeping a secret journal during the course of our marriage: our life together had necessitated much independence of thought and deed. No; what I could not understand, or rather conceive of, was how any such journal, having been nowhere in evidence at the time of Arabella's death, had appeared in timely fashion at Gibbous House. Nor could I fathom that she had met me by design and perhaps at another's behest.

I turned the leaves of the diary rapidly through Arabella's callow musings, more rapidly still through her swoonings over her tutor Cadwallader, and the veiled hints as their illicit relationship progressed to elopement. I was stopped short by an entry for January 12th 184_:

> *'I am in receipt of a communication from Septimus. I am loath to broach its contents with my Husband; viz. that we are summoned to Northumberland; that there I shall learn something to my advantage. That pronoun being underlined with a savagery that precludes any mention of the missal to Cadwallader.'*

It seemed an affectation to refer to her husband by his familial appellation. Perhaps it was a measure of the distance between them, evidence of the fading of romantic love in the presence of more ardent needs of a pecuniary kind. I wondered how Arabella had revealed their joint summons without showing Septimus Coble's hand. Her journal gave no clue. The following entry read:

> *'Post coach north, from the Golden Cross.'*

Thereafter came a pause altogether in the journal's entries. One month had passed before she wrote another word, and there she wrote one only:

'*Quickened!*'

The script foreshadowed that of the most recent entries, in so far as it quavered, perhaps due to some great emotion. Arabella's next entry was more businesslike – and less terse:

'I wish that in my dealings with Coble I had bargained better. However, the man was immovable on the matter of income and interest, swearing that if I did not take the capital sum of one thousand pounds, I should receive nothing at all. In truth, I was glad to leave, and to take the sum offered. I shudder yet at the prospect of suffering Cadwallader's fate...

No matter, one thousand pounds I have and not a penny more. One can but hope that it is sufficient to see the unborn child some way to majority, at least until I can acquire some prospects of my own. That or fulfil the task they have set me of finding their unwitting mark.'

I continued to read as quickly as I could, noting with interest that my brief reconnaissance on the East India Docks had been no more painstaking than her own. She had inveigled herself aboard the recently arrived cutter in the knowledge that I would likely meet her on the gangplank. A smile was

on glassware. Behind the chimerical beast were five sealed jars: they contained the major organs of a human being, save the skin. I was sure I knew where the missing item might be found.

Where the light had penetrated the dark and dust-covered room I knew not. All drapes had been drawn against the daylight and there was not so much as a candlestub in any sconce. It occurred to me that there might be some marking on the wax-sealed lids of the jars, and there was sufficent light to descry the hieroglyphs, perhaps those of this phara-onic disembowelling. My fingers traced the letters H and C.

Heathfield Cadwallader.

Chapter Twenty-four

Plainly, Arabella had been quite justified in her fear of meeting her first husband's fate: I had no intention of suffering any such demise. The silent gatekeeper's identity was now self-evident, and I wondered just how long Heathfield Cadwallader had remained mute and rigid in the gatehouse before I had stumbled on his preserved relict. Still, the man had achieved immortality of a sort.

On arrival in the library, I encountered the purported Edgar Allan engaged in mortal combat with a recalcitrant bottle of claret. The man appeared to be assaulting it with a complicated arrangement of levers and a metal spiral. Opalescent beads of sweat adorned his flushed forehead – perhaps from his exertions – although I surmised it might have been a while since his last enlivening refreshment. He acknowledged my entry with a rolling eye and punctuated his explanation with much grunting and several tosses of the head to prevent his forelock obscuring his already limited vision.

'The – ah – four-square – oh – pay – mmm – tent wine-stopper – uh – removal tool!'

This last word emerged four-square between a shout of triumph and the squeal of an inconvenienced pig, as the stopper was revealed to be impaled on the metal spiral but, unfortunately, still firmly inserted in the neck of the bottle. The remainder had smashed at the reporter's feet, one of which was promptly lacerated through the sole as the man attempted to recover his balance.

The man was to be admired for his bravery in embracing the innovatory, but I could not help thinking that this latest device was no advance on the admirable Reverend Henshall's much simpler patent.

To summon aid for the still hopping reporter, I pulled a handle without much hope of it ringing to any effect. It hung limply between two shelves that contained ancient philosophical writings interspersed with books adorned with vaguely familiar glyphs. I removed one at random: the shapes were similar – but not identical – to those on the documents that had magically appeared during my interminable coach journey from London.

A scrap of paper fell from the book: the lettering was in the Roman style: *As above, so below*, it read. I pocketed the book and the paper, thinking to glean a clue as to the meaning of the glyphs.

Mindful of Allan's difficulties with the claret, I seized a decanter of jerez and poured us both a good draught. I savoured my own whilst admiring his ability to remaining upright on one leg while spilling nary a drop.

*

Somewhat alarmingly, the bell's summons was answered by the diminutive academic. It pained me to no small degree that the man thought nothing of loitering in the servants' domain, but any such pain was overwhelmed by astonishment at the fact that he would meet their responsibilities. It should have pleased me inordinately to order the fellow about, but I was less enamoured of the idea since, evidently, the dwarf would willingly perform his duties.

As Mr Dryden said, 'Bold knaves thrive', so I summarily despatched the midget to fetch such swaddling and medicaments as he saw fit. The journalist evinced a pallor rather paler than that to which even he was wont, and as I stepped forward to guide him to a chair he fell in a dead faint, fortuitously enough into one of the more comfortable furnishings in the room. Well upholstered and with a rich, if grubby, brocade covering, it seemed in better condition than many of the other pieces. The gilt on one of the elegantly turned legs was misfortunately tarnishing under the flow of the journalist's own red ink.

Jedermann returned in his customary crustacean manner, scuttling toward Allan with enough bandaging to supply one of Miss Nightingale's hospitals and a variety of vilely coloured liquids in bottles of various shapes. Allan, whose faint had been as transitory as any glory he might have aspired to as a writer, reared up in the chair in fright at the professor approaching him.

'There is nothing about which you must be worrying, Mr Allan; among my studies there is the small matter of a medical degree. I am completely and utterly immersed in the mysteries of the human organism, thanks to several years' study of cadavers under... Well, no matter, what is that surgeon's name to a man bleeding profusely, if not to death?'

Upon this, the little man advanced on Allan with a demeanour that enabled the inflicting of the quite noxious-smelling liquids, one by one, and an amount of cloth wrapping that would evince to the innocent observer a heroic episode of the gout. I addressed the professor with as peremptory a tone as I could muster: 'I am surprised that your religious sensibilities permit such tasks on the Sabbath.'

The smallest of grins widened his puckered little mouth.

'Mr Moffat, as you know, I am not of the Jewish faith, but even if I were, what kind of religion would not per-mit succour to the injured on account of the day of the week?'

I was not ignorant of this aspect of Judaism: Arabella had justified many quite unlikely acts by what one might, or might not, do on Shabbat. Furthermore, she had explained to me the role of the Shobbas Goy, who might perform any prohibited task on the Sabbath on behalf of the frum. On our few intimate occasions she honoured me with this appellation. One could not but admire such practicality.

The reporter was still trembling after the professor's ministrations and I suggested that he might hie himself to a spare chamber that he might recover the better.

The professor kindly offered to see the man to a room; the reporter appeared to me to be quite horrified at the prospect.

I was obliged, by an overwhelming curiosity as to the reason for this, to offer mine own services.

We made slow progress to the vestibule, Allan's arm draped around my shoulder, as his uninjured plantar was seemingly ill-prepared to bear even half of its owner's weight. I allowed myself a smile as we passed through the taxidermic grotesques, imagining the pair of us as a human equivalent of the two-headed equine monster recently despatched by Cullis Major.

The dining room remained in a state reminiscent of the aftermath of a Roman feast, platters and dishes containing remnants of food covering the table's surface. I heard the scratch and click of rodent claws on the parquet and pondered the liberation of a cat or two from the west wing.

Manoeuvring through the clutter of the vestibule was difficult and not accomplished without curses – or the barking of Allan's shins on sundry furnishings. We mounted the stairs and Allan, though it cost him some effort, addressed me for the first time since we had left the library. 'I have dissembled, sir. I have made my own investigations: there is little I do not know – or suspect – about the Cobles.'

Humouring the fellow seemed the best course, therefore my reply was succinct: 'Do tell, Mr Allan.' Although I confess I stifled a yawn.

'Not here, Moffat.'

It was uncertain whether he meant not on the staircase or at Gibbous House; furthermore, I suspected my yawn had not been quite so well suppressed as I had hoped. In any event, he forbore to speak further as we passed through the *trompe l'oeil* and I manhandled him into a chamber whose door, being a heavenly blue, was one of the first few leading off the corridor. The man was deceptively heavy despite his ascetic appearance.

It was a room unvisited by myself in my earlier explorations. More generously appointed than others, I felt I detected the hand of the Bedlamite designer of the house: the room was large, but not so large as to accommodate the violent commingling of styles and designs the furniture brought to it. Messrs Sheraton and Chippendale were both represented, but not by any complete suite of items. The toilette was the one and the chair before it the other.

One particularly large cabinet was as vulgar and vibrant a piece of Chinoiserie as ever I had seen. A Persian kilim served as barrier to such light as the single small window admitted, although the bed was equipped with drapes as would have performed this obstruction more happily. A larger version of the kilim covered the majority of the cracked and splintered floorboards. It looked as though it had been rolled out for display with little care for symmetry or use: in fact a significant proportion lay under the bed, and one corner climbed the large cabinet as if in hope of escape.

Depositing Allan upon the bed with as much ceremony as he deserved, a packet of papers became dislodged from one of my pockets and the reporter caught it deftly. My effort at retrieval achieved nothing as a suddenly sprightly Allan held the packet out of reach. Disdaining to demean myself, I did not demand its return.

He gave them up willingly after a brief application of my knife blade, through the swathe of wrappings, to the sole of his foot.

There was a satisfactory vibrato in the reporter's voice as he interrupted my move to the door.

'M-m-moffat?'

I turned and looked quizzically at the invalid, who let his words tumble forth like water at a mill race. 'Do you read the Arabic script, sir?'

'I do not, as it happens, Edgar.'

'No matter, your documents use the Aramaic. Similar, of course, how could they not be? The one is the precursor of the other; many ancient texts were written in it in the Holy Lands and beyond.'

'But who would write it now, Edgar? And why in a document meant for me?'

His voice became more steady. 'Perhaps it was not meant for you, Mr Moffat.'

I could not but concur.

'I will ask the dwarf; the damn fellow seems to think himself a polymath.'

The newspaperman's reply was to the point. 'In your place, I would not.'

'And for why?'

'The man is not to be trusted, least of all by yourself, I think.'

I advanced toward him with a meaningful look at his swaddled appendage.

'There are rumours, that is all. Unnatural rites, blood-drinking, sacrifice.'

He looked almost affronted when I laughed in his face. 'My dear fellow, such rumours abound . They are merely fear of the Other.'

His crest had not fallen quite so far, even so. 'Well, Mr Moffat, in any event the man is a strange cove and appears to wield quite some influence in the affairs of Gibbous House, and so of course... '

'In mine,' I finished for him.

He gave a slow nod as much as if to agree with some inner voice as with me.

'I knew who you were. News comes in many forms, and not everything appears in typeface. I have made it my business to cultivate the coachmen on the Alnwick stage. So many passengers are indiscreet to some degree, still more so in the inns through which they pass. A man may learn much in low bars and coaching houses for the price of a gin and water.'

'So you are less the reporter and more the spy, Mr Allan?'

He revealed himself a true journalist by refusing to be insulted by the jibe.

About to take my leave, my sleeve was tugged in the manner of a beggar in the street; I shook my arm, angry at this presumption on my person.

Predictably, he cringed, shrinking into the bolster. Nevertheless, he addressed me once more. 'A moment, Moffat, a moment only. What if the script should be but encypherment, a feint?'

I enquired as to what he meant, though I knew well what it was, since the idea had occurred to me scarce a quarter-hour ago.

With the zealous proselytising manner to which we had both been subjected by the policeman, he began to regale me with an account of substitution codes and cypher wheels and I knew not what else. He was anxious that I know that the papers might not feature simple transliteration by transposition of the letters between alphabets, but that any or all of these arcane techniques might well have been employed to confound an accidental reader. He finished by reiterating: 'The essential thing, Moffat, the *sine qua non*, as it were, is of course a sample of the Aramaic alphabet.'

I asked him how he proposed I should acquire such a thing. He gave a sly look and said, 'I am sure you would get no satisfaction from merely asking the professor to write one for us. A man of your talents will find a way, Mr Moffat. No one could evade the police for quite so long without some ability as well as luck.'

This may have been true, but there surely was no manner of means by which the so-called Mr Allan might have known the breadth of talents I did possess, nor how accustomed I was in employing them.

Chapter Twenty-five

I left him abed. He had raised matters that would bear consideration. I resolved to accost Miss Pardoner in her chamber, or wherever she might be, to glean some further intelligence concerning the crab-like curator of the Collection.

Hesitating momentarily before the teal of the door, I reflected again how little such colours – which I had noted she liked to affect in her dress – suited her colouring. I should have preferred to see her in rich burgundies, carmines and the shining black of Norwich bombazine. I gave the signal knock of a seasoned molly-house visitor and received for answer the alarmed cry: 'A moment, if you please!'

A moment it proved to be: Miss Pardoner appeared at the door, her Hispanic colouring made still more attractive by a certain flush. She motioned me in a little breathlessly, a curious conical item of polished hardwood in her hand. She saw me eyeing the curiosity and held it up for display, demonstrating a screwing motion of the base; the upper part of the cone separated and, by a convoluted contraption involving a transverse expanding bar, continued to widen as each half was forced apart from the other.

'It is a glove stretcher, Mr Moffat.'

She gave me a look that dared me to challenge her. I did not. The item was not unfamiliar to me: Arabella had owned one, and it was indeed purposed for stretching the fingers of a lady's glove. However, my late wife had demonstrated other – more imaginative – uses on occasion.

Miss Pardoner sat on her bed and pointed to the chair before her toilette. I nodded my thanks and turned the delicate seat toward her. She had not secured or even closed the chamber door after my entry.

'Miss Pardoner, I come in search of conversation, nothing more. We may adjourn to one of the public rooms if you would prefer, the library perhaps?'

To my surprise she nodded vigorously. I was disappointed that she thought so much of decorum, as I had believed her above such things.

We did not repair to the library, after all. To my utter astonishment, the dining room appeared to have received some attention, although from whom I knew not. Nevertheless, the used crockery and cutlery had all been removed; no empty wine bottles stood sentinel over napery, only randomly scattered crumbs bore witness to the table's former condition. Ellen Pardoner and I sat at the head of the inordinately long refectory table and I began my interrogations.

'The professor seems an interesting fellow to be so far from civilisation, does he not?'

Naturally, the woman chose to reply with a question. 'Do you consider us quite so uncivilised here in Northumbria, Mr Moffat?'

'Even Alnwick is hardly Vienna or Berlin or any other of the groves of Academe friend Jedermann claims to have attended,' I replied, a little sharply.

Miss Pardoner appeared to have recovered some of her poise, for the telltale corner of her mouth had risen once again. 'Oh, I doubt the professor has misled us to any extent in the matter of his scholarship.'

I tried another tack. 'But why here? Why not London, or Edinburgh? What could possibly have brought him here? Was he summoned by Coble?'

She sighed, a tutor before a particularly obtuse student.

'Why would you go to a wild and relatively isolated place, Mr Moffat?'

'I would not,' I said.

'But you have,' she rejoindered.

'I have come for profit, as you well know, though I doubt I shall see any great quantity of it. It is beyond belief that anyone associated with this absurd notion of "Collection" is motivated by any sort of pecuniary gain.'

Miss Pardoner ignored my peevish tone and offered, 'Not all advantage is monetary, sir.'

'Humbug! Miss Pardoner. I will have an answer.'

My palm smarted a little but the sound of its contact with the wood of the table was distinctly gratifying. That Miss Pardoner did not flinch was less so.

'The professor is carrying out important research.'

'Indeed?' It was my opportunity for the sardonic smile. 'Of what kind?'

'Scientific, historical and religious, Mr Moffat.'

Her fervour demonstrated that I had been mistaken in considering her incapable of any utterance devoid of irony. I informed her that whilst I found such pursuits noble in the abstract and the singular, in practice and combination I believed that no good could come of them.

Miss Pardoner looked down at her hands for a moment or two, seemingly intent on finding a smut or fault on her soft skin, 'There are others who believe the contrary, Septimus Coble having been one of them.'

Since I cared not a fig what Coble had believed, I merely asked, 'Jedermann, does he speak many languages so well as English?'

His English was at times – as I had noted previously – so very near perfection as to be that of an educated native son. The odd cadences and Bohemian consonants were barely perceptible. It was evident to me, however, that certain humours caused him to fall more often into pitfalls, grammatical and syntactic. Miss Pardoner informed me that: 'the professor is more than proficient in most modern European Languages, although his native German owes more to Bavaria than Prussia, I would say.'

This I absorbed with some incredulity, believing Miss Pardoner no more able to differentiate between a Münchener burgher and a Prussian Junker than I myself. In any event, I changed the object of my enquiries.

'Scientific research, you say?'

'Oh yes, matters arcane and little known even among—'

She stopped, and of a sudden her hands became once more of particular interest.

'Indeed, outwith the publications of the Royal Society for example?'

For answer I received a nod.

'Come, Ellen! Surely the man is not some... alchemist?'

Her head came up sharply. 'The professor has an interest in such things, yes... But there are other more important areas of scholarship for him.'

'Well?'

'Vitrolium,' she gave out sullenly, as if revealing a secret vice.

'And what might that be?'

Miss Pardoner straightened her posture as if about to give a recital, which perhaps she might have been.

'V.I.T.R.I.O.L.V.M. that is *Visita Interiora Terrae Rectificando Invenies Occultum Lapidem Veram Medicinam*. Visit the interior of the Earth; by rectification thou shalt find the hidden stone.'

I laughed.

She shook her head.

'Jedermann believes he has found an original manuscript which explains the manifestos.'

'Manifestos?' Such lofty subjects truly did not interest me.

Again her gaze fell to the hands in her lap; she spoke with her head down in answer to the question I had not posed. 'The Rosicrucian Manifestos.'

'So?'

'The document he has found was written by John Dee. The greatest mind of the Elizabethan Age.'

I disdained to inform her that the mystical nonsense that I had heard at second hand whilst in the Edinburgh Asylum had led me to a quite different estimation of the man.

'What has this to do with me?'

'Do you not feel yourself meant for great things?'

It seemed that Jedermann possessed sufficient charisma to render Miss Pardoner partial to – if not involved in – his bizarre researches. Or perhaps the reasons for Miss Pardoner's partiality had more to do with her affection for Maccabi. It mattered not a whit to me. I resolved to do all in my power to break the conditions of the discretionary trust and wrest the control of my inheritance from the hands of this lunatic and his acolytes.

We sat in silence for a while. Through the windows the reddening sky alerted me to the fact that the Jewish Sabbath would soon be over. No doubt still more food would be served as it had been on those occasions when Arabella had honoured the traditions in my company.

The long dining room was appointed with a generous fireplace, an inglenook that would have accommodated my entire household and an inferno fit for Beezlebub himself. There was not a stick of wood, or smut of ash, in the voluminous grate. It had not been cold in the room during the Sabbath repast, which by custom had begun after sundown, and it was not uncomfortable now.

Leaning to the side, toward Miss Pardoner's seat, I laid my palm on the parquet floor. The wood was warm. It was not likely that Gibbous House was possessed of a hypocaust, although I supposed anything was possible. Miss Pardoner – after an uncharacteristic flinch at my proximity to her person – spoke. 'It is steam, sir, driven through pipes under the floor. The professor tells me it is modelled on an innova- tory system of the last century designed by Mårten Triewald. For a large greenhouse in Newcastle, in fact.'

'And the engine?' I queried.

'Below, sir, the fire is below.'

'I wonder that I have been excluded from that part of the house, Miss Pardoner.'

'As have I, sir. Perhaps it was assumed you would have no interest in it.'

She said this innocently enough. Since it might well have been true, I chose to let it pass.

'In any event, whilst there is no lack of available wood for the fire, where are the strong of arm to feed the beast? Surely this is not in Cullis's remit as well?'

For answer I received a shrug.

Miss Pardoner's manner toward me had changed some- what; I was most disappointed in this development – this demure and respectful aspect was not stimulating in the least. Provocation seemed best suited to my purpose.

'Are you much in the company of Maccabi, Miss Pardoner?'

'I am more in his company than in yours.'

'Of late that is not so, surely?'

'I should be more plain, Mr Moffat. I find your company diminishes me.'

I laughed. 'I think even the company of Satan himself would do little to diminish you, Ellen.'

Her visage assumed a more familiar aspect.

'That remains to be seen.'

'Well, forgive me if I have put you out of countenance. I meant no harm. Shall we not share a friendly libation?'

Her answer remained unheard as a drawn-out grinding sound filled the dining room. One would have thought it the progress of a capstone up the side of a pyramid, so loud was it. The noise appeared to emanate from the enormous fireplace. The soot-free stone of the rear of the inglenook drew back to reveal the professor. 'A libation? A capital idea! Most capital!'

He beamed at the both of us from the depths of the empty hearth.

Chapter Twenty-six

With an élan quite disproportionate to someone recently emerged from behind a fireplace, the professor's tiny feet skittered across the parquet to a magnificent, if dilapidated, sideboard. The rich walnut's topmost surface was a repository for tantali and decanters of every shape and size; a few dusty bottles stood guard amongst the undoubtedly valuable crystal. The professor surveyed the glassware with a gimlet eye then picked up the dustiest of bottles before announcing: 'My friends, let us partake of the Elixir Ordinaire! No pale imitation from La Maison Pernod Fils for we three, let us sample Doctor Pierre's original and best receipt and banish the woodworm from the soul by a generous application of the spirit of the wormwood.'

The professor removed from a waistcoat pocket a silvered object remarkably like a spoon, of a size with one suitable for the consumption of a pudding save for the fact that there were several voids of rectangular shape in the metal of the bowl. From a long pocket of his frock coat he removed a paper bag and placed it on the sideboard.

Opening a door below, which gave an agreeably musical creak, he removed three small stemless glasses. Glasses marshalled on the sideboard, he placed a white cube beside each of the vessels.

He eyed both of us.

'Sugar cubes: a splendid innovation, are they not?'

He placed the not-quite-spoon over each glass in turn and poured a generous measure of a particularly foul-looking liquid over a cube and thence through the voids in the spoon's bowl. Handing each of us a glass, he said, 'Absinthe! Aged and amber, the green spirit has departed but its strength remains.'

It was quite the vilest thing I had ever tasted; Miss Pardoner's aplomb while drinking it put me quite to shame, while the professor seemed to favour the Slavic method of disposing of the disagreeable taste of a spirit by throwing the entire contents of his glass at once – with venom – toward the back of his throat. He smacked his lips and said, 'Another?'

I declined politely and was rewarded with a sneer from both companions.

At precisely that moment the door opened wide and Maccabi entered, followed by a comical entourage consisting of Mrs Gonderthwaite – bearing nothing – and two simple-looking fellows carrying vast covered platters of silver. These fellows had thus far not been in evidence at any time. Maccabi caught my eye and shook his head. Quite what he meant by that, I knew not.

The two salver-bearers were as like as twins, and, furthermore, were sufficiently low of forehead to allow a criminal bent to their nature, according to the journalist's theories. Certainly this facet of their appearance did little to commend a level of intelligence above that of a simian, any more than the clatter of the salver lids that both let fall to the floor in the act of presenting the evening's repast. A large roast of beef filled the one to overflowing, a medley of vegetables and a prodigious quantity of potatoes covered the other.

At this point we none of us were seated. I took my place at the head and gestured the hesitant Maccabi to be seated. Mrs Gonderthwaite's back was already receding; the brothers primate, however, stood slack-jawed in mirrored pose on either long side of the table.

'Out!' I bellowed, and thereby ascertained that their capacity for communication reached the basest human level. Leave they did, turning cartwheels as they did so.

The professor proffered a prayer in a language unknown to me. As he finished, I remarked that the fare seemed quite civilised. His voice was oleaginous.

'You yourself decreed that this household should not run in accordance with ritual; I trust that you forgive me the prayer of thanks I offered for our victuals, even so?'

For reply I gave him a grunt. Three of those seated looked expectantly from the heaped platters of food to the remaining person. Maccabi rose stiffly and began apportioning the food. He served it mechanically and without flourish, his movements driven by ratchets and gears, but smoothly nonetheless.

As he filled Miss Pardoner's plate he reached a zenith of

graceful mechanisms, worthy of Merlin's Swan, and I admired the control the man seemed to have over his emotions. Miss Pardoner began exercising her silverware with gusto ere Maccabi had reached his seat, but perhaps he did not notice, as his eye continued to be drawn by any other thing – sentient or otherwise – that it could find. He did not eat much of the first course and nothing at all of the second, as it turned out.

The professor made several miserably unsuccessful gambits in the game of conversation but could find no partner or opponent around the table. The chink and chime of porcelain and cutlery were all the noise to be heard in the cavernous room and the rhythm of dinner aided me not as I pondered how to extract a fair copy of an ancient alphabet from the diminutive scholar. Un-summoned by any bell, the phantasmal Mrs Gonderthwaite appeared, flanked by her para-human acolytes, who bore further covered chargers. These serving dishes were laid down as gently as could be expected by such unskilled hands. Mrs Gonderthwaite threw out a skeletal, if imperious, finger toward the long sideboard and the two servants scurried gibbon-like to perform a pantomime involving the opening of several drawers and doors before the recovery of four dessert plates. The lady herself removed our dinner plates to a dumb waiter that I could not remember being wheeled into the room.

Oyster plates were placed upon larger plates revealed by the removal of the main course. This corruption of the lately fashionable service à la Russe appeared to amuse the professor greatly, as he took delight in raising his oyster-fork and spoon from their correct position to the extreme right of his plate and winking prodigiously at me.

We were not served oysters. To my surprise, all manner of other shellfish was revealed by the hairy paws of the silent servants, but no oysters. There were abalone, clams, mussels, winkles, cockles and scallops, all served on the shell. Maccabi's platter apart, the mute fellows spooned generous portions onto the plates and their environs, allowing very little food to sully the linen or our clothing, and then withdrew.

Mrs Gonderthwaite announced in a surprisingly masculine and sturdy voice for one so unsubstantial, 'Only two courses.'

She turned smart as a hussar to leave, but I stopped her, saying, 'I hope our guest is provided for?'

She did not deign to turn back, but gave a graceful nod over her shoulder before vanishing through the double doors.

The crustaceans were cleared from our oyster plates with a minimum of fuss. The professor in particular went at his portion with a will that I found a little queasy, given his own crab-like attributes; I was only grateful that lobster, crayfish and the like had made no appearance at the table.

Frustration, not surprise, was my lot on realising that our household staff would make no reappearance that evening: the prospect of despatching Maccabi to the kitchen with the crockery was once again tempting, but I scented better sport in having him in the room.

The duration of the meal seemed an inordinate time to be without something to slake the thirst, and I was surprised that no wine had been forthcoming from the cellar or the sideboard. I was about to offer some liquid refreshment to the assembly when the professor once again sprang to his feet and tap-tapped to the long sideboard. He picked up a heavy crystal decanter; thumb and forefinger pincered around the neck, he eyed the contents as he held it up to the light.

'Red. Bordeaux, who knows how it will taste?' he said, as he found glassware and proceeded to fill it. He did not do so in the manner of a refined oenophile, rather poured great gouts into the bowls as though the decanter were a pitcher and the crystal goblets the meanest pewter tankards. He drained his own glass and refilled it before approaching the table with our own.

'It is poor stuff,' he said.

He seemed awfully partial to such a poor exemplar of vintners' wares, taking another great draught from his glass on taking his seat once more. Looking round at our dining companions, I noted that they were rapt in contemplation of the tiny figure. Perhaps he was the possessor of Mesmer's animal magnetism; if so, I found myself completely immune to it.

He sported a shirt of once-fine linen, whose collar was over-large to the extent that no amount of starch could possibly have held it upright. Naturally, the shirt itself was too voluminous for his diminutive frame. The procurement of a tailor's services was not among the dispensations he made from the income he doubtless received from my estate. The trews, jacket and waistcoat had seen the benefit of needlework subsequent to that of their manufacture, but this seemed inexpert enough to have been his own handiwork. His garb was indefinably grimy in some way, yet there were no stains of the scholar's blotted ink, the gourmand's spilled morsels or the sweat of honest labour. Still, there was something odd about it, as if below the ring of his collar lurked a dully squamous patina over his flesh.

He seemed provoked to a certain nervosity, by what I did not know. He fidgeted and wriggled like a child with a secret and I asked him, quite bluntly, what lay behind the fireplace.

Chapter Twenty-seven

'There will be time for such later, Mr Moffat,' he said, and I fancied I caught a glimpse of scaly skin as he slipped a finger into the collar of his not-quite-white shirt.

Miss Pardoner clapped her hands and cried, 'A game! A game!'

Maccabi stared stolidly to his front. Jedermann bared his teeth in a gruesome smile and I noted he was in possession of a solitary canine, though it was of tolerable length, and it leant him the air of an aged wolf. He countered the proposal. 'But what to play, Ellen? What to play?'

'The cards, perhaps?' she simpered, and I confess I felt an urge to beat the woman to her former boldness or let her die in the attempt.

'I had rather die than play another hand of Whist,' I said.

Maccabi looked directly at me. 'I had rather thought so, since your strength might more likely lie in speculation.'

'Ach, I am not for the cards,' said the professor, although whether excited or under some stress, I was not sure. 'A parlour game, that is it!'

'With respect, Professor, are we not a little above the Minister's Cat?'

The prospect of such entertainments filled me with horror.

'What then?' asked Miss Pardoner, and her expression reminded me that she claimed to be not yet one and twenty.

'Oh, I don't doubt that the professor might have some idea. Edify us, Jedermann, do,' I urged.

The professor's reaction was to begin bringing forth from the surprisingly numerous pockets about his person crumpled scraps of paper in various shapes and conditions. Having assembled a pyramid-like mound, he began to smooth out each and every one, apparently in order to peruse what might be written on them.

The greater majority of pieces were immediately restored by means of re-crumpling to their former quasi-spherical states and re-sequestering in one or other of his pockets. For the rest there remained three sheets of a similar size: viz about that of a sheet from a reporter's notebook. They appeared for the moment to be blank, as far as I could ascertain.

The dwarf then began tearing small rectangular pieces from each of the three sheets, of a size that might contain one written word. He then wrote something on each scrap and turned them face down to the table. The fidgeting had stopped, though his eyes glittered, and he swept them over the company before letting out in a rush, 'So! A game, a diversion, a pasatiempo, a bagatelle!'

He paused and, still aglitter, his gaze passed over us again, before he added, 'But edifying! Ameliorative! Improving!

How very worthy! Moffat, you are truly a remarkable fellow.'

The professor began an elucidatory ramble on the conduct of his diversion. Each word that he had written on the paper scraps came from a different language. He emphasised that the language might not be rendered in Latin script. Proposing to give each of us one in turn, he enjoined us to keep it concealed from the others. We were to hearken to his expert pronunciation of the word in isolation, then to his use of it in some witty aphorism or proverb, and finally we were to decide whether or not we held the mysterious word in our hand.

It sounded uncommon dull for an entertainment, even by the abject standards of a parlour game. Nonetheless, there were only smiles in view from my companions. The professor slid a scrap in our respective directions, and we were obliged to rise and recover them to our seats. Jedermann then gave out what I presumed was a word in stentorian tones, although he was unable to prevent it sounding ridiculous:

'Pea-yat!'

I was none the wiser on looking at the paper carefully concealed in my palm.

The dwarf's voice filled the cavernous dining room once more with a longer chain of folderol which sounded something akin to: 'Loo tche eemyet pee-yat vragov tchem sto drooz-yei lozh-nykh.'

There was no mark on my paper indicative of Chinee, and so I remained convinced that the word was not mine. But this part of the game gave me great hope: the quotation of the word in context could not possibly provide any help to a player of it. Therefore, what purpose did it serve other than to gratify an overweening vanity on the part of the professor concerning his skill as a linguist? I was in great hope of turning this self-regard to advantage.

Still less to the purpose was the professor's no doubt erudite translation of this – so he claimed – ancient Slavic proverb as: 'Better to have five enemies than one hundred false friends.'

Both Maccabi and Miss Pardoner's smiles had grown wider, indeed I believed that my ward's shoulders were shaking slightly and she appeared to be at pains to maintain her self-control. On collecting herself a little, she announced: 'The word is not mine.' And with an unladylike snicker she revealed her paper. 'Five' was written in a skilled and legible hand.

Maccabi's smile became a smirk and I hated him for it.

'Nor mine,' he said and he revealed a word that I recognised, as Arabella had once written it out for me:

ഡ൮ന

It meant five.

The colour rose to my cheeks as all three laughed when I turned over my paper to reveal

ПЯТЬ

I marvelled that there were only three others around the table and not five, which would have rendered the supposed proverb more apposite. The professor, noting that I was not pleased at being made the butt of their joke, attempted to cajole me to better humour.

'Come, Mr Moffat, surely you agree our little charade was amusing. I had thought you would guess that the game was pure invention. In any case, I doubt you will ever forget the Russian word for five, to be sure.'

Maccabi looked smug, Miss Pardoner more so. I did not respond directly, but asked instead with how many languages he was familiar.

'Familiar? What does that mean? That I might recognise but not understand? That I might write but not speak, in the manner of Latin, Ancient Greek or Sumerian? Or that I might speak and not write, like Chinee or Hindoo?'

It was typical of him to answer a question with another of his own. He was not finished, however; like many learned men he was inordinately fond of the sound of his own voice.

'I confess to you all, by whichever criterion you choose to define "familiar", I do not, in truth, know. I do know the Hebrew, Aramaic, Greek, Latin and, as you saw, the Cyrillic alphabets, as well as many of the languages written in Latin or Cyrillic. Why do you ask, Moffat?'

Here stood the chained and padlocked gate in my path: why indeed? The man had offered me an opportunity, by himself bringing up the matter of alphabets. I resolved to feign an interest in the cursed Collection, and in particular that part of it which took volume and parchment form.

'I believe I should like, as the putative owner of such a fine repository of books as is contained in the Collection, to be the better equipped to peruse them. Oh, I do not expect to learn the cuneiform of the Sumerians, since no one has any clue what their tablets mean. No, indeed, I should merely like to know the origin of a work by sight of the script alone, and to be able to differentiate the Aramaic from the Hebrew, perhaps.'

Miss Pardoner gave a snort, while Maccabi leaped up to offer his 'kerchief that she might wipe the Bordeaux from her upper lip and chin.

The professor appeared not to notice and began, not altogether unexpectedly, to pontificate at length on the similarities and differentiating characteristics of the Hebrew and Aramaic scripts. Thankfully, and I did feel most grateful to the fellow, Maccabi kept our glasses charged through an infinitesimally detailed account of cursive strokes, descenders, ascenders and the development of the delineations of the latter from the former. In demonstrating their similarity he used a paper of the three scarcely used by the game and drew what he informed us were the Aramaic 'Qop' alongside the Hebrew 'Kuf'.

The one appeared as no different from the other save the Aramaic letter had the look of a child's letter p, and the Hebrew an angular look more suggestive of its name. Taking advantage of a pause occasioned by the dwarf's imbibing of another prodigious swallow of wine, I said, 'Most fascinating, Enoch. Would you fashion for me a fair copy of the two alphabets that I might compare them at my leisure?'

Miss Pardoner appeared to have less trouble with her wine on that occasion; she may have had a mote in her eye, though I imagine she winked at Maccabi.

The professor dipped his pen and carved the twenty-eight Arabic letters from right to left on the thick vellum sheet he had chosen, blew on them in the absence of any sand and laid down the Aramaic letters beneath them.

I thanked him and folded the stiff paper into a pocket.

We were all startled when the doors to the dining room were thrown wide, and no less surprised when the detective stepped into the room. Assuming Mrs Gonderthwaite had answered some summons to the front entrance, I felt the tickle of anger that she should presume to usher the fellow to our table and not announce his arrival, much less inform us that he waited without. He was still in his uniform, but made the politeness of removing the top hat, which he carried uncomfortably under his arm. He eyed each of us in turn.

'There is no doubt of it,' he said.

'Inasmuch as I, myself, am in doubt as to what you refer to, Constable, I should say there is considerable doubt of something,' I replied.

'It is murder, of course,' Constable Turner elucidated.

I was considering a response, when Maccabi blurted out, 'Oh come, Constable, the man fell down the hill and took a blow from a rock. Very likely he was drunk. He often was.'

The policeman gave Maccabi a look with which he seemed to take his measure and find him wanting in some degree.

'A blow from a rock was surely taken by the poor sot, it's true. It is only that I should like to know by whom the blow was given.'

It was with some disbelief that I saw the colour rise in Maccabi's face. What was the matter with the man? Did I but have such fellows about me in Cheapside, never would I have given the Peelers a second thought!

Constable Turner, in an apparent leap to unrelated matters, enquired, 'The scribbler, Allan, where is he?'

The professor informed him that the reporter had met with an 'unfortunable accident', the misstep in his speech betraying – to me at least – his own nervousness in the presence of the law. Ellen Pardoner was darting looks from Maccabi to the professor and thence to the investigator. It appeared to me that the most cool of manner in the room were the man investigating the crime and the man who had committed it.

Turner gave a nod and drew a deep breath through his nose. It was a magnificent specimen, worthy of a prizefighter at a fair, although perhaps not a good one. He released the breath, and it seemed that he had used this aspiration to calm himself or gird his loins for some prospective challenge. He said nothing.

Against my better judgement, I posed a question of my own: 'What brings you to the conclusion that the man was dealt a blow rather than the victim of an unfortunate accident, Constable?'

'It is quite simple, Mr Moffat, the rock covered with blood is on the crown of the hill, whilst the unfortunate's body was, as you saw, in the pond. It is most unlikely that he could have fallen against that rock with such force at the top of the rise.'

He was right of course; I had been careless, but, truly, who could have expected any policeman to take an interest in an accident at Gibbous House?

Chapter Twenty-eight

Turner looked expectantly at me. Being at a loss as to what expectation lay behind this regard, I offered to summon Mrs Gonderthwaite. 'I presume you have not dined, Constable? You are come too late to share our meal, but if you require some sustenance I will ring for the cook.'

He replied curtly, 'Bread and cheese, sir.'

I made my way to a fabric bell pull beside the large hearth, only to be intercepted by the professor carrying the hand bell from the dining table.

'This one, Moffat, the other is not functioning.'

The professor's eyes darted to my hand hovering beside the brocaded fabric of the bell pull, and he ran a familiar finger around his oversized collar. I took the hand bell from him and shook it violently. It made its customary unmusical sound. I bade the constable take his ease at table.

In deference to my position, Maccabi restrained himself, and offered no contribution at this point. He appeared uncomfortable, however, and once more was to be observed from the corner of the eye, continuously squirming under the obsidian gaze of the policeman. Even the professor seemed inclined to keep his counsel, apparently relieved at ensuring my use of the correct bell.

Miss Pardoner did not remain silent. She turned in her chair to examine the constable the better, pushing aside the remains of her repast to lean both elbows on the wood in a most forward manner. Her eyelids made rapid and contrived motion and she breathed a question in one word: 'Murder?'

If the investigator's visage showed any reaction to Miss Pardoner, it was only that of Theseus regarding Medusa's head dangling from his grip. I gave my ward a stern look. 'That is quite enough, Miss Pardoner. This is a serious matter. Frivolity will not aid us in the capture of the villain.'

'Murder is serious, Mr Moffat,' Turner agreed, nodding sagely at Miss Pardoner, but he said no more, seemingly content to await his loaf and cheddar.

Once more I was struck by the remarkable passivity required in this new science of detection. By the same token, I was beginning to feel as uncomfortable around the policeman as Maccabi. Still, I resolved to engage with Turner.

'So, Constable Turner, an itinerant rogue, a vagabond footpad. Do you think such a thing likely?'

He gave me the benefit of his most stony regard and said, 'I surely would, but for the lack of motive, Mr Moffat.'

'Robbery, perhaps?'

He shook his head, slowly. 'Hardly that. The corpse had a golden guinea in his waistcoat pocket.'

Maccabi's eyes started from his head, my ward gave a

gasp; my face remained composed, but I was filled with rage that I had not searched the body, since the man appeared to have been in possession of more pecuniary assets than myself at the time.

Once more the policeman fell silent. I found it difficult not to offer to ensure the guinea found its way to the surviving brother, surmising that the policeman would rather see to this himself. Maccabi, still uncomfortable in the presence of the law, stammered, 'B-but do you have your suspicions? Surely we are not suspected?'

Not we, but certainly Maccabi.

At that point Mrs Gonderthwaite appeared. The two heteroclite specimens moved in harmony behind her, although to what purpose I could not tell. There was something vaguely familiar about their simian features, as though had they been drawn by a more expert hand they would have resembled a human of my acquaintance.

I addressed the cook. 'Constable Turner will have a fresh loaf and some cheddar.'

No sooner had I said it than I wished for something more outlandish, since, on previous evidence, almost anything could be produced from the bare pantry as if from a magician's sleeve.

The woman and her hominid acolytes departed to conjure the victuals from the thin air of the kitchen. I enjoined the professor to provide the company with a libation of his choosing, the greensome foulness excepted. He skipped lightly to the task, and with an eye for Maccabi's reaction I enquired of Turner, 'Shall we each of us then expect an inquisition? I wonder which of us is in a position to claim alibi? Certainly I have enjoyed a modicum of my own company of late, with none to vouch for me. I expect others are more fortunate.'

He composed his features quickly, but not before two lines in his brow briefly indicated an interior reflection. Strangely, he replied: 'Oh, I am not concerned about such things. After all, how can we know when the fellow met his fate? A diary of movements would not help my investigation. Besides, my opinion is that what has occurred is that rare thing: a motive-less crime.'

'Motiveless? What do you mean?'

'Motive is one to the three pillars of crime detection. Except in extremely unusual circumstances, for every murderer there must be the motive for, the means by which, and the opportunity to commit any crime.'

'Speak English, man!'

'The why, the how and the combination of time and favourable circumstance. But as I say, I consider this an exceptional case.'

It now fell to me to feel less than comfortable; perhaps there was more to the marvel of detection than I had heretofore thought. It mattered not, for at that moment the constable's sustenance arrived in a most peculiar manner. The doors swung wide, but there was no sign of the cook. Instead, the pair of near-primates came in at quite a lick, the one holding a large round loaf upon his head and the other rolling a gigantic cheese before him in the manner of a child with a hoop and a stick. They stopped short at the table, near the policeman's seat, composed themselves in crude imitation of the most obsequious of footmen and laid the comestibles before our guest. They gave him an animalistic showing of teeth, which may have been a smile, and withdrew. The policeman gave a tiny smile of his own and said, 'I wonder which of the brothers is the father? There is but little of Mrs Gonderthwaite in them, save perhaps about the eyes. Well, they are short an uncle or a father, in any event.'

The professor gave a shrug, Maccabi gave one of his own, although with some stiffness about it. On Miss Pardoner's face I espied a not unexpected smirk, as she informed Turner and myself, 'At the risk of indelicacy, I am given to understand that – as to the paternity of the two – Mrs Gonderthwaite is undecided, much as she has long been undecided in the matter of the relative charms of the two possible candidates.'

What exercised my mind was my inability to imagine what the two imbeciles would do with a guinea.

The professor placed a glass of leaded crystal before me, a beautiful thing. Brilliants glittered as the candlelight caught the geometric cuts in the glass.

'Beautiful, isn't it?' he said.

I raised the stemware to eye level. 'Indeed the vessel is a thing of rare beauty. What, pray, is the unattractive liquid it contains?'

'It is a digestif, Mr Moffat. The Germans are exceptionally

blessed with a number of truly magnificent bitters, but this, good sir, is a giant among them: Kujawische Magen-Essenz.'

The liquid had the colour of the water in a well-used horse trough. Its name seemed a grandiose appellation for something quite so unappetising. Nevertheless, I sipped a little of it. It was less emetic than the absinthe, but not by a very great amount. The professor returned to his seat.

Meanwhile, the policeman was making little impression on his loaf, and still less on the enormous cheddar. Miss Pardoner had begun fidgeting, while Maccabi seemed calmer. Perhaps he had been in need of the bitters.

'Are you in need of some diversion, Miss Pardoner? Or do you wish to excuse yourself our dull male company?'

She coloured a little. 'Dull indeed, sir. Might we not elevate ourselves with a little conversation?' she enquired.

'Elevate?' I gave Maccabi a look of enquiry.

'I am sure Miss Pardoner does not think you in need of elevation, Maccabi.'

He seemed to stifle a reply.

'Well, Ellen, it seems you must make do with such conversation as the rest of us might provide, although I doubt anything I might say would prove of an elevatory nature,' I said.

At this point, the constable, having given up the unequal struggle with the cheese, asked the company, 'The reporter? Allan? 'I wonder, has he mentioned a certain name?'.

'We have passed some hours in conversation, it would be

strange indeed if none were mentioned.' I yawned, although it was yet early.

For once the policeman's detachment wavered.

'D____, sir. One name in particular, I mean to say a name of antiquity that is... '

But I knew before he uttered the name, 'Cadwallader.'

To no great surprise, Maccabi gave a start, which the policeman appeared not to remark.

Miss Pardoner asked innocently, 'The last Welsh King of Britain?'

It took some effort not to laugh, as puzzlement seeped over the policeman's features. He seemed unsure whether he was being played for a gull.

'No, miss. Heathfield Cadwallader.'

Both the professor and Maccabi gave a firm 'No!'

'He mentioned him to me, in passing,' I said.

I might have died from the look Maccabi gave me, were such things possible. From the professor's look I would have been a very long time doing so.

The constable, his face offering a negative opinion on the bitters, addressed me thus: 'In passing? I have found him monomaniacal on the subject.'

The professor scrambled from his chair and seized the nearmost bottle from the long sideboard. 'Shall we be having another?'

I waved the academic away and asked, 'How so, Constable?'

He lifted his crystal but decided against a further sip and

replaced the glass somewhat delicately over the ring it had left on the wood.

'Mr Allan made my acquaintance shortly after beginning his employment at the *Mercury*. From that time scarcely a day has gone by when he has not importuned after the fate of one Heathfield Cadwallader. A party, I should add, of whom I have never heard, much less encountered, in any capacity.'

Miss Pardoner, in a more serious tone than earlier, asked, 'But why?'

Maccabi let out a sigh and the policeman considered him momentarily before answering the young woman. 'If I might be so bold as to suggest, subject of course to Mr Allan's disposition, that he be brought below, I think it might interest you all to hear his obsessions first hand.'

'A capital idea!' I said, although, judging by the expressions of Maccabi and the dwarf, others did not share my enthusiasm. I instructed Maccabi to see to the transposition of Allan from his sickbed to our presence, and he made off to do so with more alacrity than good grace.

The doors closed behind him. The professor, his grasp of grammar recovered along with his equanimity, asked: 'Forgive me, Sergeant, but what of your investigation? Poor Cullis?'

'Constable, Professor, Constable.' He was quick to assert his true status, but a thin smile showed he was not above the implied flattery. 'It proceeds, sir, it proceeds.'

I caught Miss Pardoner's eye and became convinced she shared my own opinion that the great detective was no more nor less than a humbug.

Chapter Twenty-nine

I confess that I myself started as the doors opened again with a clatter. It seemed that Maccabi had arranged Allan's arrival with more care for its despatch than its safety. Mrs Gonderthwaite's offspring entered bearing the reporter in the manner of a litter, one brother's hairy paws were clamped around poor Allan's shins whilst the other had a firm grip on his upper arms.

He made a sorry litter, however, for he sagged quite dramatically at the middle. The brothers, without malevolence but with little care, deposited him in a chair at the policeman's right hand. Allan looked a little pale, but he must have been in better health than he appeared for he drained Turner's glass of its bitters and his grimacing worsened hardly at all.

Constable Turner allowed Edgar Allan a few moments to compose himself before abruptly bidding him 'Begin!'

Evidently, Maccabi had apprised him of the reason for his summoning for he began in a wavering voice, 'What is fear, I ask you? To phrase it mathematically' – here a nod to the professor – 'fear is the product of mystery multiplied by imagination. Which factors I must explain. I do not mean the hermeneutic mysteries of the Kabbala or of the Brotherhood of the Rosy Cross. Rather the unexplained and unexplainable in the world of the mundane. Equally, I do not mean the contrived imaginations of the novelist or playwright. No, I refer to the visceral imagination of those alone and abroad in the night.'

He hesitated at this point, perhaps concerned at the professor's bristling at the mention of the Kabbalists and Rosicrucians, which I remembered meant Order of the Rosy Cross – while the former, as I understood it, was a system of belief practised by Knights Templar, Masonic Lodges and all manner of secret societies.

'Put forward the case, a hypothetical one to be sure, of a man found delirious in a street in, shall we say, Baltimore. The man raves, crying out the name "Reynolds" from time to time. He is soon taken up. His last words might be "Lord, help my poor soul", since many call on Him for the first time at the last. The man is buried in the clothes in which he was found. They are not his own, they say, and the name on the tailor's labels does not match the one upon his headstone. So who has died? One man or two? Or is this the only Resurrection?'

His voice had grown stronger through this short oration and the white flecks on his lips resisted the sharp lick of his tongue. But he was barely begun and continued thus: 'Or shall we put another case, more empirical in essence – although perhaps lacking a body of proof? Can a man in this modern age just disappear? It would seem he can: the mere assumption of a name can change a man so completely as to place him beyond the grasp of determined pursuers. Even so, if a man plunges into baptismal waters, as it were, does he not reappear somewhere, reborn? Can he not be found if an image of the disappeared is at hand?'

At this point, Allan produced from his coat two daguerreotype portraits about the size of a small volume. One depicted himself a little younger, less careworn. He held up the other to the company for their perusal.

'*This is Heathfield Cadwallader.*'

I recognised him, certainly. So, I was sure, did the others, since he yet remained in residence in the gatehouse.

'A handsome fellow, is he not? His looks would preserve well in age, I think,' I said.

'He was a cousin, distant I admit. Impecunious too, and not above a supplicant letter, even to a relative as distant in miles as in blood. He was persistent. Many letters I threw away unread over the years, but one last missive I did open, I cannot tell you why. It was written in Newcastle and despatched on a ship across the Atlantic: a letter of quite different character. No tales of hardship, no pecuniary requests, simply a few veiled hints as to an improvement in expectations. He mentioned a large house in the north and a notary in Seahouses, but he was not more specific. My own letter of encouragement went unanswered.'

He picked up his glass, by now quite drained of bitters; the professor nimbly arose and filled it with more of the same.

Allan sipped absently and cleared his throat before continuing. 'Some years later, it – ah – behove me to depart the Americas. Being experienced in the Fourth Estate, I thought to try my hand in Northumberland. I took a position at first with *The Journal* in Newcastle, with a view to finding my relative and seeing if his expectations had been met. At first, I enjoyed uncommon luck. The Office of the Turnpike Authority had had occasion to deal with a Mr Heathfield Cadwallader. It seems my relative had been in the habit of travelling between York and Newcastle on the stage, whilst taking the opportunity of relieving the more gullible passengers of their valuables at cards. He was little suspected at first, being in the respectable company of a wife. He was warned off the coaches in Newcastle at a date shortly before that of his letter.'

Cadwallader appeared to have been a resourceful enough fellow, I was intrigued that he had met so grisly an end.

Somewhat abruptly to my mind, Miss Pardoner took her leave of the company. Maccabi, the reporter and myself stood, as ceremony dictates. A nimble dismount from his seating arrangement proved too much for the professor on this occasion, and it seemed the policeman also cared not for such niceties. Allan seemed disinclined to continue, staring at the table surface as if some clue could be discerned in the grain of the wood.

It was Maccabi who roused him from his contemplations.

'And you were not so successful, thenceforth?'

Allan gave a start, as though he had been in Baltimore or Brooklyn rather than across the table.

'Ah no. I spent several months in Newcastle. I heard nothing, not in the public saloon bar nor the finest restaurants. Despondency filled me, I confess.

'Early one morning at the turn of the year, I sat, wrapped in my topcoat, at a wharf on the quayside. I confess the previous evening had ended in ignominy, when the landlord of a nearby public house had evicted me with some force. The sandstone wall beside the wharf had served me quite well as a cot. Of a sudden, a large, black bird alighted beside me. I am obliged to tell you that I am possessed of an unreasonable fear of all birds, particularly those of the genus corvus.

'Quickly, though yet unsteady on my feet, I ran up the nearby stairs. Carved from the ubiquitous sandstone, these vertiginous flights join the riverside areas with the centre of the town. The Morrigan pursued me with much flapping and cawing. Despite my fear, I looked back over my shoulder at the bird, missing my step on occasion. I know now as I knew then that such behaviour on those stone stairs was foolhardy. Still, what a man fears will fascinate him also, don't you think?'

He paused, wiping a sleeve across his mouth, lately flecked with white.

'I breasted the top of the stairway, ran pell-mell down a chare, narrow and dank and slippery underfoot from uncollected pure. The bird followed, cawing close to my ear. I stumbled, threw my arms up to protect my head and recognised the bird as *Corvus corax sinuatus*: a traveller as far from home as myself. Any here who know the true nature of fear will not be surprised that I fell into a dead faint.'

Edgar Allan darted a look at the policeman, at which the latter raised his eyebrows and gave a diffident shrug of his shoulders. The reporter began to speak once more.

'Ah... I was shaken awake some time later. One would suppose that I had been lucky not to suffer some assault or larceny on my person. On checking my pockets I found them no more empty than before, so perhaps luck played little part in it after all. The waking hand belonged to – ahem – a member of the Northumbrian constabulary.'

Again he looked at the policeman's most inexpressive face. Truly, the man was an incompetent liar; one wondered how he had made any kind of fist of the writing trade, much less journalism.

'The incident with the bird had shaken me to the core, and I prevailed upon the constable to join me in a drink for restorative purposes. We emerged from the dingy alley and repaired to the Scotswood, a ramshackle but welcoming establishment. We took a porter for the body of it, as proof against the cold. The man remarked upon my accent, claimed he found it strange, and the conversation became an interview. He asked me why I was so far from home. I explained I was looking for a distant relative, that I had traced him to Newcastle and that the trail had vanished, as though the man had been plucked from existence by the hand of an unseen deity.'

Once more, he stopped short. He fiddled with his collar

and the bottom of his waistcoat, seeming remarkably uncomfortable in his clothes. Suddenly he threw out a forefinger toward Constable Turner.

'You! Turner, put aside this nonsense! Tell your part of the story.'

Chapter Thirty

Turner seemed unperturbed by the outburst.

'I informed Mr Allan that such disappearances were not uncommon. Indeed, I myself had heard of a mysterious matter occurring in rural Northumbria. A man seen in the company of a respected notary and not heard of since. Rumour abounded as to his fate, naturally enough.'

Here Allan interrupted, having recovered a little of his poise, but remaining prone to excitement. 'It was Cadwallader! Imagine that!'

The professor's glass shattered on the floor.

'Imagine!' I said equably.

Equable was not a word one could have used to describe the look Maccabi gave me at this point. The professor seized the hand bell and rang it vigorously. As the dissonance faded, I bade the policeman continue.

'Nothing more to say. I spoke with several notaries in the north Northumbrian region and none seemed disposed to throw any light on the matter.'

The professor let out a breath like an old bellows. Maccabi's parade ground spine was mollified a little, at least until the irrepressible reporter declared: 'But I know he visited John Brown of Seahouses.'

'And if he did? How came you by this information?' Maccabi said, then wiped his spittle from the table with a sleeve.

'A journalist's sources are confidential.'

Maccabi looked as though he believed that confidentiality's battlements could be easily stormed, could he himself but grasp the throat of the newspaperman. The cracked bell rang sourly again, more to provide distraction than out of impatience, no doubt.

As the professor placed the bell on the table, Mrs Gonderthwaite appeared, broom in hand. The woman's appearance was quite fey enough to allow for the gift of second sight, although it might have been that her lack of substance enabled her to listen at doors undetected.

'It seems Mr Allan is over-excited,' I posited. 'We should have allowed him a little more time in recuperation, perhaps?'

There were enthusiastic nods. The professor offered to escort Mr Allan to his chamber. I thought it a capital idea. Mr Allan seemed less enamoured of the idea, shrinking from the professor's touch as they left the dining room. Allan, still less than fully ambulatory, hopped and skipped ahead of the scuttling gnome.

'I thought we'd never be rid of them, Jedediah.' I smiled at the louring lumpkin. The policeman, as taciturn as ever, said nothing.

'What you will, Mr Moffat,' he sneered.

'Indeed so, Jedediah. '

We all three stood close to the tapestry bell pull beside the fireplace. I looked into the huge space in the hearth. I could see no mechanism. What lay behind and whence had the professor come earlier? I looked again at the length of tapestry alongside the fireplace. The professor was in the habit of summoning servants with the cracked hand bell. I waved at the moth-eaten pull.

'Would you mind?' I asked, looking at Constable Turner.

For answer he gave a perfunctory tug on the cloth. It proved sufficient: I heard the sound evocative of Ancient Egypt once more, and the stone to the rear of the inglenook grated to the side. As grimily cinereous as the fireplace was pristine, a passage led off to who knew what.

'After you, Jedediah,' I said.

Scant steps into the passage, which inclined downward from the outset, the diameter of the corridor was constricted by two vast examples of columnar statuary. Maccabi sidled past for the way was strait indeed. Constable Turner followed.

My eye was caught by the two statues, for though the *couloir* darkened somewhat a few yards ahead there was sufficient light to descry the lineaments created by the unknown mason. To the right was a man-like figure, although of gargantuan size. As I looked closer, I could see that no cold chisel had formed this representation: the piece seemed to be moulded from red clay. There had indeed been skill in it. In the huge head's face the lines were as sharp as the features themselves were blunt.

Their physiognomy revealed that no paragon of beauty had been discovered by the hand fashioning the clay. The mouth looked not so much cruel as coarsely incapable of expression. A low forehead indicated a base, unthinking nature, whilst the Mongolian cast to the eye brought to mind the brutal warriors of the Khan. The figure was naked: anatomically accurate and of proportionate size.

The modeller's whim made the gap between the two statues all the narrower. Facing the clay giant was a female figure of equally exaggerated dimensions. A cruelly beautiful face had been chiselled in the soft, red Collyhurst. This figure too was naked, save for a peculiar shaped shawl on her shoulders. A very fine chisel indeed had been applied to the delicate areas.

Maccabi turned back. 'Are you coming, Mr Moffat?'

'But where are we going, Maccabi? Besides, there must be time to admire those things worthy of it on our way, don't you agree?'

'What? Oh, those.'

I pointed at the erect member on the male statue. 'Perhaps these are religious figures?'

'Folkloric, Mr Moffat,' Constable Turner interposed. 'The lucky fellow, I believe, is a representation of the Golem of Prague, while the woman, most likely, is a dybbuk.'

It was quite worth suffering the policeman's smug look to see the slack dangling of Maccabi's jaw.

I knew the legend about the monster of reanimated clay, but was forced to enquire about what a dybbuk might be.

Maccabi answered, 'A dybbuk is a possessive spirit. The shawl shape on her shoulders represents the dybbuk. The woman is just a woman.'

'A remarkable example nevertheless,' I observed.

I squeezed between the guardians and drew up to the others. At this point the passage was yet wide enough to allow us to walk abreast. The ceiling was unusually high, but lighting was there none. Maccabi drew out a lucifer match and struck light. We descended into Hades.

It was hot indeed. Turner was the first to loosen his collar and abandon his coat. It lay behind us on the rough stone floor of the passage, relict of a burned scarecrow. The heat became almost unbearable before Maccabi dispensed with his own coat and thus allowed me to do the same.

There were arcane, almost runic scratchings in the walls of the passage, even before the masonry walls gave way to the rough hewing through the rock beneath the house's foundations. Yet still it was hot. We had walked several chains, although not yet a furlong, and while the descent was not precipitous it was remarkable. None spoke, although all were hard-pressed not to pant in the manner of hounds after a fox.

At first it was merely dark. But the further we descended, the more the white shirts of my fellow troglodytes seemed to assume a faintly vermilion tinge, and the dark became more a crepuscular gloom. By this time, possibly by dint of an advantage in years over the good policeman, Maccabi was to the fore.

He stopped suddenly. There was no cry of surprise or alarm. He said nothing, merely pointing a forefinger ahead of him into a red glow. Turner and I reached Maccabi at the same moment.

'Are you previously unacquainted with this part of Gibbous House, Mr Maccabi?' I asked.

Answer came there none. Following the direction indicated by his forefinger, I looked into a large chamber bathed in a hellish-red light. Vast heating stoves filled the half of it. At any one time three or more of the stoves' doors yawned, throwing out red light into the room and beyond.

A great deal of activity greeted our gaze: dozens of tall and dark-skinned bodies fed the maws of the fiery beasts with coal and the occasional piece of furniture, for the remainder of the room contained pieces as eclectic and possibly as valuable as those in the famed Collection.

I turned to the policeman.

'A most wasteful source of heat for a house lacking so much glaziery in its windows, wouldn't you say?'

'That would depend, Mr Moffat,' he said.

'On what?'

It was Maccabi, seemingly in possession of a tongue once more, who answered, 'On whether such machines do serve some other purpose.'

The Ethiops continued their task, oblivious to our observation. Maccabi made to wave an arm to attract their attention, but Turner laid a hand on his arm. 'They are likely deaf and dumb; it would serve no purpose.'

It was true that none could have worked many days in the cavernous room without becoming as deaf as stone, although we had heard nothing, even at the very end of the passage. On the threshold, it was uncommon loud. I stepped back a pace and the noise vanished as if it had never been.

We retraced our steps in silence. I strained to hear any faint echo of the industrial cacophony in the underground chamber; there was none. As I stooped to recover my coat from the passage floor, I caught sight of the initials 'HC' hacked into the rock of the wall.

A shiver racked my bones and I pondered the circumstances that had led from the carving of the initials to the hideous thing keeping vigil in the gatehouse of the estate. The other two recovered their own garments. Maccabi dashed the dust from his own, his lips tightening with each blow from the flat of his hand on the worsted.

The statues straitening the passage looked less imposing from the reverse approach, although the Golem's attributes remained impressive. The figures were not quite so well illuminated as before, since the entrance before us remained obdurately closed.

'I presume there is a lever on this side too, Jedediah?' I asked.

'How should I know?' he replied, somewhat snappishly I felt.

'Have we more lucifers?' enquired the practical policeman.

Maccabi replied in the negative and the two of them set about feeling the environs of the featureless stone before us.

'There is nothing,' Maccabi said, although Turner continued his tactile examination of the blank wall.

'There is always something,' I remarked. 'I believe at last I begin to understand the workings of the lunatic mind responsible for this most peculiar home of mine.'

With that I returned to the statue of the Golem, and rendered his glory into a less erect state. The familiar grate of heavy stone echoed in the passage and the wall drew back to reveal the dwarf, grinning like a natural.

'Welcome, welcome back from the Underworld, gentlemen.' The professor threw back his head and laughed, an outburst that looked most peculiar from one of his stature.

Maccabi started for the mannikin, hands outstretched as if to throttle the air above the fellow's head and bellowed, 'Slaves!'

'Slaves?' The professor hopped nimbly to the side, although in no danger from the much taller Maccabi – until such time as the latter approached him on his knees.

'They are not slaves! Although they might well have been!' he continued.

'It is a strange kind of freedom enjoyed below the ground, Professor,' the policeman offered.

'Ach, they do not want to leave. What would they do here?'

'Likely give rise to all sorts of rumours and fanciful tales,' I interposed.

The academic straightened to the limit of his short stature.

'Septimus Coble and I bought these men some years ago from an American planter. They have been paid a working wage ever since. Should they wish to leave they may.'

It seemed to me that he knew full well they would not; could not.

The policeman was saved from preventing Maccabi assaulting the diminutive academic by the arrival of Miss Pardoner in a state of some agitation. Maccabi forced his hands behind his back and recovered himself sufficiently so as not to alarm the young woman.

In truth, she spared him not the briefest glance. I had never seen her so lacking in self- possession and I felt a stirring at the prospect of inducing such a commotion in her myself. I hoped that the time would come soon.

Chapter Thirty-one

She was not so discomposed as to be hysterical. The colour in her cheeks was high indeed, however, and she shrilled breathlessly, 'Professor, come quickly, the journalist, he's... ' She did not finish, her hand merely flew to her mouth and she began to chew the knuckle of her forefinger distractedly. The professor scampered toward the doors leading from the dining room. All followed, as bizarre a retinue as ever trailed behind anyone, much less a dwarf.

Edgar Allan was not dead. The violence of his fit indicated that he might soon be so, or at least wish that he were. His head seemed half as big again as when last I had seen him, the whites of his eyes were a solid carmine, his lips were stretched wide and he gnashed as many teeth as would be visible in a flensed skull. It seemed foolhardy to approach his thrashing limbs. The pitcher and basin that had presumably been standing on the table at the bedside lay shattered on the floor, the pieces standing guard over something most unsavoury.

Foolhardy or not, the professor braved the flailing arms of the invalid and produced a curious arrangement of gutta percha, a flat disc and two small wooden cylinders. These latter parts inserted into his ears, he approached the afflicted writer boldly and – evading teeth and arms deftly – placed the disc on the fellow's chest. With remarkable sang-froid he remained still, head on one side, apparently listening for something. Abruptly he leaped back and snatched the contraption from his person.

'Bah! What can you expect? That man Leared is nothing but a damned charlatan. I doubt if anything from the exhibition will amount to less than his ridiculous stethoscope.'

Clearly, the apparatus had not functioned as advertised, although what that function might have been, I had no idea.

The writer's distress continued unabated, his back arching from time to time in simulacrum of the most flexible of Indian fakirs.

'How long has he been so?' The professor asked Miss Pardoner.

'I do not know. The seizure was as you see it but a minute before I came to summon you.'

Her eyes darted to the side as she spoke.

Perhaps she did not want to admit to a moment of panic and some undue delay caused by it; from what I presumed of her character I felt that unlikely. Maccabi, predictably, hovered at her shoulder, constantly on the point of lending a comforting arm before deciding again to allow propriety its due.

The professor addressed him sharply: 'Jedediah, my medical bag. From my room if you please.'

He was almost through the door when the policeman called after him, 'No need for haste, not on his part.' A long finger pointed at the frozen contortion that could not truly be called the writer's final repose, although he would never move again.

'The bell,' said the professor.

Miss Pardoner, stepping carefully to avoid the contents of the shattered chinaware, moved to exercise the pinchbeck pull mounted in the wall over the nightstand. It was a large and intricately cast piece of tarnished brass, whose base was formed in the image of a metallic corvid trapped in the substance of the wall, beak agape in protest at the indignity of being drawn from it repeatedly, with never a hope of escaping the plaster.

Miss Pardoner gave a sharp cry as she drew the bird out; no blood was evident but it seemed that in the young woman's haste to summon Mrs Gonderthwaite the raven's beak had pecked her. She sucked her palm greedily. I thought this a little excessive for what must have been a scratch, but took pleasure in it nonetheless.

The detective became suddenly animated. With a sharp glance toward the professor and myself, he enquired of Miss Pardoner, 'How came you to find... Mr Allan so?'

'I was in the kitchen, instructing Mrs Gonderthwaite to prepare a broth for...'

She nodded at the late reporter.

'And?' The policeman looked smug.

'And the bell rang from – well – from this room. I bade the cook continue preparing the soup and—'

She gave a poor impression of a woman about to swoon; it was most extraordinary. Maccabi, clearly taken in, made toward her, perhaps lest she fell. Miss Pardoner stepped backward out of his reach.

Meanwhile, Constable Turner, having bumped the professor aside with a bony hip, lifted each of the departed's hands in turn, inspecting them minutely. Without turning from the cadaver, he said, 'Moffat, you're an observant fellow, with which hand did this poor fellow write?'

'Left,' I replied, not caring to acknowledge the compliment.

'I thought as much.'

He turned his attention from the body and took no care of the faecal matter beside the bed. He removed a jeweller's loupe from his pocket, screwed it into his left eye socket and peered at the raven's head from every angle, taking great care not to touch it.

Suddenly he leaped back, swivelled and seized Miss Pardoner's right hand. She gave a squeal of protest and the policeman was indelicate in his treatment of her in turning it over to examine the palm. He held it up to show the rest of the company. It was unblemished.

'You are a lucky woman, Miss Pardoner,' Turner said.

'How so?' I asked.

'The bell pull is covered in a liquid, although it has dried and is now merely tacky, no doubt. I wonder whence came the nux vomica?'

He gave a meaningful look at the people in the room, much as if he hoped to extract a confession by the power of his glare.

Perhaps it might have worked had Mrs Gonderthwaite not arrived and, alarmed by the crowded bedroom, thrown up her hands in shock, causing the soup to bespatter the white trousers of the policeman's uniform. The soup must surely have been no more than moderately hot, since the fellow gave but one piercing scream.

Mrs Gonderthwaite left forthwith to find the accoutrements to repair the mess in the late reporter's chamber. The policeman cut a comical figure, holding the stained white material of his uniform trousers away from his private parts, far too much the gentleman to remove them in the presence of a lady. In the meantime, he gasped, 'Maccabi, I hold you as guarantor for Miss Pardoner's pledge to remain on the premises.'

As Maccabi began to bluster, I interrupted, 'Should that task not fall to me, Constable?'

'As you like! Someone must.'

He spat it out, either excited out of his phlegmatism by the warming properties of the broth or simply by the prospect of arresting someone, at last, for something. At this point, Maccabi finally expelled something intelligible from his mouth. 'You can't think... surely not... '

It was evident that constable did indeed 'think', and that Maccabi knew he did.

'I shall require, in that case, that Maccabi summon from Alnwick Mrs Catchpole, wife to the turnkey of the House of Correction, so that we may transport the miscreant to a place of confinement.'

Maccabi showed himself for a lovesick fool by seizing the fellow by the arm and hissing into his face, 'It was I, I saw off the hack!'.

The policeman shook off the offending hand and, raising an eyebrow, said to the handsome Jew, 'I did not take you for any kind of herbalist, sir.'

The dwarf stepped nimbly over to the policeman and beckoned him to lean his ear downward, the better to whisper a confidence. I thought this uncommon rude, although the detective's face offered as many clues as the most inept of criminal might. The professor exclaimed, 'Gentlemen, lady, follow me if you please.'

We followed the scampering gnome, some less reluctantly than others. Down the stairs, through the phantasmagoria of furnishings in the atrium, then through the dining room and the various bizarre collections until we reached the vivarium, just before the library. In addition to the vitrines behind which slithered creatures invisible in the darkness of the room, there were rows and rows of exemplars of every kind of plant imaginable, and some that were not. I doubt that I would have been able to identify even the tenth part of their varieties, had I been wont to try.

In addition to being dark, the room was uncomfortably warm, as alien as the tropic forests of Martinique and, perhaps, as sinister. The horticultural specimens stood atop long benches, the edge of whose surfaces were of a height with the professor's eyebrows. The benches were more than a cloth-yard deep, and at the very back I could see a space dedicated to the most exotic of the orchidae, their colours fighting valiantly against the general gloom. The dwarf reached under the bench and withdrew a rough stool, the like of which, in a more conventional household, might conceivably have been used for milking a cow. The professor skipped nimbly atop it and made a deep and mocking bow. 'Gentlemen, lady, before your squinting eyes our very own Jedediah will pluck the fruit of the *Strychnos nux vomica* and save the fair maiden from durance vile.'

The little man grinned and snickered and for the first time I felt some semblance of fellow feeling for him, both of us knowing that for all Maccabi's prodigious knowledge of the local avian riches, his botanical expertise was such that he could provide no answer that would incriminate himself.

Maccabi turned listlessly to the bench and grasped a plant without looking at it. He gave quite a start when the Dionaea muscipula trapped him as surely as Venus herself had inveigled his confession. The dwarf looked at Constable Turner and gave a vigorous shake of the head.

'Well, miss, your gallant has failed you,' the policeman said.

'It does not follow that Miss Pardoner is responsible, Turner,' I said.

'I know that none of these plants is *Strychnos nux vomica*, for it is, in fact, a tree. Do you now propose my arrest? Certainly the professor would know the tree itself and perhaps where, in this lunatic house, one might find it.' I awaited answer from the policeman.

He said nothing. I added, 'Perhaps we might consider more than means and opportunity. You said it yourself, there are few motiveless crimes.'

It was some surprise to me that I had unwittingly absorbed so much of the policeman's earlier lecture on the science of detection. It occurred to me also that the man might have wished that he had not proselytised quite so much on behalf of his new religion. Miss Pardoner, who had hitherto been most surprisingly mute, enquired, 'Motive? Means? Opportunity? What have these to do with such hideous crimes?'

I feared a further tiresome exposition from Constable Turner, but we were saved by the intervention of a no less tiresome, if more diminutive, didact: the professor.

'I shall explain. A fascinating subject, detection.'

He looked around, as if for applause. Maccabi appeared quite distracted, staring fixedly at a point on Miss Pardoner's bosom. Turner had a bemused look: I supposed him amazed at finding a conversationalist more boring than himself.

Miss Pardoner seemed about to interrupt the great man, but he finally deigned to answer her question, after a fashion.

'Imagine, dear Ellen, that you have robbed me of a valuable

repeater watch. Later you are found dead, strangled – it might be with a scarf, perhaps yellow – in a side-street in Newcastle.'

With this the mountebank produced, with a theatrical flourish, one such scarf from an inner pocket. He winked at me.

'So, let us say I have motive: viz the watch. I have means: exemplum – a supply of scarves, of an unusual colour I admit. But opportunity? Why, I was here all the time. Alibi is the best defence against such accusations. Suppose I had been in New-castle? Suppose I owned such a scarf as was found – begging your pardon, Ellen – around your graceful neck? What motive would I have to snuff out the life of such a beautiful creature as yourself? Besides, I have a new and different watch.'

The dwarf gave a leer worthy of an escaped convict in a molly house. Miss Pardoner looked to be biting the inside of her cheek, whether in an effort to prevent a blush or a laugh, I was not sure. I, however, was neither embarrassed nor amused, being preoccupied with the professor's glaring hints to me about my activities in Newcastle.

Professor Jedermann's lecture was not yet finished. 'So, in dealing with a civilised and logical mind, one would presup-pose opportunity, means and motive, before one might suppose the guilt of persons accused.'

I could not resist. 'And the mind of a lunatic? What would that presuppose? Especially if the lunatic were a mur-derer?'

Maccabi, and most surprisingly Miss Pardoner began to speak at once, before manners prevailed and Ellen spoke at an unaccustomed pitch, 'But that means it could be anyone. Maccabi, the professor, the servants. Anyone!'

She did not point at me, but the omission of my name did not prevent Maccabi from doing so.

The policeman held up a large and calloused hand, palm out. He shouted, with some distemper, 'Enough.'

The effect was rather spoiled by the after effects of his sudden encounter with the soup, and the manner in which these caused him to bend at the waist to evade the touch of the wet cloth of his trousers. Still, it was enough to ensure the professor did not proceed to regale us with a history of the study of the mind from Aristotle's *De Anima* to the work of some modern academic whom he had no doubt met in Leipzig twenty years before.

'The reporter's room will be sealed until the arrival of the coroner from Alnwick. You, Moffat!'

I made an obsequy, but the fellow was far too self-absorbed to note the irony.

'At your service, Constable.'

'Is there no one here to be trusted to fetch the coroner?' he asked.

'I think we might send Cullis and even expect a return before sunrise,' I replied.

'A letter. Might I have the necessary, Mr Moffat?'

'Certainly, let us all repair to the relative comfort of the library.'

Chapter Thirty-two

The company of five clustered around an escritoire of white wood. The professor had had to move aside some impressively heavy, if unspeakably filthy, damask drapery to reveal the beautiful piece standing between two of the high-arched windows in the right-hand wall. I fancied I had seen something similar at the Great Exhibition some years ago. It was most definitely a lady's escritoire, intricately carved with rustic figures, harts, hinds, hares and bucolics idling in leafy bowers; a less indolent cowherd led four cows and a calf along the carved wooden back plate. The white wood had yellowed with age; a shepherd and shepherdess reclined at each side of the writing surface, mooning at each other whilst serving as truss and bracket between the desk and the back plate. Neither nib nor knife had made so much as a scratch on the pristine writing surface, nor had any stray gobbet of ink stained the wood.

The professor pressed the centre of an exquisite rose that formed the centrepiece of a panel above the cattle and their keeper. The cattle and cowherd shot forward, revealing a drawer constrained by spring and lever. The professor stood on the tips of the toes on his tiny feet and withdrew a single sheet of vellum, a ball of wax, a pen and inkwell. He laid the items on the writing surface.

'We are not so modern here as the late Mr Allan, and can offer no miracles of contemporary calligraphy. Please, Constable, wait here while I fetch you a chair.'

The diminutive professor was as good as his word, although it cost him much barking of shins on the ornate legs of a chair that, quite literally, dwarfed him. He was not helped in his endeavours by the heavy ormolu-mounted candlestick that teetered on the rich, if tattered, fabric of the chair's seat. The candlestick was after the style of Caffieri and was as emetically rococo in style as to have come from the hand of the master himself. The midget, still huffing, placed the candlestick on the bureau and motioned the detective toward the chair.

Constable Turner did not demur before the interested gaze of the rest of our company, perhaps he was proud of the careful and elegant handwriting I observed from behind his left shoulder. The note was succinct.

Hepplewhite,
A matter for the Coroner is here at hand at Gibbous
House. Accompany the bearer of this missive, Cullis.
Constable Turner

He signed it with a flourish and finally removed his tongue to the confines of his mouth once more. He sealed the sheet using only the sealing wax, after warming it over one of the candles in the over-decorative stick. I reached for the letter, but Maccabi seized it before me and dashed away in search of Cullis.

'Miss Pardoner, Mr Moffat, Constable. Let us be seated in comfort. I shall pour us some refreshment.'

Those two followed the little man. I lingered a moment by the beautiful white-wood writing desk. I pressed the exquisite rose centrepiece, just for the pleasure of seeing the secret compartment spring open once more. A small packet of oil-skin, about the size of a snuff box, lay in one corner. I turned my back to the room the better to hide it from the others.

The oilskin was not secured, merely wrapped around a small resinous block of a familiar brown substance. Perhaps the writing desk had spent some time in the notary's office in Seahouses. I pocketed the opium and pushed the compartment shut. Turning to the room, I bellowed at the professor, 'For pity's sake, Enoch, just a good oporto, and none of that damnable green filth!'

He almost dropped the absinthe but could not save the sugar; the cube skittered across the floor to disappear under Miss Pardoner's chair. Placing the bottle on the long board, he scuttled to the chair and burrowed under Miss Pardoner's skirts to recover it. That young woman remained in a state of remarkable equanimity throughout the performance. Her own raised eyebrow answered mine in reciprocal fashion.

The professor, the sugar cube now in his mouth, retired to the lowest of the chairs in the room, an expression somewhere between a leer and the beatific smile of a saint. He let out a contented sigh. 'Miss Pardoner, if you please, some music.'

She arose without reply and strode to the far corner of the room. Seated before a piano, she looked over her shoulder and said, 'Mr Moffat, would you be so kind?' She pointed at the music on the stand before her. Naturally, I was delighted to be so.

It was an old-fashioned instrument, with none of the innovations of Erard or Babcock. A vile green in colour in the main, it featured gilt-scalloping on the edges. The keys were an inversion of the modern custom, the natural being black and the accidental white.

Ellen Pardoner gave a laugh. 'A Viennese school piano, Mr Moffat. A Stein Klavier. Who knows, perhaps Mozart himself played on this very one?'

'Perhaps,' I said.

I looked at the proliferation of black markings on the pages before her: they were as meaningless to me as the strange alphabets the professor was so proud of knowing.

'What will you play?' I asked her.

'Why Mozart, of course.'

She began to play. It was both beautiful and sad.

I turned the pages and noted the occasional crabbed note in the margin, often monogrammed with a floridly cursive M. The music finished. The professor's and the policeman's applause was augmented by that of Maccabi, who must have entered during the entertainment. I asked my ward in a whisper, 'What was it?'

Her answer was abruptly drowned by the professor's excited yelp: '*Fräulein Pardoner, sollen wir nicht singen?*'

'Oh fie, Professor, not again!'

Fie indeed, I thought. Miss Pardoner was uncommon fond of romances, it seemed.

Maccabi and the dwarf were now positioned on the French-window side of the hideous piano, as excited as boys at keyholes. The professor's chest was as puffed out as that of any pouter pigeon. I believed I saw the slightest upward turn of Jedediah's mouth, as if he were the elder indulging an excitable youth.

'*Ach ja!* Play it! Play it! Mozart's finest!'

Miss Pardoner began to play, accompanying her own pleasant contralto, the professor's reedy tenor and Maccabi's manly baritone. The policeman looked on as stoically as might have been expected. It was a round – or a canon, if you will. My grasp of the German language was sufficient to discern the title as being '*Leck mich im Arsch*'. It was not hard to imagine Mozart issuing such an invitation: there were rumours that he told Archbishop Colloredo to 'kiss my arse' more than once.

We repaired once more to chairs near the vast fireplace. The professor poured us each a glass of jerez and rang the cracked bell.

'Do you carry that with you everywhere, man?' I asked.

'As you saw, some of the bell pulls have been,' he pondered his next words for a moment or two, 'adapted to better purpose.'

'I find it nothing short of miraculous that anyone answers the summons of so unsound a chime, much less so distracted a soul as Mrs Gonderthwaite. The woman cannot possibly hear the summons, wherever she might be,' I posited, looking the mannikin squarely in the eye.

'Well, you are aware of the nature of sound, surely, Mr Moffat? As Galileo said, "Waves are produced by the vibrations of a sonorous body, which spread through the air, bringing to the tympanum of the ear a stimulus which the mind interprets as sound."'

My heart sank at the prospect of another lecture from the academic homunculus.

'The frequencies of such vibrations may be measured, you will allow, Mr Moffat?'

I nodded wearily.

'There are those who believe that animals hear more frequencies than do we, did you know that, Mr Moffat?'

'Any fool knows that, Professor,' enjoined Maccabi. 'We do not hear the half of birdsong, and how beautiful it would be to hear the entire canon.'

The fellow wore a simpering look worthy of a heroine of a sensationalist novel.

The professor sounded displeased at the interruption: 'Quite so. Although we do not hear them, it is said that sounds of low frequency may cause feelings of awe and fear in humankind. In my examinations of Mrs Gonderthwaite, I have noticed a peculiar sensitivity to audible low frequency sounds. I persist with this bell as part of my ongoing research.'

He appeared on the point of clacking the cracked bell once more when Mrs Gonderthwaite entered the library. Perhaps she had heard some sound inaudible to the rest of us. I felt the woman appeared according to her own whim, rather in the manner of the faery folk. She addressed the professor but looked at me. 'If there is nothing further, I should like to retire, sir.'

The policeman answered by means of a question. 'I trust the room is sealed?'

The woman replied that it was indeed.

'In that case,' Turner went on, 'I see no reason to keep any of you from your beds. I shall wait here for the coroner.'

I looked at the watch: it was past eleven. I stood to allow Miss Pardoner to take her leave and resolved to follow after a polite interval. Maccabi followed her, whilst the professor lingered as if wishing to share some confidence, but finally he left after a few moments of uncomfortable silence. I made to leave. Turner held me back with his arm, fixing a cold gaze on me.

'Be careful, Moffat. There is more at work here than you can know. You would do well to leave Gibbous House this very evening.'

I scoffed at his presumption, and brushed his arm away.

'You would do well to remember that I am master of this house, Constable.'

'Allan was not a man to keep his own counsel, Moffat. I have heard much of your... abilities. They will not be enough. You play into their hands, sir.'

'Whose hands?' I laughed. 'Do you not think I am a match for an ageing dwarf, a slip of a girl and that dolt Maccabi?'

The man's spittle dampened my cheek. 'Curse your arrogance, you fool. There is more at work here than you can know. Mark my words, Moffat, leave – while you still can.'

I left him in his chair.

Chapter Thirty-three

I was awakened by Mrs Gonderthwaite in the darkest hours. She wore a nightshirt – thank the lord – but the light of the moon through the window offered an unwanted glimpse of her figure's silhouette. She bore a seven-branched candelabrum aloft and informed me that the coroner had arrived. She led me below, floating before me like a phantasm from some tale of the imagination.

I followed her to the library, where Hepplewhite awaited. Of the policeman, however, there was no sign.

The coroner, though not tall, was rendered less so by a marked stoop. It was all I could do to look him in the eye, in fact. His dress was uncommon shabby, with altogether too much grubby linen emerging from his coat sleeve, and his boots had long been strangers to any kind of blacking. I adjudged him a man of about sixty years, although his movement seemed vigorous still. Pince-nez adorned his handsome nose, and his hand flicked rapidly and often at the tattered black ribbon hanging from their side. He held out a surprisingly calloused hand, and I surmised he was a country doctor rather than any rarified medical specimen.

'Hepplewhite,' he barked.

'Moffat,' I returned.

'Where is the cadaver?' He fiddled with the filthy ribbon.

'It remains undisturbed, where the fellow drew his last.'

I waited for him to ask the whereabouts of the policeman, but he did not. The man merely looked up at me expectantly. Signalling Mrs Gonderthwaite that she was to light our way, we made our way to Edgar Allan's room.

The skeletal housekeeper selected the appropriate key from a bunch with no hesitation, although I could see nothing especial to mark it out from the others. The lock opened smoothly, as though it had received frequent and thorough oilings. Carrying the candlestick before her, she led us to the bedside. Even in the dim light of the candle, poor Allan's rictus remained as alarming as before. His limbs and body had stiffened in the pose occasioned by the violent spasms preceding his demise.

Hepplewhite grunted and poked at the corpse with a bony finger. Beckoning Mrs Gonderthwaite with the same, he moved around the bed to look at the body from the other side.

'A drinker, Mr Moffat?' he asked.

'No more than some.'

'Hah, and more than others I'll be bound!' The bony finger peeled back a lifeless eyelid and he nodded.

'An apoplexy, no doubt. Had he,' a pause and a look to either side, 'means?'

The physician imbued the words with a lubricity such as a Cheapside whore might save for a drunken earl.

'I haven't the slightest notion, Doctor. Why do you ask?'

'Arrangements, dear fellow. We shall have to make arrangements.'

It seemed to me that the man had no more interest in the cause of Allan's expiry than in the Eastern Question; perhaps that was why the policeman's absence had thus far remained unmentioned by him.

'Constable Turner believed that there were some suspicious aspects in the matter,' I began diffidently.

'Nonsense!' the man bellowed upward. 'If that were the case, why then is the numbskull not here?'

With that the quacksalver thumbed his waistcoat pockets and jutted his jaw up at me as if daring me to gainsay him.

And it was true that I could not.

We repaired once more to the library, and I dismissed Mrs Gonderthwaite to whatever nocturnal pursuits she enjoyed. Despite the early hour, the coroner was looking wistfully at the sideboard with its variety of libations fair and foul.

My watch showed that it was yet four of the morning. I looked vainly for the absinthe; perhaps the professor had taken it to his private apartments. I dearly hoped so. For spite, I poured the coroner a measure of the professor's foul bitters. I took a glass of jerez out of courtesy.

'So, Dr Hepplewhite. What now?' I enquired.

'We must expedite the burial, Moffat. We could learn much from the customs of others.'

'You know so much about them? I find that strange.'

The man's face coloured. 'I buried Septimus Coble!'

I may have affronted his dignity, but I believed his blushes to be more indicative of a lie. The interruption of the professor prevented me from pursuing the matter. 'Ah, I think we may relieve your concern in such matters.'

Hepplewhite looked at him in dismay, sensing a rapidly disappearing opportunity.

'Ah... hem... My fee, at least.'

The professor smiled. It was not pleasant, merely a stretching of lips to expose the teeth such an avid consumer of green spirit deserved.

'Oh no, Hepplewhite. You will receive both your fee and such monies as you would normally disburse on the disposal of a gentleman without family or means.'

'Let's have a drink on it,' said the coroner, and he held out his empty glass toward me.

I filled his glass and addressed the professor. 'Ah, it is my belief that the law is quite strict on the disposal and interment of human remains, Professor. I hope no law will be broken under my roof?'

He laughed. 'Moffat, what do you take me for? Besides, the Anatomy Act has long since become law in your wonderful country.' He looked nervously to the walls of books.

I had followed the progress of the Anatomy Act of 1832 into law, with the interest of a professional, one might say, regretting the profitable business to which its passing had put an end shortly after my arrival in London in 183_.

'I doubt you are a licensed anatomist, Jedermann,' I said.

'It matters not, I have a paper in Allan's own hand containing instructions for the disposal of his body, in the event of his death.'

He offered me a tattered piece of vellum. I did not take it from him, but viewed the contents from where I stood. The spidery script looked similar to the hand I had seen in the notebook belonging to the reporter. It had not been written with his beloved fountain pen, however. The professor thrust the paper at the coroner, who barely looked at it before stuffing it in a pocket.

'Splendid,' he said. 'Everything seems to be in order. If I might trouble you for the sum of twenty guineas?'

I turned my back on the both of them.

Chapter Thirty-four

From the vantage point of an armchair as tired-looking as I undoubtedly was, I watched the dwarf and his confederate, heads close, hugger-mugger, whispering at the other end of the room. The subject of their susurrations was undiscernible by me and I confess I did not care.

Truly, I felt a stifling lethargy in the vast and rambling house that I had never felt in the attic rooms of Cheapside. It was an effort to keep track of the clock and calendar under the weight of the grotesquery encountered at every turn. To be sure, meals arrived more or less as expected, at least with regard to the time and place, if not in their manner. Nevertheless, it seemed to me that I had been at Gibbous House for a lifetime and not a matter of days. Perhaps the demise of Allan would have put me in better countenance if I myself had had a hand in it. I wondered which of them had truly committed the crime. The servants? Not without instruction to do so. Ellen? I could not decide whether I hoped it were so or not. Maccabi? No, I felt there was a hollow at the heart of him, some scruple that would have prevented him taking a life. Unless, of course, Miss Pardoner asked him to do so. The Professor? Much more likely, but why?

Beyond the French windows the mulberry dawn stained the sky. My brown study had lasted more than an hour. Perhaps I had slept. Perhaps the ennui had overcome my senses. There was something I needed; it would not have been wise to seek it within the grounds of Gibbous House. Not a second time.

In the full light of day the coroner left, surprisingly without breaking his fast. Cullis, stoic and mute, handed the him up into the driver's post of his own chaise, which was in no better condition than the horse in its traces. I enjoined the professor to accompany me to the dining room. He clacked his broken bell, honoured me with a malicious grin and we awaited the insubstantial Mrs Gonderthwaite.

The dwarf, from the perch fashioned by the box balanced on his chair, cocked his head at me and raised an eyebrow. 'So, Mr Moffat, I have work, the Collection. What are we to do with you?'

The goblin seemed set on provocation, but I would not give him the satisfaction.

'I am master of quite a considerable estate, am I not? I should think that would be quite sufficient employment for a gentleman,' I said.

'We will pass gently over the matter of gentry, Mr Moffat. However, did you not understand the terms of the legacy? You can sell nothing!'

The mouth offered another variation on a smile no less mirthless than the earlier grin.

'Nothing? What about the inn? At Seahouses?'

He squirmed atop his ludicrous seating arrangement.

'Ah, the mute... John Bill... '

Such papers as I *had* read insisted only on the giant's being kept in employment and I told him so, before continuing, 'In addition, I could not find the inn entailed as part of the Collection nor the property of the estate. I have need of the fellow here, I think. What I do not require is the ownership of a fisherman's tavern.'

'Ah, very well. You may be right. I will check the appropriate papers.' The pitch of his voice rose.

'You will not,' I said.

Perhaps he cursed himself for allowing me to interpret it as a question. Whatever the case might have been, I felt a little uneasy at his unexpected capitulation and sure that he was hiding something else.

The dining table was in some disarray post the cavalcade that the serving of breakfast entailed in Gibbous House. As usual, the fare had been unaccountably fine from kidney to kipper. Equally fine at that moment, to my eye, was the figure of Miss Pardoner, hindered though it was by her own unfortunate eye for colour. This same orbis ocularis caught my own.

'Well, Mr Moffat, it is a fine day: I imagine you will be busy,' she said 'I am informed by the good professor that I am completely at liberty, free from obligation or duty.'

'Perhaps you have some vigorous and manly activity in mind for your unexpected leisure?'

Maccabi, opposite me, gave the young lady a look of warning or murderous intent. Perhaps of both.

'I rather thought we might take a trip to Alnwick, you and I.'

It was most satisfying to receive a similar look from Jedediah Maccabi for my pains. More pleasure still accrued in the issue of instruction to prepare whatever carriage and beast might conceivably manage the twenty or so miles – without mishap on the part of one and expiry on the part of the other. My faithful retainer left the table with commendable alacrity, evinced by the shattering of his glass as his coat-tail knocked it to the floor.

The professor was blessedly silent. Perhaps I had bettered the midget at last.

'Well, Miss Pardoner, if you would be so good as to prepare yourself for the chaise, I shall await you afront the house, in a quarter-hour, shall we say?' I said.

Her eyebrows quite reached the fringes of hair that reflected her disregard for the finer points of cosmetology.

'I am as ready to depart as yourself, Mr Moffat. We might await the carriage together outside.' She smirked.

'It is indeed a fine day,' I allowed.

I turned to bid the professor adieu, but he was rapt, carving something in the fine, if scarred, wood of the table. Peering at it closely, it was revealed as pure nonsense:

$$\text{`}x^2 \approx -1 \text{ if } p \approx 1.\text{'}$$

The dwarf looked up, knife pointing at my heart. Then he drew the knife twice across the equation in a savage cross of negation.

Miss Pardoner's complexion suited the late-spring sunshine. She seemed to lift her face toward it as though she were some exotic tropical bloom. Cullis was holding the reins on the chaise when it limped around the corner. He drew the light carriage to a halt and leaped down, surprisingly nimbly. Lifting a hand to where a forelock might once have been, he turned on his heel, taking care to spit as he did so.

I handed my ward up to the seat. It was gratifying that a chaise had turned out to be available. Miss Pardoner and I sat uncommon close, for the carriage seated only two – and those of long acquaintance. Being on the point of laying on with the switch in an effort to persuade the cadaverous jade to effect our forward momentum, I was somewhat surprised, and not a little pleased, to feel the young lady's hand on my thigh.

'Please, Mr Moffat, let us take a turn around the outside of the house. The track is reasonably kept.'

My face must have betrayed some emotion, for she continued, 'Fie! Mr Moffat, I shall not eat you, I wish merely to point out something about the house that you may have omitted to remark.'

Ellen Pardoner removed her hand, but a playful smile lingered on her face. I persuaded the nag to movement and the tiny chaise set out along the track in circumnavigation of the house. My attention and efforts were concentrated, I confess, solely on keeping the miserable specimen in motion. The young woman again laid her hand on me. 'Stop, Mr Moffat. You should look.'

She held a long arm outstretched toward the house, finger pointed at one of the towers of the east wing. In common with every aspect of Gibbous House, the cloister between the towers of the wing did not run true. Not only the three towers of the east, but also the four spires of the west wing were visible from our vantage point on the track.

'Do you but count them, sir, and be mindful of their number.'

Perhaps I gave the horse a harder tickle than it deserved, but thankfully it moved forward at a quicker pace. She had not finished.

'And count the entrances to your fortress, sir.'

I had counted twelve by the end, when I drew the chaise to a halt before the main entrance to the house.

She looked intently at me, saying nothing.

I toyed with suggesting that this could be our fortress, but impatience moved me. 'Miss Pardoner, I should like to be on our way,' I began.

'Seven and twelve, Mr Moffat, imagine! Would it surprise you greatly to discover that there are fifty-two windows and that they contain in sum three hundred and sixty-five separate panes of glass?'

'My dear young lady, it would not surprise me if this house

had a bell tower and hippopotami in the mansard roof. Now may we at last depart?'

Her lip protruded somewhat. 'Gibbous House is a Calendar House, Mr Moffat. A rare thing. There is power in numbers.'

'A Calendar House? What is... ?'

Then I remembered the seven towers or spires, twelve entrances and the fifty-two windows with their three hundred and sixty-five panes of glass.

'I see, according to the days of the week, months of the year, weeks in the year and so on? What is the point of that?'

I ignored Miss Pardoner's knowing smirk and persuaded the bag of bones to forward momentum once again.

Chapter Thirty-five

The ride to Alnwick passed in relative silence, and, pity though it was, Miss Pardoner's hand made no more assaults on my dignity. I drew the chaise to a halt in front of the Old Cross Inn in Narrowgate, and handed her down.

'Some luncheon is in order, I think,' I said.

She brightened a little at the prospect and I received as close an approximation of a simpering smile as her strong features would allow.

Robson being in attendance, I wasted no time in instructing him to find livery for the chaise and its attendant beast. He in turn despatched a lout possessed of a low forehead the equal of his own.

'What delights has your dear mother available today, Robson?' I enquired.

'Mutha's deed,' he replied.

'I am so sorry to hear it, Robson. Was it sudden?'

He laughed, offering an unpleasant view of his gappy teeth.

'Ay it was, fowerty yeeahz gone.'

I remembered how little I had understood the fellow on first meeting him and enquired merely after the available vittles.

They proved more than adequate: a vast game pie and a brace of pigeon washed down with ale. Miss Pardoner savoured her own with a smacking of the lips that I found less than genteel, but all the more stimulating for being so.

Robson cleared the dishes, letting only a few pie crumbs sully our apparel. Miss Pardoner again tested the boundaries of decorum by sprawling somewhat in her chair and asking, 'So, Mr Moffat, what diversion is planned for our visit to Alnwick?'

'My purpose here, Ellen, is twofold. I plan to hurry Maccabi's Jewish tailor along in the matter of my wardrobe.'

I took a draught of beer and the woman's impatience got the better of her. 'And the second?'

'We are in need of more staff at the house, no matter what the professor says,' I replied.

She laughed. 'I do not think any person would be so desperate as to seek employment in Gibbous House, Mr Moffat.'

'We shall see, Ellen. Our second port of call is the Alnwick Gaol.'

The young woman betrayed no great discomposure at this intelligence. No doubt the tic in her left eyelid was occasioned by the somewhat fœtid atmosphere in the inn.

I paid Robson with the last of my dwindling funds. The weather being as clement as before, my ward and I walked arm in arm along Narrowgate through the Market Square and along Bondgate until we reached a mean bow-windowed shop next to the Globe Inn, immediately before the Hotspur Tower itself. The weathered sign hanging over the door read 'E. Salomons, Gentleman's Tailor'.

As Miss Pardoner crossed the threshold, a minuscule bell tinkled absurdly, with little hope of overcoming the racket of the machine behind which the eponymous stitcher was toiling. My ward looked around the cramped shop, her curiosity clearly aroused by the inordinate number of military uniforms hanging from rails and piled in heaps wherever the furniture allowed it.

The tunics were the madder red of Her Majesty's proud regiments of foot. Miss Pardoner's clumsy inspection of one engendered the toppling of a particularly towering heap. Salomons gave a start such as might have been deemed an apoplexy had it but lasted a few moments longer.

'*Gai kukken afen yam*,' he said, once he had calmed himself.

'We are a little far from the sea for that, Mr Salomons,' I replied.

Once again I felt grateful for the education in matters Semitic that my late wife Arabella had afforded me, it being most pleasing to inform the tailor that I would not be accepting his invitation to void my bowels into Neptune's kingdom.

Gesturing at the heaps of tunics, I asked him, 'A strange place to be sewing uniforms for the British Army, is it not, Salomons?'

'A man would not get rich making fine clothes in Northumberland.'

Miss Pardoner was now holding a tunic to her torso and admiring herself in a mirror.

I addressed the tailor, 'Now, you know me, sir. My clothes; are there items ready for use?'

I leaned over the rough table that struggled to bear the weight of his machine. He shrank a little, licked dry lips and croaked, 'One or two, if... if... you would go to the garderobe.' He gestured at a curtained-booth to the rear.

It was cramped. I saw no reason to discomfort myself further by drawing the curtain. I removed Maccabi's boots, trousers and topcoat and let them fall to the floor. Miss Pardoner, more the pity, continued to preen in the mirror. Salomons brought me an armful of clothing. The quality of work was surprisingly good: the nap of the material was exquisite to the touch, and the fit, if not perfect, showed my figure to good advantage, at least judging by Miss Pardoner's sudden loss of interest in the looking-glass.

'These clothes are acceptable, Mr Salomons.' My words brought him up sharp. 'I should like to wear these; would you parcel whatever else is ready?'

He began nodding and hopping from foot to foot, and set about packing the clothing. Presently, he handed me a parcel of easily manageable size – had the chaise been larger. No matter, it would improve the upholstery for our return to Gibbous House.

The hopping did not stop, and I wondered if there were some peculiar quality to the flags of the shop's floor. In the event it was not so: the tailor was merely summoning the courage to ask for payment. I left him my promissory note, which he was foolish enough to accept.

Maccabi's finest apparel still lay on the floor of the booth and I felt a fair exchange was no robbery.

The chaise stood in front of the window containing the infamous 'dirty bottles', proving that Robson was capable of fulfilling a simple instruction. The state of the vehicle itself indicated that the liverymen were not. It was so filthy that it was quite conceivable that the fellow with the low forehead – doubtless some relation of the landlord – had merely driven the chaise to the nearest common land and left it unattended. Still, a polished carriage was hardly required to visit a gaol.

The horse made incremental progress uphill on St Michael's Lane to Green Batt; Miss Pardoner kindly pointed out the location of the Alnwick Scientific and Mechanical Institute, informing me that the professor had been known to lecture there in the past. I turned our carriage up Percy Terrace and we drew to a halt after about a furlong. To our left was a grimly grimy building constructed in the ubiquitous sandstone. It was small, but looked secure.

I looked to Miss Pardoner. She was plucking at her lower lip with a gloved thumb and forefinger, and remained distracted the while I helped her to the ground.

It seemed a building of no great antiquity, despite the grime. A utilitarian cube, it looked exactly what it was: a place of refuse, a gaol in a provincial town. There was little evidence of adherence to the precepts of the late Bentham, a fact that I remarked upon to Miss Pardoner. Her reply was succinct.

'So advanced a thinker's theories are scarcely likely to have been adopted here.'

I reflected that she might have held some affection for his outlandish theories concerning the equality of the sexes.

Chapter Thirty-six

The entrance did, in fact, boast something so sophisticated as a bell pull. It was hardly a surprise to see that for decoration the handle bore a facsimile of a lion. I grunted with the exertion required to operate the mechanism, and Miss Pardoner covered her mouth with a hand.

The summons was not answered with any particular promptness and I was grateful that the weather was clement. The nag seemed quite content to shuffle its hooves and remain contemplative in its traces: I didn't doubt it was far too lazy to walk a yard or two, much less bolt.

In the due course of time the sturdy door swung wide and a lugubrious visage appeared atop a giant of painfully thin figure. Such were his dimensions that his head seemed enormous by comparison. His etiolated complexion was not improved by a cast of features that suggested only the most esurient of characters. He held out a grasping hand.

'Pleased to meet you, Mr Moffat.'

I took his hand, saying, 'You have the advantage of me, sir.'

'Gideon Catchpole, at your service.'

His voice was as sickly sweet as laudanum – and would undoubtedly have been as soporific if suffered at length. He turned to Miss Pardoner and took her hand in both of his.

'Ellen, it is so long since you have come to succour the unfortunates.'

A certain glee surfaced through the laudanum as he uttered the word 'unfortunates', and I thought any guest of Mr Catchpole's establishment might indeed consider themselves unfortunate. I resisted any temptation to ask how the man had guessed my own identity and hoped that it irked him that I did so.

'So, Catchpole, are you gaoler, turnkey or some other functionary here?'

There was no sign of outrage at the insult, save a slight stiffening of his pitiful body, whereupon he said, 'None of these, least of all gaoler, Mr Moffat, since my establishment is not a gaol, but the Alnwick House of Correction.'

It was a petty thing, but neither did I give him opportunity to inform me of his station, and merely enquired whether Miss Pardoner and I might have a tour of the building. He led us inside; it was as dark and damp as a cave and this, perhaps, accounted for Catchpole's invalid colouring.

The accommodations lined the outer wall of the building. Each heavy, iron-bound door was shut and would have opened onto a large stone-flagged area seemingly dedicated to Mr Catchpole's comfort whilst at his post. A comfortable-looking winged chair was too far from the large desk in the centre of the room to encourage much endeavour.

On the other side of the chair a sandstone column rose to the rafters. It was decorated with sundry rings, which in turn were festooned with chains and manacles various. A filthy boy in scarcely less filthy rags cowered at the foot of the column.

The cells seemed unlikely to allow more than the rudest of cots within and numbered some thirty. There was a further door to the exterior in the rear wall between two of these tiny rooms. Catchpole's fiefdom was the Model Asylum writ exceedingly small, and I had to strain hard not to shudder at the sight of it.

'Tea!' he bellowed, but we were hard put to discern the word, for the cacophony that had erupted on the inmates realisation that someone had entered the House of Correction was injurious to the ear. It truly was like a Bedlamite hospice, and far worse than any gaol I had had occasion to visit in the past.

Miss Pardoner and I nodded our assent, since to speak was futile. Catchpole despatched the boy with a kick: he scuttled on all fours to the door at the rear. He left it banging in the breeze, but I was glad of the little light it allowed into the dingy place. Catchpole picked up a large staff bound with iron. It was like a beadle's staff, but appeared less suited to ceremonial than to brutal functioning.

Which theory was short in the proving, as he hammered the head with menace on the first cell door. He himself said nothing, but the sound was greeted with shrieks and shouts of 'The Warden', before a silence less comfortable than the earlier pandemonium descended.

Catchpole spoke, his right hand stroking the staff all the while. 'While we await the tea, Mr Moffat, what is your business here?'

'I require a menial, possibly two, for service at Gibbous House,' I replied.

'How can I provide these? All are here for expiation of crimes,' he sneered.

'Not so, Catchpole, surely you have a trollop or indigent that may be released on my parole?' I looked him keenly in the eye and the hand stopped its movement on the staff.

'But, sir, my stipend is dependent on the number of guests I entertain.'

The soporific voice betrayed just enough avarice to leave me in no doubt as to his meaning.

It was evident what he was; the cringing boy had been proof enough of that, without considering the behaviour of the inmates. I cared not for their fate at this man's hands, but I grabbed his throat, knocking the staff aside.

'Know me, Catchpole, for one who would have you as that boy, on all fours, a cringing, whimpering dog.'

Really, I did require some release of passion soon. I had meant only to terrify the skinny wretch, but still knew it would have given me a great deal of pleasure to encounter him in the dark of night. Of course he followed my argument beautifully, replying, 'Yes, of course, sir, would you like the tour?'

I released him, and he continued to babble. 'Damn that boy! Where is the tea?'

Miss Pardoner drew up beside me, and I felt her hand brush against mine. My manner of persuasion must have affected her, as she was fully flushed. There was more to this woman than I had previously thought, or I was very much mistaken.

Catchpole moved to open the door that he had earlier belaboured with the staff. The cells were as cramped as they appeared from the exterior. This one had no cot, only straw; a figure, apparently female, lay atop it surrounded by a litter of infants of whom the eldest might have been five. Catchpole waved his staff, the children shrieked and the woman shrank into the corner.

'Thief, three penny loaves at the Shrove Tuesday market.'

He slammed the door. The next cubicle contained a male. He seemed catatonic, his hair must have passed the scapulae and he sported a beard of like proportions.

'Horse thief, gypsy, does not speak. Does not move. I check him from time to time.'

'He is newly here, I think,' Miss Pardoner said. 'Less than a trimester.'

'You are correct. I have never seen him eat or drink, although he must, else he'd be dead.' He sounded disappointed.

The next door revealed a young woman of about Miss Pardoner's age. She herself had turned away from the sight. She was chained about the waist and wrists. It was easy to see why; she still bore the marks of the damage she had earlier inflicted upon herself.

'Murderess, awaiting trial. Drowned her own in the Coquet.' He slammed the door with some vigour.

The third door revealed a columnar recess; a woman of about thirty sprang out to the length of her own chain as we all leaped back as one. She screamed a name.

It was the most surprising thing about our visit, not least because there was no one present by the name: 'Jedediah!'

Catchpole employed his staff of office to encourage Jill to return to her box. I raised an eyebrow at Miss Pardoner, who shook her head. I took this to mean we would not yet discuss the coincidence. I tugged at the fellow's sleeve; his shoulders, such as they were, heaved after the exertion of returning his captive to her rightful place.

'Catchpole, I want some harmless trollop and a strong-backed dolt; kindly show me someone suitable. We are not here to marvel at curiosities.'

The boy arrived with the tea. The china looked remarkably good, if ill matched, and the boy carried it in on a silver salver of fine quality. He deposited this on the table, and there being only one chair we remained standing to partake of the infusion. Duty done, the boy dropped to all fours and scuttled to his former post.

'What about him?' I said.

Catchpole spilled the greater portion of his tea. 'Ah, nnnn-nno, ah that is... '

I stepped toward him.

'It's my son!' he shrieked.

'We'll take him too, I think. Shall I ask him?'

But the boy was already at my knee like some hound by its master. Catchpole seemed disinclined to argue. We finished our tea as Catchpole brought out a woman of, it seemed, middle years.

She had been engaged as a pot-woman in the past in several of the town's places of entertainment, and had been incarcerated for supplementing her income by providing additional diversions. It was hardly to be believed, to look at her. Perhaps the depredations of Catchpole's hospitality had not been easily borne. Mary Cotton was her name, and she dipped a clumsy courtesy on pronouncement of it.

The second party to emerge from durance vile was a broad-backed fellow with a high forehead but no sign of intelligence behind it, his eyes dull and flat. It was all he could do to utter his name: 'James Bill'.

I asked him if he were kin to the mute in the Coble Inn, but might as well have asked the sandstone pillar, for he answered only 'James Bill'. I informed Catchpole that the parolees were to be ready at ten of the following morning, at which time a carter would await their persons outside the House of Correction. Miss Pardoner and I made our way out, the dog-boy scampering at my heels.

The boy's animal characteristics did not confine themselves to the canine: he hung from the rear of the carriage like a performing monkey all the way to the Cross Inn. I enjoined Robson the landlord to find somewhere for the chaise and instructed him in the matter of the cart for its human cargo.

He was pleased to offer us rooms for the night, but not so pleased as I to accept them.

We dined in much the same style as on my previous visit to the inn: simply but well. My pleasure was only ruined by a loud and, in time, quite drunken fellow who was making great play of approaching the 'dirty bottles', pretending to touch them but running away at the last minute. It was a childish pursuit and I became so heartsick of the nonsense I repaired to my bed, faithful dog-boy at my heels.

I awoke in sudden fashion. The dog-boy was at the foot of the bed, dreaming of chasing rabbits or perhaps his own father, whimpering and growling emanating from him in equal degree. I did not think that this had awakened me.

There was a knock at the door, tentative and light of touch. I was not displeased to discover Ellen Pardoner as the author of it. Her face was flushed and she was in her nightgown. The moonlight shone through the hall window behind her. I savoured the outline of her limbs and waited.

'Let me in, at once.' I did so willingly. Miss Pardoner sat on the bed and looked at me. I said nothing.

'Lie with me,' she said. 'Tell me of the evil you have done.'

We passed an hour enjoying the comfort of strangers. Her quiet moans were stifled by a bolster and, where necessary, my hand. She left the moment her breathing had steadied and did not look back as I watched the door close behind her.

The dog-boy slept through our most satisfactory encounter, and long after. I, on the other hand, did not enjoy a long return to sleep. I woke with a start, but did not know why. Although my room was above the public bar, there was no sound of carousal or dispute to indicate that Robson was still at his post. I dressed quickly: shirt, trousers, but no boots, and felt in my pocket for an item that might prove useful, if I were lucky.

As I descended the stairs, cat-footed, a noise gradually increased in volume. By the time I had reached the foot of the stairs, it seemed to be the dying breaths of a water buffalo. In fact it was the foolish drunk who had earlier been playing with the cursed bottles. He lay supine, maw agape on one of the longer tables in the room, one of the nearest to the self-same glassware.

I heaved him to his feet using the front of his waistcoat. He seemed barely sensible to his surroundings or to me. I pivoted him away from me using his shoulders and pushed him to the floor. In no time the yellow scarf was around his neck and my knee was in his back. Just before the death-rattle came I dragged him upright and swung him nearer to the bottles, until his flopping arm draped gently over the neat stack.

'It appears to be true, one shouldn't touch those bottles, my friend.'

I made my way back to the room, where I was greeted by a sleepy eye from the dog-boy. The sleep that came, although it may not have been that of the just, was surely that of the sated.

*

The knock at the door awoke us both before the meagre light crept through the dusty window. I had not undressed, but called out that I was as yet in my déshabillé. I told the boy to guard the door. After a suitable time, I opened it. It was Robson, looking a little piqued.

'Sir, thiz summat ah-full happent! Doonstairs.'

'What is it that it may not wait until a man has shaved?' I asked.

'It's turrible, ah-full, a divvent na... ' he spluttered.

Caring not what he did or didn't know, I told him I would shave before descending and slammed the door in his face. The water in the porcelain was clean but very cold; soap and a mug had been provided, but best of all a bone-handled razor. It proved very sharp and I pocketed it once I had made use of it.

I made to leave the room, noted the dog-boy at my feet, took hold of an ear and lifted him so that he might look me in the face.

'Dog-boy, do you think you might walk like a man in public? At Gibbous House you may do as you please, but until then you will walk upright in civilised manner. Do you have a name?'

I would have sworn he intended to bark. Instead, he gave answer in a voice as rusty as an unused hinge: 'Job.'

'Well, Job, pleased to meet you,' I said, offering a hand. His own came up like a terrier's paw, and then took mine more or less like a gentleman.

In the public bar the deceased drunkard was still embracing the infamously cursèd flasks; Miss Pardoner was standing near the entrance; I smiled, but she did not. Nor did she blink, frown or acknowledge our recent intimacy in any way. I was not entirely sure whether I was pleased – or not – at this reaction. Robson was smearing tankards whilst standing behind the bar. Also in attendance was the coroner and a policeman. I wondered that he had not buckled under the undoubtedly heavier burden that Constable Turner's unexplained absence must have placed upon him.

The coroner eyed me nervously. 'Mr Moffat, we meet again. My cousin – ah – enjoyed your visit to his humble place of work.'

Although dissimilar in shape and size, the cousins shared a certain curve of avarice to the mouth and a glint of greed in the eye, and I realised why the warden had known who I was.

'As did I, sir, as did I,' I replied.

'You heard nothing?' he asked.

'I slept like an innocent.' I looked to Job. 'Did you hear anything?'

'No, sir.'

These words came no easier to him.

I was a little puzzled as to why the coroner was asking such anodyne questions, until the policeman offered his only observation on the matter.

'Died o' fright. Bottles. Everyone knows not to touch the bottles.'

The coroner looked at me and shrugged. He leaned over the cadaver, pulled the shirt collar gently away from the neck and immediately replaced it with a great deal more haste. He licked his lips.

'Who was he, Robson?'

'Traveller, ca-yum on the co-acch. Divvent kna his na-yum. Nivver will now.'

The coroner stiffened his spine, tugged at the bottom of his waistcoat and declared: 'An apoplexy caused by extreme fright. Clear as day. Robson, two guineas for the removal and arrangements.'

Robson looked somewhat put out at this, but handed over two gold coins and some silver, withdrawn piecemeal from a pouch strung around a grubby neck. The coroner took the sum with the alacrity I had come to expect from him. Whether corrupt or simply lazy, he seemed disinclined to mention what he had seen on the cadaver's neck. With a curt bow to myself and Miss Pardoner, he left the inn, the police-man trailing behind him.

Robson informed me, somewhat sheepishly, that as the hour was now nine the cart might be late at the House of Correction, since he would be using it to deliver the unfortu-nate fellow to his final destination. I asked him at what time we could expect to leave Catchpole's place of work, intending to set off – together with my new retainers – for Gibbous House from there.

'Haff past, Mistah Moffat. His last trip willunt be a long yin.'

Robson was as good as his somewhat difficult to understand word. We set off northward at precisely half past the
hour by my timepiece. Catchpole had merely bundled the two
parolees out of the door and slammed it behind them without
even the slightest glance at his son.

Neither of the two had aught by way of possessions, save
the clothes on their backs. I instructed Bill to drive the cart
and enquired of the slattern if she knew the whereabouts of
their destination. She replied with a toothless cackle, 'Wuh
aal know Gibbous House, Mr Moffat.'

'Get you there then, as best you can. Do not think to play
the absconder. You would regret it, I assure you.'

Job hanging limpet-like from the rear of our chaise, Miss
Pardoner and I set out at a somewhat faster rate than the cart
– despite our nag's customary lethargy.

We had left the cart far behind us by the time we reached
the Lion Bridge. Thankfully, Miss Pardoner did not share
Maccabi's passion for matters ornithological. I was equally
grateful for the young woman's unusual ability to remain
silent on occasion. Nevertheless, I interrupted my own reverie
on the pleasurable events overnight to ask her, 'Did she mean
Maccabi? The woman in the cell?'

I took my eye off the road ahead, safe enough at the jog-
trot pace of our horse. She looked uncomfortable, something
I had all too seldom succeeded in making her. She licked her
lips and the words came out in somewhat of a rush.

'Yes, I mean no. Well... ' At which point she hung her head.

'Ellen, tell me.' I placed a hand on hers.

308

She was not to be fooled and shook off my comfort as though it were an irritating fly.

'Very well, the woman claimed that Maccabi had... had compromised her.'

I was surprised at her timidity of expression.

'Really? Perhaps, there is more to Jedediah than I thought,' I said.

'Or less,' she said bitterly and she sat in stiff-backed silence for the remaining hours of the journey.

Chapter Thirty-seven

We arrived a little after one, in expectation of lunch. A wait of reasonable duration produced no welcome at the door, despite repeated applications of the monkey's-head knocker. Abandoning the chaise at the entrance, we took the track around to the rear entrance. The door was ajar, and we made our way into the deserted kitchen.

'Ellen, check Mrs Gonderthwaite's quarters.'

I looked around the kitchen, running a finger over the dust on the range. It seemed better not to ponder where the food came from or how it materialised from such an unpromising source. Miss Pardoner returned, two spots of colour in her cheeks.

'She will be here presently. I took the liberty of telling Mr Cullis to attend at the same time, since he was also there.'

I laughed and, after a moment, she permitted herself to do the same.

My anger at being kept waiting by these menials was greatly offset by the anticipation of introducing the new staff to the rest of the household, especially to Maccabi. His continued absence was surprising. That of the professor was not; the fellow seemed always to be in some distant part of the house engaged in some no doubt arcane and bizarre pursuit. Truly, I had doubts about the man's sanity.

Mrs Gonderthwaite floated in, as insubstantial as ever, followed by Cullis with his clumsy gait: a phantasm followed by a troll. I informed them that there would be three new members of the household arriving shortly; Mrs Gonderthwaite and Cullis were to prepare rooms and make any other arrangements for their arrival – after preparing a suitable luncheon. I escorted Miss Pardoner out of the kitchen, preferring not to dwell on the peculiar methods that might be employed in that place.

Job had reverted to his earlier mode of perambulation and followed behind us on all fours. He was suprisingly nimble, indeed he seemed more comfortable so, and evaded any encounters with the piles of furniture in the vestibule.

We chose to await the arrival of luncheon in the library, that being my favourite room. It was not that it was any less outré than the room filled with the taxidermist's phantasmagoria – there was, after all, a riot of clashing styles and many a thousand rare and unlikely books. No, it was that it was the only part of the house that retained a sense of grandeur, that was not overpowered by furnishings or filled with a menacing claustrophobia. Besides, as in most of the reception rooms, there was a plentiful supply of beverages.

It had been in my mind to take Miss Pardoner into my confidence, as I wished to share the problem of the encoded papers. I had long felt a certain nostalgia for the early days with Arabella Coble, and I fancied that my ward was a woman of character – if not necessarily good. Job had scampered to the French windows and was stretched out in the pool of sunlight painting the parquet floor. I bade my ward sit with me at one of the ancient but exquisite tables in the room. A lone candle in a seven-branched candelabrum stood on it.

I withdrew the papers from a pocket in my frock coat, struck a lucifer match on the sole of my boot and lit the candle. Handing Miss Pardoner one of the papers, I held the other over the guttering flame. She raised a solitary eyebrow at me over her blank sheet; I tilted mine toward her and watched her composure falter as she watched the symbols appear. I laid the page on the table, took the other from her and warmed it at the flame. Leaning closer toward her, I said, 'I have it in mind that these are encyphered messages. They came to me in a packet with details of the settlement. They may be from old man Coble, they may not. Perhaps they are from Arabella, perhaps not. Will you help me with them?'

'And how would I do that, Mr Moffat? What do I know of cyphers?' Her smirk was most irritating.

'Come, Ellen, whatever you do or don't know about cyphering, two minds are better than one, are they not?'

'Perhaps,' she said.

Both pages had some five lines of the alien script inscribed upon them. I withdrew the professor's rendition of the Hebrew and Aramaic alphabets from a pocket and placed it beside them. I whispered, without quite knowing why, 'The journalist believed it might be as simple as transliteration and substitution for the Roman letters. It seems likely, for who would expect me to have the Hebrew, much less Aramaic?'

'No one, I'm sure, Mr Moffat.' She gave a laugh. 'So what to do? Substitute A for Aleph, B for Bet and so on?'

'I cannot believe it would be so simple,' I replied. 'But perhaps we should try it – if only for the purpose of elimination.'

'It is not worth the effort,' she said. 'Can you not see that these are not words?'

Springing to her feet she walked over to the exquisite white-wood escritoire. She withdrew some sheets of paper from the secret drawer and I thought I perceived the tiniest of starts when she discovered the packet of opium was missing. Her composure was quite recovered when she returned with the paper.

We began, or should I say Miss Pardoner began, by making a very good fist of copying the symbols from the parchment onto the paper. Wisely, she had chosen to apply herself to the briefer of the two sheets.

She gripped her pen lightly, but her penmanship did not strike me as particularly feminine; her strokes were bold and confident and if the loops on the descenders seemed a little ungenerous, it had a pleasing effect. Stopping suddenly, she sighed. 'Well, that's of no use at all.' She gestured with the pen nib at the last symbol. 'Do you recognise it?'

'I don't know, woman!' Perhaps I was a little sharp.

'It matters not in any case, Mr Moffat.' She jabbed at the letter with the nib once more. 'Look carefully at it.'

It was the symbol from the inn's sign. A symbol I had seen in the books in the asylum. A symbol that appeared in Arabella's diary.

'Is it not familiar, sir?' She looked keenly at me.

'Indeed, I confess I have seen it, but I know nothing of its meaning.'

She whispered clearly to herself alone, 'How can that be?'

I proposed a beverage of some kind, pointing out to my ward that the writers of my acquaintance often turned to the spirits for guidance. She laughed and said, 'The Armagnac,' and it was clear that Miss Pardoner was privy to more of the house's secrets than she cared to admit.

The good Cardinal Dufour having provided once again, I warmed the spirit in the glass and enjoyed the aroma, eying Miss Pardoner over the rim of the glass as I did so.

'The professor, does he strike you as,' I thought for a moment, 'reliable?'

'In what sense? In the manner of an expensive clock?' she asked, mouth twitching.

Clearly she wished to draw me out, and I felt it unwise to declare my true impressions of the man's character.

'He seems a little, if I might phrase it so, excitable.'

'He is a genius, Mr Moffat, one must make allowances.'

She sat back in her chair and took a generous mouthful of the Armagnac.

I attempted to turn my thoughts to the problem at hand,

but in point of fact my head was as empty as those of the twins. Perhaps I slipped into reverie, but it seemed short-lived. I was brought to myself with a start when Miss Pardoner gave the table-top a mighty wallop with the palm of her hand, crying 'Ha!' in the manner of the most dissolute baronet winning at Hazard in Crockford's Club.

'You have it, Ellen?' I asked.

'No, sir. But I will tell you the name of this symbol and the name of the man who created it.'

The name of the glyph was Monas Hieroglyphica, which meant nothing to me. Its inventor was John Dee, which did, as did the symbol itself since I had seen it more than once before.

I remembered the patient then known as Moffat refused me access to but two books during the years that I remained his plaything. Both had been written by John Dee. He often slept with one or other under his bolster. Once I tried to slip the book from under his guarding hand and he swept the back of that hand fiercely against my cheek. My skin was cut by the heavy ring on his finger. How could I have forgotten the signet on that ring? It was John Dee's glyph and, further-more, said ring had not been on the patient's finger the day that I became Moffat.

My face must have betrayed something of my shock to Ellen.

'You see!' Her eyes shone, but I had not the slightest clue as to why. It was patently nonsense, but I decided to humour her; after all, what else had I to do?

'And so you present me with a further puzzle, Ellen,' I said equably.

She was not beaten yet, however, and shewed me two letters at the beginning of each version of the message. The first was א; the second was ב.

'There, you see.' She spoke fiercely, daring me not to see it.

I saw nothing but the Hebrew letters Aelph and Bet and presumed the other the Aramaic versions, which the professor had pronounced Alep and Beth.

'There are no words on this paper. Save perhaps one and that is a word belonging to neither of these languages.'

I confessed that I was none the wiser for this information.

She ran a fingernail under a group of five letters in both languages, and stabbed a forefinger at the Hebrew for emphasis. Her elegant hand had written 'מפפאת'

'Do you see now?'

There seemed no point in dissembling, I knew that Hebrew did not, in general, represent vowel sounds in the script, with the exception of the letter Aleph.

'One might imagine that someone was trying to write Moffat.'

I was not happy with this development; it sat ill with me that my name should appear on the document when the will itself had been so vague about the person who might be the beneficiary, viz 'The husband of Arabella Coble, if such person there be.'

Therefore, in spite of my certainty that the mysterious

message had mentioned me, I sought to cast some doubt on it.

'My dear girl, surely it is naught but a marvellous coincidence! Look at the rest, a random assortment of letters indeed.'

'Perhaps they are not words, but they are not random.'

The door having swung on its hinges, the professor entered. I gathered the greater part of the papers and placed them on my chair beneath the seat of my trousers. Miss Pardoner, meanwhile, had begun writing on one of the remaining blank sheets. Naturally, the professor, having the inquisitive nature of all men of science, peered over my ward's shoulder to ascertain what she had been writing.

'Ach, a poem, *ein Gedichte*. I hope it is suitably romantic and full of love,' he said, giving her a lascivious smile, which made his absinthe-ruined teeth still less attractive.

'Shall I read it, Professor?' The professor's head still loomed over her shoulder as she gave me the most expressive wink.

'Yes, yes, too much of science makes Enoch a dull fellow.' He let out a laugh that might have cracked a looking-glass had there been one to hand.

> *Nor ever so big, as the snout of a pig,*
> *this tiny bud makes home in a fig,*
> *or perhaps a flower, whose petals unfold*
> *with a gamy fragrance, if a fellow is bold.*

She looked innocently up at the professor, and asked, 'Did it please you, Professor?'

His eyes had crossed momentarily and he ran a finger round the inside of his collar. Clearing his throat, he opined, 'An interesting verse, although of uncertain metre.'

He spied our Armagnac and scuttled off in search of a glass.

Mrs Gonderthwaite arrived and announced the arrival of luncheon in the dining room, and all three of us drained our glasses before leaving.

My astonishment was great indeed when I saw the paucity of the fare on the long table. There was a pair of loaves, but sadly no fish: only a large and mouldy cheese of indeterminate type. There were four long-corked bottles on the near end of the table that looked much like porter bottles. Mrs Gonderthwaite had departed the dining room without so much as a backward glance.

Maccabi was in attendance. He caught my eye and gestured toward our feast.

'There are outstanding accounts at most of the suppliers in Seahouses,' he said simply.

'Well, let us settle them,' I suggested.

'We are short of cash,' he replied.

'There must be something,' I protested.

'Ahh... ' But I did not allow him to finish.

'You mean to tell me that the two idiot boys are more solvent than the household?'

Rather than wait for an answer, I seized one of the bottles and confirmed that it was indeed porter. We took our seats and then the four of us made desultory inroads on the meagre fare.

Chapter Thirty-eight

We had eaten, if not our fill, then as much as we could stomach of the victuals on offer when Maccabi let out a sigh. I asked him the cause of this exhalation.

'I am tired, Mr Moffat. Sick and tired,' he answered.

'For why, you have a comfortable position here, have you not?' I enquired.

He laughed. 'It's comfortable enough while there are funds sufficient to eat. But don't imagine I am advantaged in any pecuniary manner, Mr Moffat.'

This, perhaps, accounted for the deeply unfashionable style of his attire, the best of which I had left at Salomon's. I let him alone; there seemed little point in needling him as his funk ensured there would be no satisfactory reaction to it.

I turned my attention to the dwarf, perched on his strange arrangement of box and chair.

'Enoch, you must have been busy at something most important when Ellen and I returned. I had thought you might attend our arrival.'

He squirmed on his high-chair and sniffed loudly. 'Ah,

yes... yes I was busy with the inventory!' This last came out at a rush. He gave a broad smile, as though pleased with his ex tempore invention.

'Really?' I said. 'There is no full inventory of the contents of the house?'

He looked puzzled for a moment then, 'Why, there are the papers of entailment, among those that you were... delinquent in reading at the notary's.' He ran a forefinger along the side of his nose.

'But these are not comprehensive, since you are making an inventory?'

'No,' he replied and stopped short, realising that he had perhaps chosen the wrong untruth to conceal whatever nefarious activity he had been engaged in.

'Splendid, Professor, you have quite made my day, and, indeed, I presume Jedediah's also. We shall waste no time in ascertaining with which goods we might realise an efficacious sum in the shortest of times,' I said.

I rose from my chair. Maccabi did the same, but seemed momentarily torn. We made our courtesies to Miss Pardoner and, as we turned to leave, I remarked that the professor was on the dining-room table, a foot-stamping rage worthy of the flax-spinning dwarf in the tale by the Brothers Grimm.

Of course, liquidating assets was not simply done. I had to recover the notarised papers from my room. The lists of effects were generally arranged under headings of whichever room they might be in, but that was not to say that some item had not been moved. Therefore, however methodical we might have been, there was nothing for it but to check each item we inspected against the list.

There were not a few disappointments arrived at, despite the promise of these pages. A sixteenth-century chest bearing some heraldic devices was listed as being in the professor's chamber, whilst it plainly was not. On discovering it, I found it contained a mountain of male intimate apparel in less-than-pristine condition. Maccabi had high hopes of a pair of Sheraton satinwood chairs, until these items were to be found beneath 'Kettles, large, copper, two' on page sixteen of the kitchen inventory.

At last we came upon an item that was not listed as being in any location in the house: a French commode. The curves were beautiful, and the whole was veneered in a quite delightful Japanese lacquer. Despite my suspicion that its designer might well have been Van Risamburgh, it would only have fetched, at best, a dozen guineas – were we even able to find a buyer.

Far more gratifying was the discovery of a drawerful of sovereigns beneath those containing paper and gimcrack jewellery.

'Not a word, Maccabi.'

'Not a word, Mr Moffat.'

I gestured to him to fill his pockets and began to do likewise. On the arrival of Mrs Gonderthwaite in the atrium, I closed the drawer as seemly as I could manage. She seemed more animated than I had ever seen her, nostrils flaring to

such an extent that they seemed gaping voids quite disproportionate to the rest of her face.

'Mr Moffat,' she enunciated carefully, voice taut as a piano
string, 'there are two' – the hesitation was deliberate, but not
one of deliberation – 'persons in the kitchen. They claim to
be in employment here. Is it really possible that these are the
new servants you mentioned?'

At the last her voice seemed to rise above high-C.

'It is no idle claim, madam. I would have thought you glad
of the help. Put the woman to work and send the man
through to us.'

Although plainly less than overjoyed by the prospect of
these subordinates, her anger did not affect her gait. The
woman merely floated off as she always did, borne aloft this
time on a cloud of disapproval.

It was a matter of more moments than strictly necessary
before the dull-wit James Bill made his appearance. I indicated to the two of them to transport the commode to the
exterior. Even though as many sovereigns again as had made
their way into pockets various remained within, James Bill
lifted it with tremendous ease and a cacophonous rattle of
coins. It fell to me to open the door while Maccabi looked
on, gape-mouthed as a dolt.

'Maccabi, a cart if we have such a thing, something larger
than the chaise if not.'

He went, mouth still lolling, to the rear and through the
kitchen to the outbuildings.

I stood outside with James Bill. There was little prospect

of, or point in, conversation. Thankfully, Maccabi was relatively swift to return, particularly so in light of the conveyance on which he did so.

The cart's two wheels had not the benefit of spokes or iron rims. The wood was rough and unfinished and I doubted not that the bench seat to the front had already inflicted grievous wounds on Maccabi's posterior. The taciturn Bill clearly had more sense than I had given him credit for, since he manhandled, although it were not so strenuous, the commode into the rear of the cart.

'The gatehouse, Maccabi,' I said.

He gave me a quizzical look and I answered it so. 'Indeed, no, I prefer to walk.'

It was a measure of quite how poorly the vehicle was made that I was waiting at the side door of the gatehouse ere Maccabi brought it to a halt in front of me. Again, James Bill set to without prompt and the commode was as quickly on the ground as Maccabi. The door was not locked. I pushed it open and made for the door behind which Heathfield Cadwallader kept his rigid vigil. The key was yet in the lock so I turned it and beckoned the two of them to follow me. It required the two of them to manoeuvre the piece through the narrow door. As it happened, Maccabi was to the fore, and was entering the room with his back to its contents. A question which had been in my mind for some time was answered by the thud as Maccabi fell to the floorboards in a dead faint.

Looking quickly around the room, I noted the same plain furnishings as before; it seemed the room had remained undisturbed since I had stumbled upon Heathfield Cadwallader. I opened the sovereign drawer in the commode, handed one to James Bill and began removing the remainder to the drawers beside the chair in which Cadwallader's effigy had been enthroned.

James Bill continued worrying at the gold coin with his blackish teeth for a few moments before secreting it in a pocket. The commode drawer was empty at last and I turned to look at the inert form of Maccabi. It was clear he would soon run to the jowly dissipation that was oft the fate of large-framed, golden-locked fellows, for with his physiognomy in relaxed state the firm jaw-line hinted at an incipient surrender to gravity. On my giving him a nudge with a toe of my boot, he began at last to stir.

Bolting upright, he seemed fit to swoon once again, on sight of Cadwallader.

'It's... it's... ' he spluttered.

'Indeed it is. For ever preserved in his youthful glory,' I said.

He would never look older. Something in the preservation process had tanned his hide to leather, making it seem like the dried skin of a bat's wing. His head appeared as devoid of life as those of the wax-figures on display in Baker Street.

'Come on, Maccabi, there are matters to attend to at the house,' I said, handing him up and propelling him through the door of Cadwallader's sanctum.

On locking the door behind us, I pocketed the key, where

it gave a satisfying clink against an unknown amount of gold coin.

Maccabi wisely decided to convey to James Bill that it had fallen to him to drive the cart back to wherever it had come from. So Maccabi and I set off on foot in a silence conspiratorial, if not companionable. Nevertheless, he was not long comfortable in it, and soon addressed me more civilly, and indeed less formally, than at any previous time. 'Moffat, what manner of thing was it? It looked like him, but... '

His voice fell away, and it was clear that either the fellow had been completely oblivious to Cadwallader's fate, or he should have been making his fortune at the City of London Theatre in Bishopsgate.

'Well you know what happened, Jedediah. Are there not hundreds of other specimens of this handiwork in the house?'

It was a little cruel, true, to badger him thus, but I simply could not believe that he was unaware that the professor was more than a malevolent midget. He made no reply and the glum look that settled on his features had the same effect as his earlier unconsciousness.

We were met at the door by Miss Pardoner. There was a high colour in her cheeks and her breath came shortly. 'Oh! Jedediah!' she exclaimed. 'The professor would like to see you, in the withdrawing room.'

This was most interesting, because the withdrawing room was the very room I had been unable to find since arriving at the house. Short of climbing through the window from the outside, I could see no way of penetrating its mysteries – and I worried that since I could not find my way into it from the interior, I would no more be able to leave it. Besides, I did not wish to break any more expensive glass panes than absolutely necessary.

'Excellent,' I said. 'I should like to speak with the professor.'

'Oh no, Mr Moffat, he was most explicit, Jedediah.' Miss Pardoner seemed quite agitated.

'May I not go where I will in my own property?'

I did not raise my voice, although I would have been quite justified in doing so.

'Please, Mr Moffat, I must speak with you, alone.' She stamped a foot and, like most coquettish affectations, it did not suit her.

This remark put a quite different complexion on the matter, as did the dark looks that Maccabi darted at myself and the young lady as he turned out of the furniture-crowded atrium into the dining room and beyond.

With her almost customary presumption, Miss Pardoner seized my arm and dragged us both to my left, toward a phalanx of furnishings that obscured any possible entry to the disused – save by the felines – west wing. Slightly to the right of the centre of the wall stood an armoire large enough to house the clothing of a giant. It too had been an object of interest to me when Maccabi and I perused the list of entailment. Lighter in colour than mahogany, it nevertheless boasted that noble wood's fulgent appearance. Each door was adorned with a finely turned handle, one of which Miss Pardoner laid hold of in a savage manner and pulled toward herself with equal ferocity. She entered the gigantic closet, dragging me behind her.

Imagine my disappointment when we immediately exited the rear of this wardrobe in like manner to find ourselves confronted with the door to the west wing. She turned to me. 'Mr Moffat, it is not pleasant, and the odour is unfeasibly strong, but it is the only way... '

'To ensure we are undisturbed and safe in confidentiality?' I laughed and she gave me a look of pity before leading me into the disused part of the house.

I had been low and mean in Cheapside; I had been in the company of pure-finders, sewer-hunters and the mud-larks of the Thames, but never had I suffered an assault on my olfactory organ such as was effected by the crossing of that threshold. Still worse, no sooner had we set foot in the first room – and it was not obvious what the purpose of this room might be – than a hissing and spitting began, as though a herd of cattle were roasting on a hundred broaches.

My understanding of what my ward had to tell me was not helped by her insistence on whispering, although there were none to hear but several hundred cats. What I did glean led me to believe that the cats were not, in fact, listening. I failed to hear a single one of them laugh.

It was about my vellum parchments. The letters alongside my name that Ellen had begun to decipher earlier were symbols from the Kabbala, as understood by a group she referred to as the Order of the Rosy Cross: this much I knew already.

The other sheet was more phantastical still; it referred to an interpretation by John Dee of the meaning of both V.I.T.R.I.O.L.V.M. and *The Chymical Wedding*. The writer intimated that the reanimation of corpses was not only possible but might even have been achieved. Furthermore, the text hinted that a party so resurrected might enjoy remarkable longevity. The name of a certain Comte de St Germain was mentioned in this context. I recalled that he had been a *cause célèbre* in London a century ago. I remembered from Giacomo Casanova's memoirs that he had thought the Comte 'The King of Imposters and Quacks', who had once claimed the ability to melt diamonds. There seemed to be much from this second sheet indeed. I admit I was brought up short by Galvani and his experiments on animal electricity. Later, Mary Shelley's *Frankenstein* was mentioned as though it were not a work of the most unlikely fiction. The resurrection of Osiris and the book of Thoth merited a note in the margin,

'Reassembly of parts? Impossible, there must be another way.'

I began to think that the professor's plans for me might mean more inconvenience than I thought, but since I was not entirely sure of the extent of Miss Pardoner's involvement in the matter I merely said, 'Really, Ellen, I have never heard such nonsense in my life.' The laugh escaped from my lips despite the seriousness of her demeanour.

'What is it that you think he does here, Mr Moffat?'

Quite simply, I had to confess that I had not the slightest idea.

Chapter Thirty-nine

The young woman's eyes were watering quite as much as my own. I had been hoping that we were about to retrace our steps and leave through the Pantagruelian wardrobe. However, Miss Pardoner broached a new subject. 'About the Madwoman,' she said.

'Madwoman?' I asked, surprised by this rare incidence of the butterfly mind. In my experience, many women were surprised that we males were quite unable to read their minds or make similar grand leaps of intuition, when they themselves possessed so great a talent for the association of incongruous ideas. She had hitherto seemed above such things.

'The woman in the House of Correction!' Again that stamp of the foot was unconvincing.

'What about her?'

It was difficult to maintain elocutory standards while attempting not to breathe. Consequently, Miss Pardoner obliged me to repeat myself before replying, 'She worked here, before.' Her eyes glittered in the darkling gloom and, I suspected, not entirely due to the feline stench.'

'Indeed,' I said. 'The usual thing, was it?' I asked.

'Oh yes, quite usual. The professor dealt with it.' A sniff escaped her.

'Well, a satisfactory ending, I would have thought.'

'She went quite mad, began to carry a wax doll, a hideous thing, it looked as though it had been fifty years in an attic. It was a representation of a newborn infant. She took it with her everywhere, heaven knows whence it came, perhaps it formed some part of the Collection.'

She stopped for an understandably short breath. 'She refused to work, began following Jedediah wherever he went, demanding that he acknowledge his child. Eventually, a ruby ring was found amongst her effects in her room. The professor melted the doll down for candles.'

'And you feel sorry for her?' I asked.

'Whatever for? The ring was mine, Mr Moffat.'

At last we escaped the rank atmosphere of the west wing. I believed the best solution would have been a significant number of faggots and some judiciously applied lucifer matches. It was probable that the stench clung to my new clothes and I believed I would not readily forgive my ward for it. We went swiftly to the library; I was in need of drink to clear the smell from my nostrils.

The professor and Maccabi were doubtless still about their business in the withdrawing room.

I turned to Miss Pardoner. 'Some of the professor's green fairy?'

'Yes, even that would taste better,' she retorted.

'Yes, it might, but it would be a damned close thing. I have a better idea.'

I consulted the cardinal's learned work on the Forty Virtues once more and withdrew the dwindling supply of Armagnac from its hiding place.

The professor seemed to be possessed of supra-natural ability to sniff out a spirit almost ere the cork was drawn, since he and Maccabi appeared before the first drop was poured into the glass.

'Marvellous, marvellous, just the thing!' he said, and he hurried with his peculiar gait to furnish his companion and himself with suitable vessels. Resignedly, I charged the extra two glasses and was fortunate to husband the liquid sufficiently well to cover the bottom of my own.

I had remained standing, as much to keep the diminutive professor at a disadvantage as to allow such air as was circulating in the library to dissipate the rank stench of the west wing. As ever, the dwarf affected not to notice, although I noted his chest seemed to inflate to improbable proportions.

'There are additions to our household,' I informed the professor, although surely Maccabi had told him.

Before he could answer, there was the sound of scrambling along the flooring. Clearly Job's canine habits encompassed the full range of traits; his hair was sticking up at the rear like the ruff of an angered setter and the manner of his stretching, whilst still on all fours, suggested he had slept in the sunlit parts of the library for the entire afternoon.

Maccabi looked on aghast as Job came to heel at my side. The professor, however, leaned over the boy and patted his head. Job snarled and growled at him. My admonitory 'Down, boy!' might have been more forceful, but my heart was not in it. Besides, it was possible that the odour of felines was responsible for the dog-boy's tetchiness.

'How shall we pay?' asked the professor.

'That is not your concern, not now,' I replied.

The dwarf moved a hand across his face. I noticed a patch of skin on the back of it, furfuraceous, as though he had spilled some dangerous fluid and had not made sufficient haste to wipe it away.

'And yourself, Professor, what diversions have you enjoyed in my absence?' My eyes were still on the hand, now fiddling with his collar.

'Diversions? My times have been dedicated to the work.' He glanced at Maccabi as he uttered the final word.

'What is it that you do, Professor? Aside from hoard a miscellany of unnecessary proportions?' I asked.

'You would not understand, Mr Moffat,' he replied, his grammar recovered along with his composure.

I did not pursue the matter further. The fellow would have fabricated some nonsense, and I was sure the exercising of his imagination in such a task would have given him a modicum of pleasure at my expense.

'What poor apology for sustenance will appear before us this evening, I wonder?' I asked of no one in particular.

It was improbable that our table would return to its former standard anent its quality before we had settled our accounts.

Maccabi gave a smirk. The professor merely declared, 'There will be meat tonight.'

I could not account for the shudder I gave on hearing this.

The table once again was laid for service à la Russe, in the house style. To whit: there appeared to have been some confusion as to what constituted a knife and what a fork; consequently a random selection of both could be found on either side of the large under-plate. It was safe to presume that Mrs Gonderthwaite's simian offspring had been charged with preparing the table.

Judging by the alacrity with which the professor pounced on the nearest of several bottles of wine, I was not the only member of the household relieved that, temporary state of impecuniosity notwithstanding, the cellar remained full. We took our seats, and the door opened.

The baboon-like boys swaggered in, each bearing an enormous covered salver, which – if it were not plate – we could have melted down for enough coin to settle a year of butcher's bills. Placing the platters haphazardly on the long table, each removed the domed lid of their salver with a flourish. To my left was an enormous roasted haunch, a little long in the bone for beef and, it had to be said, a little stringy looking. To the right was a long and lugubrious face I recognised.

The horse had pulled his last chaise.

The meat was well seasoned and had a flavour somewhere

between beef and venison. The Gallic palate had long been used to the pleasures of the equine at table, the professor was pleased to inform us. He seemed a little disappointed that none had refused to partake of the unusual repast. Evidently the head itself was mere decoration; the salver-bearers, however, having taken a fidgety station standing by the wall, eyed the horse's ignoble head keenly if any diner made move toward it.

'I think it best Maccabi makes course for Seahouses and the settlement of our accounts on the morrow,' I said, 'before we eat our remaining beast.'

'The mare still lives, and the roan, the other seems to be sickening for something,' said Maccabi.

'All the more reason to ensure the matter is resolved tomorrow, Jedediah.' I gave him a look that had the desired effect, for he held his peace.

The fidgeting boys cleared the platters with more diligence than they had delivered them, perhaps wishing to avoid the inevitable taint of dust on their own supper, should they let them fall. They did not return, and it seemed that the rest of the cutlery had been laid out in vain, save for the professor's, as he was in the process of some dental excavation with the aid of a fish knife.

More to interrupt this emetic pursuit than out of any real desire, I said, 'I thought we might all charge our glasses, Professor, and withdraw to the room so appropriately named.'

'Ahh, it is in need of the cleaning!' he spluttered.

'As the rest of the house is not?' I laughed.

Maccabi shifted in his seat. Miss Pardoner looked on with bored disinterest.

'Nevertheless,' he began, but I did not allow him to finish.

'Notwithstanding your objections, I think we shall repair to the withdrawing room, sir.'

I rose abruptly from my chair and moved to help the little man from his contraption a little more forcibly than he would have liked.

There was no evidence of a room between the vivarium and the library on passing from one to the other, despite the possibility of peering through the exterior windows into one such. Even so I was greatly surprised when the professor took hold of the bell pull beside the huge fireplace in the dining room. The stone rolled back and we made to enter the passage. Miss Pardoner's look of disinterest had disappeared to be replaced by one of considerable excitement. The perspiration on her upper lip affected me greatly.

By the time we reached the twin statues of the Golem and the dybbuk, my ward seemed quite beside herself, and was incapable of restraining herself from touching the Golem when we reached it.

The professor had no interest in the Golem this time. He extended a finger and proved the extent of anatomical detail lavished on the carving of the dybbuk. No sooner had he inserted his finger, than a huge slab of the red sandstone slid away to reveal an entrance in the side wall of the passage. The three of us followed the professor into the darkness.

Chapter Forty

The reason for the inky-blackness became obvious when the space it filled was revealed to be sufficient only to encompass the four of us – in what the late Mr Edgar Allan would have undoubtedly termed 'Indian file'. I, being immediately behind Jedermann, felt him fidgeting at around the level of my abdomen; attempting a cuff, I missed by a country mile and struck my hand painfully on something long and rigid.

It must have been a lever of some kind, for it behaved as one and opened a hatch-like affair about four feet in height and two in breadth, about three feet from floor level. This was the entry into the withdrawing room. I boosted the dwarf sufficiently for him to clear the hurdle and enjoyed his acrobatic efforts to land safely on the other side.

My ingress was easily effected, as was that of Maccabi. If we had been looking forward to Miss Pardoner's efforts to preserve her dignity in making her entrance, we were roundly disappointed. The young woman gathered up her skirts and swung a shapely limb into the room. Pivoting gracefully on it, she swung in the other in a quite satisfyingly disgraceful manner.

The professor pushed the hatch door to and revealed to me that we had made our entrance courtesy of Mr Gainsborough. A close inspection of the portrait revealed a faint signature at the bottom right, but it was the high quantity of oil in the paint that convinced me. I wished it had been one of his conversation pieces; it would have most diverting to discuss 'Conversation in a Park' with Miss Pardoner.

There was nothing strange about the room, save the lack of a conventional entrance. The ceiling was high, the walls appeared geometrically sound and in conformity with what I had presumed from exterior observation.

It seemed to be what its name dictated, a pleasant room for the entertainment of guests in an intimate setting after a dinner of formality.

'What is it you do here, Professor?' I asked, looking around for any clue.

'Researches; with books and papers.' He slid a look at Maccabi.

'Would not the library be the perfect location for such endeavours?'

'It is quiet here.' This time his glance fell on the Reynolds alongside our painting of entry.

'Indeed it is, but you have a plethora of papers in your chamber also, surely?'

Miss Pardoner sidled over to the Reynolds and began

fingering the brushwork absently. The professor's nervous gaze became fixed on her hand.

'Ah, I do not keep refreshment in my room. I find I need some... libation to aid my concentration,' he said.

He trotted over to the long sideboard and proved himself in great need of such help. His eyes remained on Miss Pardoner's hand, which was now touching the intricate carving of the Reynolds' gilt frame.

'Look!' she exclaimed. 'What strange designs, they look like the Hebrew letters.' Her eyes were wide, but far from innocent.

'And see here, halfway up, a Star of David; how peculiar! The frame is not symm—'

She had laid her palm on the religious symbol: there was a click and an unmistakably mechanical sound. The start the professor gave was prodigious. I was more than startled that he held on to his glass.

Miss Pardoner evaded the advancing portrait, if not with grace, with success. The professor had covered his face with his hands. I walked around the portrait, where a metal table had extended from the wall. Underneath I saw something that I believed to be a rack and pinion arrangement, like that of the cog railway between Middleton and Leeds. This was not, in fact, the most interesting feature of the table: it appeared to have the benefit of runnels and perforations designed to drain it of who knew what fluids to a container just beneath the table.

The table shone as if polished; there was not a single

blemish upon its surface and I surmised the nature of the liquid that the professor had spilled on his hand.

'An interesting thing,' I said, 'so much effort to hide a table, even one for so special a purpose.'

The professor removed his hands. 'You have no idea what purpose it serves.'

'I know that Rembrandt's Doctor Tulp would have preferred it to his own red deal,' I replied.

This appeared wide of the mark, for I saw the dwarf acquire a neck as his shoulders relaxed at this last.

'Naturally, the coroner had good reason to leave the journalist's relict in my hands; equally naturally, I satisfied my own curiosity. He was quite right to leave the matter to me, since, as you see, I have facilities far superior to his own.' His self-satisfied smile would have provoked Saint Peter to choler.

Maccabi seemed also to be relieved at the turn of the conversation, as though a tiger pit had been avoided by sheer chance. He cleared his throat. 'So, no mystery, Moffat, simply the diligence of the professor. We thought you would prefer not to be troubled by such indelicate matters.'

Quite aside from his impudence in addressing me so, I was displeased that they both considered me such a dupe as to be taken in by this misdirection.

'So, a burial is it? Here at Gibbous House, outwith consecrated ground? Surely not?'

I could not but accompany these words with a half-smile at the two of them, and no more could Ellen Pardoner.

The professor's coughing fit, if simulated, was most

convincing indeed. Unfortunately, I was unable to smite his back mightily, as Miss Pardoner most solicitously attempted to take care of the fraud. I turned to Maccabi and said but one word: 'Drink.'

He was wise enough not to interpret this utterance as an offer and plundered the sideboard for a suitable flask, pouring a simple brandy for the four of us.

Miss Pardoner and the dwarf engaged in a little wrestling as she attempted to ensure his sipping of the spirit and he endeavoured to secure a gentleman's draught of it.

In any event, I grew tired of the midget's theatricals and demanded, 'Jedermann, where is the body?'

The professor broke off his attempts at wresting control of the brandy. Tilting his head upward, he looked me in the eye and asked, 'Does it matter?'

I felt I should be wary in answering this question, so I posed my own.

'How can it not?'

'The important thing is the tenth intellect, or the human soul,' he said.

It was moot whether it were possible to discourage the windbag, but for the sake of provocation I sighed.

'Immortal or otherwise, I cannot believe in it.'

'Avicenna's floating man demonstrates that you are wrong not to do so.'

'How is that?' I asked, hoping the lecture would not be too long. I ran my hand absently along the rack under the metal table. My ward interposed with the answer while the professor continued to find something interesting in his glass.

'Imagine yourself suspended in the air, isolated from all sensation. You are floating. You cannot even feel your own touch on your body. You still think; you are aware of your physical self, are you not?' Her eyes took on a silvered look as though tears might come at the thought of being suspended so.

'How can I know, never having experienced such a thing?' I said.

The professor spat out a single word, 'Sophistry', before yelping loudly as he stubbed his toe on the leg of the metal table.

Miss Pardoner rushed to the dwarf's aid and fussed over him in a disproportionate manner. I was no longer concerned about the whereabouts of the late journalist's mortal remains: there had been something left on the rack after all. A tiny square of some material midway between paper and leather. If I knew not the location of the corpse, I knew what had been done to it.

Inspection of the Gainsborough's frame revealed a tiny carved menorah on the left hand side. I pressed it and made my exit, leaving the three of them behind me. It required only a few moments of blind groping to find a lever at the other end of the extremely short passage. I reflected that the manner of gaining entry to it was more appealing. Once at the statues, on rendering the Golem detumescent, I heard the familiar sound of the heavy stone moving and stepped out of the fireplace into the dining room.

It was pleasurable indeed to be in my own company at last. I thought I might take a turn outside in the hope of clearing my head, for it had been stuffy in the withdrawing room. It was no conscious decision to turn to the left once outside the front door, to walk past the exterior of the east wing until I reached the window offering the view into the withdrawing room.

Despite the short time it had taken to reach its window, the room was empty; the artistic efforts of Messrs Gainsborough and Reynolds were reattached to the wall and there was no trace of spilled fluids on the floor. Perhaps the three of them had repaired to their respective chambers, but I doubted it were so.

There being nothing of interest to see through the window, I decided on prolonging my excursion. It was not quite full dark, but it was well past what I had called the gloaming as a boy. At the end of the wing, I spied light emanating from a library window. The dwarf was asleep, mouth agape, sprawled in a chair, tiny legs dangling a good twelve inches from the floor.

On turning at the end of the wing, hard by the French windows, I was startled by a whimpering and growling. Clearly Job had decided that the library was his domain, for he had remained in it throughout dinner and thereafter, I supposed. I opened the French window, for it was not locked, and hissed, 'Job, for pity's sake, quiet.'

To my great surprise, he stood erect and begged my pardon fulsomely in his still rusty voice.

'Well then,' I said, 'let us rest a while, Job. Like friends.' Job made himself comfortable on the floor; I made my way wearily to my chamber in the hope of a night undisturbed by dreams.

Chapter Forty-one

It was not to be so. My sleep was disturbed by an endless cycle of the interview with the Keeper and the strange visitor that had resulted in Moffat's release, and therefore my emergence from the egg of Bedlam. In the manner of dreams, there seemed to be something about the events that I had failed to grasp. A sense of something happening off stage; a feeling that the dialogue spoken by the actors contained a meaning occult to me. Most unsettling of all was a feeling of familiarity surrounding the tall and vaguely exotic fellow who had accompanied the doctor that day. I could not say if it was his manner, voice or appearance that caused this feeling.

It was with some ill humour that I greeted the company at breakfast the following day. My mood was not improved by the arrival of yet more bread and cheese. Maccabi looked relieved to be despatched to Seahouses to pay the estate's outstanding bills. The professor appeared less delighted by this development.

Miss Pardoner, the professor and I departed the dining

room for the more comfortable surroundings of the library. Job scampered to meet me, and only a very stern look prevented his licking my face. Miss Pardoner covered her mouth, but the movement of her shoulders rendered this stifling nugatory. The professor had busied himself with refreshments, chiefly for his own gratification. He was considerate enough to confine the absinthe to his own glass – I was pleasantly surprised to be presented with a jerez, even though it was in a somewhat inappropriate tumbler. Ellen Pardoner received the same, although with the benefit of stemware.

The young lady and I took seats. The professor remained standing, his back to a shelf of books, his stature measuring off scarcely four rows. It seemed the position of someone about to give a lecture, so I felt the need to avert such a torture by saying the first thing that came into my head.

'Professor Jedermann, I would know something about you, whose destiny seems so bound to that of my own.'

He gave a smile that so far from touched his eyes that they seemed to have turned to glass.

'My life is not so interesting a subject,' he said.

'Begging your pardon,' my ward interjected. 'I am most interested, sir.'

Some life returned to the professor's gaze, but good humour was not what had animated them.

'Very well. What is it that you wish to know?'

'Your secrets,' I said. This time Ellen Pardoner did not attempt to hide her amusement.

The dwarf evinced his usual linguistic discomfiture. One

could only guess which secrets he would choose to conceal, but – would the truth be grammatical, or the lies?

'My family are or was from Transylvania. If I may say so we were of the highest rank. I have wandered far. I wander still, I may wander for ever, or at least to the end of my days. My father was... well, it is of no consequence. My mother died in childbirth. I have no brethren, only my father's legitimate offspring. My young half-brother outgrew me by the time he was ten years old. I did hate this boy and he did hate me. My father did not stint on my education, my tutor was the last of the Medici. I enrolled at the University of Vienna at the age of fifteen. The respect I earned from my mentors brought me also to a position in that institution. Apart from a time studying with Fichte in Berlin and some research conducted in Leyden among the effects of Pieter van Musschenbroek at the university there, I spent my life in Vienna until the year 1820.

'Imagine my feelings when my loving father sent his first letter to me, in December of 1819. Imagine my feelings when he informed me that the little prince was coming to Vienna. He went by the name of the Comte de St Germain, although this was no more his name than Jedermann is mine. I rather think that it was my half-brother's little jest. You may have heard of a certain Comte de St Germain's exploits in London a century ago? No matter.

'At the time I was conducting experiments based on Galvani's theories. You may know of Galvani's nephew? No?'

The professor broke off and lifted a heavy volume from a

nearby shelf. I saw from the spine that it was a copy of The Newgate Calendar for 1803. My pondering of what possible use for such a tome the dwarf might have was cut short, when he began to read.

'He died very easy; and, after hanging the usual time, his body was cut down and conveyed to a house not far distant, where it was subjected to the galvanic process by Professor Aldini, under the inspection of Mr Keate, Mr Carpue and several other professional gentlemen. M. Aldini, who is the nephew of the discoverer of this most interesting science, showed the eminent and superior powers of galvanism to be far beyond any other stimulant in nature. On the first application of the process to the face, the jaws of the deceased criminal began to quiver, and the adjoining muscles were horribly contorted, and one eye was actually opened. In the subsequent part of the process the right hand was raised and clenched, and the legs and thighs were set in motion. Mr Pass, the beadle of the Surgeons' Company, who was officially present during this experiment, was so alarmed that he died of fright soon after his return home.

'Some of the uninformed bystanders thought that the wretched man was on the eve of being restored to life. This, however, was impossible, as several of his friends, who were under the scaffold, had violently pulled his legs in order to put a more speedy termination to his sufferings.

The professor broke off his reading and traced on the leaf with a finger until he found what he next wished to impart.

'The experiment, in fact, was of a better use and tendency. Its object was to show the excitability of the human frame when this animal electricity was duly applied. In cases of drowning or suffocation it promised to be of the utmost use, by reviving the action of the lungs, and thereby rekindling the expiring spark of vitality. In cases of apoplexy, or disorders of the head, it offered also most encouraging prospects for the benefit of mankind.

'My brother attended several less ambitious experiments of my own at my chambers on the grounds of the University.'

He stopped suddenly, and not for the first time I felt some pity for the little man, who was absently – vainly – stretching neck and spine to make himself appear taller.

'There was an argument. Of course. Brothers argue. Amongst humans it has always been so. The old stories are not universal truths, Mr Moffat. I have ever found my sympathies with Cain and Esau.'

He broke off to recharge the glasses.

This time, I received the more suitable of the two glasses. Ellen Pardoner raised her eyebrows at me over the rim of the tumbler. The dwarf assumed his former post before the ranks of books, and stuttered slightly over the first word: 'My work was the cause of the disagreement. I had been in communication for a number of years with several learned men, concerning consciousness, the soul, the self. I believed that there really must be some Vital Spark, which was the motive for life and being. I had received letters from Aldini himself, although he believed me too literal in my appreciation of his uncle's experiments and his own. Whilst studying briefly with Fichte in Berlin, I had met a man who introduced me to the Rosicrucian texts.

'I asked my brother for a loan to continue with my experiments. I did not mention the mystical aspects of my work. In any event, he did not understand even the simplest of Galvani's experiments. He was a Philistine in the temple of science, and I threw him out of my rooms at the university. I have not laid eyes on him to this day. To stay in Vienna became unsupportable for me. I wandered. Perhaps I was always fated to do so.

'In 183_, I received a letter in Szczecin: a packet that had followed me for some years, from palace to slum, university to hospital. It was an offer of employment, signed by Septimus Coble. It was a matter of several months to reach this place. Coble was already frail, though he survived much more than a decade after my arrival. Perhaps the young woman in his care preserved his vitality.'

I had not perused my former wife's journal in its entirety, but I could remember no reference to the professor in the earlier pages. The professor slipped into silence at this point and I, for one, was most grateful for it.

My ward had developed some strange agitation about her

eye, and a few moments later a most alarming jerk of the head. The stamp of her foot alerted me that the young woman was attempting to apprise me of her wish that I accompany her out of the library. The dwarf, by the book-shelf, was twirling a watch in his fingers, for all the world as though he needed this link to the temporal plane. In short, he was as oblivious as to her intentions as all men are to the musica universalis.

Miss Pardoner took my hand and led me to the fireplace in the dining room, whence we made our way to the hid-den room. I looked her square in the eye as I operated the mechanism hidden in the dybbuk's intimate parts and fol-lowed indecently close behind her as she entered the short dark passage.

Chapter Forty-two

Feigning ignorance of the exact location of the lever to open the entrance, I reached around Miss Pardoner and enjoyed the proximity of the confined space. There was, in fact, nowhere for her to find relief from my presence, but I was encouraged that she appeared not to try. Placing my hand on the lever, I jerked it forcefully and Miss Pardoner gave a little cry – although I was sure the handle had not touched her person. The painting swung away from us and I enjoyed the moment of assisting Miss Pardoner's entry into the room from behind. She did, it must be admitted, look a little flushed as I landed softly on the polished boards.

'Well?' I asked.

'We are here so that we might not be observed.' Her eyes slid to the window.

'An excellent situation, Ellen,' I replied.

To my great surprise she stepped backward. I made as if to catch her by a slim wrist, but she evaded me easily.

'Mr Moffat, we are here because I have confidences for your ears.'

'Words of love – or passion?'

'Are you so shallow that you do not comprehend the danger you are in, sir?'

There was heat in her words; it pained me to realise that it came from anger.

'I think, Miss Pardoner, I am more than a match for a dwarf who is halfway to Bedlam and that handsome dolt Maccabi. Besides, what is your concern for me?'

'You do not concern me in the slightest, Mr Moffat. My purpose here is quite specific.'

'Then why take me into your confidence?' I lifted an eyebrow, at which the young woman heaved a sigh.

'Because you, sir, are part of his plans and there is none other here in whom to confide, more's the pity.'

'Plans? Crackpot schemes, more like,' I scoffed.

She was not amused. 'I do believe you are so dull as not to have guessed what the professor's plans for you are.'

Suddenly she turned to a rosewood table on the far side of the Reynolds. A handsome, though dilapidated, damask-bound volume lay atop it. From the distance of several feet, one could see that the pages of the book were well-thumbed. To my astonishment she seized the tome and threw it toward my chest. I was so shocked I made quite a poor fist of catching it.

'I assume you have not read this, Mr Moffat. You must indeed be a trifle dull if you do not see its significance after having done so.'

I turned to the flyleaf and read the handwritten note: 'To

Enoch from John William Polidori, Mary's wonderful book. Let the truth ever be stranger than fiction!' The title page shewed me the name of a work I recognised – a succès de belles lettres from perhaps four decades previously. I read the opening lines. 'It was on a dreary November night that I first beheld my man completed... '

I tossed the book onto the nearby sofa. 'Truly, does the professor think such a thing can be achieved? Is he quite insane?'

For answer Miss Pardoner pressed the Star of David carved on the Reynolds' frame; the strange table emerged clicking and whirring into the room. It was not empty. Judging by the dimensions of the thing, the remains of the policeman were lying on it. It was hard to tell, since most recognisable features had disappeared with the skin.

There was no doubt of it, even so. What the late disciple of detection would have termed a 'clue' to his own identity stood four-square atop the skinned flesh: to whit, the policeman's top hat. I removed it gently from the abomination on the table.

A leaf from a notebook fluttered onto the raw meat. I lifted it, a corner between thumb and forefinger, and read the policeman's last notes:

Heathfield Cadwallader – knew too much? Professor – mad? Evil?

It was hardly illuminating and I reflected that the science of detection had done him little good in the end.

Miss Pardoner appeared little disturbed by the sight of the charnel house relict, staring composedly into the distance somewhere over my shoulder.

'Forgive this dull student, Ellen,' I began. 'Would you be so kind as to explain the necessity for fear on my part?'

'Oh, you are a most exasperating man,' she spat.

'Indeed? So much more entertaining, I find,' I replied.

'Let me ask you something, Mr Moffat,' she went on. 'Do you think that you alone in the house are not what you seem?'

In that moment, her face seemed to offer some indication of a strain whose cause I could not fathom and I thought perhaps that, at the very least, she had been less than precise in the matter of her age.

'And what are you, if not my ward? Abandoned and unwanted daughter of impoverished clergy? Bluestocking acolyte? What?'

My voice may have been a little above the conversational, as her eyes widened at this last.

'I have seen you mark my appearance, sir. No doubt you have seen that I am no pale English lily. What am I? What should I be in this house of David?'

It ocurred to me that the Sephardi had been expelled from Spain in great number and that her forefathers might have been among their number.

'There is change in the world, sir.' Her eyes glittered and there was something of the fanatic evident in the excessively toothy expression occasioned by her drawn-back lips.

'We stand with permanence on the threshold of discovery.

Each day brings new knowledge and science into our lives. There are those who will stop at nothing to advance their own knowledge.'

She moved to the frame and pressed the Star of David once more, returning Constable Turner to his hiding place behind the Reynolds.

'Why, pray, does this require the skinning of a policeman and a reporter?'

'He mounts his failures as trophies by means of the taxidermical art,' she said simply.

'Failures?'

'Having murdered the unlucky, he attempts reanimation by the power of electricity.' She looked to the floor. 'You will be next, you are wanted for a particular reason. That must be the meaning of the coded messages to you.'

'What reason?'

'That I do not know,' she replied, still gazing at the floorboards.

'And for God's sake, how have you not stopped the lunatic already?'

I was, I confess, quite belligerent, though I gave not a fig for the victims.

'We must be prepared for the unlikely eventuality of his success,' she replied.

Chapter Forty-three

Clearly the dwarf was not the only person on the premises with a tenuous foothold in the real world. I stepped forward and grasped the woman's chin. The spark in her eyes had most definitely not been struck on the flint of passion. No matter, I spoke calmly. 'Do you mean to tell me that Alasdair Moffat is here at the whim of some scheme dreamt up by a Mittel European madman and his equally deranged acolytes?'

'They will call us the heroes of science,' came the unsatisfactory answer.

I released her chin. 'Well, Miss Pardoner, though clearly that is not your name, I am surprised that you expect me to go calmly to my fate.'

She inhaled deeply through her nostrils and let out a long sigh.

'I do not, sir. My belief is as yours – that the professor is a deeply misguided man.'

My eyebrows must have looked most peculiar at this point, as I raised them to an exceptional degree.

'Perhaps disturbed?' she offered. 'In any event, I believe he has no hope of success. I am more interested in you than your part in the Professor's schemes.'

Sadly, this development could not be further explored, as the Gainsborough swung open and the professor's head and shoulders appeared over the lip. He gave no evidence that he had heard any part of the conversation, merely requesting that I give him a hand to make entry to the room. Seizing him by his jacket was perhaps not what the dwarf had in mind, but he contented himself with straightening his jacket in a most dignified manner.

A look passed between him and the woman; whether it meant I was in more danger or less, I could not tell.

'One might think you were a man of science yourself , Mr Moffat,' he said. 'But for your singular lack of curiosity.'

Enoch Jedermann gave a leer at the purported Miss Pardoner, though I could not begin to guess the reason for it.

This particular room still made me feel uncomfortable. The impossibility of its existence, coupled by the incontrovertible proof offered by the view through the window from outside, not to say our presence in it, brought me close to nausea.

'By the by, Professor, how is it done? This room, how do we pass from the vivarium room to the library without going through it?'

The little man laughed until he passed into a coughing fit. On recovering himself he said, 'It is all done with mirrors.'

A strange thing to say, as I had yet to remark on the

presence of any in the house, save for on the ceiling of the midget's own chamber and in the *trompe l'oeil* painting through which his chamber and others were reached.

Miss Pardoner, Jedermann and I had passed the hours until lunch in the library. Conversation between the two former had been animated and, to my distracted ear, brittle. Perhaps, as I was, Ellen Pardoner was unsure at to what the professor had heard of our conversation. In any event I took no part in theirs, preferring to ponder the phantastical plot into which I had seemingly fallen. There seemed no possible reason for me to have attracted the attention of either the late Coble or the professor. Although my own origins were lost behind Moffat's, they did not include anything remarkable enough to attract the attention of those interested in the extremes of scientific endeavour. I felt my only connection to Gibbous House was that which my association with Arabella Coble had afforded me.

In the random manner of the house, luncheon was served at a quarter before two, which time heretofore had not seen any prandial activity. Maccabi had returned from restoring the good name of the household among the commercials in Seahouses. Sadly, he had not thought to return with any supplies, preferring instead to arrange delivery at some unspecified time.

The professor prefaced the entry of the two naturals by informing us that we were to be treated to one of his favourite dishes from the English cuisine.

'And furthermore,' he went on, 'it will serve as a tribute to the late Mr Allan, who informed me that he liked it also.'

This proved to be jugged hare delivered by the two off-spring of Mrs Gonderthwaite in their acrobatic style. I enquired of the professor as to its suitability for observant Jews, with regard to dietary laws.

'There are no blunt knives in this house. I drained the blood myself; for the thickening, you understand,' was his reply.

'Is it really your favourite dish?' I asked, although I was unconvinced concerning this gruesome-sounding activity.

It was impossible to think of the dwarf's careful preparation of the beast without an image of the late constable intruding. Miss Pardoner, I noted, ate nothing but a few potatoes perched on the side of her platter, far distant from the tiny portion of the dish she had allotted herself. Maccabi picked at his food, but I could not swear I saw him actually swallow anything.

I grew impatient, wanting the meal to end and the chance to quiz Miss Pardoner further concerning the professor's plans. Bearding the man himself seemed a foolhardy idea, although I was tempted. Finally, Jedermann cleared his plate, dismounted his high-chair and announced his departure on 'Collection business'. He was through the door before I could challenge him, but clearly this was merely a euphemism for the experiments connected with his madman's plot.

Maccabi excused himself, thank goodness, citing the need to check on the welfare of the horse he had used on his excursion, since it had done more work in the last week than in many a year.

I turned to the woman calling herself Ellen Pardoner. 'So? Might I know your real name?'

'Ellen will do,' was the reply.

'Tell me, Ellen, what is my involvement in this plotting? How did it come about?'

She seemed unimpressed by my seductive tones. 'I will show you tonight,' she said. 'Wait for my knock at your chamber door. The professor will leave his room at about two. We will follow ten minutes behind.'

'But surely he might be anywhere in this sprawl of a building by that time.'

'Ellen', choosing to ignore the peevish tone, retorted, 'I know where he will be.'

I should have liked to spend the rest of the day in the idleness beloved of the rich and borne uneasily by those less fortunate. Instead I brooded and paced like the hero of some novel by one of the brothers Bell. In my impatience to learn more I forwent dinner, sending word via Job that I was indisposed. It was my hope that this would encourage an earlier withdrawing from the dining room and that I could make my rendezvous with Miss Pardoner all the sooner.

Chapter Forty-four

The professor's progress announced itself in the staccato tapping of his boots as he passed my own door; it was only a moment or so after the hour of two, just as Ellen had predicted. She was still more accurate in her forecast of her own appearance, since the scratching on my door began precisely ten minutes later.

She held a finger to her lips, and pointed down the passage toward the hidden entrance. Opening the door with extreme delicacy, she peered onto the gallery and beckoned me forth. Once the door was shut behind us, she whispered, 'No more than a whisper until we reach the other side.'

'The other—' I began, but she cut me off with a savage motion of a flat hand.

It seemed expedient to follow her meekly downstairs.

In the cluttered atrium, she withdrew two 'kerchiefs from somewhere about her person. She held one to her nose and offered me the other. The cloth was redolent with a most astringent smell. I sneezed.

'Wha-what is it?'

'Camphor. It is better than the cats,' she said.

I led the way to the large armoire and occasioned our entry through its rear to the west wing.

'You may speak normally now,' she said.

I refrained from remarking that it was hardly possible with the 'kerchiefs clamped to our faces, and asked, 'Why does he come here?'

'You will see, and perhaps hear, too.'

The camphor did little to help the streaming of our eyes, and so there was some doubt about the former.

The tenebrous gloom offered only vague shapes against an indistinct background. It was impossible to gauge the dimensions of the room we were in. The noise of the felines ensured that we could safely bellow Methodist hymns without fear of discovery. Ellen stepped confidently into the darkness, and I followed closely, pulling her towards me. She half returned my embrace before hissing, 'Have a care, Moffat. We do not have much time.' She softened her voice, adding, 'Though we may well – later.'

We reached a wall after some paces that I wished I had had the presence of mind to count. Every step was marked by the rub of one or another cat against my legs. Miss Pardoner's sharp look indicated that I had been unsuccessful in stifling an unmanly scream when one particularly large specimen alighted on my left shoulder. Ellen seized the beast's tail and threw it, squalling, to our rear.

She felt along the wall until, presumably, she found the handle of a door. We passed through it into a room illuminated by a single candlestick. It seemed as though a thousand diamonds lay on a seething carpet of cats, as the single flame was reflected in every eye.

Miss Pardoner began to wade through the living sea, which parted somewhat less willingly than the Sea of Reeds had parted for Moses. Once again I fastened myself close behind her, but this time she offered no rebuke, and I was most grateful for it. In the slightly better light I calculated that the room was of a size of the dining room in the opposite wing. But I quickly realised that since nothing at all was symmetrical about the whole edifice, this observation would be of no use in determining my present location.

At the end of the room stood the candlestick, propped on a small table. Beside it, cats stood upon other cats' shoulders like some feline circus act, obscuring the doorway. Miss Pardoner seized the candlestick and waved it at the pyramid of cats and they dispersed, hissing.

Through the door the first thing I noticed was the absence of any cats at all. The second was the presence of hundreds upon hundreds of mirrors of every shape and size, covering every surface and standing in rows, facing each other like those in the Palace of Versailles.

It would have been foolish to hazard a guess at the number of candles illuminating this huge room; it might only have been a single taper, since the mirrors were not so precisely regimented as I had originally thought. Whatever the number of flickering lights, there were enough reflected images to drive a man mad if he looked too long into any one of them.

From the corner of my eye, I caught sight of a rapid movement. Miss Pardoner gave me a disparaging look as I let out a gasp, and pointed a long finger toward her own image in the nearest glass to my left. This finger she then put to her lips, whilst cupping a hand to her ear.

There was a rise and fall of an indistinct voice. On occasion a word was recognisable, if the voice reached the volume of a shout. We stood still; the woman raised her eyebrows at me when the name 'Moffat' became audible, followed by the noise of expectoration. She put her mouth to my ear and whispered, 'We will walk this aisle, mark you well the mirrors. Look at your image.'

She strode off and demonstrated by her confident gait yet another unladylike – and exciting – quality. After a few seconds spent admiring her long limbs' motion beneath her skirts, I did as I was bid.

At first I noted nothing untoward. Suddenly one mirror seemed strange. I stopped, unable to fathom what disturbed me about the image. I caught the reflection of my own eye; it had a reddish tint in the white, like a gin-soaked drunkard's or a minor demon's. This particular mirror had been silvered with some strange substance that gave the reflected image a crimson hue. The effect was quite pleasing withal. Nevertheless, I paid close attention to the reflections, as the woman had instructed me. At first, it seemed it was all a matter of colour; in one such I appeared the very model of an Ancient Briton in modern dress, so woad-like was the colour of my skin.

The ranting voice had become a little louder in the interim, such that it was now possible to discern German, Magyar and the occasional Latin tag.

Miss Pardoner had stopped at an intersection of mirror rows, her arms folded. It wanted only the tapping of a foot to render the picture more ridiculous, to my mind. She jerked her head to indicate that we should turn left. As we did so her fingers pointed at the mirrors, reminding me to pay attention to them.

Shade and colour played no part in these mirrors' peculiarities. The first to my right had some fault in the glass itself and appeared to throw a second silhouette in my reflection, as though an imperfect copy of myself stood slightly behind me and a half-step to one side. Doubtless the professor could have explained this apparent implausibility according to some sophisticated corruption of Descartes' Law. I found it merely peculiar. He could not have explained the appearance of three simulacra of myself in the smooth and faultless surface of the next looking glass. There seemed no reason for this triplication of my image, but move we all four did, in harmony of motion, as though in some stately dance.

Miss Pardoner gave her own gasp at this moment. I turned to look at her reflection on the other flank. The image was unmistakably hers. However, the pleasing if unorthodox arrangement of her features and figure had been subtly distorted as to make of her as hideously ugly a creature as had ever been seen outwith establishments of low entertainment. My own reflection appeared perfectly usual alongside this harpy.

There were but few mirrors remaining to the end of this particular aisle, and though I did not peer too closely at the reflections, any glimpse of a reflected image was sufficient to provoke a certain nausea. Miss Pardoner stopped squarely in front of the last mirror on the right, obscuring any view of a reflection. Once more her dumb show enjoined me to remain silent and listen.

The ranting, bellowing madman was revealed to be the professor, though his words were barely comprehensible. There seemed a little more English in the content than before. Of a sudden, the woman stepped away from the mirror. Once again my composure was not what it might have been.

It seemed I had been transformed into a homuncular version of myself, great of chest and uncommon short of leg. Some further peculiarity of the glass had rendered my teeth as hideous as those of the professor.

Miss Pardoner spoke without deference to volume. 'Do you see?'

'What? Another distorting mirror?'

'Have you been listening at all?' She started forward and I felt she but barely refrained from an assault on my person.

'To the rantings of an imbecile dwarf? Or is he perhaps quite drunk?'

The dwarf's voice shrieked 'Rudolf!' And something that might have been either imprecation or curse, but was, to my ear, Latin.

'He is arguing, you dolt!'

'With himself?' In light of her disregard for any necessity for silence, I laughed.

The tirade in the next aisle went on. Miss Pardoner took my hand and led us to the end of the next aisle. The dwarf was no more than two or three mirrors down, standing fully erect before one of them, oblivious to all but the reflection. We passed the end of the aisle and positioned ourselves that we might see the dwarf and his reflection.

The mirror's properties were the antithesis of those that had ensured my display as a dwarf, for there was a tall and handsome fellow reflected in the mirror before the professor. Yet another trick ensured that any movement was not faithfully reflected in the looking-glass. The little man's voice rose and rose; spittle covered the larger version of himself from the sternum to the groin. He looked up at the fellow in the glass and bellowed 'Rudolf!' before falling in a dead faint.

'Now do you see?'

'Should we revive him?' I asked, looking down at the crumpled form on the floor.

'He will be quite comfortable for an hour or two,' Miss Pardoner replied.

'Are you quite sure?'

The professor confirmed his continuing rude health by letting out – at one and the same time – a stertor worthy of a consumptive elephant and an expulsion of flatus that might have done for the trumpeting of the same species.

We began making our way out of the maze of mirrors. My companion's brow was quite furrowed – in concentration, I supposed. I busied myself in admiration of the sway of her skirts.

At the door to the cat-carpeted room, she turned, addressing me in the manner of a governess displeased with her pupil.

'Well, do you see your part in this?' She seemed on the brink of rage.

'A small man arguing with himself in the mirror?' I almost laughed.

She kicked out at the nearest of the mirrors. It fell backward and the glass crazed but remained in the frame.

'But you heard him, you heard him address the mirror as Rudolf?'

A shrug seemed the most expedient course.

'Rudolf Jedermann, his brother?' she insisted.

'Was it so? The man was ranting, I thought.'

'You saw the distortion in the mirror, did you not?'

'Of course.' I put a hand on her arm. She shook it off.

'I know his brother.' She coloured somewhat at this revelation. She went on. 'He comes down here to rail at his brother.'

'What nonsense, Ellen.' I moved sharply back, fearing she might prefer to kick me rather than risk more bad luck. 'His brother is in Vienna, he told me so himself.'

'You fool! The professor is drunk and he knows well that it is his own reflection – but I tell you it looks like his brother.'

It did indeed; the exact image of his brother, the man who had engineered my release into society as Alasdair Moffat. The man who had visited me in the asylum in the presence of the Medical Superintendent. That very man, so much on my mind of late, also bore an uncommon resemblance to some-one else in this room, although in a way that emphasised an entirely different set of features. Still, there could be no mis-taking Ellen for anything but the elder man's daughter. I wondered which of them knew – and resolved to keep my counsel regarding my own knowledge of it.

The young woman turned away and opened the door to the kingdom of the cats. We made our way back to our respective chambers without recourse to conversation. I lay abed but did not sleep with any conviction, noting the pass-ing of periods of stupor by the occasional leap of the moon across the sky.

Chapter Forty-five

Eleven in the morning of the following day found me in the grounds, behind the crumbling stables and other ramshackle buildings. The need for a constitutional perambulation had been occasioned by a breakfast of a bonier relation of the kipper and the kidneys of some large, but not necessarily domesticated, animal. Less felicitously, this hour found me also in the company of Jedediah Maccabi.

The quality of the fellow's conversation had been painfully brought home to me in the past by his fascination with the avian phenomena peculiar to Northumbria. At this particular time, however, he was boring me with the history of the Border Reivers and his own belief that one Robert Moffat had been murdered by the ancestors of the current Earl of Annandale, John Hope Johnstone, whose father had been the Honourable Member of Parliament for Dumfriesshire. On his asking me if I were in any way at all related to the last leader of Clan Moffat, I scarce managed to refrain from smiting him about the ear and bade him accompany me in silence until we made some distance from any outbuilding.

This part of the estate was as yet unknown to me. It seemed scarcely worthy of exploration – before us stood wooded lands as impenetrable as the dark forests of Bavaria. The feeling of claustrophobia that the routine and environment of Gibbous House had engendered in me did not deter me from proposing that Maccabi and I venture into that sylvan mass. He followed without great protest. Pigeons filled the gloom with their sinister two-note symphony; I caught the toe of my boot on a hidden root three or four times in as many yards. Maccabi followed with the sure-footedness of the countryman. It had been an impulse to enter the wood, one I regretted as yet another root bowled me headlong into a patch of thistles. Maccabi helped me up silently. He took the lead; I followed.

His choice of path was more felicitous than mine and both of us remained upright until he led me into a clearing lit by the late spring sun. The glade was filled with wild flowers, the colours as beautiful as a painting.

'Wait,' said Maccabi, and he held up a hand.

'Why?' I asked.

From the dark spaces between the oaks on the other side of the glade, a swarm of butterflies entered; they hovered over a large patch of what appeared to be lilies, though it was early in the year for such blooms. I decided to risk Maccabi's enthusiasm for natural history.

'Are they lilies?'

'I believe they are, Mr Moffat, though they should not be.'

'What are you talking about, man?' I felt heat rise in my face.

'Do you know what they symbolise?' he asked.

'I doubt I care.' My eye was caught by the butterfly swarm, suddenly joined by yet another horde, all the colours swirling, darting.

'You should,' he said. 'Some say they represent resurrection.'

By this time there must have been several hundred butterflies. For the briefest instant every one stopped the beating of its wings. The swarm assumed a columnar shape and I imagined I saw the outline of a man within it. Just as suddenly the shape dissolved and the butterflies flew away. The petals of the lilies appeared to have wilted and fallen under the weight of the insect swarm.

'Others say that the lily represents death,' said Maccabi.

To the left of the depleted flowers were two gnarled stumps, the smooth tops showing that the trees themselves had been felled long ago. I sat on one and motioned to Maccabi to sit. It was quite surprising that the man was not married, he cut so handsome a figure. He had no need to acknowledge his origins and could quite easily have swept any daughter of the new nobility off her feet and into an unsuitable marriage. I could not imagine why he had not. He seemed quite preoccupied and I took great pleasure in interrupting his reverie.

'Jedediah, are you the professor's man? Or were you Coble's?'

He looked at me closely, as if to find some subterfuge writ large upon my face.

'I am, sir, my own man,' came his cool reply.

'I think, Jedediah, that you are my man. If not . . .' I stopped, putting a hand on his knee.

He shifted uncomfortably, my hand slid from his breeches. He cleared his throat.

'That is not among my sins, Mr Moffat,' he said.

'I am pleased to hear that there are others, Jedediah. But I will know, nonetheless, are you my man now?'

He bit his lip. 'I am not your lackey. The professor is nothing to me, however.'

'I'm glad to hear it.' I clapped him in manly fashion on the back. 'But you are a Jew?'

He jerked, as I had tight hold of the hair at the back of his neck. He squeezed the words through the pain as I twisted my grip. 'Not by birthright. I have my mother's colour. My position is... complicated.'

This last emerged accompanied by the gasp he gave as I released his blond locks.

'Birthright? There is so much importance attached to such an insignificant matter. Esau was right, don't you agree, Jedediah, it has no more value than lentil soup?'

He did not answer, indulging in a twice-vain effort at a smoothing of his hair.

'In the spirit of our new-found understanding, tell me, Jedediah mine, what plots am I caught up in?'

The look of incredulity he gave me enraged me sufficiently to seize his hair once again and demonstrate that he was indeed mine.

*

Afterward, when he had finished vomiting, he explained my situation. The professor, he said, intended to murder me and reanimate my corpse by means of a huge electrical charge that would be generated with the help of the vast furnaces below ground. It was of some satisfaction to me that Miss Pardoner had been sincere with me. Maccabi further claimed that Cadwallader, the reporter, the policeman and countless others had been nothing more than preliminary experiments, proofs that what the professor intended was possible. I remarked that thus far such proofs had self-evidently been elusive. I could have smitten him mightily when he said, 'Perhaps not.'

The taxidermy was surely, as the professor himself had earlier said, no more than a hobby, his very own *violon d'Ingres*. Maccabi did mention the professor's concern that his brother Rudolf would arrive to ruin his schemes. He concluded his account by informing me that I could expect my own resurrection within a very few days. I confess I felt a little nauseous myself at that point.

As we made our way back through the dense woodland, I braced Maccabi once again. 'So, how do you come to be here, Jedediah?'

'In the same way as so much of what you have seen here.' He did not amplify further, until I lifted my hand.

'I was collected by Septimus Coble,' he said bitterly, and he gave me a look that informed me that no kind of physical assault would draw more from him. Nonetheless, his earlier claim to be his own man was clearly bravado of the most empty kind.

At the least, Maccabi had confirmed the half of what the putative Miss Pardoner had intimated. It exercised my mind greatly that I could see no way to turn this situation to my advantage, short of disposing of the entire household and making off with such portable effects as would raise the most capital in London.

Chapter Forty-six

On arrival at the library, the sight of the professor deep in conversation with Miss Pardoner, at altogether too close quarters, greeted us. She took a step backward from the gnome on noting our arrival. It seemed to me that Miss Pardoner had been instructed by someone or other to maintain some control over the professor. I wondered if it might be the senior Jedermann – and to what lengths he expected the woman to go. Perhaps she stopped short of inappropriate relations, but the dwarf held his hands over his lower abdomen as he turned to greet us.

'Mr Moffat, good day once again!'

The man was as transparent as polished glass. He moved a hand to wipe some drool from the side of his mouth and my stomach heaved as I saw why he had used both hands to obscure any view of his trouser front.

I returned his greeting.

'Are you quite well, Mr Moffat?' the strumpet asked, smirking.

'Indeed, I am. The better for seeing yourself.'

I was grateful that my own tailoring was more generous than that of the professor for, despite my recent use of Maccabi, Miss Pardoner had provoked a familiar reaction with her impudence.

Clapping my hands, I instructed Maccabi to serve us with libations ad libitem. It was pleasing to note he did not demur, although Miss Pardoner gave him a strange look. I wondered if she was surprised or disappointed. Jedediah served my own jerez last and I hoped for his own sake he meant no insult by it. In any event, as I was the host that was as it should be. He returned to the long board and served himself a port, which he drained at a draught before recharging the glass.

'Professor,' I began, 'are all of your family as travelled as yourself?'

'Some wander, some do not.' His syntax had returned with his composure.

'I wondered, perhaps, is it quite impossible that I might, at some distant time, have encountered a sibling of yours? Travelling, as some might put it, incognito?'

Miss Pardoner gave a slow wink.

'I doubt it, Mr Moffat. I doubt it very much.'

Which statement, in its linguistic perfection, indicated that he was telling the truth, or was at least entirely comfortable in the lie.

However, Miss Pardoner's ocular hint had persuaded me that an encounter with Rudolf Jedermann had been entirely possible. I wondered if it might also be possible to draw out the dwarf on the subject of his half-brother – or at least to gain some inkling of the alternative plans that man might have for me.

'Rudolf, your brother,' I began.

He interrupted with something that might have been 'Stiefbrüder'.

'Quite,' I continued. 'Rudolf, an important man, no doubt?'

'If you think fame for its own sake important,' he replied.

'Well respected. Not given to scatter-brained schemes?' I asked.

'No, he is a practical man, but most unscientific.'

'How so? Is it not possible to possess both qualities?'

He snorted and scampered to the decanters, pouring himself a generous volume of the first thing he laid a hand on. He cut a quite ludicrous figure, his over-generous and grubby shirt collar had all but escaped the confines of his jacket; the cloth of said shirt hung so low as to emerge from the tail of the same. The overall impression was of an urchin who had burgled the contents of a gentleman's press.

He gulped. 'Entirely so, Mr Moffat. Unless you are a superstitious peasant.'

I wondered how his relative would have reacted had he heard this insult.

'I assume he continues to dismiss your... ' I hesitated, 'experiments.'

'He would, did he but know anything of me, or my research. I have told you, I have not spoken to him these last twenty years.' It was the whine of a bullied boy.

'Yet you know something of him?' I countered.

'How could I not? They talk of him all over Europe.' I heard the bitterness in his voice.

'What is it to you?'

'He is famous, fêted throughout Europe. He preys on the foolish; did the name he pretended to in Vienna not hint at the tomfoolery he spreads among the credulous?'

I remembered he had mentioned the Comte de St Germain.

He nodded his head with vigour. 'Himself a famous charlatan. My brother repeats the Wonderman's outrageous lies in salons and ballrooms and people believe him a great philosopher and scientist.'

It was most satisfying to see the little man struggle with a rage greater than himself, aware that there was nothing he could do to relieve it at that time.

Just then, Miss Pardoner said, 'You share an interest in the Rosy Cross, Professor. You have told me that at least.'

'We are in agreement about some things, not others,' he replied.

'Ah,' I said. '"As above, so below"!'

The professor's eye yellowed visibly, as though suddenly jaundiced by sheer malevolence.

'That is one thing about which we are agreed.'

He turned on his heel in a miniature parody of dudgeon and scuttled from the room.

The young woman turned to me and declared, 'I should not provoke him if I were you.'

I silenced Maccabi's snort of laughter with a look, and replied to her, 'Provocation of the mite will change nothing regarding his intentions, but it may distract him from his preparations for them.'

I lifted my glass to the both of them, drained the inferior jerez and strode out of the French windows into the fresher air of the flagged area outside.

The day was sunlit, hazy. It occurred to me that I had not seen Job Catchpole for the best part of a day, upright or on all fours. In the distance I could hear loud whistles and wordless calls. Over the rise a flock of sheep appeared, their progress too purposeful not to be under the guidance of a shepherd. As famine follows feast, Cullis, brandishing a shepherd's crook a good cubit taller than he, ambled over the horizon. Darting around the rearmost ovines, nipping at their heels, was the dog-boy. There seemed little point in trying to reform his strange behaviours; I was sure he would have occupied Edinburgh's Medical Superintendent for many years.

The sheep, Cullis and his helper came to a stop at the edge of the flagstones. Cullis removed a battered piece of millinery that fell between cap and hat, but likely began life as neither. Clearing his throat, he said in his scarcely penetrable accent, 'Ah thowt wuh could eat wunnathuh sheep.'

'A splendid idea, Cullis. See to it,' I replied.

Again, he tugged at nothing in the area of where a forelock would have been had he yet been blessed with sufficient hair. The flock set off toward the rear of the house and its dilapidated outbuildings. I hoped Cullis would not be dilatory in supplying Mrs Gonderthwaite with the mutton.

For want of other diversions, I followed shortly after. Job, on two legs for once, held Cullis's crook and kept the sheep at bay on the far side of the small courtyard. The bleating of the sheep was loud indeed, and even at a distance of some yards I could see their eyes rolling. Given the time of year, the dearth of lambs was most perplexing. In fact there had been only the one, as far I had been able to ascertain.

In the courtyard itself, the giant Bill held the sacrificial lamb before his chest. Clearly, it would not be mutton after all. The beast was struggling mightily, but to no avail. The lamb's own chest, abdomen and loins were presented toward Cullis, who once again was wearing the blood-blackened apron. Before him was the wicked blade I had seen a few days earlier. It seemed as though the struggling sheep's eyes followed the blade, which glinted in the milky sunlight.

It was ruthless – and hardly quick. There was little doubt that Cullis's method of despatch was brutal. The noise of the animal's suffering, however, was outmatched by the distress of the rest of the flock, which finally dispersed in all directions as the chosen one breathed its last. As drenched in the blood of the sheep as Cullis was, nary a drop had fallen on the giant imbecile, whose expression had remained vacant throughout. I reflected that some, more squeamish than I, would have considered an absence from that evening's dinner.

That repast was not indelibly marked on my memory. It must indeed be true that tastes are quickly jaded. The oddities of Gibbous House had already palled for me. Despite the poetaster Cowper's assertion that variety was the spice of life, it seemed to me that an incessant flow of the unusual was equally as boring as the slow trickle of the undifferentiated. Prior to bidding the assembled company good night, I informed Maccabi that he would be driving myself and all who cared to accompany me to the Coble Inn in Seahouses on the morrow. Even a visit to a shoreside inn would provide relief from the oppression I felt in Gibbous House. Besides, it seemed the most quotidian component of my inheritance – and I was in sore need of something, anything, of the mundane.

Chapter Forty-seven

Having unwillingly broken our fast on oatmeal, Miss Pardoner and I stood afront the main entrance to the house. It was a little cooler than it had lately been, although the sun was brighter in the sky. Maccabi rounded the corner with a din one might have associated with a blacksmith at his anvil. He sat in the driver's seat of a four-wheeled carriage: it could have been a calash – if its condition were due to age – but its lines bespoke a barouche, albeit one that had long remained unused in a particularly filthy location.

This vehicle was being drawn by what might loosely have been termed our last pair of horses. The one withered jade familiar from previous excursions marched in tandem with a healthier looking specimen a full three hands shorter. This beast was healthier in so far as it consisted of a quite considerable amount of flesh; its swaying could conceivably have been occasioned by the effort required to hold up the enormous barrel of its gut. This horse had the misfortune to be on the off-side of the traces and was quite disturbed by the periodic clank of the metal wheel rim against the steel-shod mudguard.

Maccabi stood straight-backed and with far more dignity than the dilapidated state of the carriage warranted.

I was about to hand Miss Pardoner up to the seats in the rear, when the professor burst pell-mell from the house. 'Wait, wait. I shall come too! Yes, I will,' he bellowed.

He scuttled to the off-side. It was exceedingly difficult not to laugh at his attempt to swing himself aboard, and using the mudguard as purchase resulted in an ignominious fall. This, however, removed the cause of the incommodious din made by the vehicle when in progress, so the little man did not suffer in vain. Maccabi applied the switch to the withers of the horses and, after a glare from the wall-eyed bag of bones to the left, the carriage trundled northward toward Seahouses.

The faded paint on the board outside the Coble Inn described a beached fishing vessel with nets spread on a sandy shore quite unlike the rock-strewn beaches to be found not twenty yards distant. The door to the one-room alehouse was ajar and, judging by the din emerging from it, the enterprise was somewhat more lively than on the occasion of my last visit. We stepped back as a brawny fellow cartwheeled out of the entrance, gouts of blood threatening our clothing as he did so.

I nodded at Maccabi, in the hope that he would precede us all and clear a safe passage to the counter. The professor, however, had other ideas, letting out a childish laugh as he barrelled through the door and the mêlée on the other side of it. This at least allowed us to make our own way through, since the dwarf had laid about him with mean little kicks to the shins of the combatants. The stature of their assailant not coming up to their expectations, he made his way to the bar unscathed: we received many puzzled looks from inebriated dolts who were quite unable to reconcile the blows received with our passage moments afterwards.

John Bill stood behind the counter, rhythmically tapping a keg whilst observing the mayhem on the public side of the bar. I reached the counter and held up three fingers before turning to Miss Pardoner and raising my eyebrows. She continued the dumb show by holding up first three fingers on her left hand and then the index of her right, before turning it to her own bosom. John Bill, clearly more conversant with such intercourse than I, clattered four tankards on the counter. I felt this clatter more through the vibration of the counter than of my tympanum, since the brawl had continued after the brief hiatus caused by our arrival.

The mute landlord of the Coble Inn produced a large tin plate and a ladle from under the counter. He made sufficient noise with these to attract the attention of the rest of the clientele, who then floated away like driftwood on an ebb tide.

All save one. A hunched figure, the man was swarthy and vaguely familiar. His topcoat was cunningly cut to make the least of the hunch of his back. His cracked voice was instantly known to me, but it was left to his words to reveal to me whence I knew it. 'Hah, I cut a gibbous figure, don't I, Scotchman? Nearer home than you ought to be, now, I'll warrant.'

The professor's smile was quite queasy; Maccabi had turned most pale. Miss Pardoner said, 'Septimus, Septimus, you look so lively for one who has passed away.'

The man smiled. 'You are mistaken in me, miss.' He pointed a crooked finger toward me, 'I'm sure this gentleman will acknowledge my identity.'

He looked familiar, that much was true. Dislocation was the problem, or perhaps attire. As when meeting a bare-buttocked bishop in a brothel, the incongruity delayed recognition. At least until he said, 'Ha, Scotchman! You have evaded the catchpoles, at least.'

I laughed. 'I doubt the Northumbrians will care much for the Fantoccini, my friend.'

The professor continued to look shifty and sick by turns; Maccabi attempted an interjection that was rendered unintelligible by a stutter. Miss Pardoner revealed some indignation with a stamp of her not-quite-dainty foot.

'Septimus Coble, will you stop this nonsense. I know you, you are known to all, save—' she broke off and jerked her head in my direction. It was not a gesture redolent of society.

The man's accent was not so strong as I remembered it, although there were traces that could have been attributed to Romania or the Romany. He was somewhat better dressed, which perhaps gave the lie to his guise as an itinerant street entertainer. Still, there was something else that seemed at odds with my recollections. As he spoke, I fancied for a moment that his diction was more careful, as though there were some problem with his jaw.

'My lady, were I this Septimus Coble I should know your name, it seems. Why not tell me it, and I will pretend to the title for your sake?'

This gallantry was undermined by a large gout of spittle and the alarming sight of his dentures shooting forth from his mouth. He caught them deftly in his hand and replaced them.

'Mr Ash's vulcanite is not the match of Josiah's porcelain, I fear,' he said, shaking his head. That may have been the case, but his difficulties perhaps accrued from the likelihood that he was not the first owner of the dentures. Furthermore, he had evidently not been in the habit of wearing them long.

'I am Ellen Pardoner, as well you know, since I have been more than a little time in your household, sir.'

'Enchanted to meet you, Miss Pardoner,' the man replied, taking her hand in a most presumptive manner. The young woman removed it sharply from his grasp before the withered lips touched her flesh. A guttural laugh issued from between the vulcanite teeth, which briefly emerged once more from the thin mouth.

Miss Pardoner's eyes darted from side to side and, most uncharacteristically, it appeared that her bosom was heaving. Maccabi's expression was now that of a beagle mesmerised by a fly. The professor was chewing his lower lip, still unaccountably silent. I seized the moment. 'How then shall we call you, sir?' I asked.

This provoked a fit of something between coughing and laughing. On recovering himself – and his teeth – he announced, 'My names are legion,' before laughing, for want of a better word, demonically.

'Perhaps you might furnish us with your preference for convenience's sake?' I ventured.

Miss Pardoner let out a snort. On turning to the others of our company she must have viewed the expressions of the professor and Maccabi in much the same way as I, for her eyebrows rose and her mouth formed as pretty a facsimile of the letter 'o' as ever had been seen. The stranger winked at one – or all – of us:

> Wise Solomon, Puck or Harlequin,
> these am I, mayhap their kin:
> dearest Bill says what's in a name?
> I concur and say the same.

This last word was somewhat strangled in expression as my hand had grasped the villain's throat and was squeezing mightily.

'A name, sir. False or true, but a name I will have.'

One last squeeze accompanied the last word of the ultimatum. This time the man failed to catch his dentition as it fell and it pleased me greatly to kick it to the corner.

'Sholomum, Sholomum Coh-wem,' he sputtered, already feeling the want of his ill-fitting teeth.

The professor's eyes widened, most likely at the coincidence of the initial letters of the fellow's name. Maccabi turned a shade most unbecoming to the blond of his coiffure;

I fancied I could see the working of his mind in the darting of his eyes hither and yon. It seemed uncommon slow in producing much enlightenment, as his brow remained knotted for several moments after I enquired of Mr Cohen as to his business in Northumbria.

'No bishness, shir,' Cohen said, examining the floor about him for his dentures. 'A trip fo' pleshur shimply.'

Miss Pardoner handed him his teeth.

'And to visit distant relatives,' he went on.

The professor seemed relaxed for the first time since we had laid eyes on this familiar – to the others, at least – stranger.

'What relatives?' the dwarf asked.

'Distant relatives. Far from here, or not so far, my dear.' The man giggled.

Perhaps he was mad; I had long thought that there was nothing madder in the world than a poet – and his own tendency to rhyme evinced their least-appealing characteristic. Besides, if the fellow had suffered in one of the professor's experiments, who would not be driven mad by being one moment dead and the next alive? It seemed preposterous that any such experiment should ever have succeeded.

Having drained my own tankard, I waved it at the company and at the mute landlord. Miss Pardoner despatched what must have been a three-quarter-full pot with some panache, a single stray drop requiring rescue by her nimble tongue thereafter. I waggled my tankard in Cohen's face; he smiled and nodded, but not too vigorously.

All save the professor fell on the recharged vessels with alacrity, that man being hindered by his lack of stature and his unwillingness to beg assistance. Finally, Miss Pardoner took pity on him and handed the tankard down from the counter.

At last the dwarf felt able to make conversation and addressed Mr Cohen.

'Ahm... Cohen you say? Visiting the King of the Gypsies? How interesting!'

The Middle European 'r' was quite something to hear; it rendered the word itself so interesting as to be ludicrous.

'Visited, sir, the Faas are visited and I return thence, I came here to fritter a few—'

He broke off, most assuredly because my hands had neared his throat once more.

The professor was not finished himself. 'A Gypsy Jew? Or a Jewish Gypsy? How exotic!'

Both Maccabi and Miss Pardoner looked at the professor sharply, the former with the eye roll of a maddened mare and the latter in dumb incomprehension. I didn't know what to make of it, until Miss Pardoner said, 'Gypsy, Jew? Outsiders both; neither beyond assuming a lacquer of belief or custom to avoid persecution, Professor, is that not true?'

The stranger straightened – as much as his hump would allow – and pronounced, '*Solomon Cohen, Gypsy Jew, bids you all a fond a-dieu!*'

I would have had the truth of it from him as to his revivification or imposture, whichever it might have been. However, he was out of the door before I could lay a hand on him, and

I reflected that an afternoon of normality had proved beyond my reach after all.

The warped door had scarcely closed behind Cohen when all left present began to talk at once; save, of course, our host. It would have been all too easy to assert myself and insist on being heard first, but I decided against it, in the interest of seeing who would prevail on the others to defer to themselves. It was Maccabi: 'I saw him. I saw him, I tell you. Chest still and the reek of death upon him!'

I winced at the shrill pitch of his voice. Miss Pardoner's riposte lacked this same womanish timbre. 'Yet we all saw him just now, did we not? The unfortunate teeth were no disguise at all, surely?'

'It was not he,' said the professor.

I took this to be truth, or at least a confident lie, since he had not mangled the grammar of it.

'How not?' protested Miss Pardoner.

'I will show the impossibility of it,' the professor hissed.

'Impossible,' said Maccabi, although from his demeanour it was unclear what was, in fact, impossible – a living Septimus or the professor's disproving of such.

'Drink up, then, and show us, Jedermann, I am weary of the beer and this hovel,' I said.

Chapter Forty-eight

Having sorted a few coins, I slapped them on the bar. The removal of my hand was hindered by the great weight of John Bill's huge paw lying atop it. He leaned forward and forced something into the fob-pocket of my waistcoat. It bulged significantly since it shared the space with a timepiece, but I did not see what it was. The hand was removed from mine and placed firmly on my chest. It was all I could do to remain standing after stumbling backward several paces.

We departed the Coble Inn, for my own part without great regret.

It was no surprise that our carriage had not been made away with; no self-respecting thief would have stolen such a thing. We assumed our seats and I tapped Maccabi's shoulder, saying, 'Gibbous House, man! Quickly!'

The dwarf interposed immediately. 'North Sunderland, Jedediah, the cemetery.'

The carriage limped the few necessary miles inland. In the village, which seemed to have relinquished once-dear pretensions to the status of town, the sandstone was blackened and miserable looking. The streets themselves were deserted and we made rapid progress to the aforementioned cemetery. It was well kept; the grass between the headstones was short – and if the headstones themselves listed like so many drunks, not a one was obscured by moss or lichen. The carved names were therefore easy to read: Wilsons, Butterfields and many a Darling reposed beneath the green turf. In the furthermost corner, next to the only ill-cared-for section of the perimeter wall, stood a plain, square-edged stone. Decorated with the Star of David, it bore the simple inscription:

Septimus Coble 1760–1852 Gone to a Better Place

The professor bellowed, 'See!', as though by volume alone he could make the charade any more believable. For whoever the mysterious Mr Cohen had been, were he not Septimus Coble, it was no more likely that the founder of the Collection lay beneath that headstone. Furthermore, if Coble were indeed dead, it was inconceivable to me that he would have escaped being a subject for the professor's hobby and that he did not, even yet, stand stiff and glassy-eyed somewhere within Gibbous House. I chose not to dwell on the other, more phantastical alternative.

We boarded the carriage once more. The professor, Maccabi and Miss Pardoner began an interminable dispute about the mating habits of the Willow Warbler. Though it might have been some coded exchange designed to exclude me, I had no desire to expend the effort to listen, much less decipher it.

After about an hour, Miss Pardoner indicated that she was feeling some discomfort and was in need of relief. Maccabi halted the calash, Miss Pardoner hopped nimbly down without assistance and I said that I would keep watch to ensure her privacy. This offer was made not from any sense of decorum, rather out of a desire to irritate Maccabi. The woman disappeared behind a large shrub. I kept a close and careful watch, drawing great pleasure from learning that certain parts of her person were not quite so swarthy as her face.

Shortly after the wheels began turning once more, my enjoyment was despoiled by the professor's whispering in my ear, 'Did you see it? Did you see the Bonny Black Hare?' He whistled a few bars of a song popular in rural taverns, until he caught my eye.

It was late afternoon when we reached Gibbous House. Bidding the company farewell, for I was surely tired of it, I repaired to my own chamber. On removing my topcoat, I lay supine on the bed. My hand brushed across the bulge in my fob-pocket, and I withdrew something wrapped in quite grubby paper. The strange patterns left by inky fingers looked both beautiful and meaningless. Removing the paper, I saw that it was a crudely carved chess piece: a pawn. Surprisingly, perhaps, it was white. After a few moments pondering why a mute publican would give me such a thing, I caught sight of the paper beside me on the bed. Something had been written, in a daintily formed hand, on the inner side of the pawn's erstwhile wrapping:

> *Strings pulled by divinity?*
> *Or cousins' consanguinity?*
> *What is inside the humble pawn*
> *could be consumed once withdrawn.*
> *The time to do so cometh soon,*
> *sup ye well, with a long spoon.*

Which poetastery, whilst being less than illuminatory about the purpose of this valuable gift, at least left no doubt as to the identity of the giver. Replacing the pawn next to my watch, I crumpled the paper and tossed it out of the window. Supine once more, I contented myself with imagining a successful hunt for the Bonny Black Hare.

A knock at the door roused me some hours later. Miss Pardoner entered the room after an indecorously short interval. 'Dinner will be served shortly, Mr Moffat.' She sniffed the air. 'A window is best left open, from time to time, in the chamber of a solitary gentleman, sir.'

'My dear, you might have prevented my solitude – and if you had, I doubt that I should have behaved as a gentleman,' I replied.

The hoped for blush was not forthcoming, instead I received a clicking of the tongue worthy of a governess to a spoiled son. She turned on her heel without further communication and I attended to my toilette and my dress.

*

The three members of the household stood glass in hand by the fireplace in the dining room. There seemed no arrangement of their persons that would meet any criteria of compositional harmony, but the professor flanked by the robustly healthy figure of Maccabi and Miss Pardoner's own unfeminine height looked particularly ill posed. The dwarf greeted me as a molly-house owner might on opening the door to a drunken sailor. 'Ah, Moffat! How wonderful! Stupendously so. Well met, fellow!'

It seemed the glass in his hand had been recharged more than once.

'Good evening, Jedermann. You seem uncommon well disposed.'

'Indeed. Maccabi has informed me that our provender has been delivered at last. There is now bread, fresh baked by Mrs Gonderthwaite this day,' he enthused.

'A strange delight in the provision of so basic a foodstuff, Enoch?' I remarked.

'Bread is more necessary than other food, Flavel said,' Miss Pardoner offered.

'You should cite such Presbyterians more accurately, Ellen,' I winked here, 'as bread is more necessary than other food, so the meditation of death is more necessary than other meditations.'

The professor was for a few moments quite helpless with laughter, and Maccabi handed me a glass of jerez. Miss Pardoner studied a crack in the wood panelling beside the fireplace.

The repast was, in content, the equal of earlier efforts. The manner of its presentation was superior: neither simian servant appeared and we were served by the landlord of the Coble Inn's brother and Job Catchpole, upright for the most part, under the supervision of Mrs Gonderthwaite.

We had scarcely finished a post-prandial port before Maccabi and the professor made their excuses. Doubtless they were bound for some experimentation that required stronger stomachs than mine. My hand was fumbling idly in an outer pocket. The packet of opium was still in it. I took it out, unwrapped the oilskin, showed the resinous block to my companion. I had used such things only rarely, but that night I felt the need of it as never before. Events seemed outwith my influence, yet I would not flee, only take the brief refuge that the fruit of the flower might offer.

'Do we have the accoutrements to partake of the heavenly flower?' I asked.

Miss Pardoner's eyes gleamed; she did not seem such a one as would partake of the poppy.

'We surely do. What artefact is missing in this house? Such a thing has yet to be conceived of, or it would already be here, Mr Moffat. Shall I fetch what you need?'

Her head tilted to one side in a manner that I had no doubt indicated she was overcome with desire, and I was not one to resist a repetition of the recent night's pleasures.

'Please do.'

She was not long gone before returning with a pipe and tray that was more than the equal of John Brown's of

Seahouses. Ellen Pardoner knelt at my feet, and her unusual stature allowed her to continue to look me in the eye as she prepared the pipe. I took it from her and sucked the stem, the clouds and the moon filled my head. After drawing deeply and severally, I began to feel the languor prior to the dreams: it struck me suddenly that the gleam in her eye had had nothing to do with her own desire for opium.

Chapter Forty-nine

My feet seemed bound together. I stood on a white square, and a black square lay immediately in front of me. Beyond that another white square, then a black and so on. Birdsong filled the air, although I could not swear that I was outside. Opposite me, across four squares, Maccabi stood at stiff attention like a Prussian. He was dressed in black. I hobbled forward two squares. Maccabi remained still. The professor's laugh echoed as though he stood in an empty theatre, although he was nowhere to be seen. In front and to my right, dressed in an unaccustomed black bombazine, stood Miss Pardoner, her eyes staring as though blind. The next moment she held a dagger high above her head and I was impelled to grab both her wrist and her throat – but I could not. Miss Pardoner's hand descended and shook me awake.

My arms were pinioned, as were my legs. I lay on a table similar to the one on which I had seen the gruesome remains of the policeman, though this table was not hidden behind a painting in the withdrawing room. It was possible to move my head slightly to the side; on doing so I was greeted by a view that – in other circumstances – might have been quite pleasant: namely, Ellen Pardoner's lower abdomen. Behind her I could see red sandstone, and it was clear that we were somewhere under the house.

The professor continued to laugh. From the corner of my eye I could see him dancing, hopping from foot to foot, like Rumpelstiltskin around his fire. His voice, quavering, instructed Maccabi, whom I could not see, 'Jedediah, examine our subject. See that he is healthy.'

I could not turn my head to the other side, only return it to a central position where I could see nothing but the dark of the rough-hewn rock. It was a matter of sensing the movements of Maccabi's hands, rather than seeing them. He removed something from my fob-pocket and carefully slipped it into my right hand. It was not my watch. He leaned his ear to my chest, looking into my face as he did so. He gave a slow wink, put a finger to his lips and stood up. He removed the gag deftly: it was one of my own yellow 'kerchiefs. His meaty hand clamped over my mouth, he bent once again, this time to whisper in my ear, 'When you can, remove the pawn's head and drink the contents.'

He flinched at the roar I let out once his hand had quit my mouth. I spent no more than seconds struggling against the bonds. The leather, although butter-soft, was as strong as any cord. The dwarf spoke directly to me for the first time. 'Ah, Mr Moffat, you are returned from your travels in the perfumed land?'

The oath I swore was as satisfying as it was futile. Miss

Pardoner's shape receded and I saw her pick up a metallic object. It had the look of a knight's helm, although the lines were smoother and more rounded. After she fitted it to my head, it felt as though I had grown the clypeus of a housefly. The metal was hard against my nose and flared outward over my mouth, leaving my nostrils free to breathe. For how long remained to be seen.

The deprivation of my visual sense did nothing to improve the others: the lack of ocular stimulus merely prevented the filtering of unwanted noise. The dwarf's voice was often audible, issuing instructions that I did not understand. Footfalls echoed on the sandstone floor of the underground chamber. Occasional affirmations and single word questions were spoken by Maccabi or Miss Pardoner. A minute might have passed, or a day, and there was no way to discover which. Eventually, there were no more footsteps and something resembling conversation began.

'I have it in mind to wait for the storm,' said Jedermann.

'Why wait?' Miss Pardoner enquired.

'Two reasons: perhaps it will require more power than the voltaic pile can generate.' He stopped.

'Go on,' the woman urged.

'He means that the corpse should not be inanimate too long.' Maccabi said.

'Quite so.' The professor was in agreement. 'Maccabi, check the rod.'

'Let Miss Pardoner go; I'll stay in case of,' he hesitated, 'complications.'

'I am more than a match for a tethered man.' Miss Pardoner sounded quite peevish.

'Besides,' the dwarf added, 'Ellen will prepare the subject. I trust her hand with the dosage.'

Footsteps, quick and hard-stamped into the sandstone, receded, signalling Maccabi's departure for the rooftops.

'Now?' Miss Pardoner asked.

'Not yet. Check the bonds. I *will* wait for the storm, young woman.'

Hands grasped the leather cuffs binding hands and feet. Two large leather straps were already cinched tight across my thighs and chest. Miss Pardoner's hand checked these thoroughly; she was unable to force a finger between strap and flesh. A stiff collar prevented any movement of my head save to turn it slightly to the left; the large buckle at the right of my neck accounted for the impossibility of doing so to that side. She slipped a finger under the metal face-piece toward my mouth. I bit it savagely, only letting it free after she had twisted my private parts with her free hand. The pain was indescribable, and lasted the longer for my inability to double over and alleviate it. Most notable of all was the complete failure of any scream of pain to emerge from Miss Pardoner's lips. Her footsteps evoked her mannish stride as she went toward the professor.

'He may need a strong dose,' she said.

Maccabi's return was heralded by the rapid beat of a running man's footsteps.

He panted a little as he declared, 'No more than an hour. Perhaps as little as half that time.'

'Excellent.' The professor's voice held a lascivious tone. I heard a drawer being opened, the clink of glassware and the burbling of a liquid poured.

'Did you check?' Maccabi whispered.

I felt his hands at my right wrist and a sharp pain as the blade sliced through to my skin. He came to the other side of the table and began fiddling with the other wrist strap. In the hope that my actions were obscured, I pushed the pawn up under the face-piece, bit off the wooden head and allowed God alone knew what substance to pass into my throat.

The taste was quite bizarre; it brought memories of nettle soups from childhood days in Largs, which in itself was no pleasant matter. There was also an astringent hint of the new world fungi Psilocybe, whose tartness almost brought me to vomiting. Since any emetic reaction might well have killed me under such restraints as I then was, I swallowed like a Limehouse molly. The lower portion of the chess piece was concealed in my right hand; the head of the pawn had fallen I knew not where.

Suddenly, the beating of my heart was loud in my ears, and then I felt as though it had supplanted my brain in the cranium. Patients in the Model Asylum had been subjected to dosages of these mushrooms periodically. In my early days there, before my association with the learned lunatic who had died in my clothes, the Keeper had been wont to despatch me to Leith, where tattooed sailors late off ships from the

GIBBOUS HOUSE

Americas would hand me packages of dried fungi. I had purloined some of the contents only the once: the fearsome
visions had quite terrified a thirteen-year-old boy.

My temporal disorientation was worsened by the potion.
Whether it was a distillate of extracts or an infusion of the
basic ingredients, it appeared to be strong. At least that was
what I told myself as I looked down at my own supine form
on the table. I could see, or believed I could see, the underground chamber I was being held in. The dwarf wore some
kind of linen smock over his usual attire, as did the others.
Maccabi's and Miss Pardoner's, however, reached only to the
knee. The professor's trailed along the sandstone floor. He
wanted only some kind of white hood to complete a child's
picture of a diminutive phantom.

A conversation was in progress: it was audible but seemed
to be in frequencies that I was unable to hear as speech. It
sounded like what some fanciful whalers had once described
to me as the Song of Leviathan. As though such monsters
could sing. The rhythm of my heart was erratic; my head
seemed to expand and contract in sympathy. When the beat
was rapid, I heard snatches of the conversation. Miss Pardoner held a flask of some kind and I heard her say, 'Digitalis.'

The professor's answer was lost in a clap of thunder. The
brightest light I had ever seen seemed to follow it after only
a moment.

I saw Miss Pardoner move towards my body on the table,
lift the face-plate slightly with what must have been an
injured finger and pour the contents of the flask into my

mouth. It was very strange to taste extract of witches' gloves whilst viewing it being poured into the body on the table, but not half so strange as the intolerable pain I felt in my chest.

Chapter Fifty

Within and without, as above so below, a coruscating light, scenes from childhood and youth: these were no description of my experience – and neither did any bearded keeper of the keys turn me back from any gate. The sensation of floating above my corporeal form had ceased with the first spasm of my heart. Far from feeling weightless, I felt heavier than the soul of Job. There was a feeling of disconnection, but I could not see in any case; perhaps I *had* ceased to hear. The smell of violets mingled with the most intimate scent of a woman. I felt a huge jolt and someone, Miss Pardoner perhaps, removed the mask from my face.

There was a bitter metallic taste in my mouth; the quite pleasant admixture of odours had been replaced by sour ammonia. The wet cloth of my trousers accounted for this; it might have been worse. My torso felt as though I had fallen beneath the hooves of a post coach pair. I could not speak; my eyes had not yet become used to the ambient light. Turning my head to the left, I saw the professor, a demented gleam in his eye. He turned to Maccabi and Miss Pardoner. 'He lives!'

Whether he shouted this in triumph or delirium, I did not know. Maccabi's face wore a decided smirk. Miss Pardoner's expression told only of the most astonished incredulity.

It was pleasing to know that my time on earth was not yet over; I had only wished, however, that it were somewhat less painful in that moment.

Miss Pardoner, in a voice less confident than ever I had heard from her, exclaimed, 'It is done, a resurrected man. A wonder of the age... it can be... I could... '

Maccabi's roll of the eyes should have meant something to me, but it did not. I found my tongue.

'Let me up!'

Miss Pardoner pulled a pistol from some part of her attire and instructed Maccabi to loosen the bonds. Once he had done so, I found I was unable to sit up without assistance.

'Perhaps the pistol is unnecessary, Ellen.'

The barrel did not waver.

'There are people you must meet, Mr Moffat,' she said.

'There is time enough for that, Ellen.' The dwarf, eyes darting hither and yon, continued. 'I would prefer to spend a few days examining the phenomenon.'

Maccabi finally tired of my efforts to rise and helped me to a sitting position. A few moments passed before I was able to speak.

'Very well, Professor. I am at your disposal. It seems I am incapable of flight in any case.'

I began a coughing fit that I thought might ruin all their plans.

The bed was uncomfortable, or I felt uncomfortable in it, for it was not mine. The giant mute had been summoned by some means or other to the underground room and had carried me pick-a-back into the house, up the staircase, and onto the bed in which Edgar Allan had died. In truth, I was not so incapacitated as to have needed this assistance, but it suited me to appear to be so. All the same, it took more than a few minutes – and several unsuccessful attempts – to set foot on the floorboards. Moving silently was also difficult; stifling the grunts of pain as I moved required considerable fortitude.

The door was locked. As I released the handle, the door rattled with a sound like a tree trunk being battered against it. I surmised that the behemoth Bill had been stationed to guard against my egress. Retreating to the bed, I attempted to consider my position. It was quite fruitless – my mind wandered to the most inconsequential matters. For example, it occurred to me that it was strange that the landlord of the Coble Inn and his sibling suffered both from gigantism and an inability to speak. Of course, John Bill, former fisherman and lately publican, had lost the power to speak after a dreadful trauma; I wondered if his brother had ever possessed the power of speech. The suspicion that perhaps the former condition had been caused by an excess of consanguinity did occur to me.

Such nugatory ramblings kept me from devising any sort of plan of action, much less escape. The concoctions thatI had ingested, both voluntarily and under duress, must have affected me greatly, for I fell into a deep and dreamless sleep.

The hand at my throat belonged to Ellen Pardoner. The restorative powers of sleep had had little effect against my condition, for the start I gave was quite weak enough to convince her that I was of little danger to her person. She was in the company of Maccabi. Circumstance appeared to be conspiring against encountering anyone alone, save the mute. I hoped very much indeed that this was some indication of the trust, or lack of it, between my captors.

'Can you sit up, Moffat?' she asked.

My grunts were the only answer I could offer, as I demonstrated the physical proof that I could. Perhaps my inability to devise a stratagem for an escape was not so great a blow after all.

'Have you a drink?' I managed at last.

She laughed. 'Are you sure you'd like what we offer?'

Maccabi produced a silver flask, such as a huntsman might take with him in pursuit of the fox.

She took it from him, and took a manly draught. Maccabi cleared his throat. 'Of course, Ellen might easily have taken a prophylaxis for any drug that it might contain.'

I had already taken the silver vessel.

'Indeed she might, but I am past caring.'

My own consumption was the equal of Miss Pardoner's, although the gasping that ensued had been entirely dissimilar to her own short intake of breath in reaction to the cognac. In any case, I believed Maccabi had been offering an explanation for the matter of the white pawn, rather than any warning. Evidently, they had a use for me yet.

Whatever the restorative potential of sleep might have been, the spirit of the grape evinced more of it. Admittedly the gasping had inflamed my thorax somewhat, but my mental faculties had enjoyed a most welcome amelioration.

'So, I am returned from the dead. What now, Miss Pardoner?'

I cast a brief look at Maccabi: he seemed to find the floorboards most interesting.

'You are Rudolf's, if we can keep you from the professor's laboratory table,' she replied.

'Rudolf's? Are we not all masters of our own destiny?' I asked.

She laughed. 'Who here – or anywhere – is not the puppet of another?'

'And to what purpose? Whose is this marionette?'

I made a ridiculous face and jerked my arms.

Ellen Pardoner looked down the not inconsiderable length of her nose.

'There are things you do not know. Rudolf will explain. ' She was looking into the distance at some far-off possibility.

'Do you really think I will have any part of some crackpot scheme headed by a known fraud?' I asked.

'There is something of a pious fraud involved,' Miss Pardoner allowed.

Maccabi coughed. 'Perhaps we could leave you to the professor?'

My own feeling was that I was more than a match for the dwarf in strength and cunning, if not in intellect. However, even such allies as these two might be, I thought, were at least temporarily of use.

'So? When cometh the hosannas and palm-fronds?'

I almost touched the raven-shaped bell pull, but Miss Pardoner slapped my hand away from it.

'Quite so,' I sneered. 'Indeed, it seems I am more valuable than a reporter. I am giddy with pride at so high an estimation of my worth.'

'What is it you want? I can send Maccabi,' she offered.

I was somewhat taken aback that she had allowed me to isolate them so easily. There must have been some triumph visible in my expression, for she added, 'In fact, we shall both go, the more quickly to attend to your desires.'

Forbearing to mention that I was in no fit state to take literal advantage of such an offer, I merely requested some broth and bread.

Chapter Fifty-one

They left. The two did indeed make a handsome pair. Even so, it was plain to see that, of late, Maccabi adopted the moon-calf manner much less often in the lady's presence. I stared at the ceiling, counting cracks as numerous as a crone's wrinkles, hoping that some peace might engender the tiniest inkling of a plan. It was not to be so. The swinging of the door on its protesting hinges presaged the damnable dwarf's entrance in the most bumptious manner: 'Moffat! Does it feel strange! Another's skin? Or your own? The tingle of electricity fills you, does it? Are you animated by the vital spark?'

His enthusiasm was giving me a headache to accompany the pain in my thoracic region.

'No,' I replied and attempted to reassume a supine position, in the hope of feigning sleep sufficiently well to rid myself of the pest.

Needless to say, respite was not so easily come by. The midget withdrew a miniature wooden mallet from a pocket in his frock coat. Despite his earlier deriding of Leared's invention, the gutta-percha contraption was draped around his neck like some badge of office. He made no use of this, however, contenting himself merely with a manic tapping of various joints and limbs, all the while muttering 'remarkable' or 'astounding' as each word took his fancy.

The man must have been possessed of the most overweening conceit to have believed that he had truly brought a man back from the dead. Resurrection was as foolish a concept as a trip to the moon.

Finally, the dwarf had garnered sufficient information – or merely tired of its gathering – for he secreted the gavel-like object about his person, clasped his hands behind his back and began pacing the room. It seemed he was rehearsing some lecture to be presented to some body academic at some future time. Given the content and the rambling nature of its delivery, that future seemed far off indeed.

In fact, I heard only snatches of it. The simulation of sleep translated itself into an intermittent dozing and the professor's words intermingled with dreams that seemed no more bizarre than any event that had thus far come to pass in Gibbous House.

While I dreamed of floating in some ill-defined body of water, the midget evoked the names of Galvani and Faraday, promising that his work would be accepted as both culmination and revelation of the true purposes of these men. At some point he passed into the realms of theology: he cried out to Rosenkreuz to acknowledge him as his true interpreter. I was just near enough to the surface of the Lethe to reflect that

Science and Religion, whether in collision or collusion, was a dangerous combination.

The mouth of the whale was closing over me when I awoke with a start. I should have laughed had I not been fighting for my life. For some reason, the dwarf had pulled a chair up to the side of the bed and was attempting to stifle me with a bolster. Shoving him away with as much force as I could muster, I bellowed, 'Are you mad, sir? Have you not just performed the marvellous feat of reanimation on my own self? Do you think to murder me now?'

He had the look of a sulking child. 'I had it in mind to try again.'

It cost me a great deal to get myself upright and throw him out of the room. I followed him, since the door might be re-secured later and no giant sentinel stood without. After an initial, vain attempt to pursue him down the stairs, I contented myself with following him at slightly more than invalid pace to the dining room. As he passed through the doors, I heard raised voices emerging from that room. By the time I had made my way there, a civilised company of not three, but four persons was there to greet me.

A man as tall as myself stood next to Maccabi, who was an inch or two taller than the both of us. He was as dark as Jedediah was blond, and dressed in quality cloth, all of it black save the cotton of his shirt. He was a handsome-looking gentleman. He raised his eyebrows at Ellen, Jedediah and his half-brother, then held out a hand to me. 'Rudolf, Rudolf...

Jedermann, why not? I am pleased to make your acquaintance once again.'

'Again?'

'I had thought you quite cured of the mania, last time we met,' he said.

So he had, and there was no mystery as to the means by which such a man might have convinced the Medical Superintendent of Edinburgh's Model Asylum to release a man whom he knew to be either mad or a murderer.

The professor seemed unable to stand still in his halfbrother's presence, now scuttling to the long board, now walking over to stare at something most compelling in the wainscoting.

'Get us all something for our throats, Enoch,' I said.

He gave a movement of the shoulders as though trying to shake off something unpleasant that had fallen from the sky.

'Port?' he asked.

Miss Pardoner, naturally, replied in the affirmative. Maccabi nodded his assent. Rudolf Jedermann uttered the word '*Magenwasser*!'

The dwarf seemed hard put to control a cringe. I myself felt a flutter, but only at the memory of the taste of the foul schnapps. Perhaps my feelings were all too visible, for I was presented with a glass of port.

The stranger drew himself to his full height, lifted his tumbler and declaimed 'Zum Wohl!'

A snigger escaped me as I saw the self-same ritual repeated in miniature by Enoch. He must have been looking at me, although it was hard to tell with his eyes so slit-like. There was room enough for hatred to seep forth, however. The taller Jedermann looked at me expectantly: I raised my glass and sipped a little of the ruby liquid.

Rudolf turned to his half-brother after the briefest of glances at Miss Pardoner.

'Has he been told?'

'What should he be told?' asked the midget.

Without taking his eyes from the professor, Rudolf hissed, 'Tell him, Esther.'

Miss Pardoner sighed. 'I have tried, sir. Are you sure this is the man? He is so uncommon dull. Perhaps if yourself explained?'

The young woman avoided my eye.

'Very well.' Jedermann let out a sigh of his own.

'Moffat, it is a long story – as old as... well. Will you listen?'

'Perhaps I might, if a further port is forthcoming.'

Rudolf flicked a hand toward Enoch, who recharged my glass, spilling only a few droplets on my shoes.

'Who am I, Mr Moffat?' he began, although clearly expecting no answer. He looked into the far distance for a moment before continuing.

'Am I the son of a European prince? Am I an imposter, able to convince people of most unlikely truths? I come from a family of remarkable longevity. I have told people that I am five hundred years old. It is a useful lie. Others have used it before.'

At this point, Miss Pardoner and the professor nodded, clearly familiar with these words.

'Are we meant to die? Three score and ten seem hardly sufficient to learn all there is to know, don't you think? Wandering and persecution? We have wandered longer than my brother Enoch's namesake, yet we are still outsiders.'

He gave me a pointed look. Presumably my yawning had irked him.

'My brother is a great scholar, Mr Moffat. He believes that resurrection is possible. I know that it is not.'

The professor started, but his half-brother held up a hand and stilled him.

He had come so close as to allow spittle to fleck my chin. Stepping back, he took a shuddering breath. 'There are legends. Folk tales of most unlikely longevity in the Carpathians, but by no means restricted to such places. These fictions are to be encouraged, Mr Moffat. Do you know why?'

I shook my head, uncertain whether I was talking to an abject Bedlamite or the greatest mind since Da Vinci.

'Imagine someone, from an ancient family perhaps, who lives an extraordinarily long life. Not a half a millennium, no, of course not. But, let us say, for argument's sake, one hundred years. Two? In our scientific world, our world of 'investigative experimentation', would not members of such a family become the subjects of terrible tortures in the name of science? You, Mr Moffat, will save such people from this fate.'

Regrettably, I wasted some of the port by ejecting it through my nostrils.

Rudolf, or whoever he might really have been, raised an eyebrow. 'Oh, I do not mean my brother's ridiculous experiments. A Moffat died in Edinburgh, did he not? But even so, you are here yet.'

Maccabi appeared to be examining the cornices of the room. Miss Pardoner's eyes showed white all around the iris. The professor looked as though he believed Cain a suitable figure for emulation.

'I care not for science and proofs, Mr Moffat,' he continued. 'In the final account, the word will do. There is no intention in numbers, they are what they are. Would that everything in this world were so. I live as if it were. It has much to recommend it.'

I poured my own port; the dwarf appeared to be in the grip of some apoplexy.

The professor, having exhausted himself with his fit, collapsed in a swoon. Miss Pardoner rang the cracked bell, which this time summoned, quite unsupervised, the twin naturals. These two bore the academic away – to their credit– with the minimum of capering, just one ill-advised skip that caused the huge dome of the professor's pate to meet with the door frame.

I had summoned some composure in the meantime and addressed the professor's half-brother.

'And what purpose was there in the charade of your brother's experiments?'

He laughed. 'Why, I am going to make you famous. The

resurrected man. The true secret of the strange longevity enjoyed by some.'

I could make no sense of his words and he knew it.

'You will be presented in society. Fêted at expositions. You will, in short order, be the most notorious man in the world. And then you, and I, will be exposed as a fraud.'

'To what possible end?'

'The end is the end. An end to prying into certain parties' circumstances. When a lie is so much more credible than the truth, it is invariably taken as such, you see.'

'Do you think I will go along with this nonsense?'

I cleared my nostrils of a few remaining drops of port.

'The Model Asylum is still a lively concern.' He looked with disdain at the reddish liquid spattered by his feet.

'What of it?' I made to grab his shirt-front, but he eluded me.

'I paid a great deal for copies of certain... case histories.'

It would have been beneath me to ask precisely what he meant.

'Then you know that I am cured.'

Still feeling the rigours of the professor's mad attempt to reanimate someone not actually dead, I sat in a chair at the head of the table. He followed. He towered over my seated form and said in a voice filled with sand and glue, 'Come now, we both know how Moffat escaped the chains of lunacy.'

'In that case, how can I be of use? I am no resurrected corpse.' Bile rose in my throat.

'I did not pay so much for some case histories. Specious

reports on medical research, death certificates – all of these could and can be bought – should one have enough money. I mean to present you before a select group in Vienna; once my proposal is accepted you will accompany me on a grand tour.'

'It will convince no one of anything,' I said.

'Of course not, but I mean to discredit others as well as myself. '

His eyes glittered. A man excited by the prospect of destroying others and preserving himself.

'Forgive me, but I still do not understand.'

'The followers of the Rosy Cross, the philosophers, the adepts; they all see through a glass darkly,' he gave a short, bitter laugh, 'but still they see. I mean to use you to close their darkling window on a world they should never have glimpsed.'

I said nothing, believing the man almost as mad as his half-brother.

Chapter Fifty-two

Rudolf Jedermann's self-possession returned, summoned by an interrogative cough from Maccabi.

'Ah, Herr Jedermann. What is to become of Gibbous House?'

His composure was not so firmly fixed, since he turned on Jedediah, his brow close to touching Maccabi's own. 'What?' he bellowed. 'This palace of infinite varieties? This carbuncle? This monstrosity? I do not care!'

Jedermann's head advanced with each outburst and Maccabi was soon pinned against the long board. It might well have been the second occasion on which I had truly witnessed someone being browbeaten.

'Gibbous House is mine, is it not? Maccabi, I shall decide its fate,' I interjected.

Miss Pardoner's customary snort preceded any reply from Maccabi or Jedermann.

'You will do, Mr Moffat,' said Rudolf Jedermann, 'as you are instructed. Free will, in any case, is an illusion. Even fools can stumble on some truths, on occasion.'

Finding at least the second part of this statement not

incompatible with my own reading of the situation, I concluded that any protest would scarcely be material.

Moving close to Maccabi, I clapped him hard on the shoulder, saying, 'Jedediah, grasp that bell and summon us some provender, I find that having been dead is quite a stimulus to the appetite.'

I turned toward Jedermann. 'Unless, of course, I am bound for the Inquisition before nightfall?'

Some impediment required clearing from his throat. He answered, 'We will depart soon enough.'

The familiar dissonance of the hand bell somehow managed to ensure the arrival of Mrs Gonderthwaite in less time than it ought to have taken her to come from the kitchen.

'Dinner?' I said.

'It is barely five in the evening, Mr Moffat,' Mrs Gonderthwaite asserted.

Quite how she achieved the appearance of looking down her nose at me – despite being a good hand's breadth the shorter – I could not say.

Jedermann, a smile on the lips, if not in the eye, said, 'I think we might wait for Enoch's recovery. We'll be five for eight, Mrs Gonderthwaite.'

Which serendipitous rhyme proved that if the man had not set foot within Gibbous House previously he was conversant with its household.

Mrs Gonderthwaite departed; we three males looked at each other as if expecting someone else to begin some interchange. Miss Pardoner clapped twice and said, 'Cards, gentlemen!'

We repaired to a smaller table with an appropriate number of lower chairs. This ensemble was situated in the corner furthest from the likely entry point of any comestibles. The seats were comprehensively padded and the fabric, though fine, was as faded as a spinster's looks. Gilt had been rubbed from the wood by friction at some long time past, judging by the dust on that which remained. The four of us sat: Miss Pardoner with her back to the very corner of the room and thus with a good view of the dining room in its entirety. I sat opposite and felt the less comfortable with my back to any potential ingress or egress. The door through to the horrors of the taxidermist's lair was within my sight line, but that was all. Maccabi sat at my left hand, Jedermann to my right.

Miss Pardoner opened a drawer in the table itself and produced a bundle that consisted of a yellow silk kerchief. She eyed me as she undid the knot. From this cloth she produced a tired-looking deck of cards. The woman smiled at those around the table and proceeded to deal the cards face up into two distinct piles. To her right she seemed at first to be collecting the deuces and treys, as in the other stock she placed a seven, a king, an ace, a knave and a nine before placing anything other than a low-pipped card to her left. At that it was merely a six of spades. Finally the cards were all apportioned and I had noted that all suits from two to six were at her left hand and the remainder at her right. She opened the drawer once more and swept the supply of lower value cards into it.

It seemed that a round of Speculation was not in prospect.

'Well, gentlemen. In honour of our esteemed visitor,' a nod here to Rudolf Jedermann, 'I propose a game of Schafskopf – or Skat, if you prefer.'

The fellow so honoured let out a sigh, rather than a whoop of excitement.

'I do not know the game, Ellen,' I said.

'We are four; one must sit out, each in his turn. You shall be first, Mr Moffat,' and she began to jumble the remaining cards in an inexpert fashion. She dealt out every card, ten to each of the three players and the remaining two into something she called the 'Skat'.

Jedermann picked up his cards and threw them down immediately.

'These are not correct. The suits... ' He became silent.

'Herr Jedermann,' Maccabi's voice was oily, 'it is quite simple... '

He pointed out the equivalents, mentioning acorns, bells and leaves, whilst allowing that the count would recognise the hearts at least.

They began the bidding, or reizen, as Jedermann termed it. I paid no attention whatsoever, leaving a reverie about murdering the three of them only when actual play began. This was also difficult to follow. Contrary to my expectation, Maccabi laid the first card; Miss Pardoner followed according to the clock, which was less surprising. Jedermann played the diamond jack on the led hearts and took the trick for his own. The hand was played out and subsequently the tricks and the cards therein were perused by each player. Then there was a chattering of jackdaws as unfamiliar words were interspersed with arguments over the value of the tricks won. At no time did anyone note the scores claimed.

Miss Pardoner gathered up the cards, passed them to Jedermann and came to stand behind my chair.

'I shall help you with the game, Mr Moffat,' she said. I supposed that by rights Maccabi ought to have taken his turn to be a spectator.

The cards were dealt. I understood even less of the bidding with sight of the cards being bid on. It was with some surprise that I came to realise that, as the winning bidder, I was to begin play proper. Miss Pardoner's hand lay lightly on my shoulder, near the neck. Each wrong selection was followed by a fierce pinching of her fingers on my person. I suffered some degree of pain before selecting a card that met with her approval. The game proceeded with some discomfort for me. Clearly, Miss Pardoner was a player of some skill as I won that particular hand. This did not mean that I understood the jackdaw chatter any better than before.

It was with some relief that I learned that Miss Pardoner would not be assisting my play thereafter. Jedermann left the table with speed and made for the long board. He did not return with any refreshment for the remaining players.

This time during the bidding, which I began with one of something, Miss Pardoner queried, 'Will you go?' There was a short pause, and thereafter, 'One more?'

'Ah... t-two,' I stuttered.

'No, will you go?' Again she waited and repeated, 'One more.'

In fact, Maccabi was at turn to bid; I mentioned this. A kick from a sharp-pointed shoe followed this observation, and Miss Pardoner hissed, 'Will... you... go?'

'Of course not,' I said. I had no intention of going with Jedermann Senior, though I admired her efforts to disguise her question.

Maccabi said, simply, 'Three.'

The game finished after one more round, Jedermann declining to rejoin it. Perhaps Miss Pardoner was the winner, but it might well have been myself, or even Maccabi, for all I had understood of the play. The young woman and Maccabi engaged in some chatter concerning Sevastapol, remarking that the Turks owed the British yet another favour for having routed the Russian bear. I was tempted to intervene at this point and enquire why Her Majesty should aid one savage over another – but I doubted that the company would have welcomed the interjection. I found their interest quite remarkable.

Jedermann appeared to be a practised drinker, refilling his glass at the long board more than severally and patrolling the length of the dining room without the slightest misstep.

The professor and dinner arrived in quick and cacophonous succession. The former barrelled through the door in a state of noisy inebriation, a bottle of spirits in each hand. The latter made an entry by the simian sons of Mrs Gonderthwaite that surpassed any they had previously attempted.

One or other of the boys was seated atop an exquisite, if battered, silver trolley. It was something more suited to the transportation of delicate patisserie from kitchen to dining room in Verrey's of Regent Street than a hirsute youth. He himself was carrying a huge tureen of silver similar in quality and condition. A piece of flatware was balanced on his head, something the lowness of his brow facilitated. The noise was occasioned by the rattling of the silverware he carried and the cutlery in his pockets, which were being agitated – rather more than necessary – due to the rate at which the whole commotion was propelled into the room by his sibling's efforts. The meal was served before any of us had taken a seat, each boy managing to produce a relatively clean porcelain soup bowl from about their respective persons.

Yet again, the food was of delightful quality, as though Mrs Gonderthwaite felt a need to compensate for the manner of her food's delivery with her efforts in its production. It was most diverting that the broth, once tasted, was revealed to be a particularly fine Palestine soup. I hoped that I myself would prove to have as little to do with Jerusalem as the artichokes from which it had been made.

The remainder of the meal passed in a pandemonium of noise and fine viands, my own favourite being a very fine pheasant. Whence it had come, I had not the faintest idea, but it was both plump and succulent. Best of all, my teeth were not inconvenienced by any shot. When the last dish and knife had been removed, Maccabi bade the professor to remain seated and went himself to dispense the port. The professor appeared incapable of walking the short distance to the long board, in any case.

'Du! Maccabi! *Warsht ner stinkender Arschloch*!' The professor was, indeed, drunk. He fixed me with a baleful, rolling eye.

'It ish not a game. Serioush eksh-esp— Sciensch!'

Rudolf laughed. Miss Pardoner shot him a look containing a little less respect than customary. The dwarf spat on the floor and busied himself with his drink. His temper remained hot.

His half-brother looked at me. 'We'll be leaving around midday, Moffat.'

'Will we?' I asked.

'Most assuredly,' came the reply. 'You are, of course, most welcome to gather any portables to bring with you. Surely there are things you would like to bring? Things portable and convertible, eh?'

He laughed long and hard this time. At last he said between wheezes, 'You'll be ready at noon.'

The professor was not a soporific drunk. He continued to wriggle in his chair, muttering, whispering and occasionally shouting. I sensed that Miss Pardoner, at least, felt embarrassment on his behalf, though his own half-brother did not. Maccabi had the look of someone lured into sitting with a senile uncle through the bait of an attractive cousin. Conversation, for whatever reason, was desultory.

By eleven Miss Pardoner – and Maccabi – had retired to their chambers, and the two Jedermanns and I seemed locked in a relatively silent contest to be the last to take to their bed.

Eventually Rudolf took a gracious leave. I, too, took my own shortly after, choosing not to remain alone with the drunken dwarf. Perhaps I should have done so.

Chapter Fifty-three

A last look at the repeater by the light of the moon revealed the hour to be three. Sleep came – as it often does – at the moment at which I had despaired of it. The blessed relief was undisturbed by dreams and seemed all the shorter for it. I awoke sweating and coughing, although the smoke coming into the room from under the door was wispy and hardly dense.

The door was not locked. Swinging the door wide enabled me to consider how to penetrate the mound of furniture blocking my egress. It might have been possible to wait for the fire to burn through it, but it occurred to me that a choking death would have been my fate long before it could do so. Putting a shoulder against the rear of a large armoire proved nugatory. Perhaps it was full. I found it strange that the efforts required in moving such an enormous and weighty piece had not disturbed my slumber.

The smoke had become a little thicker: it was an irritant to the throat but no more. The room itself, however, was hot, and although I was still in my déshabillé, a sheen of perspiration covered every inch of my exposed skin. Nevertheless, I began to dress, reasoning that it were better to force the flames to consume a few layers of wool and cotton before my own flesh.

The sheen had become a flood by the time my boots were on. I smashed the small window with an elbow. A few bright flames licked at the edges of the door frame, although the armoire itself still seemed to resist the conflagration. Head and shoulders through the empty window frame, I looked downward. There seemed no hand- or foothold to facilitate a gingerly executed descent down the wall itself. In addition, it seemed I would have to remove my topcoat, as I was on the point of becoming wedged in the aperture. Worst of all, the window looked out onto the stalls of the yard, but there was no sign of straw, nor hay, nor anything at all to break what was sure to be a precipitous fall. The remaining glass fell inward as I jerked out of the opening. My topcoat fell in a heap to the floor as I shrugged it off.

The varnished wood of the armoire was blistering now, whilst the flames themselves had nibbled at the edges of the piece. Picking up the porcelain from beside the bed, I threw it to the floor in as petulant a gesture as to which I had ever been provoked. The bourdeloue, thankfully empty, landed safely on my topcoat. Despite the lack of satisfaction at destroying something, it was pleasing to have some hope aroused in my breast by the glimmer of a stratagem for escape.

Having dropped the topcoat out of the window, I watched it fall gracelessly and with some momentum, it being of quality material. The bedclothes followed in quick succession, all a-bundle. I was grateful that I had chosen the least luxurious of possible accommodations, since the mattress from the rude cot followed these in its turn with only a modicum of force required to ensure its passage through the narrow opening. The armoire was truly alight now. I pushed the cot to the wall beneath the window. The bed enabled me to clamber feet first through the window facing inward. The conflagration was making alarming progress across the room. I hung by my hands from the window frame for a few moments, contemplating the long fall. Perhaps my resolve hardened before the flame touched my fingers, but in any event I loosed my grip.

Despite my preparations, the landing left me a little stunned. It was some moments before I felt I might safely move. That I did not do so was entirely due to the knife at my throat. Cullis's grimy hand was wrapped around the haft and his ill-cared-for teeth loomed above it. His breath smelled as though he had been chewing sheep-droppings to sweeten it.

'Divven't think I divven' na!' he said.

Judging silence the best course, I kept mine.

'It was 'ee. Yiz killed worlad!'

Indeed, I had; but I was at a loss to know how he knew it, since the policeman, before his unfortunate demise, had been unable to discover the identity of the murderer. There was a sharp pain and I felt blood trickle down my neck. Cullis collapsed, insensible, upon my person. Shoving him aside I stood and saw the rock in the dog-boy's hand.

'Well done, Job Catchpole! I am indebted to you.'

The boy stared mutely for a few seconds, then knelt to tend to the wound in Cullis's scalp.

He looked up briefly. 'Go,' he said.

Flames were visible through the window from which I had dropped. The servants' entrance was a matter of a few steps to my right. The handle on the door was hot to the touch.

Skirting the building took no more than a minute or so, even though there was some stiffness of the joints after my fall. There were no flames apparent from the outside. Finding the main entrance locked from within, I used the lion's head bell pull more in hope than expectation. The summons was answered as quickly as ever it had been during my stay at Gibbous House. The door was opened by Miss Pardoner, whose unfashionable coiffure was enlivened by the effect on it of the lady's having recently enjoyed some energetic activity. Combined with the flush in her cheeks, it gave her an alluring look.

'Quickly!' she gasped. 'The house is afire.'

I refrained from comment, feeling that the singed aspect of some of my attire, not to mention my hair, was response enough.

She grasped my arm and dragged me into the entrance-way.

'Rudolf! He is with Enoch. Below. He must be saved.' She looked me in the eye with such imprecation as led me to think she truly believed some altruistic spark glowed somewhere within me.

'I'll need money; you'll make sure you have it when I return.'

She gave a look as though she had just smelled Cullis's breath.

'You'll get your reward,' she said.

On looking up at the gallery, it was obvious that the wall-paper hall of mirrors was curling with the heat. The hand-painted *trompe l'oeil* mirror concealing the access to the bedrooms had been the first to suffer the effects of the conflagration. It seemed the fire set outside my own bedroom door had thus far been confined to the apartments of the members of the household proper. As I passed through into the dining room, I could have sworn I heard the crack of heated glass.

The refectory table resembled a culinary battlefield, in as much as wine spilled like blood and broken vittles covered the surface of the table like cavalrymen at Balaclava. I reflected that I had surely struck my head in my fall from the window, if such nonsense could enter it at so inappropriate a time. At the head of the table, apparently insensible from drink, was the giant, Bill. The noise emanating from his gaping mouth was sure indication that he lived yet.

The entrance in the inglenook fireplace was open, though the underground passage looked as dark as ever. I passed between the Golem and the dybbuk and wished for a light. A familiar hellish glow infused the red sandstone of the passage walls, and passing Heathfield Cadwallader's message I felt a brief queasiness in my stomach. The light from the chamber containing the infernal machine was not so bright as on my previous visit, and the Ethiops were conspicuously absent. The moving parts of the machine seemed sluggish, as though it were tired or drugged. As a consequence, the great chamber was a little quieter, with relative silence prevailing as the great wheels paused at the apex of each rotation. A faint screaming could be heard at these moments.

I turned left, skirting the sandstone. It was still devilish hot, although clearly the machine was not producing so much calorific power as before. It seemed advisable to keep my distance from the mechanical Leviathan. The sandstone wall at first followed the contours of the machine, running parallel at a distance of some yards from it. After some twenty-five yards, the wall veered to the left, opening out into a vast and empty cavern. In the opposite wall there was an opening, and a faint light emanated from it. The screaming had become louder, but the words were indiscernible and the voice unrecognisable.

To my initial relief, the further I put the machine behind me, the cooler it became. By the time I had reached the central point of the huge cavern, my breath was visible in the air. I shivered, and of course it was cold, but I could not account for the icy feeling in my spine. By the time I reached the opening, my teeth were clacking like a dowager's needles. The screaming voice was Enoch's, the language indecipherable. I crossed the portal and felt nauseous at once.

In the centre of a small chamber was the kind of table atop which I had previously been strapped. Now Jedermann Major was tightly bound to it with familiar-looking leather strapping. He was not responsible for the screaming. His half-brother gibbered and capered, seemingly oblivious to my presence. The dwarf's wing collar was in the process of taking flight from his person. His hair, such as remained, appeared to have been affected by some of his beloved experiments with electrical current. One shoe was missing and most remarkable of all was the evidence of his excitement protruding from the front of his trews. Perhaps the shortness of his legs contributed to its striking appearance. Evidently the constant movement of his head and darting of his eyes had effected the parlous state of his shirt collar. Then the twisting of his neck and head halted. His gaze fixed upon my person. 'Moffat!' was the only intelligible utterance among the stream of what I presumed to be invective.

The dwarf leaped at me, fingers extended toward my eyes. His fingernails drew blood from my cheek as I stumbled backward against the examination table. The homunculus straddled my chest and, revolted by the proximity of his most private parts, I threw him off with a great heave. Such was his rage or madness that he was totally undeterred by the blow he received from the corner of the table upon his pate. From somewhere about his person, he produced a large knife. In his tiny hand it appeared like Domenico Angelo's smallsword. Thankfully he had never studied in the Soho School of Arms. The razor I took from my pocket made short work of the tendons in his wrist and the knife fell to the sandstone floor.

The pain had a calming effect on the midget, the frantic movement of his head subsided and a keening noise replaced the crazed ranting. A boot to the temple put a stop to this last, for a time.

Releasing Jedermann from his bonds, I awaited the expected effusions of gratitude.

'You fool, Moffat!' he said. 'I needed to know!'

'He seemed more likely to be extracting information from you, when I arrived,' I opined.

He spat; most likely the gag had been uncomfortable.

'Why knock him senseless, man? I need to know if they are close?'

'Who?' It seemed a reasonable question.

'Those in the shadows, *les eminences grises*, those who look for such as we.'

It made little sense to me. Perhaps the insanity was a family trait.

'Close to what?' I offered, out of courtesy only.

'To me, to you, to our plans. Where there are those who are othered, there are those who would see them gone.'

I reflected that his feelings of persecution might have some basis in fact, if any scintilla of truth existed in his strange tale. Nonetheless I wasted no time in assuring him that I would play no further part in his scheme, as I could sooner foresee my end in gaol than in any successful conclusion to his plan.

'Whether you will or no, I cannot be caught here in Gibbous House. Not by them.' For the first time he looked truly fearful.

'Indeed, we should leave. The house above is afire.'

He held me back as I turned to leave. Pointing to his

unconscious sibling, he said, 'Bring him. I need to know what he told them.'

'He is your brother, sir, carry him yourself.'

Chapter Fifty-four

A wait of some minutes ensued in the dining room in front of the fireplace. Eventually Rudolf struggled into the room with his neck wreathed in the dwarf's disproportionately long arms. Loosening this grip by means of the tips of fingers and thumbs, he relieved himself of his burden. Enoch must still have been insensible, for his fall to the floor provoked no reaction, not even a groan or exhalation of air. There was no sign of Bill: I suspected he might have been in the grip of the drunkard's punishment – namely the nausea and headache that truly deserved a name of their own.

A judiciously applied kick to the supine form of the professor roused him from his slumbers. He seemed more – or less – himself, in as much as he was not raving. Neither was he silent, however, being given over to a mumbling that might have been some arcane prayer, or simply cursing under his breath. His physical wellbeing was well attested to by the alacrity of his arrival at the doorway out of the dining room into the vestibule. That is to say, he left both his elder sibling and myself in his wake.

Rudolf Jedermann bestowed a half-smile upon me as Enoch squealed in pain upon seizing the door knob. I would have hoped that an intelligent man would have taken this as warning not to open the door itself, however we all three were thrown backward by the blast of hot air that ensued once the foolish midget had done so. None of us was so dull as not to realise the futility of making our egress via that route, therefore we scampered pell-mell through the rooms leading to the library, the professor smashing a few of the vitrines in the vivarium as he passed, whether out of concern for the slithering creatures within or for some other less altruistic motive, I did not know.

The French doors at the end of the library were already open. Framed within the opening were Maccabi, Mrs Gonderthwaite and Miss Pardoner. The latter had a stiff arm around the sharp shoulders of the wraith-like housekeeper, who seemed to be racked with pain or, indeed, grief. Miss Pardoner merely looked uncomfortable. Maccabi looked, as ever, like a blond – if handsome – dolt. That this company parted before us like mist was as well for them, since the three of us were travelling at quite a lick, for fear of encountering the lick of any pursuing flames.

'Are they out?' Mrs Gonderthwaite enquired in a voice like the bellow of a birthing cow.

I was so put out by this most uncustomary outburst that I quite forgot to wonder what on earth she was talking about. Naturally, Miss Pardoner clarified matters. 'The twins, her boys!'

EWAN LAWRIE

'I haven't seen them,' I said.

The professor broke off from praying or swearing, whichever it had been.

'I told those boys, I told them! Set the fire, do not stop to admire it!'

This last word was somewhat strangled in his throat, as Miss Gonderthwaite's hands were firmly clamped around it.

It was Maccabi who released the housekeeper's grip on the professor's person, whereupon the woman seemed truly to become the ghostly figure she resembled, lapsing into a soft keening and trembling as if on the point of being blown away on the next gust of wind.

We all stood on the flagged area outside the library, shivering. The weather was unseasonably cool. I could hear a clacking, like a chattering of arthritic crickets. If we found it cool, the Ethiops surrounding the terrace were feeling a mighty chill, their teeth being the source of the noise.

Looking to the professor proved of little use, as he was intent on massaging the bruising to his neck. I spoke instead to Maccabi. 'What do they want?'

'How should I know, Moffat?' came the less than helpful reply.

'Are they dangerous?' The voice belied his status as Europe's foremost mountebank, and I suppressed a snicker at Rudolf Jedermann's discomfiture.

Miss Pardoner gave a bellow and a series of grunts and clicks. The tallest of the men enunciated carefully: 'We need quitclaim, an affidavit.'

'Whatever for?' I asked.

For reply, he opened a leather pouch, about the size of a small bag of flour, and tipped its contents on the ground.

The gold glinted in what meagre sun penetrated the cloud.

'A quitclaim is for property,' Maccabi said.

'And what have we been, if not owned by him!' He thrust a long finger toward the dwarf, who had recovered himself enough to flinch at this.

'But you are not slaves, nonetheless,' Maccabi said. 'I will sign an affidavit stating your entitlement to the coin.'

'Will you indeed, Jedediah?' I asked, more for form's sake, I confess. Any tussle with the Ethiops would most likely have ended badly for ourselves.

'Best you fetch pen and paper then, Maccabi,' I continued, and the lout set about procuring these requirements in the library behind us. He returned more rapidly than he left, with a few pages torn from some invaluable tome, a pen with a dripping nib and a singed air about him.

The affidavit was drafted and signed and the twenty or so blackamoors left with rather more dignity than was left to us. Whither they went, I do not know, but sincerely I wished them luck of their gold and their affidavit, for I doubted either policeman or footpad would care a fig for the latter.

A loud noise came from behind us. To me at least it was not entirely unexpected – I had seen enough of the effects of fire on buildings in London. We ran around the building, all save the professor giving the perimeter the widest possible berth. On reaching the drive before the entrance, Miss

Pardoner and the professor gave a cry. The dome that gave the house its informal sobriquet of Gibbous House had fallen in. Every turret, spire and tower had suffered a similar fate. The professor screamed and ran into the burning ruin.

I looked at Rudolf Jedermann. He replied succinctly to my unspoken question with one of his own: 'Am I my brother's keeper?'

Maccabi started after the foolhardy midget. Miss Pardoner held him back, saying, 'Three deaths are enough for that place.'

I forbore to point out that – by my own reckoning, at least – considerably more than three had met their ends, either directly or indirectly, due to the existence of Gibbous House. Besides, I cared not a whit for any of it, or any of them. Clearly Miss Pardoner held the blond Jew in some regard or affection, else she would have allowed him his grand gesture of saving the professor.

'Are the horses safe?' I asked of no one in particular.

'Why?' Rudolf Jedermann enquired.

'I am taking my leave, sir.'

'You do not have mine to take it, Moffat,' he said, stepping in front of me.

I gave him the bare-knuckler's last punch, knocking him back with the full force of my forehead. The next words he spoke came from the mud: 'We are not finished with you yet, Moffat!'

I silenced him with a satisfying boot to his ribs.

'You'll leave us the carriage, Moffat?' Miss Pardoner was as civil as she had ever been to me.

'I'll be taking a horse and a few things from the gatehouse. You may do as you please, Ellen.'

A coughing fit seized me, but no hand reached out to soothe. Not even that of Ellen Pardoner. All eyes save mine had turned to the ruin of the cupola. The coughing ceased and I turned to look at it myself. It resembled nothing so much as a boiled egg after being thoroughly breakfasted on: jagged edges pointing upwards, their convergence providing the barest clue to the erstwhile perfection of design and purpose. For lunatic as the imbroglio of styles and design of the house's entirety had been, the dome itself had been perfect, even beautiful. Now its relict was the backdrop for the last rantings of a madman, for leaping nimbly from joist to charred-and-burning joist was Professor Enoch Jedermann, once of Vienna, Leyden and Siena Universities, late of Berlin. His shouting was for once in English, which given his recent behaviours was surprising. More surprising still was the fact that he was naked.

'There will be no peace for you, Rudolf. Not for you, nor your Jezebel.'

Miss Pardoner coloured quite becomingly at this last, and I regretted the lack of further opportunities to be the cause of her blushes myself. However, it did reveal that only two of the three were aware of the true relationship between Ellen and Rudolf.

'Maccabi! Viking Jew! You were mine and whose are you now? You have been the imposter's catamite, I know it!'

A laugh escaped me at this; Maccabi himself looked

embarrassed, while Miss Pardoner looked at me with fascination. Jedermann senior was shaking his head.

'Moffat!' the mannikin screamed the name. Perhaps he had trod on a particularly warm timber. Then he gave a maniacal laugh as chilling as any heard in Bedlam.

'Moffat!' he went on. 'You are no more Moffat than I! Murderer, pander, thief, fratricide! I shall shout your name so that your friends may know thee for the evil thou art!'

Whilst I was reflecting on his strange diction, and who, precisely, these friends might have been, the dwarf fell screaming into the burning interior.

I left them all in front of the burning wreck, waving a cheery hand from astride the best of the remaining horses. Mrs Gonderthwaite lifted a listless hand by way of farewell. As for the others, save Ellen, they did not even glance in my direction. Miss Pardoner looked me in the eye and said, 'The Americas! I'll find you there.' I nodded to her as I rode away.

On removing the portables I had secreted earlier in the gatehouse, I set fire to it, which permitted Heathfield Cadwallader – at the last – a cremation of sorts, if not a Christian burial. A vast column of smoke was rising above the main house: as I turned my horse in the direction of Alnwick, I thought I might take Ellen at her word, board a ship at Newcastle and try my luck across the ocean. South or north, it was nothing to me; both sounded an ideal destination for a man of my singular talents.

Supporters

Unbound is a new kind of publishing house. Our books are funded directly by readers. This was a very popular idea during the late eighteenth and and nineteenth centuries. Now we have revived it for the internet age. It allows authors to write the books they really want to write and readers to support the books they would most like to see published.

The names listed below are of readers who have pledged their support and made this book happen. If you'd like to join them, visit www.unbound.com.

Zoe Aukim

Randall Abbott
Geoff Adams
Liz Ait
Amy Alderson
Deborah Allan
John Allan
Anthony Allen
Richie Allport
Clarissa Angus

Laurie Avadis
Angela Baker
Jason Ballinger
Shrewd Banana
Andy Barber
David A Bell
Tony and Mary Bell
Samantha Bendelow
Warren Bennetts

Tessa Beukelaar - van Gulik

Bill Biggles

Debra Bishop

Lucy Bowden

Sean Brady

Martin Brennan

Dougie Bruce

Joseph Burne

Ross Burton

Bill Busby

James Bushnell

Paul Carlyle

Nicola Carr

Helen Causer

Gérard Celli

Elanor Clarke

Eddie Cloke

Steve Cloke

Jake Coates

Julia Coleman

Jo Connelly

Tony Cook

Jo Copoc

Sarah Copsey

Stumpy cornah

Malcolm Cox

Dawn Cranie

Mick Cranston

Jock Crawford

Marco Criscuolo

Catherine Daly

Martin Darby

Patrick Davie

Colin & Jackie Davies

Harriet Fear Davies

Nina Davies

Rhiannon Davies

Jonathan Davison

Barbara Jean Day

Celia Deakin

Leighton Dean

Petra Dean

David Demchuk

Daniel Derrett

John Dexter

Darren 'Mr Vice' Dix

Julie Donath

Kevin Donnellon

Jenny Doughty

Connor James Doyle

Robert Dunn

Paul Dunseath

Matt Eager

Jared Ely

Marina Escalada-Romero

David Escolme

Laura Etherington
Peter Ettedgui
Mike Ewing
Jo Eydmann
Kerry Fagg
Allison Farr
Tasha Farrington
Margaret Farthing
Paul Fearon
Zulma Fernandez
Graham Fernihough
Simon Few
Flash
Rachel Flood
Andy Forrester
Steve Fowkes
Chris Frow
Ian Furbank
Mark Gamble
Adam Garland
Annabel Gaskell
Paul Giblin
Carya Gish
Jackie Glassar
Danny Glover
Iain Graham
Mandy Graham
Mike Graham

Neil Graham
Cosy Gray
Michael Green
John Grindrod
Sophie Hall
Christine Hamill
Jay Hamilton
Jill Hand
Michelle Hardaker
Richard Harmer
Michelle Haycox
Hal Hegerty
Johnny Helmo
Angie Hemlin
D M Hemming
Sandy Herbert
David Herr
E O Higgins
Andrew Hill
Lisa Hinsley
Peter Hitchen
Andy Hodder
Paul Holbrook
Michael Horsley
Craig Houston
Stephen Howell
Laura Howes
Paula Hunter

Tim Hutchinson
Martin Hyatt
Ben Ingber
Johari Ismail
Trev Jones
John Keki
Aidan Kendrick
Dan Kieran
Mark Kilburn
Shaun Lane
Rab Larkin
Joe Lawrence
Alasdair Lawrie
Barbara Lawrie
Callum Lawrie
Donald Lawrie
Isabella Lawrie
Nancy Lawrie
Tracey Lawrie
W Tom Lawrie
Jan Lawson
Robert Lewis
Peter MacAulay
Milcah Marcelo
Alan Martin
Jane and Peter Martin
Jo Martin
Mark Mason

Matthew May
Alan McCormick
Richard McDonough
Ian McLachlan
Tom Meiklejohn
Janice Milligan
Steve Milligan
John Mitchinson
MJ
Peter Moore
Stephen Moore
Frank Morley
James Morley
Morven Morley
Stephen Morley
Mike Murtagh
Carlo Navato
Geoff Nelder
Rob Newlyn
Willow Nicholson
Andrew O'Brien
Jack O'Donnell
Jenny O'Gorman
Mike O'neill
Jackie Oliver
Justin Ollerton
Par Olsson
Michael Paley

Carole Parker

Julia Parker

Bryn Parry

Alison Paxton

Andy Pegg

Richard Penny

Nick Petch

Jennifer Pickup

Justin Pollard

Marjolijn Postma

Bev Proctor

Huan Quayle

Christy Ralph

Rajkumar Rao

Steve Rea

Helen Richardson

Jamie Richardson

Paul 'kaffa' Richardson

Beth Roestenburg

Joanne Rogerson

John and Sue Rosie

Kev Ross

Susan Ross

Catherine Rossi

Ron Saint

Vanessa Schmidt

Jim Scott

Maureen Scott

Simon Scott

Tracy Scotting

Sue Sharpe

Lynne Sheppard

Kevin Sherratt

Clint Simpson

Wendy Smart

Janet Smith

Samantha Smith

Gus Sparrow

Perry and Gill Spencer

Rita Spencer

Teresa Squires

Angie Stalker

Christopher J. Steele

Jason Stevens

Julian Sutton

Sallie Tams

Adam Thomas

Kevin Thompson

David Thorne

Simon Tierney-Wigg

Vicki Timings-Thompson

Mike Tompkins

Lynne Tott

Michael Tucker

Stuart Watt

Aliya Whiteley